Chronicles of the Cheysuli: Book Three

LEGACY OF
THE SWORD

Jennifer Roberson

CORGI BOOKS

LEGACY OF THE SWORD

A CORGI BOOK   0 552   13120 2

First publication in Great Britain

PRINTING HISTORY

Corgi edition published 1988

Copyright © 1986 by Jennifer Roberson O'Green

This book is set in Times

Corgi Books are published by Transworld Publishers Ltd., 61-63
Uxbridge Road, Ealing, London W5 5SA, in Australia by Transworld
Publishers (Australia) Pty. Ltd., 15-23 Helles Avenue, Moorebank,
NSW 2170, and in New Zealand by Transworld Publishers (N.Z.) Ltd.,
Cnr. Moselle and Waipareira Avenues, Henderson, Auckland.

Reproduced, printed and bound in Great Britain by
Hazell Watson & Viney Limited
Member of BPCC plc
Aylesbury Bucks

This book is for C. J. Cherryh
who is, quite simply,
the best.

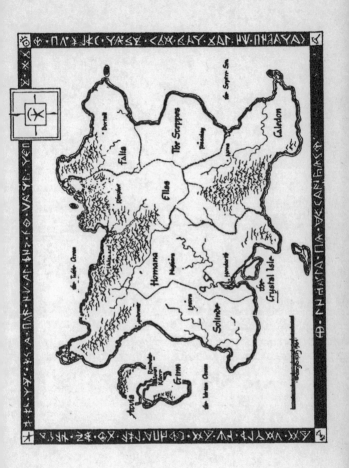

Part 1

1

Hondarth did not resemble a city so much as a flock of
sheep pouring down over lilac heather toward the glass-
grey ocean beyond. From atop the soft, slope-shouldered
hills surrounding the scalloped bay, grey-thatched cottages
appeared to huddle together in familial affection.

Once, Hondarth had been no more than a small fishing
village; now it was a thriving city whose welfare derived
from all manner of foreign trade as well as seasonal
catches. Ships docked daily and trade caravans were dispatched to various parts of Homana. And with the ships
came an influx of foreign sailors and merchants;
Hondarth had become almost cosmopolitan.

The price of growth, Donal thought. *But I wonder, was
Mujhara ever this – haphazard?*

He smiled. The thought of the Mujhar's royal city – with
the palace of Homana-Mujhar a pendent jewel in a magnificent crown – as ever being *haphazard* was ludicrous.
Had not the Cheysuli originally built the city the
Homanans claimed for themselves?

Still smiling, Donal guided his chestnut stallion through
the foot traffic thronging the winding street. *Few cities
know the majesty and uniformity of Mujhara. But I think
I prefer Hondarth, if I must know a city at all.*

And he did know cities. He knew Mujhara very well
indeed for all he preferred to live away from it. He had, of
late, little choice in his living arrangements.

Donal sighed. *I think Carillon will see to it my wings are
clipped, my talons filed . . . or perhaps he will pen me in a*

11

kennel, like his hunting dogs.

And who would complain about a kennel as fine as Homana-Mujhar?

The question was unspoken, yet clearly understood by Donal. He had heard similar comments from others, many times before. Yet this one came not from any human companion but from the wolf padding at the stallion's side.

Padding, not slinking; not as if the wolf avoided unwanted contact. He did not stalk, did not hunt, did not run from man or horse. He paced the stallion like a well-tamed hound accompanying a beloved master, but the wolf was no dog. Nor was he particularly tame.

He was not a delicate animal, but spare, with no flesh beyond that which supported his natural strength and quickness. The brassy sunlight of a foggy coastal late afternoon tipped his ruddy pelt with the faintest trace of bronze. His eyes were partially lidded, showing half-moons of brown and black.

I would complain about the kennel regardless of its aspect, Donal declared. *So would you, Lorn.*

An echo of laughter crossed the link that bound man to animal. *So I would,* the wolf agreed. *But then Homana-Mujhar will be kennel to me as well as to you, once you have taken the throne.*

That is not the point, Donal protested. *The point is, Carillon begins to make more demands on my time. He takes me away from the Keep. Council meetings, policy sessions . . . all those boring petition hearings –*

But the wolf cut him off. *Does he have a choice?*

Donal opened his mouth to answer aloud, prepared to contest the question. But chose to say nothing, aware of the familiar twinge of guilt that always accompanied less than charitable thoughts about the Mujhar of Homana. He shifted in the saddle, resettled the reins, made certain the green woolen cloak hung evenly over his shoulders . . . ritualized motions intended to camouflage the guilt; but they emphasized it instead.

12

And then, as always, he surrendered the battle to the wolf.

There are times I think he has a choice in everything, lir, Donal said with a sigh. *I see him make decisions that are utterly incomprehensible to me. And yet, there are times I almost understand him . . . Almost . . .* Donal smiled a little, wryly. *But most of the time I think I lack the wit and sense to understand any of Carillon's motives.*

As good a reason as any for your attendance at council meetings, policy sessions, boring petition hearings . . .

Donal scowled down at the wolf. Lorn sounded insufferably smug. But arguing with his *lir* accomplished nothing – Lorn, like Carillon, always won the argument.

Just like Taj. Donal looked into the sky for the soaring golden falcon. *As always, I am outnumbered.*

You lack both wit and sense, and need the loan of ours. Taj's tone was different within the threads of the link. The resonances of *lir*-speech were something no Cheysuli could easily explain because even the Old Tongue lacked the explicitness required. Donal, like every other warrior, simply *knew* the language of the link in all its infinite intangibilities. But only he could converse with Taj and Lorn.

I am put in my place. Donal conceded the battle much as he always did – with practiced humility and customary resignation; the concession was nothing new.

The tiny street gave out into Market Square as did dozens of others; Donal found himself funneled into the square almost against his will, suddenly surrounded by a cacophony of shouts and sing-song invitations from fishmongers and streethawkers. Languages abounded, so tangled the syllables were indecipherable. But then most he could not decipher anyway, being limited to Homanan and the Old Tongue of the Cheysuli.

The smell struck him like a blow. Accustomed to the rich earth odors of the Keep and the more subtle aromas of Mujhara, Donal could not help but frown. Oil. The faintest tang of fruit from clustered stalls. A hint of

flowers, musk and other unknown scents wafting from a perfume-merchant's stall. But mostly fish. Everywhere fish – in everything; he could not separate even the familiar smell of his leathers, gold and wool from the pervasive odor of fish.

The stallion's gait slowed to a walk, impeded by people, pushcarts, stalls, booths, livestock and, occasionally, other horses. Most people were on foot; Donal began to wish *he* were, if only so he could melt into the crowd instead of riding head and shoulders above them all.

Lorn? he asked.

Here, the wolf replied glumly, nearly under the stallion's belly. *Could you not have gone another way?*

When I can find a way out of this mess, I will. He grimaced as another rider, passing too close in the throng, jostled his horse. Knees collided painfully. The man, swearing softly beneath his breath as he rubbed one grey-clad knee, glanced up as if to apologize.

But he did not. Instead he stared hard for a long moment, then drew back in his saddle and spat into the street. '*Shapechanger!*' he hissed from between his teeth, 'go back to your forest bolt-hole! We want *none* of your kind here in Hondarth!'

Donal, utterly astonished by the reaction, was speechless, so stunned was he by the virulence in words and tone.

'I said, *go back!*' the man repeated. His face was reddened by his anger. A pock-marked face, not young, not old, but filled with violence. 'The Mujhar may give you freedom to stalk the streets of Mujhara in whatever beastform you wear, but here it is different! Get you gone from this city, shapechanger!'

No. It was Lorn, standing close beside the stallion. *What good would slaying him do, save to lend credence to the reasons for his hatred?*

Donal looked down and saw how his right hand rested on the gold hilt of his long-knife. Carefully, so carefully, he unlocked his teeth, took his hand away from his knife and ignored the roiling of his belly.

14

He managed, somehow, to speak quietly to the Homanan who confronted him. 'Shaine's *qu'mahlin* is ended. We Cheysuli are no longer hunted. I have the freedom to come and go as I choose.'

'Not *here*!' The man, dressed in good grey wool but wearing no power or rank markings, shook his dark brown head. '*I* say you had better go.'

'Who are you to say so?' Donal demanded icily. 'Have you usurped the Mujhar's place in Homana to dictate *my* comings and goings?'

'I dictate where I will, when it concerns you shape-changers.' The Homanan leaned forward in his saddle. One hand gripped the chestnut's reins to hold Donal's horse in place. 'Do you hear me? Leave this place. Hondarth is not for such as you.'

Their knees still touched. Through the contact, slight though it was, Donal sensed the man's tension; sensed what drove the other to such a rash action.

He is afraid. He does not do this out of a sense of justice gone awry, or any personal vendetta – he is simply afraid.

Frightened, men will do anything. It was Taj, circling in seeming idleness above the crowded square. *Lir, be gentle with him.*

After what he has said to me?

Has it damaged you?

Looking into brown, malignant eyes, Donal knew the other would not back down. He could not. Homanan pride was not Cheysuli pride, but it was still a powerful force. Before so many people – before so many Homanans and facing a dreaded Cheysuli – the man would never give in.

But if I back down, I will lose more than just my pride. It will make it that much more difficult for any warrior who comes into Hondarth.

And so he did not back down. He leaned closer to the man, which caused the Homanan to flinch back, and spoke barely above a whisper. 'You are truly a fool to think you can chase *me* back into the forests. I come and go as I please. If you think to dissuade me, you will have

15

myself and my *lir* to contend with.' A brief gesture indicated the hackled wolf and Taj's attentive flight. 'What say you to me *now*?'

The Homanan looked down at Lorn, whose ruddy muzzle wrinkled to expose sharp teeth. He looked up at Taj as the falcon slowly, so slowly, circled, descending to the street.

Lastly he looked at the Cheysuli warrior who faced him: a young man of twenty-three, tall even in his saddle; black-haired, dark-skinned, *yellow*-eyed; possessed of a sense of grace, confidence and strength that was almost feral in its nature. He had the look of intense pride and preparedness that differentiated Cheysuli warriors from other men. The look of a predator.

'I am unarmed,' the Homanan said at last.

Donal did not smile. 'Next time you choose to offer insult to a Cheysuli, I suggest you do so *armed*. If I was forced to slay you, I would prefer to do it fairly.'

The Homanan released the stallion's rein. He clutched at his own so violently the horse's mouth gaped open, baring massive teeth in silent protest. Back, back . . . iron-shod hooves scraped against stone and scarred the cobbles. The man paid no heed to the people he nearly trampled or the collapse of a flimsy fruit stall as his mount's rump knocked down the props. He completely ignored the shouts of the angry merchant.

But before he left the square he spat once more into the street.

Donal sat rigidly in his saddle and stared at the spittle marring a single cobble. He was aware of an aching emptiness in his belly. Slowly that emptiness filled with the pain of shock and outraged pride.

He is not worth slaying. But Lorn's tone within the pattern sounded suspiciously wistful.

Taj, still circling, climbed, back into the sky. *You will see more of that. Did you think to be free of such things?*

'Free?' Donal demanded aloud. 'Carillon *ended* Shaine's *qu'mahlin!*'

16

Neither *lir* answered at once.

Donal shivered. He was cold. He felt ill. He wanted to spit much as the Homanan had spat, wishing only to rid himself of the sour taste of shock.

'Ended,' he repeated. '*Everyone* in Homana knows Carillon ended the purge.'

Lorn's tone was grim. *There are fools in the world, and madmen; people driven by ignorant prejudice and fear.*

Donal looked out on the square and slowly shook his head. Around him swarmed Homanans whom he had, till now, trusted readily enough, having little reason not to. But now, looking at them as they went about their business, he wondered how many hated him for his race without really understanding what he was.

Why? he asked his *lir*. *Why do they spit at* me?

You are the closest target. Taj told him. *Not because of rank and title.*

Homanan *rank and title*, Donal pointed out. *Can they not respect that at least? It is their own, after all.*

If you tell them who and what you are, Lorn agreed. *Perhaps. But he saw only a Cheysuli.*

Donal laughed a little, but there was nothing humorous in it. *Ironic, is it not? That man had no idea I was the Prince of Homana – he saw a shapechanger, and spat. Knowing, maybe he would have shut his mouth, out of respect for the title. But others,* other *Homanans – knowing what Carillon has made me – resent me for that title.*

A woman, passing, muttered of beasts and demons and made a ward-sign against the god of the netherworld. The sign was directed at Donal, as if she thought *he* was a servant of Asar-Suti.

'By the gods, the world has gone mad!' Donal stared after the woman as she faded into the crowded square. 'Do they think I am *Ihlini*?'

No, Taj said. *They know you are Cheysuli.*

Let us get out of this place at once. But even as Donal said it, he felt and heard the smack of some substance against one shoulder.

17

And smelled its odor, also.

He turned in the saddle at once, shocked by the blatant attack. But he saw no single specific culprit, only a square choked with people. Some watched him. Others did not.

Donal reached back and jerked his cloak over one shoulder to see what had struck his back, though he thought he knew. He grimaced when he saw the residue of fresh horse droppings. In disgust he shook the cloak free of manure, then let the folds fall back.

We are leaving this square, he told his *lir. Though I would prefer to leave this city entirely.*

Donal turned his horse into the first street he saw and followed its winding course. It narrowed considerably, twisting down toward the sea among whitewashed buildings topped with thatched grey roofs. He smelled salt and fish and oil, and the tang of the sea beyond. Gulls cried raucously, white against the slate-grey sky, singing their lonely song. The clop of his horse's hooves echoed in the narrow canyon of the road.

Do you mean to stop? Taj inquired.

When I find an inn – ah, there is one ahead. See the sign? The Red Horse Inn.

It was a small place, whitewashed like the others, its thatched roof worn in spots. The wooden sign, in the form of a crimson horse, faded, dangled from its bracket on a single strip of leather.

Here? Lorn asked dubiously.

It will do as well as another, provided I may enter. Donal felt the anger and sickness rise again, frustrated that even Carillon – with all that he had accomplished – had not been able to entirely end the *qu'mahlin.* But even as he spoke, Donal realized what the wolf meant; the Red Horse Inn appeared to lack refinement of any sort. Its two horn windows were puttied with grime and smoke, and the thatching stank of fish oil, no doubt from the lanterns inside. Even the white-washing was greyed with soot and dirt.

You are the Prince of Homana. That from Taj, ever

vigilant of such things as princely dignity and decorum.

Donal smiled. *And the Prince of Homana is hungry. Perhaps the food will be good.* He swung off his mount and tied it to a ring in the wall provided for that purpose. *Bide here with the horse. Let us not threaten anyone else with your presence.*

You *are going in.* Lorn's brown eyes glinted for just a moment.

Donal slapped the horse on his rump and shot the wolf a scowl. *There is nothing threatening about me.*

Are you not Cheysuli? asked Taj smugly as he settled on the saddle.

The door to the inn was snatched open just as Donal put out his hand to lift the latch. A body was hurled through the opening. Donal, directly in its path, cursed and staggered back, grasping at arms and legs as he struggled to keep himself and the other upright. He hissed a Cheysuli invective under his breath and pushed the body back onto its feet. It resolved itself into a boy, not a man, and Donal saw how the boy stared at him in alarm.

The innkeeper stood in the doorway, legs spread and arms folded across his chest. His bearded jaw thrust out belligerently. 'I'll not have such rabble in my good inn!' he growled distinctly. 'Take your demon ways elsewhere, brat!'

The boy cowered. Donal put one hand on a narrow shoulder to prevent another stumble. But his attention was more firmly focused on the innkeeper. 'Why do you call him a demon?' he asked. 'He is only a boy.'

The man looked Donal up and down, brown eyes narrowing. Donal waited for the epithets to include himself, half-braced against another clot of manure – or worse – but instead of insults he got a shrewd assessment. He saw how the innkeeper judged him by the gold showing at his ear and the color of his eyes. His *lir*-bands were hidden beneath a heavy cloak, but his race – as always – was apparent enough.

Inwardly, Donal laughed derisively. *Homanans! If they*

are not judging us demons because of the shapechange,
they judge us by our gold instead. Do they not know we
revere our gold for what it represents, and not the wealth
at all?

The Homanans judge your gold because of what it can
buy them. Taj settled his wings tidily. *The freedom of the*
Cheysuli.

The innkeeper turned his face and spat against the
ground. 'Demon,' he said briefly.

'The boy, or me?' Donal asked with exaggerated mildness, prepared for either answer. And prepared to make
his own.

'Him. Look at his eyes. He's demon-spawn, for truth.'

'No!' the boy cried. 'I'm *not*!'

'Look at his eyes!' the man roared. 'Tell me what you
see!'

The boy turned his face away, shielding it behind one
arm. His black hair was dirty and tangled, falling into his
eyes as if he meant it to hide them. He showed nothing to
Donal but a shoulder hunched as if to ward off a blow.

'Do you wish to come in?' the innkeeper demanded
irritably.

Donal looked at him in genuine surprise. 'You throw
him out because you believe him to be a demon – because
of his eyes – and yet you ask *me* in?'

The man grunted. 'Has not the Mujhar declared you free
of taint? Your coin is as good as any other's.' He paused.
'You do have coin?' His eyes strayed again to the earring.

Donal smiled in relief, glad to know at least one man in
Hondarth judged him more from avarice than prejudice.
'I have coin.'

The other nodded. 'Then come in. Tell me what you
want.'

'Beef and wine. Falian white, if you have it.' Donal
paused. 'I will be in in a moment.'

'I have it.' The man cast a lingering glance at the boy,
spat again, then pulled the door shut as he went into his
inn.

20

Donal turned to the boy. 'Explain.'

The boy was very slender and black-haired, dressed in dark muddied clothing that showed he had grown while the clothes had not. His hair hung into his face. 'My eyes,' he said at last. 'You heard the man. Because of my eyes.' He glanced quickly up at Donal, then away. And then, as if defying the expected reaction, he shoved the tangled hair out of his face and bared his face completely. 'See?'

'Ah,' Donal said, 'I see. And I understand. Merely happenstance, but ignorant people do not understand that. They choose to lay blame even when there is no blame to lay.'

The boy stared up at him out of eyes utterly unremarkable – save one was brown and the other a clear, bright blue. 'Then – you don't think me a demon and a changeling?'

'No more than am I myself.' Donal smiled and spread his hands.

'You don't think I'll be putting a spell on you?'

'Few men have that ability. I doubt you are one of them.'

The boy continued to stare. He had the face of a street urchin, all hollowed and pointed and thin. His bony wrists hung out of tattered sleeves and his feet were shod in strips of battered leather. He picked at the front of his threadbare shirt with broken, dirty fingernails.

'Why?' he asked in a voice that was barely a sound. 'Why is it you didn't like hearing me called names? I could tell.' He glanced quickly at Donal's face. 'I could feel the anger in you.'

'Perhaps because I have had such prejudice attached to *me*,' Donal said grimly. 'I like it no better when another suffers the fate.'

The boy frowned. 'Who would call *you* names? And why?'

'For no reason at all. Ignorance. Prejudice. Stupidity. But mostly because, like you, I am not – precisely like *them*.' Donal did not smile. 'Because I am Cheysuli.'

The parti-colored eyes widened. The boy stiffened and drew back as if he had been struck, then froze in place. He stared fixedly at Donal and his grimy face turned pale and blotched with fear. *'Shapechanger!'*

Donal felt the slow overturning of his belly. *Even this boy –*

'Beast-eyes!' The boy made the gesture meant to ward off evil and stumbled back a single step.

Donal felt all the anger and shock swell up. Deliberately, with a distinct effort, he pushed it back down again. The boy was a boy, echoing such insults as he had heard, having heard them said of himself.

'Are you hungry?' Donal asked, ignoring the fear and distrust in the boy's odd eyes.

The boy stared. 'I have eaten.'

'What have you eaten – scraps from the innkeeper's midden?'

'I have *eaten*!'

Anger gave way to regret. *That even a boy such as this will fall prey to such absolute fear –* 'Well enough.' He said it more sharply than intended. 'I thought to feed you, but I would not have you thinking I seek to steal your soul for my use. Perhaps you will find another innkeeper less judgmental than this one.'

The boy said nothing. After a long moment of shocked silence, he turned quickly and ran away.

2

In the morning, Donal found only one man willing to give him passage across the bay to the Crystal Isle, and even that man would not depart until the following day. So, left to his own devices, Donal stabled his horse and wandered down to the sea wall. He perched himself upon it and stared across the lapping waves.

He focused his gaze on the dark bump of land rising out of the Idrian Ocean a mere three leagues across the bay. *Gods, what will Electra be like? What will she say to me?*

He could hardly recall her, though he did remember her legendary beauty, for he had been but a young boy when Carillon had banished his Solindish wife for treason. Adultery too, according to the Homanans; the Cheysuli thought little of that charge, having no strictures against light women when a man already had a wife. In the clans, *cheysulas*, wives, and *meijhas*, mistresses, were given equal honor. In the clans, the birth of children was more important than what the Homanans called proprieties.

Treason. Aye, a man might call it that. Electra of Solinde, princess-born, had tried to have her royal Homanan husband slain so that Tynstar might take his place. Tynstar of the Ihlini, devotee of Asar-Suti, the god of the netherworld.

Donal suppressed a shudder. He knew better than to attribute the sudden chill he felt to the salty breeze coming inland from the ocean. No man, had he any wisdom at all, dismissed the Ihlini as simple sorcerers. Not when Tynstar led them.

He wishes to throw down Carillon's rule and make Homana his own. For a moment he shut his eyes. It was so clear, so very clear as it rose up before his eyes from his memory: the vision of Tynstar's servitors as they had captured his mother. Alix they had drugged, to control her Cheysuli gifts. Torrin, her foster father, they had brutally slain. And her son they had nearly throttled with a necklace of heavy iron.

Donal put a hand against his neck. He recalled it so well, even fifteen years later. *As if it were yesterday, and I still a boy.* But the yesterday had faded, his boyhood long outgrown.

He opened his eyes and looked again upon the place men called the Crystal Isle. Once it had been a Cheysuli place, or so the *shar tahls* always said. But now it was little more than a prison for Carillon's treacherous wife.

The Queen of Homana. Donal grimaced. *Gods, how could he stay wed to her? I know the Homanans do not countenance the setting aside of wives – it is even a part of their laws – but the woman is a witch! Tynstar's meijha.* He scrubbed a hand through his hair and felt the wind against his face. Cool, damp wind, filled with the scent of the sea. *If he gave her a chance, she would seek to slay him* again.

Taj wheeled idly in the air. *Perhaps it was his tahlmorra.*

Homanans have none. Not as we know it. Donal shook his head. *They call it fate, destiny . . . saying they make their own without the help of the gods. No, the Homanans have no tahlmorra. And Carillon, much as I respect him, is Homanan to the bone.*

There is that *blood in you as well*, returned the bird.

Aye. His mouth twisted. *But I cannot help it, much as I would prefer to forget it altogether.*

It makes you what you are, Taj said. *That, and other things.*

Donal opened his mouth to answer aloud, but Lorn urgently interrupted. *Lir, there is trouble.*

Donal straightened and swung his legs over the wall, rising at once. He looked in the direction Lorn indicated with his nose and saw a group of boys wrestling on the cobbles.

He frowned. 'They are playing, Lorn.'

More than that. Lorn told him. *They seek to do serious harm.*

Taj drifted closer to the pile of scrambling bodies. *The boy with odd eyes.*

Donal grunted. 'I am not one of his favorite people.'

You might become so, Lorn pointed out, *if you gave him the aid he needs.*

Donal cast the smug wolf a sceptical glance, but he went off to intervene. For all the boy had not endeared himself the day before, neither could Donal allow him to be beaten.

'*Enough!*' He stood over the churning mass of arms and legs. 'Let him be!'

Slowly the mass untangled itself and he found five Homanan boys glaring up at him from the ground in various attitudes of fear and sullen resentment. The victim, he saw, regarded him in surprise.

'Let him be,' Donal repeated quietly. 'That he was born with odd eyes signifies nothing. It could as easily have been one of you.'

The others got up slowly, pulling torn clothing together and wiping at grimy faces. Two of them drifted off quickly enough, tugging at two others who hastily followed, but the tallest, a red-haired boy, faced Donal defiantly.

'Who're *you* to say, shapechanger?' His fists clenched and his freckled face reddened. 'You're no better'n *him*! My Da says men like you are nothing but demons yourselves. *Shapechanger!*'

Donal reached out and caught the boy's shoulder. He heard the inarticulate cry of fear and ignored it, pulling the boy in. He thought the redhead was perhaps fourteen or fifteen, but undernourished. Like all of them. 'What else does your father say?'

The boy stared at him. He hunched a little, for Donal still gripped his left shoulder, but soon became defiant.

'Th-that Shaine the M-mujhar had the right of it! That you should all be slain – like *beasts*!'

'Does he, now?' Donal asked reflectively, desiring no further answers. He felt sickened by the virulence of the boy's hate. He only mouthed his father's words, but it was enough to emphasize yet again that not all Homanans were prepared to accept the Cheysuli, no matter what Carillon had done to stop Shaine's purge.

Almost twenty years have passed since Carillon came back from exile to make us welcome again, declaring us free of qu'mahlin, *and still the Homanans hate us!*

Lorn came up to press against his legs, as if to offer comfort. It brought Donal back to full awareness immediately, and he realized he still held the redhead's shoulder. Grimly, he regarded the frightened boy.

But not so frightened he forgets his prejudice – Donal took a deep breath and tried to steady his voice. 'Do you think I will eat you, boy? Do you think I will turn beast before your eyes and rip the flesh from your throat?'

'M-my Da says –'

'*Enough of* your *jehan*, boy!' Donal shouted. 'You face *me* now, not your father. It is you who will receive what punishment I choose to give you for the insult you have offered.'

The boy began to cry. 'D-don't eat me! *Please* don't eat me!'

In disgust, Donal shook him. 'I will not eat you! I am not the beast your father says I am. I am a man, like he is. But even a *man* grows angry when boys lose their manners.'

Lir, Lorn said in concern.

Donal silenced him through the link and kept his attention on the boy. 'What punishment do you deserve? What I would give my own son for such impertinence. And when you run home to tell your *Da*, tell him also that you sought to harm an innocent boy. See what he says then.'

Even as he said it, Donal grimaced to himself. *Most likely he will send his son out to find another helpless soul.*

Contempt and hatred beget more of the same. He tightened his grip on the redhead. 'Now, perhaps you will think better of such behavior in the future.'

Donal spun the boy quickly and held him entrapped in his left arm. Before the redhead could protest, Donal swatted him twice – hard – on his bony rump and sent him stumbling toward the nearest street. 'Go home. Go home and learn some manners.'

The boy ran down the street and quickly disappeared. Donal turned at once to the victim, meaning to help him up, then thought better of it. *Why give him another chance to revile me for my race?*

But the boy evidently no longer held Donal in such contempt. He scrambled to his feet, tried to put his torn and muddied clothing into some semblance of order, and gazed at Donal with tentative respect. 'You didn't have to do that.'

'No,' Donal agreed. 'I chose to.'

'Even after – after what I called you?'

'I do not hold grudges.' Donal grinned suddenly. 'Save, perhaps, against Carillon.'

The parti-colored eyes widened in shock. 'You hold a grudge against *the Mujhar*?'

'Upon occasion – and usually with very good reason.' Donal hid a second smile, amused by the boy's reaction.

'He is the Mujhar! King of Homana and Lord of Solinde!'

'And a man, like myself. Like you will be, one day.' He put out a hand and touched the ugly swelling already darkening the skin beneath the boy's blue eye. The brown one was unmarred. 'This will be very sore, I fear.'

The boy recoiled from the touch. 'It – doesn't hurt.'

Donal, hearing the boy's fear, took away his hand. 'What is your name? I cannot keep calling you "boy," or "brat," as the innkeeper did.'

'Sef,' whispered the boy.

'Your age?'

Cheeks reddened. 'Thirteen – I think.'

27

Donal gently clasped one thin shoulder, ignoring the boy's sudden flinch. 'Then go on your way, Sef, as you will not abide my company. But I suggest you avoid such situations in the future, do you wish to keep your bones whole and your face unblemished.'

Sef did not move as Donal removed his hand. He stood very stiff, very still, his parti-colored eyes wide, apprehensive, as he watched Donal turn to walk away.

'Wait!' he called, 'Wait – *please* –'

Donal glanced back and waited. The boy walked slowly toward him, shoulders raised defensively, both hands twisting the drawstring of his thin woolen trews.

'What is it?' Donal asked gently.

'What if – what if I said I *did* want your company?'

'Mine?' Donal raised his brows. 'I thought you feared it, Sef.'

'I – I do. I mean, you shift your *shape*.' Briefly he looked at the wolf. 'But I'd rather go with you.'

'*With* me?' Donal frowned. 'I will willingly buy you a meal – even a week's worth, if need be, or give you coin enough so you could go to another town – but I had not thought to take you with me.'

'Please –' One hand, briefly raised, fell back to his side. He shrugged. It was the barest movement of his ragged clothing, intensely vulnerable. 'I have no one. My mother is – dead. My father – I never knew.'

Donal frowned. 'I do not live here.'

'It doesn't matter. Hondarth isn't my home. Just – just a place I live, until I find better.' The thin face blazed with sudden hope. 'Take me with you! I'll work for my wage. I can tend your horse, prepare the food, clean up afterwards! I'll do *anything*.'

'Even to feeding my wolf?' Donal did not smile.

Sef blanched. He stared blindly at Lorn a moment, but then he nodded jerkily.

Donal laughed. 'No, no – Lorn feeds himself. I merely tease you, Sef.'

The boy's face lit up. 'Then you *will* take me with you?'

28

Donal glanced back toward the Crystal Isle. What Carillon had sent him to do offered no place for a boy, but perhaps after. Having a boy to tend to his horse and other small chores would undoubtedly be of help.

And there is always room for serving-boys in Homana-Mujhar. He turned back to Sef and nodded. 'I will take you. But there are things you must know about the service you undertake.'

Sef nodded immediately. 'I will do whatever you say.'

Donal sighed. 'To begin, I will not countenance pointless chatter among other boys you may meet. I understand what pride is, and what youth is, and how both will often lead a boy – a *young man* – into circumstances beyond his control, but this case is very special. I am not one for unnecessary elaborations, and I dislike ceremony, but there will be times for both. You will know them, too. But you must not give in to the temptation to speak of things you should not to other boys.'

Sef frowned intently. '*Other* boys? Do you have so many servants?'

Donal smiled. 'I have no servants – at least, not as *I* think of them. But there are pages and body-servants where we will go, when I finish my business here, and I must have your promise to keep yourself silent about my affairs.'

Sef's dirt-streaked face grew paler. 'Is it – because you're Cheysuli?'

'No. And I do not speak of *secret* things, merely things that are very private. And sometimes quite important.' He studied Sef's face and then brought his right hand up into the muted sunlight. 'See this? Tell me what it is.'

Sef frowned. 'A ring?'

'Surely you are more observant than *that*.'

The frown deepened. 'A gold ring. It has a red stone in it, and a black animal in the stone. A – lion.' Sef nodded. 'A black lion –'

'– rampant, upon a scarlet Mujharan field,' Donal finished. 'Do you know what that is?'

29

Sef started to shake his head. And then he stopped. 'Once, I saw a soldier. He wore a red tunic over his ring-mail, and on the tunic was a lion. A black lion, rearing up.' He pointed. 'Like that one.'

Donal smiled. 'That soldier was Carillon's man, as they all are. So am I. But – I am not a soldier. Not as you know soldiers.'

'A warrior.' Sef dipped his black head down. 'I know about the Cheysuli.'

'Not enough. But you will learn.' Donal smiled and reached down to catch Sef's chin. He tipped up his head. 'My name is Donal, Sef, and I am the Prince of Homana.'

Sef blanched white. Then he turned red. And finally, before Donal could catch him, he fell downward to smack his bony knees against the salt-crusted cobbles. '*My lord!*' he whispered. 'My lord – *the Prince of Homana*!'

Donal suppressed a laugh. It would not do to embarrass the boy simply because he was so in awe of royal rank. 'I do not stand on ceremony. Serve me as well as you would serve any man, and I will be well-pleased.'

'My lord –'

Donal reached down and caught a handful of thin tunic, then pulled Sef up from the cobbles. 'Do not be so – *overwhelmed*. I am flesh and bone, as you are.' He grinned. 'If you are to serve me, you must learn I am not some petty lordling who seeks elevation in the eyes and service of others. You may come with me as my friend, but not my servant. I left enough of those back at Homana-Mujhar.' His voice was gentle. 'Do you understand me?'

'Aye,' Sef whispered. 'Oh . . . my lord . . . *aye!*'

Donal released the ragged tunic. *I will have to buy him better clothing, perhaps in Carillon's colors – well, that will have to wait. But some manner of fitting clothing will not.* 'You shall have to *earn* your passage, Sef.' Donal looked down at the boy solemnly. 'Are you willing to work for that passage?'

'Aye, my lord!'

'Good.' Donal squeezed a narrow shoulder. 'All I

require of you is your company. Come along.'

'My lord!'

Donal turned back. 'Aye?'

'My lord –' Sef broke off, pulling again at his ill-fitting, muddied clothing. 'My lord – I wish only to say –' He broke off yet again, obviously embarrassed, vivid color flooding his cheeks.

Donal smiled at him encouragingly. 'Before me, you may say what you wish. If you speak out of turn, I will say so, but I will never strike you. Say what you will, Sef.'

The boy sucked in a deep breath. 'I wished only to thank you for coming to my aid, and to say that usually I *win* the fights.'

Donal smothered a laugh. 'Of course.'

'They were five to my one,' Sef pointed out earnestly.

'I counted them. You are right.' Donal nodded gravely.

Sef studied Donal a moment. Then, anxiously, 'You said I may *say* what I wish. Do you mean I may ask it as well?'

'You may always ask. I may not always answer.'

The boy smiled tentatively. 'Then – I'd ask you what you'd do against five men, if *you* were ever attacked.'

'I?' Donal laughed. 'Well, it would be a different situation. You see, I have two *lir.*'

'*They* would fight, too?' Sef stared at Lorn in amazement, then turned his bi-colored gaze to the sky to pick Taj out from the crying gulls.

'They will always fight, to aid me. That is what *lir* are for.'

That, and other things. Lorn reminded him dryly.

'Then five men couldn't stop you?'

Donal understood what Sef inquired, even if the boy did not. 'I do not doubt you fought well, Sef, and that bad fortune put you on the losing side. You need not make excuses. As for me, you must recall I am Cheysuli. We are taught to fight from birth.' His smile faded into a grim line. 'There is reason enough for that. Even now, I begin to think.'

31

'Cheysuli,' Sef echoed. He stood very still. 'Will you tell me what it's like?'

'As much as I can. But it is never easily done.' Donal nodded his head in Taj's direction, then gestured toward the wolf. '*There* is the secret of the Cheysuli, Sef. In Taj and Lorn. Understand what it is to have a *lir*, and you will know what it is to be blessed by the gods.'

Sef glanced at him skeptically. '*Gods*? I don't think there are any.'

'Ah, but there are. I am no *shar tahl*, dedicating my life to the prophecy and the service of the gods, but I can tell you what I know. Another time.' Donal smiled. 'Come along.'

This time, Sef fell into step beside him.

3

In the morning the ship's captain, paid generously before-hand in freshly minted gold coin, cast off readily enough for the Crystal Isle. Donal questioned him and learned all traffic to the island was closely watched by men serving the Mujhar; the man had agreed to transport Donal and Sef only after a close look at the royal signet ring. For once, Donal was glad Carillon made him wear it.

The captain was a garrulous man, perfectly content to while away the brief voyage by telling Donal all about the Queen of Homana's confinement. He confided there were Cheysuli on the island with Electra so she could use none of her witch's ways, and they kept Tynstar from rescuing her. He seemed little impressed with the knowledge that he transported the Prince of Homana himself, being rather more impressed with how he could use the knowledge to his own best advantage in fashioning an entertaining story full of gossip and anecdotes. Donal did not doubt a tale of his visit to the island would soon make the rounds of the taverns, undoubtedly much embellished. He quickly grew tired of the one-sided conversation and withdrew with what politeness he could muster, turning his back on the man to stare across the glassy bay.

Behind them, Hondarth receded. The painted cottages merged into clustered masses of glowing white, lumines-cent in the mist against a velvety backdrop of heathered hills. Before them, the island grew more distinct as the ship sailed closer, but Donal could see none of the distin-guishing features. Just a shape floating on the water,

wreathed in clouds of fog.

He became aware of Sef edging in close beside him. The mist shrouded them both and settled into their clothing, so that Sef – wrapped in a deep blue cloak Donal had purchased for him the day before, along with other new clothing – looked more fey than human. His black hair curled against his thin face – now clean – and his parti-colored eyes stared out at the island fixedly.

'It should not frighten you,' Donal said quietly. 'It is merely an island. A place.'

Sef looked at the eerie, silent blanket of sea-spray and morning fog. Even the crying of the gulls was muted in the mist. 'But it's an enchanted place. I've heard.'

'Do you know the old legends, then?'

Sef seemed hesitant. 'Some. Not all. I'm – not from Hondarth.'

'Where *are* you from?'

The boy looked away again, staring at the deck. Then, slowly, he raised his head. 'From many places. My mother earned bread by – by . . . ' He broke off uncertainly. His face colored so that he looked younger than the thirteen years he claimed. His voice was nearly a whisper. 'Because of – men. We – didn't stay long in any single place.' He shrugged, as if he could dismiss it all. But Donal knew such things would never entirely fade, even with adult-hood. 'She died almost a year ago, and I had no place else to go. So – I stayed.'

Donal heard the underlying note of shame and loneli-ness in Sef's tone. 'Well, travel befits a man,' he said off-handedly, seeking to soothe the boy without insulting him with sympathy. In the clans, the Cheysuli rarely resorted to emphasizing unnecessary emotions. 'You are of an age to learn the world, and Hondarth is as good a place as any to begin.'

Sef did not look at him. He looked instead at the Crystal Isle as they sailed closer yet. The fog thickened as they approached, wrapping itself around the ship until it clung to every line and spar, glistening in the brassy sunlight so

muted by the mist. Droplets beaded the railing and their cloaks, running down the oiled wool to fall on the deck. Their faces were cooled by the isle's constant wind, known to Cheysuli as the Breath of the Gods.

'Will you still keep me with you?' Sef asked very softly.

Donal looked at him sharply, frowning. 'I have said I would. Why do you ask?'

Sef would not meet his eyes. 'But – that was before you knew I was a – *bastard*.'

Donal made a quick dismissive gesture. 'You forget, Sef – I am Cheysuli, not Homanan.' Inwardly he shut his ears to the voice that protested the easy denial of his Homanan blood. 'In the clans, there is no such thing as bastardy. A child is born and his value is weighed in how he serves his clan and the prophecy, not in the question of his paternity.' Donal shook his head. 'I care not if your *jehan* – your father – was thief or cobbler or soldier. So long as *you* earn your keep.'

'Then the Cheysuli are wiser than most.' The bitterness in Sef's young voice made Donal want to put a hand on one narrow shoulder to gentle him, but he did not. The boy was obviously proud as well as uncertain of his new position, and Donal had more cause than most to understand the feeling.

He pointed toward the island. 'Tell me what you know, Sef.'

Sef looked. 'They say there are demons, my lord.'

Donal smiled. 'Do they? Well, they are wrong. That is a Cheysuli place, and there are no Cheysuli demons. Only gods, and the people they have made.'

'What people?'

'Those of us now known as the Cheysuli. Once, we were something different. Something – better.' Like the boy, he stared across the glass-grey ocean toward the misted island. Finally it grew clearer, more distinct. It was thickly forested, cloaked in lilac heather. Through the trees glowed a faint expanse of silver-white. 'The Firstborn, Sef. Those the gods made first, as their name implies.

35

Later, much later, were the Cheysuli born.'

Sef frowned, concentrating, so that his black brows overshadowed his odd eyes. 'You're saying once there were *no* people?'

'The *shar tahls* – our priest-historians – teach us that once the land was empty of men. It was a decision of the gods to put men upon the Crystal Isle and give it over to them freely. It is these original men we call the Firstborn. But the Firstborn soon outgrew the Crystal Isle, as men will when there are women, and went to Homana: a more spacious land for their growing numbers. They built a fine realm there, ruling it well, and the gods were pleased. As a mark of their favor, they sent the *lir* to them. And because of the earth magic, the Firstborn were able to bond with the *lir*, to learn what *lir*-shape is –'

'*Shapechangers*,' Sef interrupted involuntarily, shivering as he spoke.

Donal sighed. 'The name is easily come by, but we do not use it ourselves. *Cheysuli* is the Old Tongue, meaning *children of the gods*. But men – Homanans – being unblessed, all too often resort to the word as an insult.' He thought again of the Homanan in the Market Square; the woman who had made the sign of the evil eye; the splatter of manure against his cloak. And all because he could shift his shape from man into animal.

Surely the gods would never give such gifts to us was there any chance we would use them for evil? Why must so many believe we would?

They do not understand. Taj floated lightly, pale gold in the silver mist. *They are unblessed, and blind to the magic.*

Why do the gods not make them see?

Blindness often serves a purpose, Lorn explained. *Sight recovered is often better than original vision.*

Donal looked directly at Sef. 'Shapechanger,' he said clearly. 'Aye, it is true – I shift my shape as well. I become a wolf or falcon. But does it make me *so* different from you? I do not doubt there are things *you* do that I cannot. Should I castigate you for it?'

36

Sef shivered again. 'It isn't the same. It isn't the *same*. *You* become an animal, while I –' he shook his head violently, denying the image, '– while *I* remain a boy. A normal, *human* boy.'

'Unblessed,' Donal agreed, for a moment callous in his pride.

Sef looked at him then, staring fixedly at Donal's face. His disconcerting gaze traveled from yellow eyes to golden earring, and he swallowed visibly. 'The – the Firstborn,' he began, 'where are they, now?'

'The Firstborn no longer exist. And most of their gifts are lost.'

Sef frowned. 'Where did they go? What happened?'

The taffrail creaked as Donal shifted his weight. 'It is too long a story. One night, I promise, I will tell you it all – but, for now, *this* will have to content you.' He looked directly at the boy and saw how attentive he was. 'I am told the Firstborn became too inbred, that the gifts began to fade. And so before they died out they gave what they could to their children, the Cheysuli, and left them a prophecy.' For a moment he was touched by the gravity of what his race undertook; how important the service was. 'It is the Firstborn we seek to regain by strengthening the blood. Someday, when the proper mixture is attained, we will have a Firstborn among us again, and all the magic will be reborn.' He smiled. 'So the prophecy tells us: *one day a man of all blood shall unite, in peace, two magical races and four warring realms.*' Fluidly, he made the gesture of *tahlmorra* – right hand palm-up, fingers spread – to indicate the shortened form of the Old Tongue phrase meaning, in Homanan, *the fate of a man rests always within the hands of the gods*.

'You said – they *lost* their gifts –?'

'Most of them. The Firstborn were far more powerful than the Cheysuli. They had no single *lir*. They conversed with every *lir*, and took whatever shape they wished. But now, each warrior is limited to one.'

'*You* have two!' Sef looked around for Taj and Lorn. 'Are you a Firstborn, then?'

Donal laughed. 'No, no, I am a Cheysuli halfling, or – perhaps more precisely – a three-quarterling.' He grinned. 'But my half Homanan *jehana* bears the blood of the Firstborn – as well as some of the gifts – and by getting a child by my Cheysuli *jehan* she triggered that part of herself that has the Firstborn magic. I have two *lir* because of her, and I may converse with any, but nothing more than that. I am limited to those two shapes.'

Sef turned to stare at the island. 'Then – this is your birthplace.'

'In a manner of speaking.' Donal looked at the island again. 'It is the birthplace of the Cheysuli.'

'That is why you go?' Sef's odd eyes were wide as he looked up at Donal. 'To see where your people were born?'

'No, though undoubtedly every Cheysuli should.' Donal sighed and his mouth hooked down into a resigned grimace. 'No, I go there on business for the Mujhar.' He felt the curl of unhappiness tighten his belly. 'What I am about is securing the throne of Homana.'

'Securing it –?' Sef frowned. 'But – the Mujhar holds it. It's his.'

'There are those who seek to throw down Carillon's House to set up another.' Donal told him grimly. 'Even now, in Solinde . . . we know they plan a war.'

Sef stared. '*Why*? Who would do such a thing?'

Donal very nearly did not answer. But Sef was avid in his interest, and he would learn the truth one way or another, once he was in Homana-Mujhar. 'You know of the Ihlini, do you not?'

Sef paled and made the gesture warding off evil. 'Solindish demons!'

'Aye,' Donal agreed evenly. 'Tynstar and his minions would prefer to make the throne their own and destroy the prophecy. He wishes to have dominion over Homana – and all the other realms, I would wager – in order to serve Asar-Suti.' He paused. 'Asar-Suti is your demon, Sef, and more – he is the god of the netherworld. *The Seker*, he is called, by those who serve him: *the one who made and*

38

dwells in darkness.' He saw fear tauten Sef's face. 'In the name of his demon-god, Tynstar wishes to recapture Solinde from Carillon and make the realm his own, as tribute to Asar-Suti. And, of course, his ambition does not stop there – also he wants Homana. He plots for it now, at this moment – but we know this, so we are not unprepared; we are not a complacent regency in Solinde. And so long as Carillon holds the throne – and his blood after him – the thing will not be done. The Lion Throne is ours.'

Sef's hands were tight-wrapped around the rail. '*You'll* hold the throne one day, won't you? You're the Prince of Homana!'

He glanced down at the attentive boy. 'Now, do you see why I must teach you how to hold your tongue? Honesty is all well and good, but in Royal Houses, too much honesty may be construed as grounds for beginning a war. You must be careful in what you say as well as to whom you say it.'

Sef nodded slowly. 'My lord – I have promised to serve you well. I give you my loyalty.'

Donal smiled and clasped one thin shoulder briefly. 'And that is all I require, for now.'

His hand remained a moment longer on Sef's shoulder. The boy needed good food in him to fill out the hollows in his pasty-white face and to put some flesh on his bones, but his attitude was good. For a bastard boy living from hand to mouth it was very good indeed.

Donal chewed briefly at his bottom lip. *Being little more than an urchin, he may not prove equal to the task. He may not mix well with the other boys. But then I cannot judge* men *by how they conform to others – how boring that life would be – and I will not do it with Sef. I will give him what chance I can.* He smiled, and then he laughed. *Perhaps I have found someone to serve me as well as Rowan serves Carillon.*

The prison-palace on the Crystal Isle stood atop a gentle hill of ash-colored bracken and lilac heather. The forest

grew up around the pedestal of the hill, hiding much of the palace, but through the trees gleamed the whitewashed walls, attended by a pervasive silver mist. Stretching from the white sand beaches through the wind-stirred forest was a path of crushed sea shells, rose and lilac, pale blue and gold, creamy ivory.

Donal stood very still upon the beach, looking inland toward the forest. He did not look at the palace – it was not so ancient as the island and Homanan-made at that – but at the things the gods had made instead. Then he closed his eyes and gave himself over to sensation.

The wind curled gently around his body, caressing him with subtle fingers. It seemed to promise him things. He knew without doubting that the isle was full of dreams and magic and, if he sought it, a perfect peace and solitude. Carillon might have banished his treacherous wife to the island, but the place was a sacred place. Donal had thought perhaps the incarceration profaned the Crystal Isle.

But he sensed no unhappiness, no dissatisfaction in the wind. Perhaps the island was used for mundane Homanan concerns, but at heart it was still Cheysuli, still part and parcel of the Firstborn. It merely waited. One day, someone would return it to its proper state.

Donal feared to tread the crushed shells of the pathway at first, admiring its delicate beauty, but he saw no other way to the palace on its green-and-lilac hill. He took nothing with him save his *lir* and Sef. And, he hoped, his courage.

The isle was full of noise. Soft noise; gentle noise, a peaceful susurration. He and Sef and Lorn trod across crushed shell. They passed through trees that sighed and creaked, whispering in the wind. They heard the silences of the depths, as if even the animals muted themselves to honor the sanctity of the place.

Sef tripped over his own feet and went sprawling, scattering pearly shells so that they spilled out of the boundaries of the pathway, disturbing the curving symmetry.

Aghast, he hunched on hands and knees, staring at what he had done.

Donal reached down and caught one arm, pulling him to his feet. He saw embarrassment and shame in the boy's face, but also something more. 'There is nothing to fear, Sef,' he promised quietly. 'There are no demons here.'

'I – I *feel* something . . . I *feel* it –' He broke off, standing rigidly before Donal. His eyes were wide and fixed. His head cocked a trifle, as if he listened. As if he *heard*.

'Sef –'

The boy shuddered. The tremor ran through his slender body like an ague, Donal felt it strongly in his own hand as it rested upon Sef's arm. His thin face was chalky grey. He mouthed words Donal could neither hear nor decipher.

'*Sef –*'

Sef jerked his arm free of Donal's hand. For a moment, a fleeting moment only, his eyes turned inward as if he sought to shut out the world. He raised insignificant fists curled so tightly the bones of his knuckles shone through thinly stretched flesh. Briefly his teeth bared in an almost feral grimace.

'They *know* that I am here –' As suddenly he broke off. The eyes, filled by black pupils, looked upon Donal with recognition once again. 'My lord –?'

Donal released a breath. The boy had looked so strange, as if he had been thrown into a private battle within himself. But now he appeared recovered, if a trifle shaken. 'I intended to say it was only the wind and your own superstitions,' Donal told him. 'But – this is the island of the gods, and who am I to say they do not speak to you?'

Especially if he is Cheysuli. Donal felt the cool breeze run fingers through his hair, stripping it from his face. The wind was stronger than before, as if it meant to speak to him of things beyond his ken.

'They know it,' Sef said hollowly. And then his mouth folded upon itself, pressing lip against lip, as if he had made up his mind to overcome an enemy. 'It *doesn't matter*.'

41

Donal felt the breath of the gods against the back of his neck. He shivered. Then he helped put Sef's clothing into order once again. 'I will not deny I feel something as well, but I doubt there is anger in it. I think we have nothing to fear. I am, if you will pardon my arrogance, a descendent of the Firstborn.'

'And I am not,' Sef said plainly. Then something flickered in his eyes and his manner altered. He looked intently at Donal a moment, then shrugged narrow shoulders. 'I don't know *what* I am.'

Donal smoothed the boy's black hair into place, though the wind disarranged it almost at once. 'The gods do. That is what counts.' He tapped Sef on the back. 'Come along. Let us not keep the lady waiting.'

The interior of the expansive palace was pillared in white marble veined with silver and rose. Silken tapestries of rainbow colors decked the white walls and fine carpets replaced rushes which, even scented, grew old and rank too quickly. Donal did not know how much of the amenities had been ordered by Electra – or, more likely, by Carillon – but he was impressed. Homana-Mujhar, for all its grandeur, was somewhat austere at times. This place, he thought, would make a better home.

Except it is a prison.

Racks of scented beeswax candles illuminated the vastness of the entry hall. Servants passed by on business of their own, as did occasional guards attired in Carillon's black-and-crimson livery. Donal saw a few Cheysuli warriors in customary leathers and gold, but for the most part his fellow warriors remained unobtrusive.

When the woman came forth to greet Donal, he saw she wore a foreign crest worked into the fabric of her gown: Electra's white swan on a cobalt field. The woman was slender and dark with eyes nearly the color of the gown; he wondered if she had chosen it purposely. And he recalled that Carillon had also exiled the Queen's Solindish women.

He wondered at the decision. *Would it not have been better to send the women home? Here with Electra, they*

42

could all concoct some monstrous plot to overthrow the Mujhar.

How? Taj asked as he lighted on a chairback. *Carillon has warded them well.*

I do not trust her, lir.

Nor does Carillon, Lorn told him. *There is no escape for her. There are Cheysuli here.*

The Solindish woman inclined her head as she paused before Donal. She spoke good Homanan, and was polite, but he was aware of an undertone of contempt. 'You wish to see the Queen. Of course. This way.'

Donal measured his step to the woman's. She paused before a brass door that had been meticulously hammered and beveled into thousands of intricate shapes. The woman tapped lightly, then stepped aside with a smooth, practiced gesture. 'Through here. But the boy must wait without – there, on the bench. The Queen sees no one unless she so orders it – and I doubt she would wish to see *him.*'

Donal restrained the retort he longed to make, matching the woman's efficient, officious manner as he inclined his head just enough to acknowledge her words. Then he turned to Sef. 'Wait for me here.'

Sef's thin face was pale and frightened as he slowly sat down on the narrow stone bench beside the door. He clasped his hands in his lap, hunching within his cloak, and waited wordlessly.

'Be not afraid,' Donal said gently. 'No one will seek to harm you. You are the Prince's man.'

Sef swallowed, nodded, but did not smile. He looked at his hands only, patently prepared to wait with what patience he thought was expected, and wanting none of it.

Knowing he could do nothing more, Donal gave up the effort and passed through the magnificent door. It thudded shut behind him.

Taj rode his right shoulder. Lorn paced beside his left leg. He was warded about with *lir*, and still he felt apprehensive. This was Electra he faced.

Witch. Tynstar's meijha. *More than merely a woman.* But he went on, pacing the length of the cavernous hall.

Electra awaited him. He saw her standing at the end of the hallway on a marble dais. And he nearly stopped in his tracks.

He had heard, as they all had, that Electra's fabled beauty was mostly illusory, that Tynstar had given it to her along with the gift of youth and immortality; so long as she was not slain outright, she – like Tynstar – would never die. He had heard that the beauty would fade, since she was separated from Tynstar. But Donal knew how much power rumors had – as well as how little truth – and now as he saw the woman again for the first time in fifteen years, he could not say if she was human or immortal; ensorceled or genuine.

By the gods . . . separation from Tynstar has not dulled her beauty; has not *dispersed the magic!*

Her pale grey eyes watched him approach the dais. Long-lidded, somnolent eyes; eyes that spoke of bedding. Her hair was still a fine white-blonde, lacking none of its shine or texture. Loose, it flowed over her shoulders like a mantle, held back from her face by a simple fillet of golden, interlocked swans. Her skin lacked none of the delicate bloom of youth, and her allure was every bit as powerful as it had been the day she trapped Carillon in her spell.

Donal looked at her. No longer a boy, he saw Electra as a man sees a woman: appraising, judgmental and forever wondering what she would be like if she ever shared his bed. He could not look at her without sexual fantasy; it was not that he desired her, simply that Electra seemed to magically inspire it.

I have been blind, he realized. *No more can I say to Carillon I cannot comprehend what made him keep her by him, even when he recognized her intent.* He swallowed heavily. *I have been such a fool* . . . But he would never admit it to her – or to Carillon.

Electra wore a simple gown of silvered grey velvet, but over it she had draped a wine-purpled mantle of sheer, pearly silk. Unmoving, she watched him. Watching her watching him, Donal made up his mind to best her.

'You come at last.' Her voice was low and soft, full of the cadences of Solinde. 'I had thought Carillon's little wolfling would keep himself to his forests.'

Donal managed to maintain an impassive face as he halted before the dais. A word within the link to Taj sent the falcon fluttering to perch upon the back of the nearest chair. Lorn stood at Donal's left knee, ruddy pelt rising on his shoulders.

As if he too senses the power in the woman.

Electra was not a tall woman, though her tremendous self-possession made her seem so. The dais made her taller yet, but even marble could not compete with Donal's Cheysuli height.

It was an odd moment. She stood before him, impossibly beautiful and immortally young. Too young. He came to speak of her daughter, when she appeared hardly old enough to bear one.

He smiled. *I have you, Electra, and you do not even know it.*

She watched him. The clear, grey-pale eyes did not move from his face, as if she judged him solely by his own eyes. Well, he knew what she saw: a clear, eerily perfect yellow; eyes bestial and uncanny, full of a strange inborn wisdom and wildness and a fanatic dedication to the prophecy of the Firstborn.

We are enemies. We need say nothing to one another; it is there. It was there from the day I was born, as if she knew what I would come to mean to her and the Ihlini lord she serves.

'I have come to fetch home your daughter, lady,' he said quietly. 'It is time for us to wed.'

Electra's head moved only a little on her slender neck. Her voice was quiet and contained. 'I do not give my permission for this travesty to go forth. No.'

'The choice is not yours –'

'So you may say.' Slender, supple hands smoothed the silk of her mantle, drawing his eyes to their subtle seductiveness. 'Think you I will allow my daughter to wed a

45

Cheysuli shapechanger? No.' She smiled slowly. 'I forbid it.'

He set his teeth. 'Forbid what you will, Electra, it will do you little good. If you seek to rail at me like a jackdaw because of your fate, I suggest you look at the cause of your disposal. It is because of *you* Carillon has made me heir to Homana and your daughter's intended husband. *You*, lady. Because you conspired against him.'

Long-nailed fingers twisted the wine-red fabric of her mantle. Her eyes held a malignant fascination. 'Your prophecy says a Cheysuli must hold the Lion Throne of Homana before it can be fulfilled. Undoubtedly all of the shapechangers think that man will be you, since Carillon has let everyone know – no matter how unofficially – that he intends to proclaim you his heir. "Prince of Homana," are you not styled, even before the proper time?' Electra smiled. 'But that is not the prophecy Tynstar chooses to serve . . . *nor is it mine!* We will put no Cheysuli on the Lion Throne but an Ihlini-born man instead, and see to Carillon's death.'

'You have tried,' he said with a calmness he did not feel. 'You have tried to slay him before, and it has failed. Is Tynstar so inept? Is he a powerless sorcerer? Or has the Seker turned his face from his servant, so that Tynstar lacks a lord?' He waited, but she made no answer. Even in her anger, she was utterly magnificent. He felt the tightening of his loins, and it made him angry with himself as well as with the woman. 'Electra, I ask you one thing: have you said this to your daughter? Do you tell *her* what you intend to do? He is, after all, her father.'

'Aislinn is not your concern.'

'Aislinn will be my *cheysula*.'

'Use no shapechanger words to me!' she snapped. 'Carillon may have sent me here, but this is *my* hall! *My* palace! I rule here!'

'What do you rule?' he demanded. 'A few pitiful acres of land, served only by those who serve the Mujhar, except for your loyal women. An impressive realm, Electra.' He

46

shook his head. 'It is a pity you hold no court. Instead, you have only the memories of what you once had the ordering of.' He smiled ironically. 'The grandeur of Bellam's palaces in Solinde and the magnificence of Homana-Mujhar. But all of that is gone, Electra – banished by your treachery and deceit. Curse not me or mine when you must first curse yourself.'

For the first time he had shaken her composure utterly. He could see it. She trembled with fury, and clutched at the silk of her mantle so that the fabric crumpled and rent. Rich color stood high in her face. 'First you must *wed* her, shapechanger, to merge the proper blood. But what is not yet done shall *remain* undone . . . and the prophecy shall fail.'

Electra stretched out a hand toward him. He saw the merest crackle and flare of purple flame around one pointing finger, but the color died. The hand was nothing more than a hand. Before a Cheysuli, the arts Tynstar had taught her failed.

'Tynstar's sorcery keeps you young now, Electra,' Donal said gently. 'But you should remember: you *are* a woman of fifty-five. One day, it will catch up to you.' He walked slowly toward the dais, mounted it even as she opened her mouth to revile him, and slowly walked around her. 'One day he will be slain, and then what becomes of you? You will age, even as Carillon ages. Your bones will stiffen and your blood will flow sluggishly. One day you will not be able to rise, so feeble will you have become, and you will be bound to chair or bed. And then you shall have only endless empty hours in which to spin your impotent webs.' He stopped directly before her. 'That is your *tahlmorra*, Electra . . . I wish you well of it.'

Electra said nothing. She merely smiled an unsettling smile.

'What of *me*?' asked a voice from a curtained opening. 'What do you wish for *me*?'

47

4

Donal spun around and saw the young woman gowned in snowy white. A girdle of gold and garnets spilled down the front of her skirts to clash and chime against the hem. Redgold hair flowed loosely over her shoulders, in glorious disarray. Her lustrous white skin and long grey eyes were her mother's; her pride was Carillon's.

'Aislinn!' It was the only word he could muster. For two years he had not seen her, knowing her only through her letters to Carillon. And in those two years she had crossed the threshold between girlhood and womanhood. She was still young – too young, he thought, for marriage – but all her awkward days were over.

He smiled at her, prepared to tell her how much she had changed – and for the better. But his smile slowly began to fade as she moved into the hall.

Aislinn let the tapestry curtain fall from a long-fingered hand. The gems in the girdle flashed in the candlelight. Gold gleamed. A fortune clasped her slender waist and dangled against her skirts. And Donal, knowing that Carillon's taste in gifts to his daughter ran to merlins, puppies and kittens, realized the girdle was undoubtedly a present from Electra.

He looked at Aislinn's face. It was taut and forbidding, set in lines too harsh for a young woman of sixteen years, but if she had heard his final words to Electra he was not at all surprised she should view him with some hostility.

The girdle chimed as Aislinn moved. And Donal wondered uneasily if Electra had somehow purchased her daughter's loyalty.

Carillon should never have sent her . . . not for so long. Not for two years. The gods know he meant well by it, realizing the girl needed to see her jehana . . . but he should have had her brought back much sooner, regardless of all those letters begging to remain a little longer. Two years is too long. The gods know what the witch has done to Aislinn's loyalties.

The girl halted before him, glancing briefly at the wolf. Donal thought she might greet her old friend, but she made no move to kneel down and scratch Lorn's ears as she had in earlier days.

Aislinn's pride was manifest. 'Well? What say you, Donal?' Her tone was a reflection of her mother's, cool and supremely controlled. 'What of *me*?'

'By the gods, Aislinn!' he said in surprise. 'I have no quarrel with *you*. It is your *jehana* who lacks manners!'

It was obviously not what she expected him to say. She lost all of her cool demeanor and stared at him in astonishment. 'How *dare* you attack my mother!'

'Donal.' Electra's voice sounded dangerously amused, and he looked at her warily. 'Are you certain you *wish* to wed my daughter?'

He wanted to swear. He did not, but only because he shut his mouth on the beginning of the word. He glared at Electra. 'Play no games with me, lady. Aislinn and I have been betrothed for fifteen years. We have been friends as long as that.'

Electra smiled: a cat before a mousehole. 'Friends, aye – at one time. But are you so certain she is the woman you would wish to keep as your wife the rest of your life?'

No, he said inwardly. *Not Aislinn . . . but what choice do I have?*

He gritted his teeth and made up his mind not to lose the battle. Not to Electra. He knew she took no prisoners. 'I imagine you have done what you could to turn Aislinn against this marriage in the two years you have hosted her.' He glanced at the girl and saw contempt for him in her eyes. Electra's eyes, so cool and shrewd. Contempt, where once

49

there had been childlike adoration. 'Aye,' he agreed grimly, 'I see you have. But I have more faith in Aislinn's integrity.'

'Integrity has nothing to do with it,' Electra said gently. 'Ask Aislinn what she thinks of bearing unnatural children.'

Shock riveted him. He stared at the woman in horror. '*Unnatural children* –'

'Ask Aislinn what she thinks of babies born with fangs and claws and tails, and the beast-mark on their faces,' Electra suggested softly. 'Ask Aislinn what she thinks of playing mother – no, *jehana* –' she twisted the Old Tongue cruelly '– to a *thing* not wholly human nor wholly animal – but bestial instead.' The perfect mouth smiled. 'Ask Aislinn, my lord Prince of Homana, what she thinks about sharing a bed with a man who cannot control his shape – *in* bed or out of it.'

He took a single lurching step away from the dais and the woman. 'What *filth* have you told her –?'

'Filth?' Electra arched white-blond brows. 'Only the truth, shapechanger. Or do you deny the gold on your arms, in your ear . . . the animals your kind call the *lir*?' An expressive gesture encompassed gold and wolf and bird.

He felt ill. He wanted to turn his back on the woman and flee the hall, but he could not do it. He would not do it. He would not allow her to win. 'Lies,' he said flatly. 'And Aislinn knows it. Do you forget? – she has known me since her birth.'

'I forget nothing.' Electra smiled with all the guilelessness of a child. 'But you have the right of it, of course . . . Aislinn knows you well.'

Donal stood his ground. 'We played together as children, Electra. Scraped knees, tended bee stings, shared one another's bread. Do you think, *lady*, such memories can be destroyed with but a few words from you?'

'I have had her two years, Donal.' Electra allowed the violet mantle to slither to her hip, exposing the low-cut neck of her gown and the pale flesh of the tops of her breasts. 'Do

you recall what I did to Carillon in two *months*?'

He did. And he turned at once to Aislinn. 'Two years is more than enough time to fill your head with lies, and she is good at that. But do you forget your *jehan*? It is Carillon with whom you lived for fourteen years before you came to Electra.'

A pale hand smoothed the garneted chains hanging from Aislinn's girdle. Her pinched face told him she did indeed recall their childhood friendship and her girlish attraction to him. 'I – believe my mother has told me the truth. We are children no longer . . . and why would she lie to *me*?'

'To use you.' He had no more time for tact or diplomacy. 'By the gods, girl, are you blind? Do you forget why she is here? She will try to bring down Carillon any way she can. Even now she stoops to perverting *you*!'

Fingers tangled in the garneted golden chains. 'But – it is not the Mujhar she speaks of, Donal . . . it is *you*. It is *you* she warns me against, knowing your animal urges –'

'*Animal urges!*' He was aghast. ' Have you gone mad? You *know* me, Aislinn – what *urges* do you speak of?'

Her face had caught fire, as if to match the richness of her hair. 'We were children, then . . . we are adults, now. You are – a man . . . and she has told me what to expect.' She averted her eyes from his, staring fiercely at the floor. 'I have only to look at Finn, if I want to see what you will become.'

'Finn?' He stared. 'What has *Finn* to do with this?'

Aislinn managed to look at him again, though the chiming of her girdle told him how she trembled. 'Will you deny that he *stole* your own mother because he wanted her – as an animal wants another? Will you deny that he stole also the Mujhar's sister – who later died because of his neglect?' Aislinn sucked in a shaking breath. 'I look at Finn, Donal, your own uncle . . . and I see what you will become.'

By the gods, Electra has driven her mad – He felt his hands clench into fists, unclenched them with effort, and tried to speak coherently through his astonishment and anger.

'We will – speak of this another time. In some detail. But

51

for now, I must tell you to have your things packed.'

'Have you gone mad?' she demanded. 'Do you think I will go with *you*?'

'I think so,' he said grimly. 'It is the Mujhar's bidding I do, not my own. Aislinn – he bids us end our betrothal. The time has come for us to wed.'

For a long moment, she simply stared. He saw how she looked at him, appraising him even as her mother had. What she saw he could not say. But her face was very pale, and there was true apprehension in her eyes.

She turned quickly to face her mother. 'He cannot make me go if I wish to stay with you.' The question, even through her declaration, was implicit in her tone.

'You have been with your *jehana* two years, Aislinn – longer than was intended,' Donal pointed out. 'Carillon allowed you to stay because you wished it. He has been overly generous, I think – but now it is time you returned to him.'

Electra smoothed the supple silk of her purple mantle. 'He is a shapechanger, Aislinn. He can make man or woman do *anything*, does he wish it.' Her cool eyes glinted as she looked at him. 'Can you not?'

Grimly, he wished he could slay her where she stood, even before her daughter.

Electra merely smiled.

'I will *not*,' Aislinn declared. 'I will go nowhere I have no wish to go.'

Inwardly, he sighed. 'Then you defy your *jehan*, Aislinn. It is Carillon who wants you back in Homana-Mujhar.' *Not me*, he thought. *Oh gods, not* me.

'And you do *not*?' she demanded triumphantly, as if she had won the battle and proved her point.

Donal laughed, but the sound lacked all humor. 'No,' he said bluntly. 'Why should I?'

Slowly, so slowly, the color flowed out of her face. Her grey eyes were suddenly blackened pits of comprehension. Color rushed back and lit her face. '*Do you mean* –'

'– do I mean I do not want you?' he interrupted rudely.

'Aye, that sums it up. So gainsay your foolishness, Aislinn, and order your belongings packed. Carillon wants you home.'

The breath rattled in her throat. 'Wait you – *wait* you –' She shut her mouth, tried to recover some of her vanished composure, and frowned at him. 'To gain the throne, you must have *me*.'

'Oh, aye,' he agreed, 'but have I ever said I *wanted* it?'

'But – it is the *throne* –' She gestured. 'The throne of all Homana . . . and now Solinde. The *Lion* Throne.' Her frown deepened. 'And yet you tell me you *do not want* it?'

'I do not,' he said distinctly. 'Do you understand, now? We were betrothed because Carillon had no sons, only a daughter – and no *cheysula* – no *proper* one – to share his bed and bear him any more children.' His eyes went to Electra, standing stiffly on the dais. 'And so, by betrothing his daughter to his cousin's son, Carillon gets an heir for the throne of Homana.' He spread his hands. 'Me.' The hands flopped down. '*That* is why I am here, no matter what your *jehana* tells you.'

Aislinn gathered the heavy girdle in both hands, wadding the chain into the soft flesh of her palms. She was pale, so pale; he thought she might cry. But she did not. He saw her reach within herself to regain her composure.

She looked at her mother. She looked at her mother, and waited.

When he could, Donal looked at the woman also. She stood but two paces from him, close enough that he could put out his hands and throttle her. He knew, for the first time, a measure of the futility Carillon had experienced, and knew himself a fool for undervaluing the woman.

Gods . . . even now she does not give up. She will hound him to his death – He was brought up short. *Which is what she wants. Even now. Even imprisoned on this island, she will do what she can to slay him . . . even to using her daughter.* He felt ill. *I cannot deal with this –*

Electra regarded him quietly. 'Do you see?' she asked. 'You may win back a part of her, in time – I do expect it, of

course – but there is a portion of Aislinn I will always hold.' Her right hand scribed an invisible rune in the air between them, as if she dallied idly. She smiled composedly. 'Her *soul*, Cheysuli wolfling. I have made that completely mine . . . and what is mine is also Tynstar's.'

Donal watched her hand, so slim and pale, as it closed upon the invisible rune. *By the gods, what has she done to Aislinn?*

He looked at the girl. She stood very still, staring fixedly at her mother, and Donal felt an uprush of chilling apprehension. *There are Cheysuli here – Electra can practice no magic.* And yet he knew, watching the woman, that she retained a measure of her power. How much or how little he could not say, but there was power in her eyes. And Aislinn, Homanan and Solindish, was completely unprotected. Vulnerable to her mother.

Before a Cheysuli, the Ihlini lose much of their power. But not all! There are still tricks they can perform. Electra may only know such tricks as Tynstar taught her, being no Ihlini herself, but I cannot say she is as helpless as we thought –

Donal looked sharply at Aislinn. He saw how pale she was, how she continued clenching the golden girdle with all its rich cold stones. Her hands were shaking, and yet her voice was quite steady, quite calm.

As if she has made a discovery, and is strengthened because of it.

'Is that why you wanted me?' Aislinn did not move. 'For the Ihlini?' She ignored Electra's abortive attempt at speech. 'And are you so *certain* your perverted magic has worked on me?'

Donal stared at Aislinn. So did Electra. The silence was unbroken in the hall.

Garnets rattled as Aislinn clutched the girdle. 'I have listened to Donal just now. I have listened to you as well, hearing you mouth all the things you have told me these past two years. And – I know you better than ever before: *I know you.*'

'Aislinn –' Electra began.

54

'*Listen to me!*' Aislinn's shout reverberated. 'I will hear no more lies about my father – *no more lies*. Oh, aye . . . I know what you sought to do – I know why you sought to *do* it! Make the daughter into a weapon against the father.' Aislinn's voice shook. 'He told me – he *told* me: once he truly loved you. But you gave yourself to Tynstar. You wasted yourself on an Ihlini sorcerer! And now you think to twist me in spirit as Tynstar has twisted my father in body?' Hysterically, she laughed, and the sound filled up the hall. 'I *do* know Donal – and he is *not* what you say he is!'

Electra's lips were pale. She stood very still on the marble dais. 'He is a *shapechanger*. What I have told you is true.'

Aislinn shook her head violently. 'What you have told me are *lies*! Did you think I would not know? Did you truly believe I would listen to that vile filth you spewed when I have known him longer than I have *you*?' Again, Aislinn laughed. 'You do not live up to your reputation, *mother*! I am amazed at how easily I saw through your plans.'

Electra's face was bone-white. Suddenly, even through the magnificence of her beauty, she was old.

But still she summoned a smile. 'Then I will tell you the truth in one thing, Aislinn – *heed me well*. I do not lie. What is mine is also Tynstar's, and I have *made you mine*.' One hand stabbed upward to cut off Aislinn's angry words. 'Wait you, girl, and you will see. Do not seek to denigrate my power when you have hardly known it.' This time, it was Electra who laughed. 'Run along, then, and pack your things. Perhaps it *is* time I sent you home to the cripple who sired a useless daughter when all he wanted was a son.'

'Aislinn, do not.' Donal's quiet tone overrode the beginnings of Aislinn's outcry. 'Let it be. You know what she is.' He touched the girl's arm. He felt her body tremble. 'Go. Pack your things. And look forward to seeing your *jehan*, who truly loves you.'

White-faced, with tears staining the fairness of her cheeks, Aislinn turned and ran from her mother's hall.

When he could better master himself, Donal turned back to face Electra. 'I am grateful to you.' He said it very

quietly. 'You have let the girl see for herself precisely what you are, and I need never say another word. You have made my work easier, Electra. I thank you for it.'

'Do you?' The overwhelming beauty was back and all the odd fragility was banished. Electra was once more herself. 'Then I am heartened. It will make it so much sweeter when my plans are quite fulfilled.'

Donal shook his head. 'You have power, lady – that I willingly admit – and no doubt Tynstar has taught you how to use it, but you forget. You forget something very important.' He forced a smile. 'Aislinn loves her father, Electra . . . and the power of that love you can never destroy.'

Electra considered a moment. 'Perhaps not,' she conceded, 'but then must we always speak of Carillon? Why not of you, instead?'

'Does it matter?' he demanded. 'You have lost her entirely.'

'Have I? No, I think not. She may believe so for now – she is welcome to that innocence – but she will soon see that she cannot deny me. I am no idle practitioner of the little love-spells other women like to think they weave. No, no – I am much more. Tynstar has made me so.' Slowly, she gathered up the red-purple mantle and draped it over one velveted shoulder. 'Aislinn is all mine. You will see it. So shall she. And in the end, I shall win.'

'What can you do?' he demanded derisively. 'What spell do you think you can cast? You have seen and heard your daughter, Electra – she is none of yours. How can you think to gainsay us?'

The woman smiled slowly, with all the seductiveness in her soul. 'Quite easily, as you will see.' Electra laughed once more. 'Surely you know the law, Donal: *No marriage is binding if it is not consummated*.'

56

she ran a hand through it. Something glinted there before
was lost and gone, her hand dropping away as she made
... she was part of her own ... she could run to the cliffs ...
the two winds that drove the ship? She set her teeth,
... that within she stopped, then glanced about and ...
... uncertain, watchful. 'I ... have sorrowful knowledge the
... mind. And then Aislinn ... 'I did.' Aislinn, to what
... she had thought ... her, I ... have bored though what
... would be made to make any demands that caught. She
... have ... and once ... even the never shining in not

5

The ship creaked as she broke swells on her way back
toward the mainland. Behind her lay the mist-shrouded
island. Already the sun shone more brightly, even as it
sank toward the horizon and set the seas ablaze.

'I am sorry for what I said to you in the hall.' Aislinn,
standing before Donal as he leaned against the taffrail,
ignored his dismissive gesture. 'I said them because my
mother made certain I would, though I did not realize it
then. She had told me so much of you, and I almost
believed her.' The lowering sun set her hair aglow. 'I
am – shamed by my behavior, which was not fitting for a
princess.' Her voice trembled. 'Oh Donal – I am *so*
ashamed –'

'Aislinn –'

'No.' She made a chopping gesture with her right hand.
Her young face was blotched and swollen with tears, so
that most of her burgeoning beauty was replaced with
anguish. 'I *almost* believed her. Though I have known you
for so long. And then, when I heard her confidence – when
I heard how she intended to *use* me – I could not bear it!
I thought of my father as I looked into your face, and I
knew what she meant to do.'

Donal turned from the rail to face her directly. 'Do you
say, then, you did not know before today what it was she
sought to do?' He asked it gently, knowing it needed to be
asked; knowing also she was extremely vulnerable to the
pain engendered by such questions.

The wind played with Aislinn's red-gold hair, though

57

she had braided it into a single plait for traveling. The rope of hair hung down her back to her waist, bright against the dull brown of her traveling cloak. Stray curls pulled free of the braid and crept up to touch her face.

Impatiently, she stripped them back with one hand as she brushed more tears away. 'I – knew something of what she intended. At least – I thought I did.' Aislinn shrugged slightly. 'Perhaps it is just that now I wish to deny what sway she held over me, so I can find some pride again.' She turned away from him. 'Toward the end, during my last days, I began to understand better what she wanted. And I knew I wanted no part of it. But I was – afraid. I thought – if I told her I wished to go home to my father, she would forbid it. So – I waited. And when I heard you had come, I thought I would ask you to take me back. But – I heard what you said to her, how you reviled her, and I recalled all the things she had told me – about what the Cheysuli can do – and I became afraid again.' She lowered her eyes.

She was young. So very young. He was unsurprised Electra had chosen to use her; even less so that Aislinn had so easily been taken in. He could not begin to imagine what it had been like for her in Homana- Mujhar, princess-born and bred by her father the Mujhar, knowing all the while her exiled mother was imprisoned on the Crystal Isle.

'Aislinn.' He put out his hands and drew her away from the railing, cradling her shoulders in his palms. 'I am sorry for the scene involving your *jehana*. But that is done now, and you must face the things that lie ahead.'

Almost at once he felt ludicrous – he was not the girl's father, but her betrothed – and here he was speaking like a wise old man when he was more ordinarily an unwise young one.

Donal smiled wryly. 'Listen to us, Aislinn. One would think we hardly know one another.'

She moved closer, seeking solace. 'I think perhaps we do not.' Her eyes beseeched his. 'Will you be easy with me? I am sometimes a foolish girl.'

'And I am sometimes a foolish boy.' Donal set a hand to her head and smoothed back the blowing hair. 'We will have to grow up together.'

Aislinn laughed a little. 'But you are already grown, no matter what you say. While I feel like an infant.'

'Hardly that. You should look in the polished silver.'

A glint crept into Aislinn's eyes. She arched her brows. 'I have.'

He tugged her braid. 'And vain of what you see, are you?' He laughed at the beginnings of her protest. 'I am no courtier, Aislinn, but I can tell you this much: you are a woman now, and quite a beautiful one.'

She touched his bare arm lightly. 'My thanks, Donal. I was afraid – I was afraid I would not please you. And I do desire to please you.'

It was earnestness he heard in her voice, and honesty, not seductiveness. And yet even in her simplicity, there was a powerful allure about her. She lacked Electra's guile, but none of her mother's power to bind a man.

He disengaged from her as easily as he could and stepped away. He could not afford to be bound.

The same Homanan sailed them back to the mainland, silent now in his astonishment at what he heard and from whom he heard it. Sef sat on a coil of rope nearby, watching Donal and Aislinn with the rapt attention of a hound guarding his master. Taj perched upon a spar high above them. Lorn, deck-bound, paced the length of the ship again and again, as if something troubled him.

Lir? Donal asked.

Something. Something. I cannot say. And Lorn would say no more.

Taj?

The falcon's tone was troubled. *Nor have I an answer.*

Aislinn clutched at the taffrail for support as the ship broke swells. Donal reached out and set an arm behind her back. 'Forgive me, Aislinn – what I must ask is harsh, I know . . . but you must realize that others have known what Electra is for years. How can you have escaped it?'

59

Her young mouth twisted bitterly. 'Oh, aye, I heard all the stories. How could I not in Homana-Mujhar? We have all heard the lays from the harpers – how it was the Queen of Homana sought to slay her wedded husband.' Aislinn looked away from him, staring instead at the mainland as the ship sailed closer. 'I heard them all,' she muttered, 'but she is my mother, and I wanted to see her. Oh, how I longed to see her!'

'Because she was the stuff of legend?' He could not let it pass.

Aislinn's chin rose defensively. 'That, too. She was *Electra of Solinde*, Bellam's daughter, ensorceled by Tynstar himself.' Her fair skin was flushed with shame. 'And I wondered: did I have any of the Solindish witch in me? I could not *help* but wonder.'

'No.' Donal shifted against the rail. 'Aislinn – you must know I do not blame you. I cannot say I know Electra well – like you, I know her through the legends – but I *do* know that what you said was what she had put into your mind. She is a witch, with powers we cannot fully comprehend.'

'And you are Cheysuli.' Aislinn's grey gaze, though red-rimmed from her anguish, was very steady. She had more of Electra in her features than Carillon, but he saw a shadow of her father in her pride and confidence. 'Can your magic not overcome hers?'

'She can use none on me,' he agreed, 'because of my Cheysuli blood. But she is free to use what she will on you. You are Homanan –'

'– *and* Solindish.' She said it very clearly. 'Do you wonder, now, if I am the enemy also? If what she said about me is true, then perhaps I *am* nothing but a tool to be used against my father . . . or even you.'

'There is no truth in Electra's mouth.' Donal tugged her braid again, and then the hand slipped under the rope of hair to press against the cloak and her back beneath the wool. 'We must make a marriage, you and I, for the sake of your *jehan's* realm. But if you have even the smallest bit

of Carillon in you, I need have no fear of Electra's influence.'

Aislinn stared fixedly at the shoreline. 'You said you did not desire the throne.' Her voice trembled just a little. 'You said – and clearly – you did not desire *me*.'

He was not a man of stone, to hear the pain in her voice and not respond. But he could not lie to her, not even to salve her pride.

'The truth,' he said gently. 'No. I do not desire you. I think of you as a *rujholla*, not a *cheysula*.'

'I am not your sister.' Her spine was rigid beneath his hand. 'And I do not think of *you* as a brother.'

She never had; he knew that. He had known it from the beginning. Before she was old enough to know what betrothal meant, she had decided to marry him.

Aislinn turned and faced him. 'We were young together, briefly; you grew up too fast. You already had your *lir* – you were a warrior, not a boy, and too soon you wearied of playing with little girls. Me. Your sister. Meghan.' She shrugged. 'You left us all behind. But now – *now* – I am trying to catch up.'

He knew what she wanted. Some confirmation there could be love between them. And he knew he could not offer it.

I will hurt her. One day . . . I will have to.

'Aislinn – let it come of its own time if the gods desire it. You are young. There is time.'

'I am young,' Aislinn agreed, 'but I am old enough. The priests will see to that.'

Donal touched her braid again. 'Aye, so they will. I am sorry, Aislinn. But I will not give you falsehood or false dreams.'

She turned abruptly and faced him. 'Do you not care for me at *all*?'

He wanted to retreat, but did not. He owed her more, no matter how horrible he felt. And he felt. More deeply than he had believed possible. He was fond of Aislinn, very fond; she had always been a winsome girl, and he had

61

always enjoyed her company. But it was girl to man, not man to woman; he had another woman for that.

'Aislinn,' he said at last, 'What you know of a man and woman has been twisted by your *jehana*. You would do well to speak to mine, to know the truth of things.'

Aislinn set her jaw. It was delicately feminine, but he did not forget what man had helped to form it. 'Alix is your mother,' Aislinn declared. 'She will think only of *you*, and not at all of me.'

'She is not blind to my faults,' Donal told her wryly. 'She knows me very well.'

'But would she admit them openly to me?'

He laughed. 'Do you think there are so many?'

'Sometimes.' She pushed strands of hair out of her face. 'They say you are much like Finn. And what I have heard of *him* –'

'From *Electra*?' Donal wanted to spit. 'Gods, Aislinn, there is nothing but hatred between them.'

'From others. You know what the servants say in Homana-Mujhar.'

He overrode her at once. 'Most of those stories are false. They are made-up things, tales to entertain those who enjoy such petty nonsense.' He shook his head. 'Do you think your *jehan* would keep by him a liege man who had done all the things the tales say Finn did?'

'He is your uncle,' Aislinn retorted. 'I think you will not admit *he* has faults.'

Donal smiled wryly. 'Oh, aye, my *su'fali* has faults. Many of them – but not so many as all these people so willingly ascribe to him.' He sighed, frowning a little. 'But – Carillon says I am more like my *jehan* . . .' He said the last part wistfully, revealing more of his feelings than he realized; knowing only he longed to be as much like his father as he could.

Aislinn looked at him sharply. He was aware of the intensity of her appraisal. After a moment she looked away again. 'You – never speak of your father. You never did. At least – not often.'

'No.' Donal turned away to lean against the taffrail, belt buckle scraping against wood. 'No. For a long time, I could not. Now, although I can, I find I prefer to keep him private.'

'Because that way he is yours, and you do not have to share him.' Aislinn stood next to him. Her nearness – and unexpected understanding – was disconcerting. He would have preferred another woman standing at his side, blonde instead of red-haired, but she was not there. Aislinn was. 'I never knew Duncan,' she said quietly. 'I was too young when he died.' She cast him a sidelong glance, then looked more directly at him, as if she threw him a challenge. 'He did *die*, did he not?'

'He died. As a *lir*less Cheysuli dies.' His tone was more clipped than he intended. But it was difficult to speak of his father's fate when he resented his loss so much. He recalled too clearly how Carillon had given him the news, saying Tynstar had slain Duncan's *lir*. Dead *lir*: dead Cheysuli. As simple as that.

Except it was not. He knew – as every Cheysuli knew – that death was the end result of *lirlessness*, but no one knew how it happened. How the life was ended at last.

Your father is dead, Carillon had said. *Tynstar slew his lir.*

Very little else had been necessary, though Carillon had said the words anyway. Even at eight years of age, Donal understood precisely what *lirlessness* meant.

'What was he like?' Aislinn asked.

'He was clan-leader of the Cheysuli. A warrior. He served the prophecy.' He thought it was enough; at least, for her.

'That says *what* he was. Not *who*.'

Donal pushed the breath through the constriction in his throat. 'He was – *more. More* than most. One man may claim he is the best hunter, another may claim the best shot, another the premier tracker. But – my *jehan* was all of those things. Clan-leader at my age, because he was the wisest of those young warriors who survived Shaine's

63

qu'mahlin. More dedicated; he knew what faced the Cheysuli and he brought them through it. He brought Carillon to the knowledge of what he was; of what he had to be. Gods . . . he gave up his own freedom in service to the prophecy, knowing he would die. Knowing Tynstar would win their personal battle.'

'He *knew*!' Clearly, Aislinn was shocked. 'How can a man foresee his own death, and then go *to* it?'

Donal put out his right hand and made the Cheysuli gesture: palm up, fingers spread, encompassing infinity. '*Tahlmorra*,' he said. 'My *jehan* had a clearer vision than most, and he did not turn away. He knew what he had to do. He knew what the price would be.'

'*Tynstar* slew him.' She stared fixedly toward the shore-line. 'There are so many legends about that sorcerer.'

'Tynstar slew his *lir*.' He shrugged. 'One and the same, in the end.'

Aislinn looked at him sharply. 'Then – he did what a *lirless* Cheysuli does? He simply walked away?'

He was somewhat surprised she knew that much. It was not often spoken of, even in the clans. Cheysuli simply *knew*. But he had not expected Aislinn to know.

'The death-ritual.' Donal's hands closed tightly on the rail. 'It is customary. But personal for each warrior.'

Aislinn shivered. 'I could never do it.'

'You will never have to.'

After a moment, she reached out and touched his arm, as if to comfort him. 'So – you came to live at Homana-Mujhar in the wake of your father's death.'

'No. I came to spend time there at Carillon's behest, not to *live* there. The Keep is my home.'

Aislinn looked at him steadily. 'And when we are wed? Do you think *I* could live in such a place?'

He shook his head. 'No, of course not. You will live in Homana- Mujhar, as you have always done. But you must know there will be times – perhaps *many* times – when I will go to the Keep. There are – kinfolk there.'

Aislinn nodded. 'I understand. My father has said I

cannot expect you to forget the blood in your veins.' She shook her head a little. 'I do not understand it – what it is to be Cheysuli – but he has said I must give you your freedom when I can. That you tame a Cheysuli by keeping your hand light.' She smiled at the imagery.

Donal did not. Inwardly, he grimaced. And yet he blessed Carillon for preparing the girl for his absences, no matter what images were used.

But she will have to know sometime. I cannot keep her in ignorance forever.

He looked past her at the shoreline. 'Aislinn – we are here. You have come home again to Homana.'

Her reddish brows slid up. 'Is not the island part of Homana, then?'

'The Crystal Isle is – different.' He thought to let it go at that, but could not when he saw her frown. 'It was a Cheysuli place long before Homana was settled by the Firstborn.'

She flicked one hand in a quick, dismissive gesture. 'Your history is different from mine.'

'Aye,' he agreed ironically. *More different than you can imagine.*

'What do we do now?' she asked as the boat thudded home at the dock.

'We see to it your trunks are offloaded, and then we shall find an inn that meets with your royal standards.' He took her elbow to steady her. 'Tomorrow will be soon enough to start out for Homana-Mujhar.'

He had thought, originally, to stay the night on the Crystal Isle, but after his bout with Electra he felt he had to leave, to take Aislinn back to the mainland quickly. The girl had been terrified her mother would use magic on her, to force her to stay against her will. And so Donal had taken her off the island alone with Sef and his *lir*, since Aislinn would have none of her mother's Solindish women with her. And now they faced the journey ahead without a proper escort for the Princess of Homana.

Well, Sef will lend some *measure of respectability to the journey, I hope.*

Donal watched silently as Aislinn's trunks were offloaded and placed on the dock at Hondarth. Sef, as had already become his habit, stood near him. The boy had been unusually silent since he had followed Donal out of Electra's palace, but then Donal knew he himself had not been the best of company. The confrontation with Electra had left a foul taste in his mouth, particularly since she had nearly accomplished what she had intended.

She almost made me doubt her daughter. She nearly made me wonder how much of Aislinn's soul is still her own. But I thank the gods the girl has her own mind, because it has saved her from her mother's machinations.

He glanced at Sef. The boy was still pale, still secret in his silences, watching as the captain piled up all the chests. The odd parti-colored eyes seemed fastened on the distances, as if the island had touched him somehow, and he was still lost within its spell.

Well, perhaps he is. Perhaps he begins to understand what it is to be Cheysuli – what the weight of history is. Does he wish to serve me, he will have to understand it.

The dock was busy with men. Donal turned to one of them, hired him with a nod, and gestured toward the growing pile of chests. 'Hire men and horses to take these to Homana-Mujhar, in Mujhara.' Briefly he showed the ruby signet ring with its black rampant lion. The man's eyes widened. 'Lose none of these things, for the Mujhar's daughter prizes her belongings . . . and the Mujhar prizes his daughter's contentment.'

The man bobbed his head in a nervous bow, accepting the plump purse Donal gave him, but his eyes slid to Aislinn as she walked unsteadily down the plank. She was wrapped in the heavy brown traveling cloak but, with her bright hair, unconscious dignity and a subtlety of manner that somehow emphasized her rank, her identity was hardly secret.

'See it is done,' Donal said clearly. 'The Mujhar will reward you well.'

The man looked at him again; at the yellow eyes and golden earrings. The cloak hid Donal's leathers and the

rest of his gold, but there was no need to show it. His race was stamped in his face; a Cheysuli, even one born to his clan instead of a throne, wears royalty like his flesh.

The man bobbed another bow, then quickly went about his business.

Aislinn, having come to stand next to Donal, watched the man closely. 'They serve you through fear,' she said clearly, as if making a discovery. 'Not loyalty. Not even knowing you are the Prince.' She looked into Donal's face. 'They serve because they are afraid *not* to.'

'Some,' he agreed, preferring not to lie. 'It is a thing most Cheysuli face. As for me – it does not matter.'

Her coppery brows drew down. 'But I saw how it grated with you; his fear. I saw how you wished it was otherwise.'

'I do,' he admitted. 'The man who *desires* to see fear in the faces of his servants is no proper man at all.'

'And you are?' She showed white teeth, small and even, in a teasing, winsome smile. 'What *proper* man takes on the shapes of *animals*?'

He was relieved to see the humor and animation in her face. So, in keeping with her bantering, he opened his mouth to retort that she should know, better than most, what it meant to be Cheysuli. She had grown up with enough of them around her at her father's palace.

But then he recalled that it was to *him* she had directed her questions, and how reluctant he had been to answer. She had been a child, a girl; he had been older, already blessed with his *lir*, and therefore considered a warrior. Then, he had felt, he had little time for a cousin with questions when there were other more important concerns.

Now he knew he had erred, even as he teased. He would have to spend time with her; he would have to educate her, so she could understand. Particularly if she were to comprehend the sometimes confusing customs of the Cheysuli, which often conflicted with the Homanan ones she knew so well.

Uneasily, he wondered if he could explain them all properly.

'We cannot stay here. We must find an inn, sup, then get a good night's rest so we may start back for Mujhara in the morning.' Donal glanced at Sef. 'You know Hondarth better than I. Suggest an inn suitable for the Princess of Homana, then go and fetch my horse while I escort the lady.'

Sef thought it over. 'The White Hart,' he said at last. 'It is not far –' he pointed '– up that way, and around the corner there . . . it's a fine inn. I can't say I've seen its *best* parts –' he smiled a little '– but I'm sure it'll suit the princess. I'll bring your horse. And should I speak to the hostler about buying another for the princess?'

Donal smiled. Sef had taken his service to heart, seeking to do everything Donal would have a grown man do. 'And for yourself? Or do you intend to walk?' He laughed as Sef's face reddened. 'Fetch back my horse and you may speak to the hostler. Perhaps he has two good mounts for sale.'

Sef nodded, bowing clumsily in Aislinn's direction, and scrambled up the dock-ramp to the quay beyond. He vanished in an instant.

Aislinn frowned. 'I have not known you to keep boys before. Especially ones like *that*.'

'I took Sef on because he is earnest and willing . . . and because he needs a home.' Donal bent to run his fingers through Lorn's thick coat. 'He is a good boy. Give him a chance, and I think you will see how helpful he can be.' He slanted her an arch glance. 'Is it not part of a princess's responsibilities to succor where succor is needed?'

Color flared in her face. 'Of course. And – I will do so.' She snugged the furred cloak more tightly around her body and turned her back on him, heading for the dock-ramp.

Donal laughed to himself and followed.

Seabirds screeched, swooping over the waterfront. Fisher-folk lined the shore, hauling in their catches. The pervasive smell of fish hung over everything; Aislinn wrinkled her

nose with its four golden freckles and set a hand over her mouth. 'How much farther?'

Donal reached out and caught her elbow, steadying her at once. 'Sef said it was around this corner.'

'Have we not *already* gone around that corner?'

'Well, perhaps he meant another. Come, it cannot be so far.'

The sun fell below the horizon and set the white-washed buildings ablaze in the sunset, pink and orange and purple. Lanterns were lighted and set into brackets or onto window ledges, so that the twisting streets were full of light and shadows. Aislinn's hair was suddenly turned dark by the setting sun, haloed by gold-tipped, brilliant curls.

Behind them lay the ocean, gilded glassy bronze by the sunset. White gulls turned black in silhouette; their cries resounded in the canyons of myriad streets. The uneven and broken cobbles grew treacherous underfoot, hidden in light and darkness, until Donal took Aislinn's arm and helped her over the worst parts.

'Maybe he meant *this* corner,' Aislinn said, as they rounded yet another.

Lir, Taj said, flying overhead. Then, more urgently, *Lir!*

Five men came into the street. From out of the shadows they flowed, bristling with weapons. Three behind and two in front. Donal cursed beneath his breath.

Aislinn hesitated, then glanced up at him. He tightened his grasp on her arm, hoping to go on without the need for conflict, but the men moved closer together. All exits were blocked, unless he flew over their heads. But that would leave Aislinn alone.

One man grinned, displaying teeth blackened by a resinous gum he chewed even as he spoke. 'Shapechanger,' he said, 'we been watching you. You with your pretty girl.' The grin did not change. He bared his teeth. 'Shapechanger, why do you come out of your forest? Why do you foul our streets?'

Donal glanced back quickly, totaling up the odds. With

Taj and Lorn, he was hardly threatened, but there was Aislinn to think about.

The man stepped closer, and so did the others. 'Shape-changer,' he said, 'Homanan girls are not for you.'

'Nor are they for you.' Silently, Donal told Taj to continue circling out of range. Lorn moved away from his leg to widen their circle of safety.

'Donal!' Aislinn cried. 'Tell them who you are!'

'No.' He knew she would not understand. But men such as these, now bent on a little questionable pleasure, might see the implications rife in holding the Mujhar's daughter. Fortunes could be made.

'Donal –!'

Black-teeth laughed. 'Who are you, then? What does she want you to say?'

'Move away, Aislinn,' Donal said. 'It is me they want, not you.'

'Is it?' Black-teeth asked. 'What does a man do when faced with a woman who consorts with the enemy?'

'Donal – *stop* them –!'

One of the men scooped up a stone and hurled it at Donal. He heard it whistle in the air and twisted, trying to duck away, but even as that stone missed another one did not. It struck a glancing blow across his cheek, smacking against the bone. And then all of the men were throwing.

He heard Aislinn cry out. But mostly he heard the cruel hatred in their voices as the men taunted him.

'Shapechanger!' they cried. 'Demon –!'

Taj, he asked, *where are you*?

About to impale the leader –

Lorn –?'

Can you not hear the man screaming?

He could. One of the men reeled away, clutching at his right leg. Lorn released him and leaped for an arm, closing on his wrist. The man screamed again, crying out for help, but the others were too busy.

Black-teeth fell away, clawing at his back. Taj still rode his shoulders with his talons sunk into flesh. Donal, left

70

with three men, drew his knife to face them.

No more rocks did they throw. In their hands were knives. No longer did he face Homanans merely out to trouble a Cheysuli, but men instead intent upon his death.

He was angry. Dangerously angry. He felt the anger well up inside, trying to fill his belly. Not once had he faced a man merely trying to steal his purse; not once had he faced a man simply wishing to fight, as men will sometimes do. Not once had he faced any man attempting to take his life. And now that he did, it frightened him.

But the fright he could overcome, or turn to for strength. It was the anger that troubled him most; the anger that came from knowing they saw him for his race, and marked him for death because of it.

When a man dies, he should die for a reason – not this senseless prejudice –

And with an inward snap of rage and intolerance, he summoned the magic.

6

He knew what the Homanans saw. What Aislinn saw. A blurring voice. A coalescing nothingness. Where once had stood a man, albeit a Cheysuli man, now there was an absence of anything.

It was enough, Carillon had said once, to make a man vomit. The Mujhar had seen such happen before, when Finn had taken *lir*-shape. Apparently it was true, for one of the men cried out and soiled himself even as Donal changed.

It was so easy. He reached out from within, seeking the familiar power. He sank every sense down into the earth. Almost at once he was engulfed by taste, touch, scent, sound and all the bright colors of the magic. He was no longer Donal, no longer human, no longer anything identifiable. He was a facet of the earth, small and humble and incredibly unimportant – until one looked at what he had done and would do, and the effect it would have on others. No Cheysuli, fully cognizant of his place within the tapestry of the gods, could possibly deny the need for loyal service. Donal, closer to the tapestry than most, did not even think of it.

The magic came at once to his call, filling him until he thought he might burst. He felt tension and urgency and utter need, a physical compulsion. *Sul'harai*, the Cheysuli called it; having no Homanan word to describe the act of the shapechange, they likened it to the instant of perfect love between man and woman. In that moment when he was neither man nor animal, Donal was more complete

72

than at any other time, for he put himself into the keeping of the earth and took from it another form.

He felt excess flesh and bone melting away, sloughing off his body to flow into the earth. There it would find safekeeping, allowing him to set aside fear for the loss of his human form while he assumed another. It was a manner of trading, he knew; while the earth held his human shape, it gave him another to replace the one he put off. But he could not say which cast was better – or which, in fact, held the essence of the true Donal.

He felt the alteration in sinew and skin. He felt the wholeness that came with being completed. He felt the vivid vitality pouring through altered veins, muscles and flesh. No more was he Donal as the others knew him, having voluntarily put off that mold. In its place was a male wolf, yellow-eyed and silver-coated. And when he heard the screaming he knew the change was done.

Donal bunched his powerful haunches, letting all his strength pour into the latter half of his body. He tensed and the fur of his ruff stood on end until he was hackled to the tail. And then he launched himself at the nearest man's chest, jaws opening to display rows of serrated teeth.

The body crumpled, collapsing beneath his weight. It crashed against the ground, blackened teeth clicking in inarticulate words of pain and horror.

I could take his throat – tear it out – watch the blood spill out to soak into the cobbles. What harm would it do? He sought to slay me. Why not slay him instead?

Wolf-shaped, Donal stood over the man, head lowered, teeth bared, almost slavering. A mist of anger and bloodthirst rose before his eyes. Everything he looked at had a fuzzy rim around it, as if it bled over into another form. Black-teeth's gurgling moan of horror was lost as Donal gave into the wolfish growl rising in his throat. And the other men, their terror-inspired paralysis vanishing, tore away.

Donal could smell Black-teeth's fear. It clogged up his nose until he was immersed in the rankness of the stench.

Tongue lolling, he could *taste* the terror. It flowed out of the man like a miasma. And for a moment, a long moment, Donal teetered on the brink. He was angry, *too* angry; he was losing himself fast. In a flicker of lucid disbelief he saw himself clearly: wolf, not man; beast, not animal.

Gods, is this *what they meant when they told me never to resort to* lir-*shape when I was angry?*

He retreated at once, lunging away from the madness. He realized how close he had come to the fine line between control and animal rage. A warrior in *lir*-shape maintained his own mind and his comprehension of things, but the balance was delicate indeed. Donal had been warned many times that *lir*-shape carried its own degree of risk. Did a warrior grow so angry that he lost himself completely within his *lir*-shape, he also lost his mind. He would become a wolf utterly, with all a wolf's savage power, awesome strength and lack of human values.

And without recourse to human form.

Donal fell back again, within and without, backing away from the sobbing man. He heard his own breath and how it rattled hoarsely in his wolf-throat; how he panted in despair. He heard also the echo of his own anger and his desire to slay the man.

I have come too close, too close – by the gods, I nearly lost myself –

At once, he sought to take back his human form. The response was sluggish, painful; he had gone too close to the edge. What was the essence of wolf in him did not wish to give up its shape.

It hurt. Donal gasped, clawing out toward the earth. He had no wish to stay locked in wolf-shape. Not when he was meant to be a man.

Then, all at once, the shapechange slipped into place. He was on one knee, one hand pressed against the cobbles. Paws turned to hands and feet, fur to hair, canines to human teeth. Man-shape once again, but he was not certain how much of the wolf remained.

Lir!

It echoed within the link. Taj and Lorn, both warning him at once.

He spun around, thrusting himself upward, one hand going up to thwart the blow. He saw Aislinn then, whom he had forgotten – a wild look on her face as she sought to stab Donal with her knife.

'*Aislinn* –'

In the bloodied light of sundown he saw the flash of the blade as she brought it up from her side. Not overhand, not slashing downward, as novices usually did. From underneath, jabbing upward, as if she knew precisely what she did.

She does . . . by the gods – *she* does –

For a moment, for one fatal moment, he hesitated. But she did not. She thrust upward with the knife even as he sought to jerk out of her way, and the blade sliced across the knuckles of one hand. He cursed, jumping back, and then he saw Sef hurl himself at Aislinn.

'No – *no*! I won't let you hurt him!'

Aislinn cried out. Donal saw the flash of the blade as Sef set his teeth into her wrist; the knife was perilously close to the boy's thin face. But Sef ignored it, shutting his teeth into flesh, and Aislinn cried out in pain.

Donal stepped in at once. But Sef's teeth had done their work; the knife fell clattering to the street. Donal prudently kicked it out of reach, then caught Aislinn's arm and one of Sef's shoulders.

'Enough – *enough*! Sef – let be . . . I have her now.' Donal caught Aislinn under both arms and set her against the wall, pinning her there with his left hand. The right one he carried to his mouth, sucking at his bleeding kuckles. He tasted the acrid salt of blood and the bitterness of futility.

'Aislinn . . . *Aislinn*!' He held her against the wall as she struggled feebly to get away. 'What idiocy is this?'

'Witchcraft.' Sef whispered. 'Look at her *eyes*.'

Donal looked. To him, they appeared swollen black with fear and senselessness. Her face was the color of death. 'Aislinn – this is *madness* –'

75

But she said nothing at all.

It was Electra. It must *have been Electra! Gods, will the woman never give up?* Still holding Aislinn, he glanced back at the man on the ground. Black-teeth was alone, deserted by his cohorts. But he remained, gibbering incoherently.

Was all *of this planned?* Donal wondered suddenly. *This attack, knowing how Hondarth feels about Cheysuli, and then, having failed, an attack from Aislinn herself?*

It made him ill. He felt the slow roiling of his belly and the hollowness of his chest.

He looked at Aislinn again. *Did Electra tell the truth? Has she made Aislinn into a weapon against her father – or even against me?*

Aislinn was still his prisoner. She had fallen into silence, staring blankly at the ground. The hood had slipped from her head to bare the rose-gold hair. It glowed brightly in the sunset.

Donal closed his eyes. He felt unsteady, unbalanced by the attempt. But then no one had ever tried to slay him before, and he did not doubt it was unsettling for any man. *I would not care to repeat it.*

You may have to, in the future. Taj pointed out. *There are enemies in every corner.*

Including my betrothed?

The *lir* chose not to answer, which was answer enough for Donal.

'My lord?' It was Sef. 'What do we do now?'

Donal looked again at Aislinn. One of the stones had struck her, bloodying her brow. He lifted his wounded hand to wipe it away, then did not. The hand dropped back to his side. *She gets no tenderness from me, until I know what she plans.* He glanced at Sef. 'Did you fetch my horse?'

Sef gestured. 'There.'

The chestnut stallion stood patiently in the shadows. Donal nodded. 'Then find us this inn you suggested.'

Sef looked at Black-teeth, still cringing on the cobbles,

and at Aislinn, bloodied and vacant. Then at Donal, who still felt distinctly ill. The eyes were huge in his thin, pale face. 'What – what will you do to her?'

'I do not know.' Donal gestured. 'Sef – show us to this inn.'

Sef, bent down and picked up the knife. 'My lord –?'

'Keep it,' Donal told him. 'But never give it to the princess, or I may lose more than a little flesh.' He sucked again at the cut across his knuckles.

'But why?' Sef whispered. 'Why would she try to slay you?'

'I think she has been – *influenced* – by her *jehana*.'

'The *Queen*?' Sef's eyes widened further. 'You say the *Queen* set her own daughter on you?'

'Or Tynstar, through his *meijha*, if it is true what Electra told me.' Donal gestured. 'Sef – walk. I have no wish to tarry here a moment longer.'

Sef no longer tarried.

The White Hart Inn was everything Sef said it was. It boasted good food, better wine, warm beds and spacious rooms. Donal took one for himself and Sef and another for the princess.

Donal led Aislinn up to her room and sat her down on the edge of the bed. Then, gently, he sponged away the dirt and blood on her face with a clean cloth borrowed from the innkeeper, along with a basin of water. Aislinn sat on the bed and let him minister to her, though at first she had flinched from his touch.

When she was clean again, though too pale, he gave the basin to Sef to return. Then he turned to Aislinn. 'Do you understand what you have done?'

He was not certain she would answer. She had not spoken since she had attacked him.

But this time she broke her silence. Slowly she looked up to meet his eyes, and he saw how her own were clouded and unfocused. 'Done? What have I done?'

'Do you not recall it?'

She seemed bewildered by his questions. 'What is it you wish me to recall?'

Donal put out his hand. She flinched back, then allowed him to touch her. Gently he fingered the lump where the stone had struck. There was hardly a mark to show what had happened, though – with her fair skin – he was certain there would be a bruise in the morning.

Yet he did not think the stone had struck hard enough to damage her memories. *Unless they were damaged before . . . by someone with reason to do so.*

Aislinn's eyes, Electra's eyes, regarded him almost blindly. Gently, he traced one brow and then the other with his fingertips. 'Aislinn, do you trust me?'

'She said I should not – she warned me I should not, but – I do.' She frowned a little. 'Is it all right?'

'Aye,' he said roughly, 'it is all right. I would never harm you. But – I think someone has. I think someone has meddled with your mind.' He leaned closer to her. 'Aislinn – there is a thing I must do. But I will not do it with you unknowing . . . or unwilling. You say you trust me – let me prove the worthiness of that trust.'

Her eyes were almost vacant. 'What would you have me do?'

He wet his lips before he spoke. 'Allow me to touch your mind.'

She put up her hand. Her fingers touched his own. But she did not still their gentle movement across her brow. 'You mean to use your magic.'

'Aye,' he admitted. 'I must. I must see what Electra has done.'

Her very disorientation seemed to lend credence to his suspicions. Aislinn merely shrugged.

Again, he wet his lips. He slipped his free hand up to cradle her head in his palms. Slowly, with great care and gentleness, he slipped out of his skull and went into hers, tapping the strength of his magic.

Gods, do not let me harm her. If Tynstar has set a trap-link, or Electra – He discontinued the thought at

once. The implications were too serious. A trap-link might well have been set in Aislinn's mind, waiting to snare him – or any other Cheysuli entering her mind – and hold him for later disposal.

Unless, of course, the trap was set to slay him.

He dismissed the thought. If such a trap existed, it was already too late.

He felt the slow consummation of his bonding with the earth. He tapped the source of Cheysuli magic, drawing it up through an invisible conduit, until it filled him with power and strength. He sliced through Aislinn's young barriers painlessly and slipped into her mind. And he faced, for the first time in his life, the full knowledge of his power and abilities. He had only to *twist* here, *touch* there, and Aislinn's will would be replaced with his own.

But the thought was anathema to him. He saw Cheysuli, not Ihlini.

Aislinn's eyes widened, then drifted closed. He saw how pale she was, how her jaw slackened so that her mouth parted to expose small portions of her upper teeth. She was his completely –

Or is she? Someone else has been here before me –!

He withdrew at once, lunging out of her mind and back into his own, badly frightened by what he had felt. Residue. An echo. A *feeling* of other sentience.

Gods – is it Tynstar? Did Electra speak the truth?

'My lord?' It was Sef, kneeling by the bed. Donal saw how pale the boy's face was; how fixed were his odd-colored eyes. And how fright was in every posture of his body. '*My lord* – did it hurt you?'

For a moment, Donal shut his eyes. He needed time to regain his senses completely. But there was none. He took his hands away from Aislinn's head, and smiled wearily at the boy. 'I fare well enough. But I should have warned you –'

'Was that – *magic*?' Sef's eyes were widening. 'Did you cast a spell here in *this room*?'

'It was not a spell. We do not cast *spells*. We – borrow

power from the earth. That is all.' Donal looked at Aislinn. 'I had the need to know if sorcery had been worked, and so I used my own.'

'Had it?' Sef whispered.

Donal did not hear him. He watched Aislinn, frowning slightly as he saw how she began to rouse. Color was returning to her face.

'My lord? Was it?'

Donal glanced back. 'What? – oh, aye. It was. But I could not discover the whole of it, or who had the doing of it. Electra, most likely – or Tynstar, through Electra herself.' He suppressed a shudder. 'But now. I think it is time we all got some rest. The princess particularly.' He glanced back at her. She seemed almost to sag into the bed, though she continued to sit: Donal set a hand onto her shoulder. 'Aislinn, I know you were merely the game-piece. But no matter how small the piece, it can overtake even the highest.'

He rose. *How in the names of all the gods am I to tell Carillon what Electra has done to his daughter?*

And then, as he turned to go, he felt a wave of heat wash up to engulf his body. And he fell.

7

The Mujhar himself poured two cups of steaming spiced wine. He had dismissed the servant, even Rowan, which was an indication in itself that the conversation was to be expressly private. Warily, Donal accepted the cup and waited.

Carillon turned. 'Tell me how Sorcha and Ian fare.'

In bed, bathed in sweat and filled with pain, Donal stirred. He groaned, inwardly ashamed of his weakness, yet knowing there was nothing he could do. The sorcery had drawn him in. All he could do was lose himself in memories he would rather forget.

'Ian has a fever,' he told Carillon. 'A childhood thing, they tell me – but he is better. Sorcha is well.' He paused. 'My jehana says the child will be born in four weeks. I would like to be with her when the pain comes upon her.'

Carillon sipped idly at his wine. But his eyes, half hidden beneath creased eyelids, were bright and shrewd. 'Provided you are returned, I have no quarrel with that.'

'Returned!' Donal lowered his cooling cup. 'Where is it I am to go?'

'To the Crystal Isle.'

'The Crystal Isle?' Donal could not see any reason he should go there. It was nothing more than a convenient place for Carillon to keep his exiled wife imprisoned. 'Why would you send me there?' He grinned. 'Or have I displeased you of late?'

Carillon did not return the smile. 'You please me well

enough . . . for a prince who has more interest in Cheysuli things than Homanan.'

'*I am Cheysuli –*'

'*– and Homanan!*' Carillon finished. '*Do you forget your mother is my cousin? There is Homanan blood in those veins of yours, and it is time you acknowledged it.*' Carillon set down his wine and paced to the firepit. His age- and illness-wracked hands went out to bathe in the heat, and Donal saw the edges of the leather bracers he wore on either wrist. For decoration, most thought, to hide the old Atvian shackle scars. But Donal knew better. Carillon needed them to guard his waning strength.

'*I do acknowledge it.*' Donal damped down his impatience and frustration. '*But I have* lir *and responsibilities to my clan. To my* su'fali, *who is clan-leader. To my* jehana, *to my son, and certainly to my* meijha.' He paused. '*Would you wish me to turn my back on my heritage and* tahlmorra?'

'*Part of that heritage places you first in the line of succession,*' Carillon said flatly, still warming himself at the fire. '*So does your gods-dictated destiny. I would have you remember* all *the responsibilities you have, for there are those to Homana as well. Not merely the Keep and your clan.*'

Donal twisted in the bed. Every portion of his flesh ached until he wanted to cry out with the pain. Fire had settled into the pit of his belly, burning relentlessly, and against his will he began to double up. Fists dug into the flesh of his belly, trying to knead the pain away, but it did not go.

'*Do you say I neglect Homana?*' he whispered through his pain.

'*Aye, I do.*' Carillon turned to face him squarely. '*You neglect my daughter, who is to be your wife.*'

Donal stared at him. The wine cup was forgotten in his hands. The frustration and rising anger melted away into shock. '*Aislinn?*' he said at last. '*But – you sent her away to visit her* jehana.'

82

'Aye. And I would have you fetch her back to Homana-Mujhar, so I may have her with me again.'

Donal felt a wave of relief sweep through him. If Carillon only wanted her brought back for company, the fetching would not be so bad. 'I will go, of course. But – surely you could send Gryffth or Rowan, or someone else. I wish to be with Sorcha when the child is born.'

'I will give you leave for that, if you are back with Aislinn in time. I have said it.' Carillon's voice was steady. 'But I think it is time you thought also of wedding my daughter.'

Donal tried to smile. 'I have thought of it. Many times. But Aislinn is still very young –'

'Not so young. Old enough to be wedded and bedded.' Carillon's tone did not soften. 'And was not Sorcha but sixteen when she bore your first child?'

'And it died!' Donal cried it aloud, thrashing against the bed. Hands were on him, pressing him against the mattress, but he did not know them. 'The child died, and Sorcha nearly did! Even with Ian the time was hard. And now that she will bear *again* –'

'It does not matter.' Carillon's voice was implacable. 'It is past time you got yourself an heir.'

Donal gestured. 'You are only forty. Hardly ancient, no matter what Tynstar's Ihlini arts have done to you. I doubt you will die any time soon. Give Aislinn a few more years –'

'No.' Carillon said it softly. 'I cannot. Look again upon me, Donal, and do not mouth such nonsense. Tynstar's sorcery took away twenty years from me and – for all I feel but forty in my heart – I cannot hide the truth forever. Not from you or anyone else.' He stretched out his twisted hands. 'You see these. Each day they worsen. So do my knees, my spine, my shoulders. A crippled man is not the Mujhar for Homana.'

'You would never abdicate!' It was unthinkable in the face of Carillon's pride.

'Abdication is hardly the point.' the Mujhar said. 'I

doubt I have so many years left as you would prefer to believe. I prefer to have the throne secured . . . and so should you. It is, for all that, a Cheysuli thing.'

Donal scowled. *'You play me as Lachlan might play his Lady. Pluck this string, that one, and the proper tune is heard. You call my Cheysuli heritage into conversation, and you know what I will do.'*

'Then do it.' For a moment, Carillon smiled. *'Aislinn is spoiled, as I have spoiled her, but she is also a warm and giving girl. I think you will find it no chore to wed my daughter.'*

But Donal could not reconcile the loss of Cheysuli freedom with the Homanan title the Mujhar promised.

Aloud, he muttered: 'I would rather wait. Not – long. A six-month. Perhaps a year.' Donal twisted. 'Surely you can see your way clear to granting me the time. And Aislinn will need months of preparation . . . women do, and she is a princess –'

'Donal,' Carillon said gently.

'Aislinn is like a rujholla *to me.'*

'But she is not your sister, is she?'

He felt the sudden desperation well up in his soul. 'But I would rather wed with Sorcha!' he shouted aloud. 'I will not lie to you – it is Sorcha who should be *cheysula* instead of *meijha* –'

'That I do not doubt.' Carillon sounded more compassionate. *'I question nothing of her honor or her worth, Donal, as I think you know. But Homana requires all manner of sacrifices, and this one is yours to make.'*

'So, you would have me play the stud to Aislinn's mare, merely to get a colt.' He said it clearly into the room at the White Hart Inn. 'Yet even the Cheysuli, who have had more cause than most, cannot sanction their women to be treated as mere broodmares.'

'I have cause.' Carillon retorted gently. *'I have cause, I have reason, I have more than justification, though kings rarely have need of anything more than whim. Oh, aye, I have all the cause in the world.'* He turned his back on the

firepit. 'I have a kingdom to rule as well as I possibly can. I have people to husband. Heirs to beget.' He smiled, but without humor. 'but then we know I failed at that task, do we not? There is only Aislinn, only a daughter from my loins.' The smile fell away. 'Do you not wed Aislinn, she will go to a foreign prince. And then we run the risk of losing Homana, into the hands of another realm. The Cheysuli, so odd and eerie in their magic, may become little more than game, once again. Hunted, branded demons . . . slain. It happened once, Donal. Can you tell me it will never happen again?'

Donal could not. He knew it would destroy the prophecy, destroy the *tahlmorra* of his people . . . destroy, perhaps, even Homana herself.

He thrashed, sweating, and doubled up yet again from the pain. With great effort, he gave the Mujhar his answer. 'I guarantee nothing, Carillon. I know it as well as you. Perhaps better, since I bear the tainted blood.' He did not smile. It was not a joke. In some circles, it was said Shaine's *qu'mahlin* should still take precedence over Carillon's peace.

But those were circles Donal did not patronize, being in no position to know them personally; did he know them, they would slay him.

'I do not do it to you.' Carillon's tone was ragged. Gone was the strength of his rank, replaced with the need of the man. 'I do it for Homana.'

Even as he forces me to do it for the Cheysuli. *After a moment, Donal nodded. 'I will fetch her back.'*

Carillon sighed and rubbed at his eyes. 'I will give you this much – you may have eight weeks of freedom when you have brought Aislinn back. It is – not long, I know. But it is all I can spare.' Twisted fingers slipped up to comb through a silvered forelock. 'I would have you fully acclaimed before the year is done.'

Donal, hearing the Homanan portion of his fate sealed, could only nod. Then he glanced up and saw the Mujhar's ravaged face.

Carillon watched him with a hunger and sadness Donal could not comprehend. It sent a chill coursing down his spine. He stared back at the Mujhar, not knowing his own face reflected the very expression that had conjured Carillon's pain. 'I have lost you,' the Mujhar said quietly. 'I am bound as cruelly by my royal heritage as you are by your tahlmorra, and I have lost you because of it.'

'My lord?' Donal's tone was soft.

Carillon sighed and waved a twisted hand. 'It is nothing. Only memories of the man whose face you wear.' He smiled faintly. 'Your father lives in you, Donal . . . you have all of Duncan's pride and arrogance and convictions. I did not fully understand him and I do not understand you. I only know that by pressing for this marriage, I have lost what little of you I once had.'

'You have me still.' Donal spread his hands. 'Do you see me? – I am not gone. I stand before you. I will ever be your man.'

'Perhaps.' Carillon did not smile. 'It simply must be done.'

'I know it, my lord Mujhar,' Donal put out his right hand, gestured defeat. 'Tahlmorra, Carillon.'

'By the gods –' he blurted, lunging upward against the hands that tried to hold him. Small hands, two sets, one toughened, one soft and delicate. Sef, he knew, and – Aislinn?

His eyes snapped open. He saw the dark wooden walls revolve until the movement dizzied him; he shut his eyes at once. A sour harshness preyed on his throat.

'Lie down again,' Aislinn said. 'So much thrashing is not good for you – it brings more pain.'

He looked at her, and did not protest as she and Sef urged him down again. The bedclothes were soaked beneath him. He shivered. 'It was *you* –'

'Not me,' she declared. 'Oh, aye, it was I who cut your fingers, but I swear I knew nothing of the poison. That, I fear, was my mother.'

Weakness washed over him. '*Lir*,' he said raggedly.

86

Here, upon the roof-beam, said Taj, though Donal could not summon the strength to look.

And I. That from Lorn, sitting by the bed.

Donal's hand moved out to touch the wolf's muzzle. Lorn nuzzled him gently, then pressed his nose into Donal's limp hand.

'Donal,' Aislinn whispered. 'I am so sorry. I did not *know* . . . I swear it. Oh gods, do not *die*. What would become of me?'

Through slitted eyes he watched her. The single braid was tumbled, as if she had spent no time on it for days. Strands of bright hair straggled into her face and he saw how furrows of concern had dug their way into the smooth flesh of her brow. Her cool, pale eyes were fastened on his face.

Gods . . . those are Electra's eyes . . . He swallowed and knew again the stripped feeling in his throat. 'Aislinn, I swear – do you *lie* to me –'

'No!' She leaned forward on the stool, reaching out to clasp his hand. 'Oh Donal, no. I do not. Sef has – told me what I did, and what you did after – to find out why I did it. He – he said you found something.' Shakily, she touched her temple. 'Is there – something in my head?'

'Some*one*,' he said wearily. 'I do not doubt it is your *jehana*'s doing, or perhaps even Tynstar's through the link to Electra.'

She paled. 'Then – if that is true, it is not that I do these things willingly. Donal – do you truly think I could mean to slay you?'

'I could not say, Aislinn.' Vacancy threatened to steal his senses from him. 'I think – I think if they have meddled with your mind . . . you are capable of doing anything.'

'Is there no way of *gainsaying* it?' she demanded in horror.

He laughed. It rasped in his throat painfully, and he hardly knew the sound. 'Oh, aye – there is always a way. But I think you would not like it . . . and I doubt you would agree.'

She stared down at the hand she held, dark against her

own, though the illness had lent pallor to his flesh. 'I will do what you wish, Donal,' she said quietly. 'How else am I to prove I am innocent of this connivance?'

'And if you are not?' He had to ask it. 'If you are not, and seek this way of advancing Tynstar's bid to throw down Carillon, you would do better to try another method.' He shut his hand upon hers almost painfully. 'I am not the one to do it – I am still too young, and lack the experience one must have – but there are those who could do it for me.' He watched her eyes and saw how she stared back. She was clearly frightened, and there was no hint of satisfaction in her manner, as there might be if she sought the test out of some perverse plan to gain his confidence. 'Even unknowing, do you agree to this?'

'Aye,' she whispered finally. 'I will – do what you wish.'

He lifted her hand. 'Then I hold you to it. You will be tested. Do you understand?'

She nodded. 'But – may I know who will have the doing of it?'

'Aye,' he said carelessly, releasing her hand. 'I will ask my *su'fali* to do it.'

Aislinn's head jerked up. *'Finn?'*

'Who better?' He looked directly at her. 'He is clan-leader of the Cheysuli. And he has had some experience with Ihlini trap-links before.' Donal did not smile.

'But –' She broke off.

'I think,' said Donal, 'we will know the truth at last.'

'I swear it,' she whispered. 'I did not *know*.'

Waves of pain radiated upward from his belly. Donal felt the cramping of his muscles and knew again the total helplessness as he curled up against the fire. Even Taj and Lorn, seeking to lend him strength, could not reach him. The pain was absolute.

'My lord?' It was Sef, bending over the bed. 'My lord – is there *nothing* I can do?'

'Watch,' Donal said huskily. 'Watch Aislinn for me.'

He heard her indrawn breath of dismay. But he had no

strength to regret his cruelty. He dared not trust her now.

He recovered. Sef brought him hot broths at first to soothe the emptiness and ache in his belly, then brought stew when Donal could keep it down and finally, after ten days, brought meat, bread, cheese and wine. Donal ate a little of each food, drank down half a cup of wine, then set it all aside.

'Enough. I will burst. More will have to wait.' He looked at Aislinn, sitting silently on the stool across the room, and saw she intended to offer no speech. 'Well, lady – I think we shall be on our way to Mujhara in the morning.'

The light from the lantern was gentle on her face. It set up brilliant highlights in her hair and painted her face quite fair, gold instead of silver, though – save for her bright hair – she had the fairness of her mother. She had changed from plain brown gown and cloak to equally plain moss-green, save for the copper stitching at collar and cuffs. An overtunic of darker green hid much of her femininity, though no man would name her boy. Her features were too delicate.

One day, she may rival her jehana's *beauty, though it be a different sort. Brighter, warmer, less cold and seductive as Electra's – well, if I must take her as my* cheysula, *better a pretty one than a plain.* Then he smiled inwardly, knowing the irony in his statement. *Already you think of making her the* cheysula *Carillon wants, when she may be plotting against your life. Fool.*

No, said Taj. *Practical.*

Realistic. That from Lorn.

Donal sat up slowly, swinging his legs over the side of the bed. He was still in his clothing, he discoverd; Sef, undoubtedly, had lacked the strength to strip him of the sweat-soaked leathers, and it was not Aislinn's place to do it. He was rank with his own stench, and ordered Sef to fetch up a half-cask for bathing at once.

Aislinn, still sitting silently on the stool, colored, clenching her hands in her lap. 'You will send me out, of course.'

'Have you not had your own room?'

'You are *in* it,' she said softly. 'When you fell, the most we could do was drag you into my bed. Sef would allow no one near you, not even the innkeeper's wife. And so *we* tended you.' She shrugged. 'We have been together here with you . . . Sef, you see, would not allow me to be alone.'

He frowned. 'Not at all?'

Her gaze lifted to meet his. 'But you said he must watch me,' she said simply. 'I have begun to think of him as my jailer – or, perhaps, your third *lir*.' She did not smile. 'He is – obdurate. You chose him well, Donal. I do not doubt he will serve you as well as General Rowan serves my father.'

'And so you have been here with me for all this time?' He shook his head. 'Perhaps it was best, but I am sorry if it caused you inconvenience. Sef is – unaccustomed to royalty.' He sat very straight, then arched his spine to crack all the knots. His midsection was extremely tender, within and without, and his muscles felt like rags. Even the *lir*-bands on his bare arms fit a little loosely – he had lost flesh as well as ten days.

He clasped each band, squeezing it against his arm. Beneath his fingers curved the shapes of wolf and falcon, honoring Taj and Lorn in traditional Cheysuli fashion. When a Cheysuli boy became a man, acknowledged so by the bonding of his *lir*, he put on the traditional armbands and earring to mark warrior status. Donal, gaining his *lir* younger than most, had worn his gold for fifteen years.

'You seem much improved.' Aislinn ventured.

'Aye. Weary and sore, but both shall pass soon enough.' He rolled his head from side to side, loosing the tautness of his tendons. 'You need not be *frightened* of me, Aislinn. I do not take retribution on the woman I must wed.'

'Must wed,' she echoed, and he saw how tightly set was

90

her jaw. 'That is it, is it not? – you *must* wed me. My father has taken the choice from you.'

'You knew that.' Carefully he rose, steadying himself by pressing his calves against the bedframe. He felt old, at least as old as Carillon – 'Gods!' he blurted. 'Have you done *that* to me?'

'What?' she demanded crossly. 'Do you accuse me yet again?'

'Am I old?' He tried to take a step forward and found it weak, wobbly, lacking all grace or strength. Before him rose the specter of premature aging, and what it had done to Carillon. *Have you made me like the Mujhar?*

Aislinn made a rude, banishing gesture. 'You can only *hope* to be like my father . . . no man can match him, Donal. Do not try.'

He lifted one hand and saw firm, sun-bronzed flesh, taut and still youthful, though the palms were callused and tough. He made a fist, and saw how quickly the muscles responded. *Not old, then . . . just – weakened. But that will pass.*

The hand flopped back down at his side. 'Aislinn –'

She rose. The stool scraped against the pegged wood of the uneven floor. 'I want to know who she is.'

For a moment he could only stare. 'Who do you mean?'

'Sorcha.' She was pale and very stiff in her movements. And every inch the princess. Donal, who had intended to ask her what had caused her change in manner, suddenly understood it very clearly.

'Ah.' He sat down slowly on the edge of the bed. 'Sorcha.'

'Who is she?'

There was no help for it, he knew; the time had come for truth. Evasion was no longer an option. 'Sorcha is my *meijha*,' he answered evenly. 'In the Homanan tongue it means *light woman*.'

Aislinn's grey eyes widened. 'Your *whore* –?'

'*No.*' He cut her off at once. 'We have no whores in the clans. We have *meijhas*, who hold as much honor as *cheysulas*.'

91

Color stood high in Aislinn's fair face. 'You see? There are many Cheysuli customs I do *not* know.' An accusation; he did not run from the guilt. 'Then it is *so*: because we are betrothed – and because my father would never allow it, having no other male heir – you cannot wed your *meijha*. You must wed me instead.' Aislinn stood rigidly before him: a small, almost fragile young woman, yet suddenly towering in her pride. 'Do I have the right of it?'

'Aye,' That only; more would be redundant.

'And – Ian?'

'Ian is my son.'

Aislinn paled. He realized, belatedly, Aislinn would probably feel a woman with a child posed more of a threat than simply a woman alone. 'A *bastard* –'

'My *son*' He pushed himself out of the cot. 'Aislinn – I know you only echo what words you have heard before . . . but I will allow neither my *meijha* nor my children to be abused.'

'*Children!*' She gazed at him in shock. 'There are *more*?'

There was no easy way. And so he told her as simply as he could. 'Sorcha is due to bear another child within the month. It is why I wish to leave this place and hasten back –'

'– to the Keep.' She nodded jerkily. 'That is why, is it not? – not that you wish to fulfill my father's wishes.'

'Aye,' he told her gently. 'I want to go home to my family.'

She stared up at him, clearly stunned as well as hurt. He saw how her mouth trembled, though she fought to keep it steady. 'Then – there is no hope for me. I am bound to a loveless marriage . . . and all because of the *throne* –'

'Aye,' he said softly. 'You have begun to feel its weight – the weight we must share.'

'Then I do not *want* it.' Aislinn's hands rose to cover her mouth. She looked directly at him. 'I will have this betrothal broken.' The words were muffled, but he understood them.

For just an instant, he felt a surge of hope well up from deep inside. *Does even* Aislinn *ask it, Carillon will have to break the bethrothal. And I will be free.*

But the hope, as quickly, died away, and in its place was futility. 'Aislinn,' he said helplessly. 'I doubt he will agree.'

'He will,' she said. 'He will do as I ask.' She drew in a trembling breath and tried for a steady smile. 'He agrees to whatever I want.'

Donal admired her brave attempt at confidence, even though it failed. But inwardly, he knew the truth. *He will not agree to this, my determined Homanan princess. Not when realm and prophecy depend so much upon it.*

But he had no heart to tell her.

8

'*Gods!*' Sef breathed. 'Is *this* where you live?'

Donal looked at the boy. His mouth hung open inelegantly as he stared about the inner bailey of Homana-Mujhar; though it was far smaller than the outer bailey, the inner one was, nonetheless, impressive. Massive rose-colored walls jutted up from the earth, thick as the span of a man's outstretched arms. The outer wall was thicker yet, hedged with ramparts and towers. The clean, unadorned lines of the walls and baileys lent Homana-Mujhar an austere sort of elegance. But Donal thought the legends told about the palace formed at least half of its fabled reputation.

And we Cheysuli built it. Inwardly, he laughed. Outwardly, he smiled at Sef. 'This is where the Mujhar lives, and the princess. I – *visit* here often, but the Keep is my home.' Donal gestured eastward. 'It lies half a day's ride from here. If you wish, I will take you there some time.'

But Sef appeared not to hear him. He twisted his shaggy head on a thin neck, staring around at the walls and towers and the liveried guardsmen passing along the walkways. In the midday sun the ringmail and silver of their steel glittered brightly.

The iron-shod hooves of the three horses clopped and scraped across slate-grey cobbles. Donal led Sef and Aislinn past the garrison toward the archivolted entrance of the palace. Though he himself preferred a side door in order to avoid an excess of royal reception, for Aislinn he would enter through the front.

94

And then, as he saw Carillon come out the open door to wait at the top of the marble steps, he knew he had chosen correctly.

Donal turned to speak to Aislinn, then shut his mouth at once. He saw how she stared at her father; he saw the shock and disbelief reflected in her eyes. Before him the color drained out of her face, even from her lips, and he saw how her gloved hands shook upon the reins.

'Aislinn –?'

'He is – grown so *old* –' she whispered. 'When I left, he did not look so – so *used up*.' Aislinn turned a beseeching face to Donal. 'What has happened to him?'

Donal frowned. 'You have heard the story, Aislinn: how Tynstar used his sorcery to try and slay your *jehan*, and in doing so aged him twenty years. That is what you see.'

'He is *worse* –' She spoke barely above a whisper. '*Look* at him, Donal!'

Accordingly, he looked more closely at the Mujhar, and saw precisely what Aislinn meant.

She sees more because she has not seen him in two years, while I – having seen him so often for those two years – do not mark the little changes. But Aislinn has the right of it – Carillon has aged. Tynstar's sorcery holds true.

In truth, the Mujhar was but forty years of age, yet outwardly – because of sorcery leveled against him fifteen years before – he bore the look of a sixty-year-old man. His once-tawny hair had dulled to a steely-grey. His face, though partially hidden by a thick silvering beard, was care-worn, weathered to the consistency of aged leather. The blue eyes, deep-set, were crowded around by clustered creases. And though a very tall and exceptionally strong man – *once* – age had begun to sap the vitality from his body. The warrior's posture had softened. Pain had leeched him of any pretense of youth.

That, and Tynstar's retribution. Donal felt a flutter of forboding. *If he grows so old this quickly, what does it mean for me?*

He saw how stiffly the shoulders were set, how they

95

hunched forward just a little, as if they pained Carillon constantly. Perhaps they did. Perhaps his shoulders had caught up at last to his knees and hands as the disease ate up his joints.

Gods, but I hope I never know the pain he knows, Donal thought fervently. He ignored the twinge of guilt that told him he was selfish to think of himself when Carillon stood before him. *Spare me what Carillon knows. I think I lack the courage it takes to face what he has lost.*

He looked briefly at the hands that hung at Carillon's sides. The reddened fingers were twisted away from his thumbs, almost as if someone had broken all the bones. And the knuckles were ridged with swollen buttons of flesh. How he managed to hold a sword Donal could not say. But he did.

Carillon is what keeps Homana strong . . . Carillon and the Cheysuli. Does he fail any time soon, it is all left to me – and I do not want it!

'Aislinn!' Carillon called. 'By the gods, girl, it has been too long!' He put out his twisted hands, and Aislinn – forgetting her royal status and the need for proprieties – jumped down from the saddle before the stable lads could catch the reins.

Donal bent over and caught Aislinn's mare before she could follow the girl up the marble steps. He reined her back, then handed the leather over to the first boy who arrived to take the horse.

Aislinn gathered her skirts and ran up the black-veined steps, laughing as she climbed. Carillon caught her at the top of them, lifting her into the air in a joyous, loving hug. Donal, watching, saw yet again how close was the bond they shared.

It is almost as if she spent no time with Electra. She nearly makes me think she is nothing but a girl not quite become a woman – but I dare not trust her. Not until Finn has tested her.

The Mujhar did not appear an aged, aging man as he

hugged his only child. The twisted hands pressed into the fabric of her blue cloak, tangling in the wool. His face, seen over Aislinn's right shoulder, was younger than ever before. But the image faded as he set her upon her feet, and Donal saw again how Carillon had grown older in two years.

'Donal, climb down from that horse and come in!' Carillon called, one arm still circling his daughter's shoulders. 'And tell me why it is that the baggage train arrived ahead of you.'

'Dismount,' Donal said in an aside to Sef. 'This is the Mujhar you face, but be not overcome by him. He is not a god, just a man.'

Sef's expression was dubious. But he shook free of his stirrups and slithered down from the saddle, scraping his belly against the leather. Another stable lad took his horse; yet a third caught Donal's reins with a low-voiced 'Welcome back, my lord.'

'My thanks, Corrick.' Donal gestured to Sef. 'Come with me.'

'*Now?*' Sef demanded. 'But – you go with the Mujhar!'

'So do you.' Donal gestured him up the stairs, and after a monumental hesitation, Sef climbed.

'You are somewhat late,' Carillon said quietly when they reached the top of the steps. 'Some manner of delay?'

'Some manner,' Donal agreed blandly.

'He was ill,' Aislinn declared. 'Someone – *poisoned* him.'

Carillon made no movement, no sound of dismay. His face tightened a little, but otherwise Donal observed nothing that indicated concern. 'Well then, you had best come in. As you do not appear in imminent danger of dropping dead at my very feet, I must assume you are completely recovered.'

Donal smiled a little. 'Aye, my lord, I am.' But he had never been good at lying.

Carillon did not seem to notice. 'Well enough. Let us leave off standing out of doors. It may be spring, but it is cold enough to qualify as fall.' He turned and escorted his

daughter into the palace as Donal, Sef and the *lir* followed.

It is not so cold, Donal thought, concerned. *Not so cold as to trouble a man*. But he said nothing to the Mujhar. He merely followed him into the palace.

'I will have you fed first,' Carillon said, 'and then *you*, Aislinn, must rest. I doubt not you are weary.'

'I have not seen you in two years,' she protested, 'yet you send me to bed like an errant child.'

'You *are* an errant child. Have you not kept yourself from me for longer than I wished?'

Her right arm was at his waist as they paused in the entry hall. He had not thickened or put on weight with advancing age, but he was considerably larger than she. 'I must speak with you, father. It is important –'

'Another time.' Carillon's tone left no room for argument, even from a beloved daughter. 'If you do not wish to look like *me* before your time, you must get the rest you require.'

Aislinn, shocked, pulled back from his side. 'Do not *say* that! You are *not old*!'

Sadly, Carillon bent and kissed her on the crown of her head. 'Ah, but you give yourself away with so valiant a protest. Aislinn, Aislinn, I have seen the silver plate. Give me truth, not falsehood; I value that over flattery.'

With tears in her eyes, she nodded. 'Aye,' she whispered. 'Oh gods, I have missed you! It was not the same without you!'

Carillon hugged her again as she leaned against his chest. Over her head, he met Donal's eyes. 'Aye, I *do* know the truth. There is much we must speak about.'

Mutely, Donal nodded. Then he cleared his throat. 'My lord, I would have you meet Sef. It is my hope you will allow him to remain in Homana-Mujhar. Let him be trained as a page, if you wish, or perhaps – when he is old enough – as one of your Mujharan guards. I think there is good blood in him, albeit unknown.'

Carillon looked at the boy. Sef was pale but he drew himself up to stand very straight, as if he already bore

sword and wore the lion in the name of his Mujhar.

'Do you wish it?' Carillon asked. 'I will harbor no boys who do not willingly accept the service.'

'M-my lord!' Sef dropped awkwardly to his knees. 'My lord – how could a boy wish *not* to serve his king?'

The Mujhar laughed. 'Well, you will be serving your prince, not your king – I think you will do better with Donal. But I suggest, first, you put flesh on your bones and better clothing on that flesh. You are too small.'

Donal marked how Carillon asked nothing about the boy's background, or how he came to be riding with the Prince of Homana. He did not embarrass the boy, nor did he embarrass Donal with unnecessary questions. He simply accepted Sef.

Sef, still kneeling, nodded. Black hair flipped down into his face, hiding the blue eye. But, for the first time, Donal saw Sef deliberately push the hair back.

As if he has accepted what he is. Well, Carillon inspires all manner of devotion. He smiled. 'Enough, Sef – few things are accomplished on stone-bruised knees.'

Sef did not move. 'My lord,' he appealed to Carillon, 'is it true you nearly defeated the Ihlini demon?'

'Tynstar?' Slowly, Carillon shook his head. 'If that is what the stories say about me, they are wrong. No, Sef – Tynstar nearly defeated *me*.'

'But –' Quickly, Sef glanced at Donal. He was asking permission to speak, and Donal gave it with a nod. 'My lord Mujhar – I thought *no one* escaped an Ihlini. At least – not *Tynstar*.'

Carillon tousled Sef's wind-ruffled hair. 'Even Tynstar is not infallible. More powerful than any I have known, it is true, because of the power he has borrowed from Asar-Suti, but he is still a man. And when faced with a Cheysuli –' He smiled grimly. 'Let us say: Tynstar is a formidable foe, but not an impossible one.'

'But –' Again Sef hesitated, and again Donal gave him permission to speak. 'I heard, once, that Tynstar had slain a Cheysuli clan-leader.'

Donal felt the sudden wrenching movement in his belly. *That* he had not anticipated.

Carillon looked at him. Compassion was in his eyes. 'Aye,' he answered Sef quietly. 'Tynstar slew Duncan's *lir*, and so Duncan sought the death-ritual as is Cheysuli tradition.'

Slowly, Sef worked it out. And when he had, his eyes turned at once to Donal. His face was a mask of horrified realization. 'Then if Taj and Lorn are slain –'

'– so am *I* slain,' Donal finished. 'Aye. It is – difficult for the unblessed to understand. But it is the price of the *lir*-bond, and we honor it.'

Aislinn's eyes widened. 'You would not do it if you were *Mujhar*!'

She meant it as a declaration. It sounded more like a question. Donal realized, in that moment, she had assumed once they were wed, the customs of the Cheysuli would not be so binding upon him. And he realized she believed he would turn his back on many of them once he was Mujhar.

'Aye,' he told her. 'Warrior or Mujhar, I am constrained by the traditions of my people. And I intend to honor them.'

'You are Homanan as *well* as Cheysuli –'

'I am Cheysuli *first*.'

He saw shock, realization, and rebellion in her face. And a mute denial of his statement.

Carillon's hands came down on her shoulders. 'You are weary,' he said in an even tone. 'Go to bed, Aislinn.'

'No,' she said, 'first there is a thing we must discuss –'

'Go to bed,' he repeated. 'There will be time for all these discussions.'

She flicked a commanding glance at Donal, as if she meant him to bring up the possibility of breaking the betrothal; he did not. He had no intention of it. Done with waiting, she picked up her skirts and ran.

Carillon turned to Sef. 'I am sure you are hungry. I suggest you ask in the kitchens for food.' He gestured and

100

one of the silent servants waiting nearby came at once. 'Escort the boy to the kitchens and see he is fed until he cannot keep his eyes open. Until the prince or I call for him, he is free to learn his way about the palace.'

'Aye, my lord.' The young man, tunicked in Carillon's livery, nodded and looked at Sef. He waited.

Sef, still kneeling, looked up at Donal. 'My lord?'

Carillon laughed. 'I see he knows his master.'

Donal gestured Sef up from the floor. 'You may go.'

Silently, Sef stood up, bowed quickly, and went with the liveried servant.

'I am sorry for what the boy said.' Carillon's tone was compassionate. 'You need no reminding about your father's fate.'

'One warrior's *tahlmorra* is not necessarily easily accepted by his kin,' Donal responded evenly. 'But – I hope the gods grant me a life as effective as his.'

'Effective?' Carillon did not smile. 'A modest way of describing Duncan's loyalty and dedication. And odd, from his son –'

'It does no good to dwell upon it,' Donal interrupted. He felt the clenching of his belly; the sudden cramping of his throat. He had said more of his father to Aislinn than he had said to anyone in a very long time. And it was no easier speaking of him to Carillon, who had known Duncan better than most. 'Tynstar defeated my *jehan*, but not before he accomplished what he was meant to.'

'Siring *you*?' Carillon's mouth twisted a little. 'Aye, he sired you – and in doing so forged the next link in the prohecy.'

The link that excluded a Homanan Mujhar. Donal wondered for the hundredth time whether Carillon himself resented the upstart Cheysuli prince as much as everyone else. So much had been given to him when he deserved none of it.

An accident of birth. No more. And yet Donal knew it was not. The gods had decreed his fate.

Carillon appraised Donal. 'For a poisoned man, you

seem uncommonly fit. Is what Aislinn said true?'

'True. And I am fully recovered.' He was not; Donal knew it. He was weary from the ride, too weary. He needed food and rest. But his pride kept him from saying so to Carillon, who faced more poor health than any man Donal knew.

'Good. Come and show me.' Carillon turned abruptly and headed toward a corridor.

'*Show* you?' Donal went after him. 'Show you *what*?'

Carillon's stride was crisp and even. His back was rigid. There was no sign of advancing age in him, save for the twisted fingers. 'Rowan!' The shout echoed along the corridor. Donal, hastening in the Mujhar's footsteps, frowned into the candle-lit passageway.

Shortly after a second shout, Rowan stepped out of a doorway. His black hair was tousled and damp, and his clothing was a little awry, as if he had only just put them on following a bath. 'Aye, my lord?'

'My sword is in my chambers,' Carillon said briefly. 'Do me the favor of bringing it to the practice chamber.'

Rowan's yellow eyes reflected startled speculation. 'Aye, my lord. At once.'

'Carillon, what do you mean to do?' Donal at last fell into step with the Mujhar.

'I mean to find out what order of skill you claim.'

'*Sword* skill?' Donal, hastening his steps yet again, shook his head. 'Carillon, you *know* –'

'– know what? That you, as a Cheysuli, claim yourself above the use of a sword? Inviolate to its threat?'

'No, of course not.' Donal bit his tongue to repress his exasperation. 'I can be wounded as easily as a Homanan – it is only . . . Carillon, will you *slow down* –?'

'Only what?' The Mujhar did not slacken his pace. 'Is it *only* that you would simply *prefer* to keep youself to bow and knife?'

'I am good enough with both!' Donal, pride stung, stopped dead in his tracks. Carillon also paused.

'Aye,' he agreed, 'you are. But the future Mujhar of

102

Homana must also wield a sword.' He stretched out his hand as Rowan came striding down the corridor with a scabbard clenched in his hand. '*This* sword,' Carillon said, accepting it from Rowan.

Donal scraped one hand down through his hair and over his face. 'Carillon.' His voice was nearly throttled in his attempt to remain calm. 'Do you forget I am *Cheysuli*?'

'I think that is impossible.' Carillon's voice, raspy now, sounded harsh in the shadowed corridor. 'You take such pains to remind me whenever the chance arises.' Methodically, he held the scabbard in his left hand and placed his right on the heavy golden hilt. At the edge of his hand, set into prongs in the pommel of the hilt, glowed the dead-black stone that had once been brilliant crimson. A blood-red ruby, called the Mujhar's Eye, and perverted by Tynstar's sorcery.

Donal looked at Rowan. He saw nothing in the general's face save a perfect blankness. *Cheysuli blankness. He uses his race to thwart even me.*

At last he looked at Carillon. 'You wish me to spar against you.'

'Aye. As we have done in the past.'

Donal nodded his head in the direction of the sword. 'You have not used *that* against me before.'

'Then perhaps it is time I did. It *is* your grandsire's sword.'

'He *made* it,' Donal retorted. 'He never used it himself. The Cheysuli never do.'

'Hale was all Cheysuli,' Carillon agreed. 'But you claim a full quarter of Homanan blood, and *that* much entitles you to learn the proper use of a sword.'

Again, Donal glanced at Rowan. And again, he saw the blank expression. *Carillon's man to the core. For all he is Cheysuli, he seems more Homanan than Carillon himself!*

Pointedly, Donal looked at Rowan's left side. At the sword sheathed there. A Homanan sword, but wielded by a Cheysuli.

Color came into Rowan's dark face. Cheysuli-born,

Homanan-bred; adversity had taught him to stay alive, during Shaine's *qu'mahlin*, by ignoring the truth of his origins. And now, though free to embrace the customs of his race, he did not. Cheysuli on the outside, Homanan on the inside; Carillon's right-hand man.

In place of my su'fali, *a proper* liege man.

But Donal did not blame Rowan. Note entirely. Finn's dismissal from Carillon's service had been initiated by someone else entirely, and aided – albeit unintentionally – by Carillon himself.

There was, suddenly, tension in Rowan's face. And Donal was ashamed. *It is not his fault. He was raised by the unblessed. Lacking a* lir, *he lacks also a heart and soul. But he does the best he can.*

'Come,' Carillon challenged, 'show me what you know.'

Donal looked at the royal sword of Homana, knowing it was Cheysuli. And then he looked at Rowan.

Silently, Rowan pulled his forth. He offered the hilt to Donal.

9

The practice chamber had no aesthetics about it. It was a plain chamber of unadorned dark-blue stone, even to the floor, which had been worn into a perfectly smooth indigo-slate sheet from years of swordplay and footwork. Each wall bore only weapons racks: swords, long-knives, spears, halberds, axes, bows and other accouterments of war. Wooden benches lined the sides for students who chose to or were ordered to watch. Wall sconces with fat candles in them lit the room with a pearly glow. Donal had been in the chamber many times in fifteen years, but he far preferred the training sessions with Finn and others in the Keep.

Carillon stood in the precise center of the smooth, dark floor. He was still fully dressed, not bothering to shed even his doublet of mulberry velvet. His boots were low-cut, of soft grey leather, lacking the heavy soles of thigh-high riding boots. And in his twisted hands was gripped the gold-hilted sword with its baleful, blackened eye.

Idly, Donal slapped the flat of Rowan's blade against his leather-clad leg. He stripped out of his cloak and dumped it onto the nearest wooden bench. Sighing, he turned to face Carillon. 'My lord, this will be a travesty.'

'Will it?' Carillon smiled. 'Then I am pleased you so willingly admit you lack what skill any soldier should possess.' He gestured sharply. 'Rowan – the door. It may be the Prince of Homana will not desire anyone to see this – *travesty*.'

Briefly Rowan dipped his still-damp head in an

acknowledging nod, then pulled the door tightly shut. He crossed his arms and leaned against the wall, watching both men in an attitude of nonchalance, yet intently aware of each.

Donal yet held the sword in one hand negligently. The hilt was unfamiliar, being made for Rowan's hand, but then the hilt of any sword was unfamiliar to him. He had spent hours with an arms-master, being drilled until he thought he would go mad, but he had always been an indifferent student. He knew, did the time come when he would have to fight, it would be with knife or Cheysuli warbow.

Or lir-*shape. This is foolishness.*

'Come forth,' Carillon invited, 'And tell me how it was you were poisoned.'

Donal's short laugh was a bark. 'I can tell you that without resorting to *this*, Carillon. And I think the answer is easy enough to come by. It was your *cheysula*, my Lord Mujhar. The Queen of Homana herself.'

'Come forth.' Carillon's tone brooked no refusal. '*I*, at least, can speak while I spar. Can you?'

He baits me . . . by the gods, he baits *me!* Donal moved forward, clad more comfortably than Carillon in snug Cheysuli leggings and sleeveless jerkin dyed a warm, soft yellow. Though he hated swordplay, he could not help but move into a defensive posture as Carillon settled the rune-kissed blade more comfortably.

Carillon grunted. 'Electra, was it? I would have guessed the Ihlini.'

'Oh, Tynstar may have encouraged it.' Donal shifted Rowan's sword until it rested more comfortably in his hands. 'But Electra had the doing of this, I am quite sure. But – not alone. She had help.'

'Who? Have I traitor on the island?'

'Traitoress, rather . . . though I think it is too harsh a word. I believe she was unknowing.' Donal touched his blade gently to Carillon's in brief salute. 'It was Aislinn, my lord.'

'*Aislinn* –!' The Cheysuli blade lowered slightly before Carillon caught himself. 'What is this idiocy?'

Donal shook his head. 'No idiocy, my lord – it is the truth. Ask the girl; better yet, ask Sef. He saw what she tried to do.'

'Come *at* me!' Carillon rasped. 'Tell me this over the sword-song!'

Donal stepped in. He parried Carillon's opening maneuver, parried again, and ducked a vicious two-handed swipe that whistled near his ear. He hissed in startled surprise, then danced aside yet again as the sword swooped back to catch him on its return.

'Say again,' Carillon ordered. 'Say *again* it was my daughter!'

'It *was*.' Donal skipped aside, blessing his Cheysuli quickness. Sparring this might be, but Carillon did not spar as most men did. He was strong enough to stop a powerful blow even as he loosed it to the full extent of the meaneuver, and so he sparred with little held back. *Except his is no longer as strong as he once was . . . gods! – he could take my head with another swipe like that!*

'Do not hang back like a fearful child!' Carillon shouted. '*At* me, Donal! I am the *enemy*!'

The royal blade blurred silver in the air, so that the runes bled into the steel and became invisible. Donal saw only the displacement of air and heard the swoop of slicing steel. He moved in instinctively, answering Carillon's challenge, and tried to turn the blow aside. But his blade was battered aside almost at once, then twisted out of his hands. His wrists and forearms cried out their abuse as he fought to hold on, but the hilt slipped from his hands. The sword fell against the floor.

Carillon took a single step forward. The tip of his blade rested lightly against Donal's abdomen, scraping softly on the gold and topaz of his buckle. 'It is your *life*, boy,' the Mujhar rasped. 'It is not *me* you face, but the enemy. Perhaps a Solindish soldier, or an Atvian spearman. Neither will allow you time to retrieve a fallen weapon.'

'Do you expect me to believe such a transparent ploy as that?' Donal snapped. 'Or do you say we go to war *tomorrow*?'

The tip pressed more threateningly. 'Not tomorrow. Perhaps the day after.' Carillon's jaw was set like stone. 'I have been receiving regular messages from couriers out of Solinde these past four weeks. Royce, in Lestra, believes there will be a full-scale rebellion before a sixth-month is past.'

'Rebellion.' Donal felt the clenching of his belly. 'You have feared it, I know . . . and you have not let me forget what might happen did Tynstar ever rally the Solindish again. But *why* would they follow him after so many years of peace?'

'Peace?' Carillon laughed. '*You* might call it that, having no knowledge of what war is. But Solinde is far from peaceful. Royce has put down insurgents time and time again, and there is talk Tynstar *does* move, even now, to unite the Solindish rebels.'

'If he does –'

'If he does, we will go to war again. Not today, perhaps not even tomorrow – but very soon.' Carillon regarded his heir. 'Now, as you know so much, tell me about Osric of Atvia.'

'*Osric!* The Atvian king?' Donal frowned. 'He is at home, is he not, quarreling with Shea of Erinn over an island title?'

'Aye,' Carillon agreed. 'But what if Osric, deciding to avenge his father's death at Homanan hands – as well as tiring of paying me twice-yearly tribute – quits quarreling with Shea of Erinn and chooses to march on Homana?'

'End the tribute,' Donal suggested. 'It would give him one less reason to consider such a march.'

Carillon's smile held little amusement. 'I instigated the tribute in retribution for coming against me the last time. Thorne paid for it with his life, leaving his son to succeed him; therefore the son must also pay for the father's folly. Do I *end* the tribute, Osric will judge me weak. It would be

108

an indication that Homana's aging Mujhar, at last, is losing strength, opening an avenue of attack for Osric. No, no – policy dictates I continue to ask tribute to Atvia. There is no other choice.'

Donal had no desire to entangle himself in the intricacies of kingcraft, even verbally. 'We were not speaking of the potential for war, my lord, but of your daughter's complicity in Electra's attack on me. Should we not finish *that* topic before we begin another?'

'Gods, but you drive me mad!' Carillon said through gritted teeth. '*Look* at me, Donal! What do you see? An old man growing older, and more quickly than anyone might have thought.' Briefly, he shrugged, and a faint wince of pain cut across his face. 'It was your father who told me Tynstar gave me nothing I would not experience anyway; that the disease would devour my body eventually *regardless* of what I did . . . and it does. *Oh, aye* – it does. Who is to say I will live to see the new year?'

'*You* are the one speaking idiocy *now*!' Donal was taken aback by Carillon's intensity. 'Aye, you grow older, but even now you wield a sword. Even *now* you defeat a Cheysuli!'

'Aye, I do. And no warrior I have ever heard of gives in to an enemy so easily.' The tip pressed close yet again. 'You speak of Aislinn's complicity? Then you had best speak a little more clearly. *Now*.'

Donal sighed. 'I cannot say for certain, Carillon. There is no doubt she was – involved. It was her hand that held the knife.' He put up his hand and wiggled his fingers. 'Healed now, and easily enough – it was not so much of a cut – but I *got* the cut because Aislinn tried to put a knife in my back. And *would* have, had my *lir* not warned me. And even then, she cut me. It was Sef who held her back.'

'Aislinn – did *that*?' Carillon's eyes were on the sun-bronzed knuckles.

'Aye, she did. But I doubt it was her decision – I am sure she was ensorceled.'

'How?' Carillon snapped.

'By Electra, my lord – who else?'

The creased lids with their silvered lashes flickered just a little. 'Aislinn is her daughter. Do you tell me Electra would stoop to such perversion?'

Donal did not smile. 'You know her better than I. Tell *me*, my lord, if Tynstar's *meijha* would.'

The breath was expelled suddenly; an explosion of disbelief and horrified acknowledgment. The sword tip wavered against Donal's abdomen. 'She would,' he whispered. 'By the gods, she *would*. And *I* sent Aislinn there –'

'My lord.' Donal did not move; not even in the face of Carillon's emotions did he dare give the sword tip a chance. 'My lord – what else could you have done? She was of an age where she needed to see her *jehana* . . . even one such as Electra.'

'Oh no . . . I could have refused. I *should* have. And now you tell me Aislinn tried to slay you?'

Donal was moved to offer any sort of reassurance, though the transgression was serious enough. He could not bear to see a man who was so strong be overcome by the plotting of his treacherous wife. 'My lord – at least she *failed*.'

Carillon was not amused by the purposeful mildness of the statement. '*This* time. But if it is true she was ensorceled, who is to say she will not try again?'

Donal drew in a careful breath. Deliberately he kept his tone light, seemingly offhand. 'There is a way. I could determine if the ensorcelment is still in effect.'

'How?'

'Let me take her to the Keep. Let my *su'fali* go into her mind.'

Carillon's brows drew down. 'Why Finn? Why not you? I know you have the power.'

'I have tried,' Donal said gently. 'There is a barrier there, the residue of someone else's presence.'

'A trap-link?' Carillon demanded at once. 'Do you say Tynstar has touched my daughter through Electra?'

'That – that is better left to Finn to determine.'

110

'Then we shell let him,' Carillon rasped, 'but only on one condition.'

Donal stared. 'You speak of *conditions* when this may be your daughter's sanity?'

'When I am forced to. And you force me, Donal.' Carillon was unsmiling. 'I set you a task. A simple task, for a Cheysuli.' Suddenly, the smile was there. 'Finn could do it. He *has* done it. That Duncan could have, I do not doubt. And now it is your turn.' He laughed. 'Are you not their blood and bone?'

Donal regarded him suspiciously. 'What would you have me do?'

'Take the sword from me.' Carillon laughed again. 'Win back your grandsire's sword!'

'From *you*?' Donal shook his head. 'Carillon, I could not. More than one realm knows what a renowned fighter you are. The harpers sing lays about you – *I* recall Lachlan's *Song of Homana* even if you do not! I would be a fool to try.'

'A fool *not* to.' Carillon beckoned with two of his twisted fingers. 'Come, Donal . . . take this Cheysuli sword from the hand of a Homanan.'

Donal swore beneath his breath. And then, invoking what skills he had learned from Finn and other warriors, he moved in against the blade. He ignored the bite of steel, concentrating instead on the surprise in Carillon's eyes, and lifted a flexed forearm against the flat of the blade in a quick, chopping motion. And then, even as Carillon subtly shifted position to try another attack. Donal hooked a leg around his ankles and jerked him to the ground.

'My lord –!' It was Rowan, moving from his place by the door, until Donal stopped him with an outthrust hand.

'Do you want the same?' he asked. 'This is between Carillon and me.'

'Donal – you do not know –'

'I know well enough!' Donal retorted. 'He goaded me into this . . . let him reap what seed he sows.'

Slowly, Carillon hitched himself up on one elbow, wincing and swearing. He glared up at Donal. After a moment he stopped cursing and nodded absently. 'Perhaps it is not so necessary for you to learn a sword after all. You are dangerous enough with *nothing*.'

Donal felt a pang of guilt and concern as he looked down upon the Mujhar. He saw again how twisted were the callused hands. 'Carillon, I did not mean –'

'I care naught for what you meant, or *did not* mean!' Carillon's shout was undiminished even by his undignified sprawl upon the stones. 'Never apologize for downing your enemy. I might have slain you with that sword; instead, you disarmed me.' He smiled. 'As I ordered.'

Donal bent down. 'Here – take my hand –'

'Tend your wound, Cheysuli,' Carillon said crossly. 'You are bleeding, and I am old enough to know how to find my feet.' He found them, pushing himself up from the floor, but he could not entirely hide a sharp grimace of pain.

Donal put a hand to his abdomen and felt the slice in the leather as well as the blood seeping through. The wound did not appear to be deep, but it hurt. Still, he shrugged. 'It is nothing. Of no account. Honor enough, in itself.' He grinned, relieved to see Carillon standing before him, apparently all of a piece. 'It is a scar gotten from Homana's Mujhar, and a token of accomplishment. I am still alive. How many others can claim that after a confrontation with you?'

Carillon eyed him suspiciously. 'You have a facile tongue. You must have got it from Alix.'

Donal smiled innocently. 'My *jehana* taught me only reverence for royalty, my lord Mujhar.'

Carillon muttered something beneath his breath and gestured to the Cheysuli sword lying on the ground. 'You may at least return my weapon to me. I may have need of more practice – for our *next* meeting.'

Donal, laughing, bent and grasped the sword by its blade. He ceremoniously offered it hilt-first to Carillon,

making a solemn production out of the gesture. The Mujhar reached out to take it with a muttered oath. His mouth twisted in a grimace of acknowledgment, but before his fingers closed on the hilt, he froze.

'The *ruby*!' The shocked outcry came from Rowan.

Instantly Donal glanced down at the stone set so deeply in the prongs of the pommel. And then he lost his smile.

Like the stare of an unblinking serpent, the Mujhar's Eye glared back at him. But no longer was it the tainted black of Ihlini sorcery. It glowed a rich blood-red.

He felt a frisson of fear and shock. 'It was *black* – it has *always* been black –'

'No,' Carillon said hoarsely. 'Before I plunged it into the purple flames of Tynstar's sorcery, it was red as the blood in my veins. Do you see? *That* is a Cheysuli ruby, Donal, set there by your grandsire's hand. Whole and unblemished, as it was meant to be, until tainted by Ihlini sorcery.'

As Carillon closed his hand on the hilt, Donal released the blade at once. And the ruby turned black again.

'*No* –' Donal blurted.

'Aye.' Carillon's voice was hoarse, uneven. 'By the gods – I understand it.' His eyes, rising to meet Donal's, were filled with sudden comprehension. 'I know now what Finn meant when he explained it to me.'

'Explained *what*?'

Carillon gestured. 'How a Cheysuli sword knows the hand of its master. How it will serve well any man who wields it, because it must, but comes to life only in the hands of the warrior it was meant for. Do you not know your own legends?'

Donal stared in horrified fascination at the black stone in the golden hilt with its rampant Homanan lion. 'I – have heard. But *never* have I seen the story proven –'

'Then look upon it, Donal. This sword was made for you.'

Slowly, Donal shook his head from side to side. 'Oh, I think not . . . I think not. I am Cheysuli, and we do not deal with swords.'

113

'A Cheysuli made it . . . as once your race made the finest swords in the world, though none of the warriors would use them.' Carillon nodded. 'Finn taught me much of the Cheysuli, Donal, and – once, for a very little while – I was Cheysuli myself.' He shrugged at Donal's twitch of startled disbelief. 'You do not yet understand, but you will. There will come a time –' He shook his head quickly. 'Never mind. What we speak of now is how this sword was made for you.'

'No.' It came a burst of involuntary sound, but he knew no other answer. 'Not – mine. It is *yours*.'

Carillon turned the sword in the candlelight, so the flames ran down the blade and set the runes afire. 'Do you see? I know you read Cheysuli Old Tongue. Decipher these runes for me.'

Donal looked at them. He saw the figures wrought in the shining steel. He saw them clearly enough to read them, and then he drew back once more. 'I will not.'

'Donal –'

'I *cannot*!' he shouted. 'Are you blind? You tell me my grandsire made this sword for me while knowing what would happen, and I *dare* not acknowledge what it means.'

'The runes, Donal. I can have them read by another. I would rather *you* read them to me.'

He took yet another step back. 'Do you not see? If that sword were truly made for me, it means I *must* succeed you. *And I am not certain I can*!'

'Why can you not?' Carillon, stricken, stared at him over the shining sword. 'Do you say I have chosen the wrong man?'

Donal clapped both hands over his face. 'No, oh no, not the wrong man – the *right* man!' His voice was muffled behind his palms. 'But how am I to follow you? After all that *you* have done?' Donal stripped the black hair back from his face. 'Gods, Carillon, you are a legend by which all men measure themselves. And you are *living*! Can you imagine how they will measure *me* when you are gone?'

114

Carillon's aging face lost its color. 'It is that, then. You fear you cannot live up to your predecessor.'

'*Aye*.' Donal sighed and let his hands drop down to slap against his thighs. 'Gods – who could? You are *Carillon*.'

'I do not want that!' Carillon cried. 'Gods, Donal, be yourself! Do not think about what others would have you be.'

'How not? There is nothing else I *can* do.' Donal caught his breath. The sparring session had sapped even more of his strength. The chamber wavered a little. He shoved a forearm against his brow to wipe the sweat away. 'Surely you must see it, Carillon. Surely you must hear it. How they worship you even as they curse the heir you chose.'

'*Curse* you –'

'Aye.' Donal's throat was dry. His voice scraped through the hoarseness. 'There are times I almost hate myself. I play the polished plate and reflect the things they see. Cheysuli. Arrogant. Believing myself better than any Homanan. And yet even as they mutter to one another how I will be *given* the Lion instead of earning it, I wonder if I am worthy of your trust.' He looked into the older man's face. 'Gods, Carillon – there are times I want nothing more than to turn my back on *you*, so I can keep a piece of myself.'

'No,' Carillon said hollowly. 'Do not think of it. Without you, there is nothing.'

Donal raised both hands briefly and let them slap down at his sides. 'The *shar tahls* say it is my *tahlmorra* to accept the Lion from you. But – I would sooner accept *nothing* from my *jehan*.'

Carillon flinched visibly. Donal saw it and realized he had hurt the man, though he had not intended to. He would not hurt Carillon for the world, not intentionally. And yet there were times he felt his very presence hurt him, because he knew himself living testimony to Carillon's failure to produce a legitimate son of his own flesh and blood.

'I care nothing for what others may think of you,'

Carillon said. 'They are fools. Homanan I may be, but I am not blind. I spent too many years with Finn to disbelieve in *tahlmorra* and a man's place within the tapestry of the gods.' One corner of his mouth twitched in an effort to steady his voice. 'There was a time Duncan himself told me how he longed to turn his back on his *tahlmorra* so he could share his life with his son. But his dedication was such that he could not ignore what lay before him, and so he met Tynstar and died. But – you should not judge yourself by others. Donal. Never.'

Insecurity suddenly overcame him. 'I know I can never be what they would have me be. I am not you.'

'Be *Donal*,' Carillon said. 'By the gods, you will be the first Cheysuli Mujhar in four hundred years!'

'Aye,' Donal agreed. 'I will have your throne one day. That is more than enough. I *will not* take your sword.'

'But it is yours. *Yours*, Donal. You must accept it now.' Carillon held it out.

Donal took a single step away. 'No. Not yet.'

'Do you deny your grandsire's wishes?'

'Aye.' Donal stared at the runes. The runes that beckoned him; the runes he had to deny. *And do I deny the power?*

Carillon drew in a raspy breath. 'Then – if not now . . . will you accept it at your acclamation?' The Mujhar smiled a little. 'Shaine gave me this sword upon *my* acclamation as Prince of Homana. Surely you could accept it then.'

'No.' Yet another step away. 'Carillon – I have no wish to strip you of your power. One day there will be no choice, but for now there *is*. And I have made it.'

Carillon's eyes, staring down at the blackened ruby, were bleak in his care-worn face. It was the face of a man who sees his own ending, when he has only just gotten past his beginning. It was the face of a man who recognizes his *tahlmorra* and all the futility and insignificance of his presence within the palm of the gods. The face of a man who, when confronted with his chosen successor, knows

116

that successor was already chosen long before.

The Mujhar looked at Rowan. 'It is *Donal*,' he said clearly. 'It is Donal, after all.' He laughed, but the sound was the sound of bittersweet discovery. 'For all Finn and Duncan told me how important *I* was to the prophecy, it does not come down to me at all.' Slowly, he shook his head. 'To Donal. I am only the *caretaker* of this realm . . . until another's time has come.'

10

Donal, mounted on his chestnut, watched sidelong as Carillon mounted his own grey stallion. Tall as he was, he seemed to have trouble reaching up to the stirrup. But he mounted. With less grace than Donal had witnessed before, perhaps, but Carillon got himself into the saddle.

The Mujhar let go a short breath of effort completed and squinted in the morning sunlight, glancing over at Donal. 'You look somewhat done in. Did you resort to the wine jug last night?'

Donal, who had resorted to nothing but his own imaginings following the confrontation with Carillon in the practice chamber, shook his head a little. 'No. I did not sleep.'

Carillon's silvering brows rose. 'Did not – or *could* not?'

Donal grunted. 'One and the same, last night.'

The Mujhar nodded. 'Neither did I.' He glanced across Donal's mount to the smaller bay horse beyond, its rider nearly out of earshot. 'So, you bring your new servant along.'

Donal drew rein as his horse fidgeted, stomping one hoof against the cobbles of the bailey. Automatically he looked for Lorn, concerned for his welfare, but the wolf waited at some distance from the horses. Taj perched upon the bailey wall.

'Now is as good a time as any for Sef to see what a Keep is,' Donal told Carillon. 'But where is Aislinn?'

'Delaying for as long as she can,' Carillon said dryly. 'She wants no part of this.'

'She said she was willing before.'

'Aye. Before.' Carillon was unsmiling. '*Before* she knew aught of Sorcha and the boy.'

Donal felt the clenching of his belly. 'Then – she told you how she found out.'

'Aye. She was – less than happy about it.' Carillon looked directly at his heir. 'We have never played games with each other, Donal – we knew one day it would come to this. Even when you and Sorcha grew close – you knew.'

Carillon, Donal knew, did not precisely accuse. But he was Aislinn's father and, though he understood Cheysuli customs better than any Homanan, no doubt he felt the relationship between Donal and his Cheysuli *meijha* was an insult to his daughter.

Donal drew in a deep breath that was just the slightest bit unsteady. 'I – know. As you say, there have been no games. And I mean no offense even now . . . surely you must see that.'

'I see it.' Carillon shifted in his saddle, as if his muscles pained him. 'Donal – I care deeply for my daughter. I would not have her hurt. But neither do I wish to trespass on Cheysuli customs.' He stared down at his twisted hands as he clutched reins and saddlebow. 'Aislinn said she wished to break off the betrothal. In the face of her tears and tattered pride, I had to refuse her, of course . . . I had no choice.'

'No doubt it is difficult for a *jehan* to deny his child anything he or she wants.' Donal made his answer as judicious as he could.

Carillon's smile was slightly sardonic. 'Aye. And, soon enough, I doubt not you will learn it for yourself. Ian is of an age to exert his needs and desires.'

'I am sorry, Carillon,' Donal said wretchedly. 'I would spare her as much pain and heartache as I could, were there another way.'

'I know that. But – I think there will come a day when you find you must make a choice.' He gestured with a nod

of his head toward the marble steps. 'And here is my tardy daughter.' Carillon motioned for one of the stable lads to lead the dun-colored mare forward.

Aislinn's shining hair was plaited tightly, then doubled up and bound with green woolen yarn. The knot of bright hair hung over one brown-cloaked shoulder. Her dark green skirts were kilted up for ease of riding, and her legs were booted to the knees. With the grace of youth she mounted, unaffected in her movements, and gathered in her reins. Like most Homanan women, she disdained a sidesaddle and rode astride.

She glanced sidelong at Donal. He saw how red-rimmed the eloquent eyes were, as if she had cried the night through; her face was a little swollen and her mouth did not hold a steady line. But her pert nose with its four golden freckles was lifted toward the sky. 'Do we go? Let us get this travesty over.'

Donal, despite the haughty words, sensed her unhappiness clearly. Aislinn was a young girl, badly frightened by what she faced, and resorted to what attitude she could in an effort to control her fear. He understood it. He had done it before himself.

Her horse was close to his own. He leaned out of the saddle slightly and caught the back of her neck, squeezing gently. 'You will do well enough.'

Her demeanor seemed less arrogant. 'Will I?' she whispered. 'Gods . . . I am so afraid –'

'Fear has its proper place – or so I am told.' He released her and reined his stallion around. 'But I think there is little need for it in the Keep.'

'But – it is *Finn* –'

'He is the last warrior you should fear. That much I promise you.'

Aislinn's hands, gloved in supple amber-dyed leather, tightened on her reins. The dun mare crowded Donal's chestnut. 'Then I hold you to your promise.'

'If you wish, I will go in with Finn. You have felt my touch before. There is little I can do, lacking the necessary

experience, but I can monitor what *he* does.' Donal shrugged. 'Would it lend you some reassurance?'

Her grey eyes, pale as water, studied him a long moment. Then, reluctantly, she nodded. He saw the twisting of her mouth. 'Aye. I want you there as well.'

He pushed the mare's mouth away from his knee before her metal bit could bang against him painfully. 'Then I will be there.'

But her fear remained. He could see it.

'Let us go,' Carillon said. 'Sooner done, is it done with.' He gathered his reins and spurred the grey stallion about. But before he could go, Rowan called for him from the top of the marble steps.

'My lord – my lord – wait you.' The general ran down the steps rapidly. 'Carillon – a courier has come. From Duke Royce in Lestra.' Rowan caught hold of one rein and held back the Mujhar's horse. 'I think, my lord, you had best hear what he has to say.'

At once, Carillon looked at Aislinn. His indecision was manifest. but even as she reined her horse closer to his, preparing to plead her case, he became more decisive. 'Aislinn – you will be safe enough with Donal. You have heard what the general has said.'

'You promised to go *with* me!'

'And now I cannot.' His tone was gentle, but equally inflexible. 'Were this testing not so necessary, I would say it could wait for another time. But it cannot, no more than can this courier.' He reached out and caught the crown of her head with one broad hand and cupped his twisted fingers around the dome of her skull. 'I am truly sorry, Aislinn . . . but I know you will be safe with Donal.'

'You give me no choice,' she accused unhappily. 'You give me no choice in *anything*!' Wrenching her mare around, she headed for the gates.

Carillon sighed heavily. 'Be patient,' he told Donal. 'She is young . . . and till now her lot as my daughter has been little more than a beautiful game. Now she knows its price.'

'I will bring her back before nightfall,' Donal promised. 'As for what she will face – there is nothing for you to fear. It is Finn who will do the testing.'

Briefly, Carillon smiled. 'After all these years, it comes again to Finn. And I think it will amuse him.' Slowly, he swung down out of the saddle and patted the horse's shoulder. 'Safe journey, Donal. And now you had best go after her before she gets so far ahead you lose her entirely.'

It was Sef, edging his horse close to Donal's, who remarked about the vastness of the Keep. 'There are pavilions *everywhere.*'

The oiled pavilions, dyed warm earth and forest tones and painted with myriad *lir*, spread through the forest like a scattering of seed upon the ground. The Cheysuli, when they could, left the trees standing, setting up their pavilions in clustered copses of oak and elm and beech with vines and bracken still intact. Surrounding the permanent encampment, snaking across the ground, stood the curving grey-green granite wall.

'It seems so, now,' Donal agreed. 'When I was a boy, there were not so many as this. But that was when we lived across the Bluetooth River, trying to stay free of Ihlini retribution and Bellam's tyranny.' He glanced around the Keep as they rode through, reining around cookfires and running children. 'This is a true Keep now, with the half-circle walls and painted pavilions. But for years – too many years – we lived as refugees and outlaws.' He glanced at Aislinn, locked up in her silence. 'It was Carillon who allowed us the freedom to come home.'

Sef's parti-colored eyes were fixed on Donal. 'It's no wonder they sing songs and tell stories about him, then. Look at what he's done.'

Donal felt a stab of sympathy for Carillon, even in his absence. *We have made him into a legend for us to idolize, and we have stripped him of his freedom, It must be more difficult for him to live up to the name, and he is the one who wears it.*

'My father is a great man,' Aislinn said flatly. 'There is no one like him in all the kingdoms of the world. *No one* will ever be able to match him.' Her grey-pale eyes were fastened with great deliberation upon Donal's face.

'Aislinn,' he said gently, 'I do not compete with your *jehan*. And I will not even when his throne has passed to me.' Trying to break the moment, he glanced around the keep. 'This is smaller now than it was when first we came here. But some of the clans have gone back across the Bluetooth to return to the Northern Keep.' Involuntarily, he shivered. 'It was cold there – too close to the Wastes. I prefer this Keep. And now – here is Finn's pavilion.'

'Another wolf,' Sef said. He pointed at the green pavilion with its gold-painted wolf on the side. 'Lorn's father?'

Donal grinned down at the ruddy wolf as Lorn snorted in surprise. 'No. More like grandsire, perhaps, did *lir* age normally. But as they do not, it makes no difference.' He jumped off his chestnut stallion even as Taj settled on the ridgepole of the pavilion. 'Come down Sef . . . there is nothing to harm you here.'

'You said that about the Crystal Isle.' Sef slid off his brown horse.

'And was there?' Donal looped his reins about a convenient tree branch and turned to help Aislinn down.

'There was,' Sef said, 'but I didn't let it.'

Ignoring the boy's superstitions, Donal ducked under the reins and scratched at the pavilion doorflap. '*Su'fali*,' he called. 'Are you in?'

'No. I am out, but very nearly in.' Finn came around the side of the pavilion with Storr padding at his side. The wolf's muzzle had greyed and grizzled, showing as much of age as a *lir* could, for his lifespan paralleled Finn's. Until his warrior died, Storr was free of normal aging.

Finn's black brows ran up beneath his silver-flecked, raven hair. But for that and a few deep lines etched into the flesh at the corners of his yellow eyes, he hardly looked old enough to have a nephew of twenty-three. The dark

flesh of his bare arms was still stretched taut over heavy muscles; his *lir*-bands gleamed in the sunlight. 'You have been a stranger to your Keep, Donal. What brings you here now?'

'Aislinn,' he said briefly, and sensed her instant tension.

Finn glanced at her. 'You are well come to the Keep, lady. Meghan will be pleased to know you are here. She is with Alix just now, but I can send Storr for her.'

'No.' Aislinn's face was tight with apprehension. 'I have not come to see Meghan. I have come because Donal made me promise, and my father insisted I *keep* it.'

'As one should, particularly a princess.' But Finn had lost his welcoming smile as he glanced again at Donal. 'This is not a casual visit.'

'No,' Donal agreed. 'Aislinn, as you know, has been with Electra on the Crystal Isle. She has been – tampered with.'

'A trap-link?' Finn's hand shot out and clamped on Aislinn's head before she could move. And by the time she *did* move, crying out and pulling away, Finn was done with his evaluation. 'No. Something else. Bring her inside.' He turned and pulled the doorflap aside.

Aislinn hung back. She looked at Donal, and he saw the terror in her face. Gently, he set one hand on her shoulder. After a moment, she slipped inside the pavilion.

Sef, like Aislinn, hung back. But for different reasons. 'It isn't my *place*,' he said. 'He'll work magic in there. I'll do better out here.'

'Come in,' Donal insisted mildly. 'What Finn will do is nothing I cannot do myself, and I do not doubt you will be witness to it sooner rather than late. It may as well be now.' He settled one browned hand around Sef's arm and ushered him into the pavilion, leaving Lorn to trade greetings with Storr – as well as the grooming ritual – and Taj to converse with the other *lir*.

Finn sat on a spotted silver fur taken from a snow leopard. As clan-leader he was entitled to a large pavilion, and he had accepted that right. Furs of every texture and color

cushioned the hard-packed earthen floor, and fine-worked tapestries divided the pavilion into sections. One of those sections, Donal knew, belonged to Meghan, Finn's half-Homanan daughter.

Thinking of Meghan reminded him that Finn had said she was with Alix. And his mother, no doubt, was with his *meijha*. Quite suddenly, Donal longed to be there as well, wishing to forget all about Aislinn and her troubles.

But he had promised, and he did not break his oaths.

A small firepit glowed in front of Finn. The smoke was drawn up to the top of the pavilion, where it was dispersed through a ventflap. Through the bluish haze, Finn's eyes were almost hypnotic.

Aislinn half-turned as if to flee, but Donal blocked her way. Defeated, she turned reluctantly back. Her fingers crept up to pull nervously at the wool binding her braid.

Finn laughed. 'You remind me a little of Alix, when first she joined the clan. All doe-eyed and frightened, yet defiant enough to spit in my face. That *is* what you would prefer to do, Aislinn . . . is it not?'

'Aye!' she answered, summoning up her own measure of defiance. 'I want no part of this. It is Donal who says I am – tainted.' Her voice wavered just a little. 'He said – she has meddled with my mind.'

Finn did not smile. He did not appear privately amused, as he so often did. His tone, when he spoke, was quiet and exceedingly gentle. 'If she has, small one . . . I will see that we rid you of it.' For a moment he studied her silently. 'There is no need to fear me, Aislinn. Do you not know me through my daughter? You and Meghan are boon companions.'

Aislinn's eyes were huge, almost colorless in the muted light of the pavilion. 'But – *I have heard all the stories.*'

'*All* of them?' Finn shook his head. 'I think not. You had best ask Carillon for more.' Now he smiled, just a little, and looked past her to Donal. 'Who is the boy you have brought?'

Donal prodded Sef forward. 'Answer him. His *lir* may

be a wolf, but it does not mean he will devour you. Any more than *I* will.'

Sef moved forward three steps. His hands were wound into the black woolen tunic that bore a small crimson rampant lion over his left breast. 'Sef,' he said softly, keeping his eyes averted. 'I am – Sef.'

'And I am Finn.' Finn smiled his old ironic smile. 'You almost resemble a Cheysuli. Donal has not brought you home, has he? As I brought Alix home?'

Color rushed into Sef's pale face, then washed away almost at once. His eyes, blue and brown, stared fixedly at Finn. 'No,' he said on a shaking breath. 'I am not Cheysuli.'

Finn shrugged. 'You have the black hair and strong-boned face for it, albeit you are too fair for one of us.' For just a moment, a teasing glint lit his eyes. 'Perhaps you are merely a halfling gotten unknown on some poor Homanan woman –'

Finn stopped. Donal, looking at him, saw the glint in his eyes fade; heard the teasing banter die. Finn frowned a little, looking at Sef, as if he sought an answer to some unknown question.

Donal laughed aloud. 'Perhaps *your* halfling, *su'fali*?'

Finn looked at him sharply. 'Mine?'

'You are no priest, *su'fali*, who keeps himself from women.' Donal, still grinning, shrugged. 'Sef himself says he does not know who his *jehan* was.'

'He was *not* Cheysuli!' Sef declared hotly.

Donal looked at him quickly, startled by his vehemence. 'Would it matter so much if he *were*?' he asked. 'What if he were Finn himself?'

Sef's eyes locked onto Finn's. So intense was his regard he seemed almost transfixed. 'No,' he said. That word only, and yet its tone encompassed an abiding certainty.

'No,' Finn agreed, and yet Donal saw a faint frown of puzzlement. Then Finn flicked a dismissive hand. 'To get to the point: Electra has once more meddled with someone's mind, and this time it is Aislinn's.' He looked at the

frightened princess. 'Sit down, girl, and I will discover what I can.'

'Donal tried,' she blurted. 'He could do nothing.'

'I am not Donal, and I have had somewhat of a more – *personal* – experience with such things as Ihlini trap-links.' Briefly he looked at Storr, lying on a pelt nearby, as if the words evoked some private memory they shared. 'Aislinn, I will not harm you. Do you think Carillon would allow it?'

She stared at the furs beneath her feet. 'No.'

Donal placed a gentle hand on Aislinn's head. 'Sit down. I am here with you, Aislinn.'

She shut her eyes a moment. And then she sat down where Finn indicated, cross-legged, across the firecairn from him.

'Now,' he said quietly, 'if Donal has done this to you, you know it will not hurt.'

'Have *you* had it done?' she challenged with a defiance that only underscored her fear and vulnerability.

An odd look passed over Finn's dark, angular face. The scar twisting across the left side of his face had faded from avid purple to silver-white with the passing of seventeen years, but it still puckered the flesh from eye to jaw, lending him a predatory expression he did not entirely require, having the look of a predator already. 'Not – precisely,' Finn answered at last. 'But something similar was done to me. It was – Tynstar. And your *jehana*. Together, they set a trap for me, and nearly slew me.' He studied her face closely, unsmiling. 'But I survived, though something else did not.'

Aislinn, startled, sucked in a breath. '*What* did not survive?'

'An oath,' Finn said flatly. 'We broke it, your *jehan* and I, because there was nothing left to do.' He reached out and touched her eyelids with two gentle fingers. 'You are not your *jehana*, Aislinn, and I doubt she has done much to you that cannot be undone. Be silent, do not fear, and forget the stories you have heard.'

127

Silently, Donal knelt down at Aislinn's side. He watched as Finn put his hands out, reaching through the smoke to touch her face. Finn ran his fingers softly across the delicate flesh of her brow, her nose, her eyelids, keeping himself silent. And then he spread his fingers and trapped her skull in his palms.

His hands held her head carefully, cupping thumbs beneath her jaw and splaying fingers through her hair. For a long moment he only looked at her pale, rigid face with its tight-shut eyes, and then his mouth moved into a grim line. He glanced quickly at Donal. 'Do you come?'

'Aye, *su'fali*.'

'Then come.' The grimness faded into relaxation, and the yellow eyes turned vague and detached. Finn was patently *elsewhere*.

Donal knew what he did. Finn sought the power in the earth magic, tapping the source as he himself had done, drawing it up into his body until he could focus it onto Aislinn. He channeled it into the girl, seeking out the knotted web of Ihlini interference. Could he do it, he would untangle the web and disperse it.

Finn's head dipped down a little in an odd echo of Aislinn's posture. His eyes, fixed and unblinking, turned black as the pupils swelled. His mouth loosened; his chin twitched once; a slight tremor ran through his body.

Donal took a breath and slipped into the link with care. He felt his knowledge of body and surroundings fade away at once, dissipating into nonexistence, until he was but a speck of pulsing awareness in a void of black infinity. It was *nothingness*, complete and complex, and yet it was the essence of everything. Earth power, raw and unchanneled, surged up around him, threatening to smother him.

Carefully, Donal pushed it back. He maintained his awareness of self and the knowledge of what he did, remaining *Donal* in the face of such overwhelming power. And slowly, the power fell back, allowing him room to move. Quickly he sought Finn and found his presence in

128

the void, the bright, rich crimson spark that was the essence of his uncle.

Su'fali, Donal greeted him.

That which was Finn returned the greeting. As they made contact, Donal felt the flare of two Cheysuli souls joined in an odd form of intercourse. Together they would locate and evaluate the residue of sorcery that resonated in Aislinn's mind, and they would free her of it.

There, said Finn within the vastness of their link.

Donal saw it. Caught in the countless strands of Aislinn's subconsciousness was a mass of knotted darkness; a spider's web. It looked tenuous as any thread, and yet he knew it was not. Tynstar's 'thread' would be tensile as the strongest wire.

Gently, Finn said. *Gently. Springing the trap must be carefully done, or it will catch unwanted prey.*

Donal crept slowly closer to the trap-link. He prepared to lend Finn what strength he could –

– and felt the sudden painful wrenching of a broken link.

Awareness exploded into a vast shower of burning fragments, hissing out one by one. Donal thought at first it was something within Aislinn, some form of ward-spell, then felt the scrape of a hand upon his shoulder. No longer was he free of his body, but bound by flesh again.

Dimly, he heard Aislinn's garbled outcry. Finn was swearing. Donal caught himself before he fell face-first into the flames, then thrust an arm against the pelts to steady himself. He was disoriented and badly shaken, feeling distinctly ill.

Angrily, he turned. 'To touch a Cheysuli in mind-link –'

But he broke it off. He saw how Sef slumped down on the fur pelt just behind, his face corpse-white in the blue-smoked air. The boy shuddered spasmodically and his mouth gaped open as if he could not breathe. Donal thrust himself up in one movement and caught Sef before he tumbled into the fire.

Donal looked back at Aislinn. Finn still held her, and by

129

the look of his eyes he had not stepped out of the link. Aislinn still drifted in the trance and Finn still sought the trap-link. But there was no doubting Donal's broken link had affected them both. The shattering had been too powerful.

Donal closed his eyes a moment. He still felt ill. His ears buzzed. Lights fired in his eyes. But somehow he managed to stand up with Sef in his arms and stagger out of the pavilion.

He set the boy down against a tree. Even as he did so, Sef began to rouse. Donal, seating himself on the ground, put his head down against his knees and tried to regain his composure.

Lir? It was Lorn, thrusting his nose beneath Donal's elbow. *Lir?*

Even as Sef stirred, Donal raised his head. *Broken link*, he told the wolf. *Sef touched me.*

You should have told him, lir. You should have warned the boy.

My fault, Donal said, and blew out a heavy breath.

Color crept back into Sef's face. He blinked, rubbed dazedly at his temple, then tried to sit bolt upright.

Donal pressed him back down. 'No. Be still. Do you recall what happened?'

Sef frowned blankly. 'I – I was drowning. I was being sucked down. It was like I was buried alive.' He stared at Donal. 'Was it the magic? Did I feel it?'

Donal sought the best words. 'Sef – what you did was done out of ignorance. I understand. And I should have warned you: never touch a Cheysuli when he has gone into another's mind.'

Sef's eyes widened. 'What could happen?'

Donal rubbed at burning eyes. His ears still buzzed, though the sound had almost faded. 'Many things, depending upon the severity of the break, and how deeply the warrior has gone. And a link is a link – in touching me you touched Aislinn and Finn. You might have injured us all in addition to yourself.'

Sef sucked in a strangled breath. 'Oh my lord, I'm *sorry* –'

Donal caught one thin shoulder. 'Do not fret. It is over with. No permanent harm was done, that I can see.'

'I was so afraid.' Sef looked steadfastly at the ground. 'I was – afraid.'

'Fear is nothing to be ashamed of,' Donal told him gently. 'It strikes all men, at one time or another, and mimics many things. You were not drowning. You were not being buried alive.'

Lorn still pressed against Donal's side. *The boy is more than frightened, lir. There is* something . . . else.

Is the boy a halfling? Donald asked.

The wolf seemed to shrug. I *cannot say. Perhaps – but I leave him to you.* Lorn turned and went back to his place on the rug by Finn's tent, sharing it with Storr.

Sef's eyes were fixed on Donal's face. 'You are – different.' he said gravely. 'Never do you make me feel a child. Oh, aye, there are times I deserve chastising, and you deliver it – but never do you treat me as if I were unworthy of courtesy. Others do.'

Donal smiled. 'Maybe it is because I am used to boys asking questions. I have a son, you see, though he lacks ten of your years.'

'A – son?' Sef sat more upright. 'But – I thought you were to wed the princess!'

'I am. But I have a Cheysuli *meijha*, and she has given me a son.' He glanced back at the pavilion, wishing to go back in so he could join again in the link with Finn.

'I didn't know that.' Sef's brows drew down in a frown.

Donal smiled. 'Does it matter? You are still my sworn man, are you not?'

'What of your son?'

'He is too young yet. Ian has years before he can serve me as you do.' He pulled Sef to his feet. 'If the pavilion is too close for you, or you feel too frightened to enter, wait here. I will be out when I can.' He released Sef's wrist, but as he did he felt something soft and supple against his

131

fingers. 'What is this?' he asked, peeling back Sef's sleeve.

It was a narrow bracelet of feathers bound around Sef's wrist. Brown and gold and black.

Sef jerked his wrist away and covered up the band with his other hand. 'A – charm.' Color blazed into his face. 'Protection against strong magic.' His eyes flicked toward the pavilion. 'I was – afraid. When – when I was given time of my own to spend as I wished, I went into the city. I – found an old woman who makes charms and love-spells.' He shrugged defensively. 'I said I was afraid of the Cheysuli, and she gave me this.' He exposed the feathered band briefly as the color ran out of his face. 'Are you ashamed of me?'

'Only if you paid her all the coin I gave you,' Donal said wryly. 'Did you?'

Sef's eyes widened. 'Oh *no*! Do you think I'm a fool? I only gave her *half* of it.'

Donal tried not to laugh and did not entirely succeed. 'Well enough, you drove a good bargain. But Mujharan prices are higher than those in Hondarth, I will wager.' He squeezed Sef's shoulder. 'There is no need for the charm. Shall I take it from your wrist?'

'*No* –' Sef took a single backward step. 'No,' he said more quickly. 'I know *you* would never hurt me,' he muttered, 'but what of all the others?'

Donal shook his head and sighed. 'There is much for you to learn, I see. Well enough, keep your ward-spell and know yourself safe from Cheysuli "sorcery" '. He turned to re-enter the pavilion, then glanced back. 'You may stay here or wander, as you like. But it will be best that you do not come in again.'

Blood came and went in Sef's face. 'No, my lord. I won't.'

Donal pulled aside the flap and went back inside the tent.

Aislinn, he saw, was slumped over, held limply in Finn's arms. He bent down at once to take her.

'No,' Finn said. 'She will be well enough. It is only the

aftermath.' Strain had etched new lines in his dark face. Like Carillon, he had once been touched by Tynstar, and it showed occasionally in his appearance and slowed reflexes. But Finn, unlike Carillon, had not lost so many years. 'It was – difficult.'

Donal knelt down quickly. 'Is she all right? Did you destroy the trap-link?'

Finn frowned. 'There was no trap-link, not as I know them. There was something, aye – you saw it as well as I – but not of Tynstar's doing. And I think Electra, even using what arts Tynstar taught her, is not capable of setting one herself. But she did work some form of magic on Aislinn. There was an echo, a residue of – *something*. I could not catch it all . . . it was too elusive. And once the boy broke your portion of the link . . . ' Finn shrugged, cupping Aislinn's lolling head as if she were an infant. 'I do believe Aislinn was somehow ensorceled to carry out Electra's plans, but I think I have ended that.'

'I hope you are certain, *su'fali*,' Donal said dryly. 'I think I would be disinclined to wed a woman who wishes to see me slain.'

Finn grinned. 'I do not doubt Aislinn has personal reasons for viewing you with some disfavor – having known Homanan women before – but I hardly think you need worry about a knife in the back in your nuptial bed.' Then the humor slipped away. 'Who is that boy?'

'A foundling. He was in Hondarth alone, living in the streets and eating what he could find.' Donal shrugged. 'He begged to come with me when I had done him a service, and so I let him come. Why? Do you think he may really be your son?'

Finn flicked him a glance from half-lidded eyes. 'I will not discount the possibility.'

Donal sat back on his heels. 'You *do* think he is –'

'I said: I would not discount the possibility.' Finn repeated firmly. 'That does not mean I claim he *is*.'

'No,' Donal conceded. He chewed at the inside of his left cheek. 'But – why should you think so? Burned dark,

he might be one of us – but he lacks the yellow eyes.'

'So does Alix. So do many of our halflings.' Finn shrugged. 'Perhaps he is mine, perhaps he is another's. There is definitely something *familiar* about him, but I think it does not matter.'

'Not *matter*!' Donal stared at him in surprise. 'How can you be so callous?'

Finn's black brows lifted. 'I will force paternity on *no* one, Donal. And he did not seem over fond of the Cheysuli.'

'He has not had a chance to know us. Given time –'

'Given time, he may find himself content to be your man.' Finn smiled. 'Not a liege man, perhaps, but a loyal companion. And I think you are in need of one.'

'I have my *lir*. They are more than enough.'

'Aye. But you will also have Aislinn.' Finn looked down on the sleeping princess in his arms. 'Odd, how she resembles both and neither of her parents. It is the coloring, I think – strip the red from her hair and make it blond, and she is nearly Electra come again.'

Donal reached out and touched Aislinn's hair, smoothing it against her scalp. She looked younger as she slept, but she was no longer a little girl. 'No. Not Electra. Perhaps she has the features, but none of the witch's ways.' He sighed and took his hand away.

'Donal.' Finn's tone was oddly serious, for a man who only infrequently sought decorum. 'I know what you face, now that you must wed her. But you are Duncan's son, and I know you have the strength.'

'Do I?' Donal looked again at Aislinn. 'I am not my *jehan*, much as I long to be more like him. And I could not *begin* to say if I share his dedication.'

'He was born with that no more than any man,' Finn said. 'He learned it because he had to. So will you.' He nodded toward the doorflap. 'Go and see your *meijha*. You owe her a little time.'

'Aislinn?'

'I will keep her with me.'

Donal felt the guilt begin to pain him sorely. 'My thanks, *su'fali*. It is every bit as difficult as you warned me, that day so long ago.'

The scar writhed as Finn's jaw tightened. 'I am not your *jehan*, nor can ever be. But I would give you what aid I can. It is only that eventually you must bear the weight yourself.' Again he motioned with the head. 'Go and see your *meijha*. I will give you what time I can.'

11

Donal stepped outside the pavilion, glad to feel the fresh air again, and found his sister in deep conversation with Sef. In all excitement of having Aislinn tested by Finn, he had forgotten Bronwyn entirely. He had not seen her for longer than he cared to admit. But then, he put her from his mind as often as he could.

No. Not Bronwyn. What Bronwyn could become.

She turned as he stepped out. She resembled their mother mostly, with Alix's amber eyes and lighter complexion, but her hair was Cheysuli black.

Or Ihlini black. In that she could take after Tynstar.

Donal shut off the thought at once. He could not clearly recall precisely how or when his mother had told him Bronwyn was not Duncan's daughter, but another man's entirely. And neither was he Cheysuli, but Tynstar himself. Tynstar of the Ihlini. No, Donal could not recall the words, but he could all too easily summon up the disbelief and astonishment he had felt.

That, and the fear.

One day, she will learn what powers she claims. She will begin to play with them. . . .

He did not want to think of that day. It had been fifteen years since Alix had escaped from Tynstar's lair bearing the sorcerer's child in her belly. Bronwyn as yet had shown no signs of Ihlini powers, but she had been increasingly moody lately. The *lir* themselves had been unable to predict when she might come to know her powers; all they could discern in her was the Cheysuli blood she claimed

136

from her mother's side, as if Alix's Old Blood were cancel-
ing out that of the Ihlini. No one but Alix, Finn, Carillon,
Sorcha and himself knew the girl's true paternal heritage,
not even Bronwyn herself. But it was possible her father's
legacy might wake in her at any time, and so they watched
her more closely each day.

She wore a gown of deepest purple trimmed with wine-
red yarn in a linked pattern of animals. Birds and bears
and cats promenaded at collar and cuffs. The front of her
skirts was hooked over the tops of her leather boots, as if
she had been running. As it was Bronwyn, she probably
had been. She rarely ever walked.

*She is wild. So wild. Someone else might say it was the
recklessness of girlhood. But – I cannot help but wonder
if there is more to it than that.*

'Rujho.' Bronwny smiled at him, exposing even white
teeth in a face darker than Sef's but lighter than her
brother's. 'I came to see you, not knowing you were busy.
Sef told me what you sought to do.' Her smile faded. 'Is
Aislinn all right?'

'Aislinn is fine. Whatever was there does not seem to be
permanent.' He glanced at Sef. 'I assume the introductions
have been concluded?'

'I told her my name,' Sef answered. 'Should I have said
more?'

'Not unless there *is* more.'

Sef looked back at Bronwyn. Donal, having seen young
boys impressed with girls before, hid a smile. He had the
distinct feeling that Sef, if Bronwyn were interested,
would spill more of his life to her than to anyone else,
including the Prince of Homana.

'Then I leave you in companionship to one another,' he
told them. 'I have private business now.'

'With Sorcha?' Bronwyn asked as he turned to go.

Donal abruptly turned back. Bronwyn as well as anyone
in the Keep knew what he shared with Sorcha. She knew
also he was betrothed to Aislinn; it was common knowledge in the clans. But Bronwyn was Aislinn's friend, and

he did not doubt she felt conflicting loyalties nearly as much as he did, if in a different way.

'Aye, with Sorcha,' he said at last. 'Bronwyn – you will give Aislinn what comfort you can –?'

Bronwyn lifted her head. She had pulled her hair back in a manner too severe for her young face, braided very tightly and entirely bound with purple yarn. The color was striking on her, but it reminded him of the Ihlini. It reminded him of Tynstar, and the lurid fire he summoned from the air.

'Aislinn loves you,' Bronwyn told him. 'When we are together – here or at the palace – she tells me how you make her feel.' Abruptly she looked away, embarrassed. 'Donal – I know what there is between *meijha* and warrior . . . but I do not think Aislinn does. The Homanans do not share.'

Donal flicked a glance at Sef. The boy listened, but he did so from behind a tactful mask. That much he had learned of royal customs.

'Aislinn must learn,' Donal said finally, knowing he sounded colder than he felt; not knowing how else to sound. 'You learned. Meghan learned.'

'Meghan and I were born of the clans.' Bronwyn's voice was pitched low, as if she recalled Aislinn inside the tent. 'There is a difference.'

Donal turned to face her directly. 'You are nearly Aislinn's age. And you and Meghan know her better than anyone. Tell me what *you* would do in Aislinn's place.'

Bronwyn clearly had never considered it. She looked thoughtful, then shrugged and spread her hands. Her expression was deeply troubled. 'I have been taught a warrior may have both *meijha* and *cheysula*. It is difficult for me to think of it differently. But – I have heard how Aislinn speaks of you, and how she dreams of the wedding and the marriage –' Bronwyn stopped short as anguish filled her eyes. 'Oh *rujho*, be gentle with her. I think she will never understand.'

'Oh, gods . . .' he said aloud, and then he turned and left them both.

He went straight to the pavilion he shared with Sorcha without paying much attention to how he got there. He was distantly aware of the normal sounds of the Keep – children laughing, babies crying, a woman singing, a crow calling – and myriad other noises. The Keep had stood so long the ground underfoot was beaten flat, fine as flour. Grass grew only in patches beneath the trees. The wall was a grey-green serpent snaking through the trees, showing a flank of stone. Donal smelled roasting meat.

And then he stood before the slate-grey pavilion he had adorned with silver paint; running wolf and flying falcon. The breeze caused the oiled fabric to billow as he pulled aside the doorflap, then passed through and set the firecairn to smoking. Blue-grey, it flowed through the interior like thin, insidious fog.

'Sorcha?' He let the flap settle behind him.

A slim hand caught the edge of the tapestry curtain dividing the sleeping area from the front section of the pavilion. He saw Sorcha's face as she pulled the curtain back, and the hugeness of her belly.

'Gods,' he said in surprise, having lost track of the months upon sight of her. 'Are you certain you will not *burst?*'

Sorcha laughed, splaying one hand across her swollen belly. 'No more than I did the last time.'

Donal crossed to her, kissed her tenderly. 'Where is Ian?' His hands went to her unbound hair and smoothed it back from her face.

'Meghan has him. I sent him out with her, to give me a little peace. Bronwyn wanted to, but –' She broke off. He knew what she would not say, because she had no wish to hurt him. And he did not blame her for her growing distrust of his sister. None of them could afford to trust too much to an Ihlini, no matter how she was raised.

Except for my jehana.

A brief grimace of pain cut across Sorcha's face. She placed a hand against the small of her back. 'A boy, I think. Again. And soon. Very soon.'

'*How* soon?' He was alarmed by the pallor of her face. Beneath his questing hand he felt the contraction in her belly. 'Sorcha – the baby comes *already*!'

'Oh, aye . . . impatient little warrior, is he not?' Her smile wavered. 'Different from Ian. Different from the first unfortunate boy.' She grimaced. 'I think – I think perhaps I had best lie down after all. Help me –?'

He guided her down onto the pallet of pelts they shared. Sorcha's tawny hair spread against the fur of a ruddy fox; he pulled a doeskin mantle over her and pushed a folded bearskin beneath her back for support. 'Should I fetch my *jehana*?'

'Not yet,' she answered breathlessly. 'Soon. But I want to share you with no one for at least a little while.' Her eyes were green. Half Homanan, Sorcha showed no Cheysuli blood. But she had been born and raised in the clan, and her customs were all Cheysuli. 'Aislinn is here,' she said.

There was bitterness in her tone, and an underlying hostility. Never had he heard either from her before. He would have questioned her about it, but he saw how her face stretched taut with effort. Her hand clung to his as he knelt beside the pallet.

'Aislinn is here,' she repeated, and this time he heard fear.

'Aye. Aislinn is here.' He had never lied to her before; he would not begin now. No more than he would with Aislinn.

'Does she know about me?'

'She knows.'

Sorcha smiled a little. 'Proud, defiant warrior, close-mouthed as can be . . . letting no one see what goes on inside your head *or* your heart. But I know you, Donal.' The tension in her face eased as the contraction receded. 'I can imagine how difficult it was to find the words.'

'Now is not the time to speak of Aislinn.' He stroked her hand with his thumb.

'Tell me what you told her.'

'Sorcha –'

'Tell me what you *said*.'

He brushed hair out of his face. The urgency in her tone worried him. 'God, Sorcha – this is nonsense . . . there are better times to speak of this –'

'*No* better time.' Her fingers were locked on his hand. 'I have borne you two sons and now perhaps another. I would bear you more willingly; I would do anything you asked me to.' She swallowed visibly. 'But I will not give you up. I will not let you be swallowed up by that witch's *Homanan* daughter.'

'Sorcha – *you* are half Homanan,' he reminded her mildly.

Sweat glistened at her temples. 'And I would open my veins if I thought it would purge me of my Homanan blood. I would cut off a hand if I thought it would relieve me of the taint. But it would not – *it would not* – and all I can do is look at my son and thank the gods he has so little Homanan in him.' She sucked in a breath against the pain. 'Gods, Donal – I hate the Homanan in me! I would trade *anything* to claim myself all Cheysuli –'

'But you cannot.' He had never heard her speak so vehemently, so bitterly or with a spirit so filled with prejudice. It seemed as if the pains bared her soul. '*Meijha*, do you forget there is Homanan in me as well?'

'Gods!' she cried. 'It is not the same with you. *You* are the chosen – *you* are the one we have waited for – you are the one with the proper blood who will take the Lion from Homana and give it back to the Cheysuli –' She shut her mouth on a cry of pain and bit deeply into her lip. Her fingers dug into the flesh of his hand. 'Oh Donal, do you see? You will leave us all behind. You will turn your back on your clan. They will make you into a toy for the Homanans –' Sorcha writhed against the pallet. '*Never* forget you are Cheysuli. *Never* forget you are a warrior. *Never forget who sired you* . . . and *do not* allow the witch's daughter to turn you against your heritage with her Homanan ways –'

141

'*Enough*!' He said it more sharply than he intended. 'Sorcha, you are doing yourself harm with this.'

'You do *yourself* harm.' Her eyes were tightly closed against the pain. 'You – do yourself harm . . . by leaving the clan behind. . . .'

'I cannot rule Homana from the Keep,' he said flatly. 'The Homanans would never accept it.'

'Do you see?' she asked in despair. 'Already they begin their theft of you.'

'I am not *leaving*,' he said. 'I will come here as often as I may. Sorcha – I am not Mujhar *yet* –'

'But you will wed the Mujhar's daughter, and he will make you *his* son instead of Duncan's –'

'*Never*.' His hand clamped down on hers. 'Not that. Never. Do you think I am so weak?'

'Not weak,' she gasped. 'Divided. Homanan and Cheysuli, because they make you so. But I beg you, Donal, do one thing for me –?'

He gave up, but only because she needed her strength for other things. 'Aye.'

'Make the Lion *Cheysuli* again . . . and your sons and daughters as well –'

In horror, he watched her knees come up, tenting the soft doeskin coverlet. The mound of her belly rolled as she cried out. What he had meant to say to her was instantly forgotten; he summoned Taj through the *lir*-link and sent him to bring his mother.

Alix came at once and met her son just inside the door-flap. 'You,' she said, 'must go.'

'Go?'

'Go. Anywhere. But go away from *here*.' Her hands were on one arm, tugging him toward the entrance. 'Do as I say.'

He did not move, being too big for her to push this way and that anymore. 'Sorcha is in pain. I would rather stay with her.'

'Loyalty does you credit, Donal –' Alix stopped tug-
g, as if she realized the futility in the effort, and merely

142

pointed toward the entrance, '– but this is no place for a man about to become a *jehan.*'

'I have been one twice before,' he reminded her. 'I let you shoo me away then – perhaps I should have refused.'

'Donal – just *go.* I have no time for you right now.' Alix – still slim in a rose-red gown – turned away from him and pulled aside the curtain. Silver clasps in her dark braids glittered, and then she was gone behind the divider. He heard her speak to Sorcha, but could not decipher the words.

Yet another outcry from Sorcha; Donal walked out of the tent into the light of a brilliant day and petitioned the gods for the safe delivery of woman and child.

And came face to face with Aislinn.

She had shed her cloak, gowned in dark green, and in the sunlight her red-gold hair was burnished bronze. Her face was very pale. 'Finn would not tell me where you were,' she told him quietly. 'He tried to keep me with him. But – Bronwyn told me the truth. I thought I should come and meet my rival.'

She was all vulnerability, suddenly fragile in the light; pale lily on a slender stalk with a trembling, delicate bloom. But she was also pride; a little bruised, a trifle shaken, but pride nonetheless. As much as claimed by any Cheysuli.

Donal drew in a deep breath that left him oddly light-headed. 'Aislinn – the gods know I have done you dishonor by keeping Sorcha a secret, but now is not the time.'

From the pavilion there came the muted cry of a woman in labor, and Aislinn's grey eyes widened. 'The *baby* –! You told me the child was due –' She broke off, covering her mouth with one hand, and her eyes filled up with tears. But almost as quickly she blinked them away. 'No,' she said. 'My mother told me tears are not the way to win a man's regard. *Strength,* she said, and *determination . . .* and the magic of every woman born –'

'Aislinn!' He caught her arms and shook her. 'By the

143

gods, girl, I am not a prize to be *won*. As for what *Electra* has told you –'

'Then how can I turn your affections to me?' she interrupted. 'Can I leash you, like a hound? Can I hood you, like a hawk? Can I bridle you, like a horse?' Her body was rigid under his hands. 'Or do I give you over to freedom, and know I have lost you forever?'

He heard Sorcha's warning sounding in his head: – *do not allow the witch's daughter to turn you against your heritage* –

'No,' he said aloud. 'I am Cheysuli first.'

'And Homanan last?' Aislinn asked bitterly. 'Is this the heir my Homanan father chose?'

His hands closed more tightly upon her arms. Too tightly; Aislinn cried out, and he loosed her only with great effort. 'You push me too far,' he warned through gritted teeth. '*Both* of you – pushing and pushing and pushing, pulling me this way and that – dividing my loyalties. What would you have me do? – divide myself in two? Give each of you half of me? What good would that *do* for you? Salve your wounded pride?'

'Give up –' Aislinn stopped dead. The color drained out of her face.

'Give up Sorcha? Is that what you meant to say?' Donal shook his head, knowing only he wanted to go away from it all. 'I would sooner give up myself.' He laughed a little, albeit with a bitter tone. 'For all that, it might be easier.'

Aislinn stared at the ground as if she wished it would swallow her up. The sun was blazing off the red-gold of her hair. 'I had no right to ask it. I know it. You have told me how it is with – *meijhas* and *cheysulas*. But – I will not lie to you. I want you for myself.' Her head came up and she challenged him with a stare. 'She has had you longer, but I will have you yet.'

Wearily, Donal pushed a strand of hair from Aislinn's face. 'You sing the same song. Were it not for me, you might be friends.' And then he recalled Sorcha's prejudice, and knew it could never be.

There came another cry from the pavilion, but this one did not belong to Sorcha. As it rose up to a wail of outraged astonishment, Donal knew the travail was done.

So did Aislinn. White-faced, she turned from him and walked regally away.

But he knew she wanted to run.

Alix did not send him away when he entered the pavilion. She did not seem to notice him at all, being too occupied with tending Sorcha and the baby. Softly he approached the partially open divider and stopped short.

Sorcha's eyes were closed; Donal thought she slept. Lines of strain were graven in her face. She looked older and very weary, but there was peace and contentment in the slackness of her mouth.

'A girl, Donal,' Alix said calmly. 'You have a daughter now.'

He could not move. He stood frozen in place, staring down at the bundled baby with her pink, outraged face as she lay snug at Sorcha's side, and knew a vast humility.

'I do not imagine you recall being in a similar position, once,' Alix said wryly. 'I do not recall it so much myself. But it was Raissa who helped me bear you, as I have aided Sorcha.'

'Granddame,' he said, and felt guilty that he had nearly forgotten the woman who had died so long before.

Slowly he knelt down beside the pallet and put a tentative finger to the perfect softness of the baby's black-fuzzed head. No Homanan girl, this; she had her father's color.

'Let them sleep. Later, you may hold the girl.' Alix rose, shaking out her rose-red skirts. Donal saw the faint shine of silver threads in Alix's dark brown hair and realized his mother, like Finn and Carillon, also aged. But less dramatically. Her skin was still smooth, still stretched taut over classic Cheysuli bones, and when she smiled it lit her amber eyes. 'It makes one aware of one's own transience, man or woman, and how seemingly unimportant

are such things as dynastic marriages when a son or daughter is born,' she said gently. 'Does it not?'

He rose also. 'You heard Aislinn and me outside the tent.'

'Bits and pieces. I was too preoccupied to understand it all.' Alix glanced back at Sorcha and the child. 'They will do well enough without us. I think we can leave them for a while.'

This time when she urged him toward the doorflap, he did not resist. He went with her willingly.

He walked with her to the perimeter of the Keep, along the moss-grown wall. Unmortared, it afforded all manner of vegetation the opportunity to plant roots into cracks and crannies, digging between the stones. Ivy, deep red and deeper green, mantled the wall against the sunlight. Twining flowers climbed up the runners and formed delicate ornamentation; jewels within the folds of the velvet gown. He smelled wet moss and old stone; the perfume of the place he knew as home. Not Homana-Mujhar. Not the rose-red walls and marbled halls, hung about with brilliant banners. No, not for him.

Even though it would be.

'Aislinn has loved you for some time, since she was old enough to understand what can be between a man and a woman,' Alix said gently. 'Surely you knew she did.'

'I thought she might outgrow it.'

'Why should she? Do you not wish for love in this marriage?' At his frown, his mother laughed. 'Oh, I know – the Cheysuli do not speak of love, seeking to keep such things impossibly private. But you will have to learn to deal with it, Donal, as your *jehan* and *su'fali* did.' When he said nothing, having no answer for her, Alix caught his right hand and stopped him beside the wall. She turned the hand over until the palm was face-up and the strong brown fingers lay open. 'With this hand you will hold Homana,' she said evenly. 'You are the hope of the Cheysuli, Donal, and a link in the prophecy. Deny this marriage and you deny your heritage.'

146

He expelled a brief, heavy breath in an expression of irony. 'Sorcha said *differently*. Sorcha said the marriage would force me to turn my back on my heritage.'

Alix squeezed his hand and then let it go. 'Sorcha is – bitter.'

'She never was before.' He shook his head in bewilderment. 'Is it because the child was coming?'

'Partly.' Alix touched him and urged him into motion once again. 'I do not doubt she was frightened as well as in pain – the birth was exceedingly easy, but she could not have predicted that. As for bitterness . . .' Alix stopped to pull a flower from the earth; delicate, fragile blossom of palest violet. 'For all these years she has known you would one day marry Aislinn, not her, but it was easy to set that knowledge aside. Now she cannot. Now she must face it, and she does not want to do it.'

'She hates Aislinn. That, I think, I can readily understand; I do know what jealousy is. But – *jehana,* she hates the Homanans as well.' Again he shook his head. 'How do I deal with *that*, when I am meant to be Mujhar?'

Alix cupped the blossom in her hands. 'A violet flower among the white is easily plucked, Donal. Easily crushed and broken. There is no protection from the others when your coloring is different.' She lifted her head and looked at him instead of the flower. 'I do not speak of blond hair and green eyes. I speak of blood, and the knowledge of what one is. Prejudiced, aye, because she is more Cheysuli than Homanan – and yet no one will give her that.'

'In the clans, people do not care. *You* are half Homanan; have you felt different from any other?'

'Aye,' she said softly. 'I spent seventeen years with the Homanans and twenty-four among the Cheysuli. But still I feel mostly Homanan; I do not doubt Sorcha does as well.'

'But she was *born* to the clan –'

'It does not matter.' She lifted the fragile blossom. 'This flower is violet. It bloomed this color. It will never be able to claim itself another color, no matter how hard it

147

tries.' She smiled and let the blossom fall to the ground, where it settled into the trembling carpet of snow-white blooms. 'Once it might have been purple. But never will it be white.'

Donal stopped walking. He turned to face his mother. 'Then – if I am that violet flower, I will never fit in with the white Homanans.'

'No,' she said. 'But why wish to fit in when one must rule?'

He turned her to face the way they had come. 'Let us go back. I want to see my son as well as my newborn daughter.'

'*Jehan*?'

The soft voice intruded into his thoughts. Donal turned, shielding the newborn body in his arms, and saw his son standing in the doorflap with Meghan at his side. Ian's black hair was curly as was common in Cheysuli childhood, and his yellow eyes were bright as he gazed at his father. But his expression was decidely reticent.

Donal put out a hand. 'Come, Ian . . . come see your new *rujholla*.'

The boy moved quickly across the floor pelts, dropping down to kneel at Donal's side. His curiosity was manifest, but he did not touch the baby until Donal pulled back the linen wrappings and showed him the crumpled face.

He glanced at Sorcha as she drifted slowly back into sleep. 'Your turn, *meijha* – I named the last one.'

Sorcha smiled drowsily. 'Isolde, then. I like the sound. Ian and Isolde.'

Donal smiled at his rapt three-year-old son. 'She is Isolde, Ian. And she will require your protection. See how small she is?'

Meghan, who had brought Ian soon after Donal had returned to his pavilion, moved forward and craned her neck to peer over Donal's shoulder. 'Black hair,' she said, 'and brown eyes, which will lighten soon enough. A Cheysuli, then, with little Homanan about her.'

148

Sorcha's smile widened, and Donal saw triumph in her eyes even as she closed them.

He glanced up at Finn's daughter. There was no bitterness in Meghan's tone, only discovery and matter-of-factness; it seemed neither to trouble nor please Meghan that she was the image of her Homanan mother: tawny-haired, blue-eyed, fair-skinned; Carillon's dead sister to the bone. And she claimed all of Tourmaline's elegance and grace, even at fifteen years. Yet she lived among the clans with a *jehan* who was clan-leader, and she felt no lack that she bore Homanan blood in her veins. No lack at all. If anything, she was more Cheysuli than most because Finn saw to it she was.

No Homanan marriage for Meghan. Finn will wed her to a warrior. Donal smiled ruefully. *But then I am sure she will have more than enough to choose from.*

He glanced up at Alix regretfully. 'Will you take Isolde? Much as I would prefer to stay, I promised Carillon I would have Aislinn back by nightfall. And – there are things to be settled between us.' When Alix had taken the baby, Donal bent forward and kissed the drowsing Sorcha softly on the mouth. 'Sleep you well, *meijha*. You have earned a sound rest.'

He rose, scooping Ian up into his arms. 'And a hug for you, small warrior. You will be busy from now on.' He glanced at Meghan. 'My thanks for seeing to him. Soon enough you will have your own children to tend.'

She laughed, blue eyes dancing in her lovely face. 'Not *so* soon, I hope. I wish for a little freedom, first.'

'Do we go?' Ian asked as Donal carried him from the pavilion.

'No, small one, only I am going. You must stay here.' He saw Lorn get up from his place in the sun by the doorflap and shake his heavy coat, yawning widely.

A cub and a bitch, Lorn observed. *How symmetrical.*

Donal snorted. A boy *and* a girl, *lir. There is nothing wolflike about either of them.*

Unless the boy bonds with one of my kind.

149

Do you say he will? Donal hoped suddenly for greater illumination into the bonding process, wondering suddenly if all the *lir* knew which of them was meant for each Cheysuli born.

Lorn paused and lifted one hind leg to scratch, doglike, at his belly. *No. Such things are left to the gods.*

Taj's shadow passed overhead. *Perhaps he will gain a falcon.*

Or a hawk. Donal nodded. *I would like him to have a hawk. How better to honor his grandsire?*

As you do yours? Lorn asked.

Donal, heading toward Finn's green pavilion, glanced sharply at the wolf. *How do I honor Hale?*

The sword, Taj said. *One day, it will be yours, as it was ever intended.*

Donal did not respond. Instead, as he approached with Meghan, he watched how Sef and Bronwyn sat together in front of Finn's pavilion, speaking animatedly. His sister's purple-wrapped braid hung over one shoulder, coiling against her skirts. Unlike Meghan or Aislinn, Bronwyn lacked conscious knowledge of her femininity. She moved and acted more boy than girl, though Donal knew she would outgrow it.

Now, as she laughed and chattered with Sef, he saw how she would lack the pure beauty Meghan and Aislinn already began to claim, but her light would be undiminished. She was his mother come again.

And who else? his conscience asked. *Is her jehan in her as well?*

He stopped by them both, still holding his son, and looked down upon them as they glanced up in laggard surprise. He saw how Sef had peeled back his right sleeve to show off the feathered band; how Bronwyn had drawn pictures in the dust with a broken stick. Runes, not pictures, he noted on closer inspection. But none were Cheysuli.

Bronwyn sprang to her feet and obscured the runes at once, hands thrust behind her back as if she meant to hide

150

the stick. Purple skirts were filmed with dust, tangled on her boot-tops, but she ignored her dishevelment. 'I heard the baby has come!'

Troubled, Donal nodded. 'The baby has come. A girl. Sorcha has named her Isolde.'

'May I see her?' Her face was alight with expectation.

'No.' He almost cursed his shortness. 'Not – now. She is sleeping. So is Sorcha. They need time alone.' He saw how her bright face fell. 'Later, *rujholla*.' And she *was* his sister, for all she was Tynstar's daughter; he hated to disappoint her. She had had no say in what man sired her.

But he dared not give her the chance to prove herself Ihlini.

Slowly the color spilled out of her face. 'What is wrong? Is it something I have done? You are so short –'

'No.' Again, he said it more sharply than he intended. Against his will, he looked once more at the runes she had drawn in the dust and then tried to obscure. Odd, alien runes, with the look of sorcery.

'*Rujho?*'

'Nothing,' he said. 'You have done nothing wrong. Bronwyn – what are those?' He would ignore the runes no longer.

She looked down in surprise at the drawings in the dust, then shot a glance at Sef. It was mostly veiled beneath lids and lashes, but he saw the silent signal.

As if she means to protect him . . . 'Bronwyn!' The tone was a command, and he knew she would not ignore it.

'A secret game,' she answered promptly. 'We took an oath not to tell.' Deliberately, she erased the rest of the runes with the toe of one booted foot.

He looked into her face and saw nothing of guile, only the expression she normally wore. And that mask he could not lift. 'Bronwyn –' But he broke it off when Finn came out of the tent. With him was Aislinn; Donal's brows slid up in surprise. He had not thought she would seek him on purpose.

Before Finn could protest, Donal set Ian into his arms.

'We must go, or the sun will set before we reach Mujhara.' He grinned as Ian locked an arm around Finn's neck and snuggled closer. Without thinking about it, Finn settled the boy more comfortably; he had had practice enough with Meghan.

Donal bent and kissed Ian briefly on the forehead. 'Care for your new *rujholla*. I will come back to you when I may.' He turned and helped a silently staring Aislinn mount her horse. Then he retrieved the reins of his own mount and swung up into the saddle. Even as he settled, Lorn was at the horse's side and Taj was in the air.

Finn reached out and caught one rein. 'How does Carillon fare?'

Donal saw the true concern in his uncle's face. For all they hardly saw one another now their paths had parted, Donal knew there remained a link that would always bind Finn and Carillon. Prince and liege man had spent five years in exile together; two more when the prince had become Mujhar. It was treachery that had parted them, and a broken oath that held.

Donal glanced briefly at Aislinn. But he saw no use in lying; she herself had marked her father's deterioration. 'He ages,' he said quietly. 'Each day – more so than most men, I think. It is the disease . . .' He paused. 'Is there nothing to be done?'

The sun shone off the heavy gold bands clasping Finn's bare arms as he rubbed idly at the chestnut's muzzle. He said nothing for a moment, but when he looked up into the sunlight Donal saw how he too had aged.

Gods, they shared so much . . . and now they share so little.

'Tynstar did not give Carillon anything he would not have suffered anyway, one day,' Finn said tonelessly. 'He merely brought it on prematurely. We cannot undo what the gods see fit to bestow upon a man.'

'He is the *Mujhar*!' Donal lashed out. 'Can the gods not see how much Homana needs him?'

Finn sighed. 'No doubt there are reasons for it, Donal.

152

The gods do nothing without them.' Abruptly he slapped the stallion's shoulder. 'Go back, then. See Aislinn safely to her *jehan*. Do not tarry here longer if Carillon is waiting.'

He serves him still . . . he would not admit it, but he does. In his heart, if nowhere else. He shifted in the saddle. 'Aye, *su'fali*. Have you a message for him?'

Finn lifted a hand to block out the blinding sunlight. 'Aye,' he said. 'Tell him I will come to Homana-Mujhar.'

'*You* will?' Donal stared. 'You have not been there in seventeen years!'

Finn smiled. 'I think it unlikely I would miss my *harani's* wedding. I will come to Homana-Mujhar.'

Donal laughed, and then he reached down to clasp his uncle's arm as it hugged Ian closely. 'My thanks, *su'fali* . . . it has been too long. I think even the servants miss you.'

'No. They miss the *stories* they told about me . . . no doubt they want fresh fodder.' Finn slapped the stallion on his broad chestnut rump. 'Go. Do not let the Mujhar fret about his daughter.'

'No,' Donal agreed. *But I will fret about mine, and with no one the wiser for it.* He motioned for Sef to mount his horse. 'Tarry no longer, Sef. I do not wish to lose the sun before we reach Mujhara.'

The boy caught his reins from the tree and climbed up into his saddle. He looked intently down at Bronwyn. 'Perhaps I will see you again.'

She still clasped her arms behind her back. Her amber eyes were slitted against the sunlight; they almost looked yellow.

'Aye. Come back. Or I will come to Homana-Mujhar.'

Sef eyed Donal. 'If my lord allows me to.'

'You will come to Homana-Mujhar, Bronwyn,' Aislinn put in. 'You and Meghan. When I am Queen, I will have to have women by me – I would have both of you.'

Finn frowned at once. 'Meghan does not belong at court. Her place is in the Keep.'

153

'*Jehan*,' the girl protested softly. 'If Aislinn needs me there, of course I will go.'

His tone was implacable. 'This Keep is your home, Meghan. Homana-Mujhar would stifle you.'

'Could I not learn it for myself?' She put a slim hand on his bare arm, and Donal saw how already she claimed a woman's gentle guile. 'The Keep will always be my home, just as it is yours. But did you not spend years out of it?'

'Aye,' Finn said harshly. 'And you have heard what such folly brought me.' His eyes were on Aislinn, but his tone indicated it was not the girl he saw. 'The witch may no longer be there . . . but her memory survives.'

12

Donal's personal chambers were, perhaps, a bit ostentatious for a Cheysuli warrior better accustomed to the Keep – and preferring it – but he could not deny that the luxuries conferred a comfort he occasionally appreciated. Thick woven carpets of rich muted tones softened the hard stone floor; woolen tapestries of every hue hid the blank rock walls. A single fat white beeswax candle set in each of four shadowed casement ledges turned the stained glass into jewel-toned panoramas of Homanan history.

The chamber was warm as well; Donal's body-servant had lighted a fire that tinged the air with the smell of oak and ash. Donal did not doubt Torvald had also set warming pans beneath the bedclothes of his draped tester bed, but he had no intention of seeking his rest so soon. The sun had barely gone down. Aislinn had been delivered. It was early yet, and a task was left to do.

On the table near the bed rested a flagon of rich red Ellasian wine and four silver goblets. Donal filled two goblets, then motioned to Sef.

The boy, hanging back by the half-open door, stared. '*Me*, my lord?'

'There is no one else in the room.' Donal smiled. 'I poured the wine for you. Will you join me in a toast?'

Slowly, Sef moved forward. He accepted the goblet from Donal's hand and peered into the wine-filled depths. Light from candles and fire set the goblet's contents aflame and bathed Sef's pale face with a rosy glow. The

155

hammered silver cast sparks of light into his eerie eyes. 'My lord,' he said, 'a toast?'

Donal raised his goblet. 'To my daughter. To Isolde of the Cheysuli.'

Sef's breath fogged the silver of the goblet as he peered nervously at Donal. 'But – shouldn't this be shared with someone other than *me*?'

Donal shrugged. 'Perhaps, were I the sort to care about such things. But, I can hardly ask the Mujhar to bless the birth of my bastard daughter.' Donal did not smile. '*You* are here with me, and I would have you share my toast.'

Sef stared at him over the rim of his silver goblet. Then, grinning suddenly, he drank deeply.

Watching the boy, Donal was glad of his companionship. He felt flat, empty, as if he yearned for a fulfillment he could not quite comprehend. He only knew he felt cheated of time with his *meijha,* his son and his daughter, and all in the name of Homana.

Sorcha has the right of it. Fearing me for a shapechanger, the Homanans will do what they can to strip my Cheysuli habits from me and put Homanan in their place.

Instinctively he looked for Taj and Lorn, knowing no Homanan in all the world could strip him of *those* habits. Because if he were, there would be no Prince of Homana. There would be no Donal at all.

Lorn lay curled upon the tester bed, half hidden behind gauzy draperies. Like Donal, the wolf did not ignore luxury when it was offered. Taj had settled upon his perch in a corner of the chamber, setting beak to wing to smooth the shining feathers.

'My lord?' It was Sef, upper lip painted with wine until a tongue reached up to carry the smear away. 'You said once I could ask you any question.'

'Aye.' Donal sat down on the nearest stool. 'Why? Have you one?'

Sef's face was very solemn in the muted wash of candlelight. 'Aye, my lord. I wondered why you do not like your sister.'

156

Donal nearly dropped his goblet. 'Sef! What makes you ask such a thing?'

'You said I could.'

Donal, still shocked, stared at the boy whose set jaw indicated a burgeoning stubbornness. 'But – *that* question,' Donal said, when he could make sense out of his words again. 'What would make you ask it? Of *course* I like my *rujholla*.'

Sef averted his eyes and stared down into his goblet, as if his brief courage had failed him. 'My lord – when we were at the Keep today . . . I –' He shrugged with discomfiture. 'I just – thought perhaps you didn't like her. I mean – you seemed troubled by something.' The eyes flicked up to meet Donal's again. 'Was it because of what Bronwyn drew in the dust?'

Donal tossed down the remaining wine in his goblet and set it down on the rug with a thump. The boy's words troubled him deeply, but not because Sef had noticed his reaction at the Keep. Because he had reacted at all.

'A game,' he said. 'She said it was a game between the two of you.'

'She told me it was – *magic*.' Sef hunched thin shoulders. 'I – I didn't want to draw the signs, but she said if I was to prove I was grown –' Color came and went in the fair face. 'She said I was to draw the same signs *she* drew, because we could make the magic stronger. But – I was *afraid*.' Sef's fingers clutched the goblet more tightly. 'I remembered what you said about Cheysuli meaning no one any harm, but – I was afraid. She said I had to. And then she – laughed.' Abruptly he drank more wine. It slopped against his face and washed over the rim of the goblet, trickling down the front of his livery. This time he did not lick the spillage from his upper lip. 'My lord – Bronwyn frightens me. . . .'

And me. But Donal did not say so.

He bent and caught up his goblet, then rose and went to the table to fill the cup again. He did not look at the boy, did not consider the contradiction between the boy's

words and his earlier actions, being too lost within his thoughts, and when he heard the voice at first he thought it was Sef's.

And then he realized it was Rowan, standing in the open doorway. 'The Mujhar desires your presence in the Great Hall at once.'

Rowan's smooth Cheysuli face, as always, expressed controlled calm neutrality. But Donal heard a faint note of tension in his tone.

He frowned. 'I have just now gotten back from the Keep. Is it truly so important?' He made a gesture that included the remaining goblets. 'Can you not join us in a drink to toast my daughter's birth?'

The candles sent a wash of light and shadows across Rowan's dark face. He wore a plain doublet of dark blue velvet, freighted with silver at the collar; it glinted in the candlelight. 'Electra,' he said, 'is free.'

Sef gasped, shocked, then drew back awkwardly into the shadows, as if he knew it was not his place to interrupt prince and general. He clutched the goblet but did not drink.

A blurted denial died on Donal's tongue. He had only to look at Rowan's face to know the truth. 'How?' he asked instead.

'We do not, as yet, have all the information we need. A messenger came –' Rowan shrugged. 'The news was simply that the Queen had disappeared.'

'From the *Crystal Isle*?' Donal shook his head. 'There were Cheysuli with her!'

'They are dead,' Rowan said. 'Simply – dead. It appears they were poisoned. As for the Homanan guards . . . once the Cheysuli were dead, Electra was free to use her magic.'

Unsteadily, Donal set his goblet down on the table. 'Cheysuli – murdered?'

He could not conceive of how it had been accomplished. Cheysuli warriors with attentive *lir* did not succumb to poison, not when they guarded a known witch. Not when they guarded the woman Tynstar called his own.

'Poison,' he said intently, recalling his bout with the same. 'Could she have grown it, or had it grown?'

'All food was brought in from Hondarth. *All* food,' Rowan said. 'The Cheysuli inspected it.'

'Tynstar,' Donal said instantly.

The faintest flicker of consternation creased Rowan's brow. 'Every precaution was taken.' His voice, once untroubled, now was underscored with frustration. 'She was guarded by Cheysuli for that very purpose. *No* Ihlini could have gotten past the warriors.'

Donal, frowning, chewed at his bottom lip. 'I would not put it beyond Electra's abilities to concoct the poison herself, with Tynstar's help. They are linked. How else could Electra have entered Aislinn's mind?'

Rowan shook his head. The firelight picked out the faintest flecks of silver in his thick black hair. 'All in all, it is less important to know how it was accomplished than to discover where she is. Where *she* is Tynstar will also be . . . and he is the one we must slay.'

'Then – it is war.' Donal felt the breath leave his chest. 'By the gods – *it is* –'

'Did you think it would never come?' Rowan said grimly. 'Did you believe the Mujhar spoke of the possibility out of boredom, having nothing else to do?'

Donal heard the faint undertone of scorn. Aye, he was due that from Rowan. Too often the general had watched Carillon's heir seek escape from princely duties. Too often that heir had turned his back on Homana-Mujhar to spend his time at the Keep.

The gods know Rowan has sacrificed enough for his lord. He would expect me to do the same.

But for the moment, he put off the guilt and lost himself in consideration. 'You wish to know where Tynstar is?' He frowned, staring blindly toward the hearth. 'He is in Solinde. He will rouse the nobles in the name of Bellam, their fallen king, *and* in the name of Electra. He needs her. To the people, she is the rightful Queen of Solinde. And he will promise sorcerous aid from the god of the netherworld

159

. . . the Solindish, having turned to such things before, will turn to it again.'

The dark flesh drawn so taut over Rowan's prominent cheekbones softened just a little. He did not smile, but a weight seemed to lift from his velvet-clad shoulders. 'You have more awareness than I expected – I thought Carillon would have to explain it all to you.'

Donal shook his head intently. 'I have learned more over the years than you may know, for all I was a poor student. But I see it more clearly now.' He thought again of Electra, free; Electra, aiding Tynstar. *Oh gods, how do we stop the carnage that will come of this alliance?* He blew out a breath and looked at Rowan. 'We will have to go to Solinde.'

There was a glint of appreciation in Rowan's eyes. 'We move an army into Solinde. Our borders are patrolled, but we will need to send aid, and soon. We cannot afford to let Tynstar breach our borders.'

'When?'

'That is for Carillon to say. But I think you will know soon enough, if you go to see him as he wishes.'

'Of course.' Donal looked for the boy. 'Sef – the time is your own. I will send for you if I need you.'

'Aye, my lord – *my lord* –!' The boy hastened forward as Donal turned to go. 'My lord – if you go to war . . . will you take me with you?'

Donal looked down on the anxious boy. 'War, I have heard, is not particularly pleasant. Perhaps you would do better staying here.'

'I'd rather go with you.' Sef's tone was defiantly adamant, but his thin face was hollowed with fear.

I am his only security, Donal realized in surprise. *He would rather go with me into danger than stay behind in safety.*

He set one hand on Sef's thin shoulder. 'I will not leave you, Sef. Your service is with me.'

The Great Hall lay deep in shadow. The candleracks were crowded with pale, fat tapers, but all had been snuffed

160

out. Donal smelled the faint odor of beeswax and smoking wicks; that, and the scent of dying coals. The firepit – a trench stretching the length of the massive hall – was heaped with ash and glowing coals. The center of the hall was illuminated only by the pit, and a single torch in a bracket near the throne.

For a moment, night-blinded by distorting shadows, Donal believed the place deserted. He stared down the length of the hall, frowning into the darkness, but then – as his eyes became accustomed to the glow from the firepit coals – he saw Carillon at last.

He sat sunken into the ancient wooden throne carved in the shape of a lion. It crouched on curling paws with claws extended, gilded with golden paint. The headpiece was a snarling face, rearing up over Carillon's head. The lion seemed almost to spring out of the darkness as if it sought prey.

The torch cast flickering light across the wood, glinting on the gold. Illumination painted Carillon's bearded face and crept down to silver the knife at his belt. A Cheysuli long-knife with a wolf-shaped hilt, made and once owned by Finn.

Donal halted before the dais. He felt oppressed by the huge hall. The arching hammer-beamed timbers loomed over his head; the far wall, full of weapons, crests and leaded casements, menaced him as it never had before. He took a deep breath and tried to steady the banging of his heart.

'Rowan – told me.' His voice echoed in the vastness of the blackened hall.

Carillon did not stir. 'Did he? Did he tell you what it means?'

After a moment, Donal nodded. 'It means war has come at last.'

Slowly Carillon leaned forward. The torch behind the throne spilled light down his back, setting the crimson velvet of his doublet aglow like a dim beacon amid the shadows of the dais. 'War was *expected*. I am not taken

unaware by the news. But – the manner of it is somewhat *un*expected.' He put his age-wracked hands to his weary face. His fingers massaged the flesh of his brow and pushed back a lock of hair from his eyes. 'Electra, with Tynstar – after all these years . . . we face potential disaster.'

Donal stepped forward. 'We face *war*, my lord. Forget those who are involved, and think only upon the strategies necessary.'

The hands dropped from the face. Carillon actually smiled. 'Do you seek to teach *me* what war is about?' But before Donal could answer, he waved a twisted hand. 'No, no, say nothing. The mood, for the moment, has passed. It is only that I recalled what she did to me so many years ago – how she nearly castrated me, without even touching a blade. Ah, no – her weapon was merely herself. Gods – *but what a woman she was*.' Stiffly, he pushed himself up from the throne. 'I do not expect you to understand. But what you *must* comprehend is that paired, they are doubly dangerous. Tynstar will use her to gather all the Solindishmen he will need – the warhost will be massive. It will be an exceedingly difficult conflict.' He moved to the torch and took it down from its bracket. 'Donal – do you do as I bid you?'

Donal watched him step off the dais and walk purposefully toward the far end of the hall. 'Usually,' he answered cautiously.

'Then do so now.' Carillon's voice echoed. 'Come with me to the Womb of the Earth.'

A grue ran down Donal's spine. The hairs stood up on the back of his neck. 'I have – heard of it,' he said. 'In the histories of my race.'

Carillon took the light with him, leaving Donal in the shadowed darkness of the throne. 'Now you will see it, Donal. Now you will go where I have gone.'

'*You!*' Donal turned to stare after the Mujhar. 'You have been to the Womb of the Earth?'

'A Homanan.' Carillon's tone was scored with caustic irony. 'Aye, I have. I thought Finn might have told you.'

'There are secret things in every man's life.' Donal

belatedly followed in Carillon's wake. 'My *su'fali* does not tell me everything . . . nor, apparently, do you.' He stopped short as Carillon halted at the edge of the firepit.

'Here,' the Mujhar said. 'The entrance is – here.'

Donal frowned. His gesture encompassed the tiles of the floor. '*Here?*'

'Blind,' Carillon muttered in disgust. 'A Cheysuli warrior – and blind.' He thrust the torch into Donal's hands and stepped over the rim of the firepit. Before Donal could blurt out his surprise, the Mujhar kicked aside unlighted wood and pushed away the residue of former fires.

Donal coughed as a layer of ash rose into the air. Carillon bent down and grasped an ash-filmed iron ring set into the bottom of the trench. Donal heard the grate of metal on stone, and then Carillon went down on one knee. His breath was ragged in his throat.

'Carillon –?' Donal moved forward at once, bending to touch one hunched shoulder. 'My lord –?'

Carillon shook his head and waved a hand. 'No – no – I am well enough. But – I think it will require a younger, straighter back.' Slowly he rose, one hand pressing against his spine. 'Give me the torch. The task is yours to do.'

Donal handed him the torch and stepped into the firepit. Frowning, he bent and grasped the ring with both hands, half-expecting to flinch from the warmth of the metal. But it was cool to the touch, though gritty with ash and charcoal.

He spread and braced his legs, gathering his strength. Then, grunting with the effort, he peeled back the iron plate that formed a lid and let it fall clanging against the stone. He stared down into blackness.

Stale air engulfed his face. Instantly he lunged backward, seeking a safer distance. 'Gods,' he said, 'down *there*?'

'Why not?' Carillon asked. 'The last man down there was me.'

Donal scowled. He knew what Carillon did. The Mujhar had only to appeal to his pride, and his invitation became a thing Donal *had* to do.

163

'I have the light,' Carillon sounded suspiciously amused. 'I will lead the way.'

'Should I summon my *lir*?' Donal said with subtle condescension, though he still felt genuine consternation.

'No. There are plenty of them where we go.' Carillon stepped past Donal and slowly made his way down the narrow stairs.

Donal was left alone in the darkness of the hall. After a moment, he followed the guttering torch.

It is a hole in the earth, Donal thought. *A deep, utterly black hole, seeking to swallow me up.* Down he went, following the Mujhar. *Carillon has gone mad. The news of Electra's escape has driven him over the edge.* But even as he thought it, he knew it was not true. Electra's escape would simply make Carillon more careful in his planning.

He could hardly see, for the torch Carillon carried smoked badly in the darkness, casting shadows into indistinct planes and hollows so that walls merged with ceiling and the steps, shallow and tapering, faded into opacity. He put one hand against the nearest wall, to steady himself.

The surface was cool, growing more damp with every step. He smelled the moldy odor of dampness, the spice of ancient stone. It filled his senses with the perfume of agedness, and his belly with trepidation.

'There are a hundred and two of them.' Carillon's voice echoed oddly in the narrow staircase. 'I counted them, once.'

'A hundred and two?'

'Steps.' Carillon's brief laugh was distorted. 'What did you think I meant? Demons?'

Donal did not laugh. His bare arms and face were filmed with clammy moisture. His hair hung limply against his shoulders and fell into his eyes. 'How much farther?'

'We are here.' The echo sounded closer. Torchlight flared up to fill the passageway and Donal saw that they stood in a space the size of a privacy closet. The Mujhar waited. Against the blackness, painted by torchlight, his

164

hair formed a silver nimbus. 'Do you see?' Carillon pointed.

Donal looked. He saw almost immediately what the Mujhar indicated: a line of runes carved into the damp stone walls. Time and seepage had shallowed the figures until they were little more than faint greenish tracings, but Donal recognized the shapes.

He looked at Carillon. 'Cheysuli built this palace. It does not surprise me that in the very foundations would be the Old Tongue runes.'

'Firstborn runes.' Carillon did not smile. 'It was your father who brought me here, Donal. With no explanation, he brought me here to show me the Womb of the Earth, so I would know what it was to be Cheysuli.'

Quick resentment flared in Donal's chest. 'You are Homanan. No man save a warrior can know what it is to be Cheysuli.'

'For four days, I did. It was – necessary.' Carillon put out a hand to the wall, seeking the proper stone. He found it, pressed, and a portion of the wall turned on edge.

A gust of stale air rushed out of the vault, but it was tinged with the tang of life. Shut up the place may have been, but it was not a deathtrap. A man could go in with impunity.

Carillon thrust the torch through the opening and the flames lit up the darkness. Donal, still hanging back at the bottom of the steps, saw the merest trace of creamy color within the vault, and the sheen of polished marble.

The torchlight was cruel to Carillon's face. Donal saw every crease, every line, every etching emphasized by the flames. But the eyes were endlessly patient.

He stepped past the Mujhar and entered the cream-colored vault. Torchlight danced and hissed, sending the shadows scuttling up walls and ceiling into cracks and crevices. The walls seemed almost to move as he entered, and he saw how the gold-veined marble took life from the roaring flames.

Lir. Lir upon *lir,* leaping out of the stone. He saw bear

165

and hawk and owl and boar, fox and wildcat and wolf. He saw all the *lir* and more, lining every inch of the marble walls and ceiling. No surface was untouched, uncarved.

'*Cheysuli i'halla shansu*,' Carillon said very quietly. '*Ja'hai, cheysu, Mujhar*.'

Donal spun and faced the man. The words had been fluent and unaccented: *May there be Cheysuli peace upon you*, and *accept this man, this Mujhar*. He almost thought it was a Cheysuli who spoke the Old Tongue. But it was Carillon, Homanan to the bone, who faced him in the vault.

He drew in a careful breath. 'Are you not a *little* premature?'

'Because I ask the gods to accept you?' Carillon smiled. 'No. Acceptance may be requested at any time; only occasionally is it given when one asks it.' For a moment, he said nothing. When he spoke again, his voice was eloquently gentle, as if he spoke to a simple child. 'Donal – you *will* be Mujhar. But it is up to you to make your peace with it if the gods are to accept you.'

Resentment flared; he thought of Sorcha, begging him not to leave his heritage behind. And here was Homanan Carillon admonishing him the same. 'My *tahlmorra* is quite clear, my lord Mujhar,' he said with a deadly pointedness. 'I accepted it long ago, since neither you nor the gods – *nor* my *jehan* – ever gave me a choice.'

Carillon did not indicate that the answer – or tone – troubled him in the least. He seemed supremely indifferent to Donal's feelings, as if what his heir thought was of no importance to him when weighed against the balance of the present and the future.

'Look around you, Donal,' he said gently. 'No man who is to be Mujhar can avoid facing his heritage. Duncan proved that to me when he brought me here. For all I am not Cheysuli, he made me see it was *your* race which made Homana strong. I accepted it and, for a brief time, I accepted the gift the gods saw fit to give me. For me, it was held within those depths.' He nodded in the direction

behind Donal's head. 'For you, it may be something else.'

Slowly Donal glanced around the vault. Gold and ivory gleamed. Momentarily he thought he saw a falcon's wing-tip move; then he saw the patch of blackness in the floor. It was a hole. A perfectly round hole, extending into the depths.

'Oubliette,' he breathed. Swiftly he looked at Carillon as the implications came very clear. 'You do not *mean* –'

Carillon's voice was perfectly steady. 'For me, it was required. For you – I cannot say. It is a thing between you and the gods.'

Donal moved closer to the oubliette. The torchlight was swallowed up, and he could see nothing past the perfectly rounded rim. Nothing at all.

And yet he saw everything.

He closed his eyes. The iron collar of comprehension was locked around his throat. 'When will the marriage be made?'

'Within the month.' Carillon sounded neither surprised nor pleased, as if he had expected the comprehension. 'It gives us time to gather guests so it can all be done quite properly. I cannot have Tynstar believing he has frightened me into this move merely to secure the throne.'

'Of course.' Donal was aware of an odd lack of emotion in himself. Shock? He thought not. Perhaps it was merely that there was no more room for vacillation. 'And the march into Solinde?'

'Within two months after the wedding.' Carillon did not smile. 'It gives you time to beget an heir.'

The flames roared in the marble vault with its ivory menagerie. 'Do you take the torch with you?'

'Of course. It is a part of the thing.'

Donal nodded. Curiously, he felt no fear, no desperation, no resentment of Carillon's calm pronouncement of his fate. He merely felt that all of it had to be done, in order to temper the links in the chain they forged.

He smiled at Carillon. '*Ja'hai-na,* my lord Mujhar. *Cheysuli i'halla shansu.*'

13

He heard the scrape of stone on stone; the sibilant grate of limestone wall against marble floor. The torch was gone, leaving only the crackle of vanishing flames in his ears and the blossom of fading fire in his eyes. When the noise and the light were gone, he was left alone in darkness.

Donal shivered. The vault was cool, but he thought the quiver through his body came from more than merely that. He was not precisely afraid, but neither was he perfectly at ease. Given the choice again, he might walk out of the vault instead of allowing the Mujhar to leave him.

He sucked in a belly-deep breath, held it a moment, then released it. He shut his eyes, seeking to measure the darkness of the vault against the darkness all men claimed, and found it brighter behind his lids. He opened them again.

'*Shansu*,' he said, to see if the word would echo. It did, but oddly, falling away into the oubliette that gaped in the floor of the vault.

He put out his hand toward the wall that formed a door. He found it silk-smooth from the skill of the master craftsman who had brought the *lir* to life. Like the walls, the door was made of marble except for the corridor side, which was dark, pitted limestone. Through the darkness, he knew this side was a perfect creamy ivory, veined with purest gold. In another palace, it would be a monument for all to admire; in Homana-Mujhar, it was a place of subtle secrets.

'*Ja'hai*,' he said. Slowly, he moved away from the wall. The edge of the pit felt near. Carefully, he poised himself

on the rim, and knelt to make his obeisance to the gods. *'Tahlmorra lujhala mei wiccan, cheysu.'*

He tucked his boots beneath him, settling his knees against the marble. His palms he pressed flat against the floor; his fingers curled over the circular rim of the oubliette. He bowed his head and opened himself to what the gods would send him.

Silence. Darkness. A perfect cessation of movement.

He sat. He felt the beating of his heart. He felt the rush of blood through his veins. He heard the quiet whisper of his breathing. He let himself go.

Slowly.

One piece at a time.

He freed himself from the bindings of his body, and let his spirit expand. He felt his awareness slipping away.

He let it slip –

– and then it came rushing back.

Light blazed up in the vault. He stared blindly at the marble wall so full of shining *lir*, and saw the shadow cast upon it.

Slender. Hooded. Cloaked.

Moving toward me –

– and the torch raised to strike him down.

Donal thrust himself upward, spinning in place at the edge of the oubliette. He saw only the outline of the shrouded figure; no face, merely two delicate, slender hands. And the torch.

The flames burned his eyes, now used to darkness, and he knew the fire would blind him.

In silence, he thrust up his bare left arm. He felt the heat of the flames as they scorched his flesh; he smelled the stench of the charnelhouse. Pain blossomed. He heard himself cry out.

Again the torch thrust for his face; again he thrust it away. He felt the burned flesh of his arm crack, and the sticky wetness of blood.

The attack had done its work. Off-balance, teetering on the brink, Donal reached out to catch the assassin's arm

and caught the flames instead. He fell backward into darkness.

With a muted scream, he stretched out his arms and tried to catch the rim.

Fingers scraped. Bone bruised. Clawing grip slipped and released.

His head, thrown back on an arching neck, knocked against the edge of the marble pit.

Tumbling.

Blind, he felt his body twisting helplessly. He had no coordination. A hand scrabbled briefly against a wall; an elbow banged; bootleather scrapped itself raw. But mostly he tumbled, touching nothing but air.

Blind. Deaf. Tasting the hot acid spurt of bile into his throat.

And then he opened his mouth and shouted a denial of his fate.

His arm dragged briefly against the silk-smooth, rounded wall. Muscles protested, stretching; he heard the chiming scrape of metal against the marble.

His *lir*-band.

Gods – I am a Cheysuli warrior! Why fall *when I can fly –?*

He thrust out both arms. Human arms, lacking feathers or falcon bones. Frenziedly he reached for *lir*-shape, but nothing answered his call.

Slow . . . it is so slow . . . I will never strike the ground. .

And if he did not strike the ground, perhaps he would not die.

He felt the air against his body. There was no wind, except air rushing past as he fell. The part of him that was falcon, the part that understood the patterns of flight realized he would have to slow himself significantly if he was to alter a downward fall into the uprush of life-saving flight.

He twitched. Sweat broke out on his body. He reached for the shapechange again.

Upside down. The jerk of trapped air against out-stretched wings.

Carefully he tipped one wing, swung over, and tried to angle a climb. But he had miscalculated. The sudden change in size and distribution of his weight sent him slicing through the air, directly at the wall. His fall was curbed, but now his momentum smashed him toward the marble.

The falcon's wings strained toward even flight. Will-power lifted him upward, veering away from the wall. And yet the oubliette, in its purity of form, nearly defeated him. The left wingtip caught the silk of the marble and the vibration ran up into his body. His direction changed. He slipped sideways into the opposite side.

Left wing snapping with dull finality.

Somehow, he flogged the air. Pain screamed through his hollow bones and reverberated in his skull. Still, somehow, he flew. Perhaps he had not fallen as far as he had feared. He flew, desperately shedding pinfeathers, and reached the edge of the pit.

Failing.

He felt the floor rise up to strike him, battering brittle bones, and then he lost the shapechange. In human-form, Donal flopped across the stone.

Sound filled up the vault. He heard it clearly: a husky, raspy, throaty sobbing, as if it came from a man with no breath left to cry aloud.

He was wet with sweat. His leathers were soaked, rank with the smell of his fear. He lay belly-down on the floor of the vault and pressed his face into the stone, compressing flesh against the bone.

No light.

The torch was gone. He lay in total darkness. But for the moment he did not care; all he wanted was to know he was alive.

His left arm, he knew, was broken. An injury in *lir*-shape translated to the same in human form. How badly the bone was broken he could not say; the dull snap of his falcon's wing indicated it was not a simple fracture. It was possible the bone had shattered. Bound, it might heal, but

it was difficult to bind up flesh already badly burned.

'*Lir*,' he said aloud. It hissed in the darkness of the vault.

He gathered what strength he could and sent the appeal through the link. *Lir . . . by the gods, how I need you!*

When he could, Donal pulled his sound arm back toward his body, doubling the elbow beneath his ribs. He tensed, levered himself up, then curled up onto his knees to sit upon his legs. The left arm he cradled briefly against his belly, rocking gently on his heels as if he were a child, but left off both cradling and rocking almost immediately. It hurt too much to move or touch the arm.

'My thanks,' he said aloud, and heard the hoarseness of his voice. 'If this was the test of acceptance . . . I would not care to repeat it.'

He tried to regulate his breathing. He tried to hoard his waning strength. *Lir*-shape was gone, he knew; he was in too much pain to hold either form. But it would do little good if he could. With the wall shut, even a wolf or falcon would know captivity.

He felt the sweat of pain drip off his face. He shut his eyes and waited.

'Donal.'

A band of dull pain cinched his brow like a fillet of heavy iron. His lip bled from where he had bitten it. He tasted the salt-copper tang. Sweat ran down his face; no more the dampness of fear.

He dared not open his mouth, even to ease his lip, or he would disgrace himself.

'Donal.' It was Carillon's voice, from where he stood at his bedside. 'Donal – Finn is here.'

His eyes snapped open. Through a haze of fever and pain he saw Finn come into the room. '*Su'fali*,' he whispered hoarsely, 'tell them no, tell them *no* –' He shifted against the bedclothes, trying to outdistance the pain. '*Su'fali*, tell them no. They want to take my arm.'

172

Carillon looked at Finn compassionately, but tension was in his tone. 'The bones are badly broken. And the burns – they could poison him in three days.'

'You cannot take his arm.' Finn moved toward the bed with Storr padding at his side. 'You know better, Carillon.'

'What do I know? That foolishness about a maimed warrior not being a useful man?' Carillon thrust out his twisted hands. 'See you these? *I* am crippled, Finn – but I rule Homana still!'

Finn bent over his nephew. 'A maimed warrior cannot fight. He cannot hunt. He cannot tend his pavilion. He cannot protect his woman or his children. He cannot protect himself.' He felt Donal's burning brow. 'You know all this, Carillon – I was the one who told you. A maimed warrior cannot serve his clan, nor can he serve the prophecy. He is useless to his people.'

Carillon stood at the bedside. He was trembling. Donal saw it in his hands, in his face; in the rigidity of his spine. The greyish pallor of shock was slowly replaced with the flush of rising anger. 'You threaten that very prophecy by sentencing him to death.'

'I sentence Donal to nothing. I will heal him. Is that not why you sent for me?'

'And if the healing does not work?' Carillon challenged. 'Occasionally it does not.'

'Occasionally, when the gods see fit to deny it.' Finn did not spare a glance for the lord he had once so loyally served. 'Donal – what happened?'

His arm pained. 'Carillon took me to the Womb of the Earth,' he said breathlessly. 'He left me there. I – gave myself up to the gods. But someone came. Someone – came at me with the torch. I – fell.' He shut his eyes a moment. 'When I could, I took *lir*-shape, but – I could not control the fall. I – could not – fly properly. And so – I hit the wall.'

Finn nodded. He glanced around for a stool, found one, hooked it over with a booted foot. In the light from a

dozen candles, the gold of his *lir*-bands gleamed. 'Nothing more,' he said quietly, sitting down upon the stool. 'Nothing more until I am done, and the arm is whole again.' Briefly he smiled. '*Shansu*, Donal . . . I will take the pain away.'

'*Ru'shalla-tu*,' Donal said weakly. *May it be so*.

He closed his eyes. He felt the encouragement of both his *lir* and the presence of Storr as well. Finn did not touch him – he merely sat on the stool and looked at Donal – but after a moment his eyes went opaque and detached. The yellow was swallowed by black.

Donal drifted. He was bodiless, bound by nothing but the pain. It flared and died, pulsing in time with his heart; he wondered if they were linked. But then, slowly, he felt the pain diminish, and the beating stopped altogether.

Am I dead? he wondered briefly, and found he did not care.

Floating –

– painlessness swallowed him.

Donal slept for three days following the healing, and on the fourth he got out of bed. In dressing he discovered there was no pain in his healed arm, no stiffness in the bone. Only new flesh, too pink against the sunbronzing of older skin.

Shall we come with you? Lorn inquired as Donal tugged on his boots.

No. I only go to see Carillon.

Taj, fluffed to twice his size as he hunched on his perch, emitted a single permissive sound. Lorn yawned, stretched, then rose to seek out a warmer place in Donal's bed. Wolflike, he turned three times in place before settling down. *Lir*like, he thanked Donal for his leftover warmth.

Donal went at once to Carillon's private solar to speak of what had happened, and found Finn and Alix there as well. He had vague memories of them standing at his bedside, discussing the state of his health; he recalled also

174

that he had tried, once, to tell them to go away, so he could get some sleep. He had slept, but he did not know if they had heeded his suggestion.

Alix sat on a three-legged stool before the fireplace, indigo skirts spread around her feet as she nursed a goblet of hot wine; Donal could see the faintest breath of steam rising from the surface. Finn sat in a deep-silled casement, silhouetted against the sunlight and framed by chiseled stone. At his feet lay Storr, eyes shut. Carillon filled a tooled leather chair with his legs stretched out before him. From the tight-drawn look of the flesh around the Mujhar's eyes, Donal knew he was in pain.

'*One* good thing has come of this. . . .' Donal shut the heavy door. 'It brought my *su'fali* back to Homana-Mujhar.'

Finn swung a booted foot. His smile was very faint. 'I said I would come to your wedding. This is not so very premature.'

'Should you be up?' inquired his mother. 'Finn told us you might sleep for days.'

'I have.' He waved her back down as she started to rise. 'And aye, I should be up – or I will take root in that bed.' He scratched idly at the new flesh above and below the heavy golden *lir*-band on his arm. 'Well, at least this way you two aging warriors may speak of old times without a hundred sycophants listening to every word.'

Carillon shifted in the chair, clutching an armrest with one hand. 'Old times can wait. For now, we need to learn precisely what has happened.' He moved into a more upright position, straightening the hunched shoulders. 'Gods . . . when I remember the howling Lorn set up . . . and Taj would not stop flying around the hall. . . .' He shook up his head. 'I left you alone in the Womb because that is the way it must be done. *Lirless*. Absolutely alone. I gave orders for *no one* to enter the hall. How could anyone have known?'

'The Womb is not entirely secret,' Finn pointed out. 'All Cheysuli know of it – though not precisely where; we

175

are taught about it as children. It is one of the first lessons the *shar tahls* give us.' He frowned. 'Still – I doubt any Homanans would know of it, save yourself. Who else is in this palace?'

'Oh Finn, you cannot expect us to believe someone from Carillon's *household* did this!' Alix shook her head. 'They are too loyal to Carillon.'

'Loyal to Carillon and *Homana*,' Finn said evenly. 'Rank aside, there is a fundamental difference between Carillon and Donal.'

Alix looked back at him levelly. The sunlight lay full on her face, leaching shadows from planes and angles to give her youth again. Donal could almost see the seventeen-year-old girl Finn had stolen from Carillon, then lost to his older brother.

But the moment was fleeting; Donal, looking from his mother to his uncle, saw only a warrior and a woman, kin to one another through their father. Hale was in their faces.

And had it not been for that jehan and Carillon's foolish cousin, none *of us would be here.*

'Foreigners, then.' Carillon scratched at his beard. 'Well, there is Gryffth. The Ellasian Lachlan sent me – was it fifteen years ago?' He frowned, plainly shocked to find so much time had passed. 'But he is the only foreigner in the palace at the moment. And Gryffth I trust with *my* life, as well as Donal's. He helped Duncan and me win Alix free of Tynstar.' Carillon shook his head. 'No, not Gryffth.'

'No,' Finn agreed. One boot heel tapped against the wall.

Donal perched himself upon the edge of a sturdy table and helped himself to wine. 'I could not begin to hazard a guess. I know there are Homanans who would sooner see me something *other* than Carillon's heir – and back in the Keep, no doubt –' he shrugged a little, mouth twisted wryly '– but I doubt any of them would wish to have me *slain* –' Abruptly, he set the wine cup down. 'No – perhaps I am

176

wrong. My reception in Hondarth was not precisely – warm.'

'What are you saying?' Carillon sat upright in his chair. 'What have you been keeping from me?'

Donal saw how attentively Finn and Alix waited for his answer. And so he told them all, briefly, of the confrontation with the Homanan and the manure that had been thrown. 'I felt it was not significant enough to tell you,' he said finally to Carillon. 'It was – unpleasant – but nothing to fret the Mujhar.' He turned the cup in circles on the wooden tabletop, idly watching how the silver rolled against the satiny hardwood finish. 'But – I *do* begin to see that not all of Homana is reconciled to the ending of the *qu'mahlin*.'

'Nor ever will be,' Finn agreed.

Alix, mute but obviously disturbed, picked worriedly at the nap of her indigo skirts.

'I am not surprised,' Finn went on calmly. 'I think there are many Homanans who care little enough that we *exist* – there is nothing they can do about that, short of starting another *gu'mahlin* – but I also think they would actively resist a Cheysuli as Mujhar. And you are next in line.'

Donal frowned. 'But would they try to have me *slain*?'

Alix's mouth was grim as she looked at Finn. 'Would they?'

He shrugged. 'It is possible. Shaine's *qu'mahlin* was a powerful thing. It bred hatred and fear upon hatred and fear, and fed off of violence and ignorance.' He glanced at the Mujhar. 'I remember what it was like when Carillon and I came back from Caledon. The purge was over, but there were many Homanans who desired to see me dead.' For the first time a trace of bleakness entered his tone. 'We would be wise not to discount the possibility that the *qu'mahlin* still exists for those who wish it to.'

'Even *now*?' Donal demanded. 'You and Carillon came back nearly twenty years ago. Time has passed. Things change. People get older and less inclined to violence.' He

shrugged. 'Perhaps there are some bigots left, but surely not enough to do Homana harm.'

Finn eyed him. 'I am fifty. *Old,* to your way of thinking, *harani.* And would you consider *me* a nonviolent man?'

Fifty. Donal had not counted up the years lately. To him, Finn was ageless. And certainly never incapable of violence. 'No,' he said distinctly, and Finn smiled his ironic smile.

Carillon rubbed wearily at his brow. 'Gods – will it *never* end? What will happen when I am dead?'

'When you are dead it will be Donal's problem.' Finn stretched out one foot and touched the toe of the boot to Storr's left ear. 'There is another problem for us to settle before that one comes upon us.'

'Such as: who tried to murder my son,' Alix said flatly. 'Oh, aye, let us turn our attention to *that.*'

Donal shook his head. 'I saw nothing clearly. Only light, fire – a shape. Someone hooded and cloaked.'

'Think back,' Finn advised. 'Call up the memory. Think what you saw before you fell.'

'Fire,' Donal repeated, recalling that too clearly. 'Flames from the torch. It was thrust at me – I threw up my arm to block it.' He suited action to words. 'I was thrown off balance – I stepped back . . . and fell.' He shuddered, recalling the sensation of weightlessness. 'I did not even hear the wall open.'

'Think again,' Finn said patiently. 'You saw a hooded, cloaked figure. Tall? Short? Heavy? Slender?' The toe caressed Storr's ear, flipping it up and down. 'Think of everything you saw – even the bits and pieces. If there is an assassin in this place, he will likely try again.'

Donal was conscious of their waiting faces, reflecting expectations. He frowned in concentration, summoning up the memory in vivid recollection. 'Much shorter than I – even you, *su'fali.* Slender. The cloak was not a large one. And I remember hands.' He sat up so rigidly he nearly overturned the table. 'Hands! The hands upon the

178

torch!' He stared blindly at Finn, seeing only the hands upon the torch. 'Slim, pale, delicate hands, clutching a torch that seemed too heavy, too awkward for a man –' He stopped short. Stunned, he turned to Carillon. 'My lord – it was a *woman* –'

Color drained out of Carillon's face and left it a bearded deathmask. 'By the gods – *say it was not Electra* –'

Finn shook his head. 'Electra is not here. Believe it – I would know it. The trap-link has bound us forever.'

Donal still stared at Carillon. 'But – what if it were *Aislinn* –'

'Oh, Donal, *no!*' Alix cried as Carillon thrust himself out of his chair.

'Have you gone mad?' the Mujhar asked hoarsely. 'Do you think *Aislinn* could seek to push you into the Womb of the Earth?'

'No more than *Bronwyn* could,' Alix said.

Donal's hand, reaching for the goblet, knocked it over abruptly. He heard the dull chime of silver rim against dark hardwood; the sibilant splatter of wine against carpeted floor. But he did nothing to pick up the overturned goblet. Instead, he looked at his mother in something akin to shock.

'How can we say that?' he asked. 'How can we say for *certain* Bronwyn would never do it?'

Alix thrust herself up from her stool. 'Have you gone *mad*?' Unconsciously, she echoed Carillon. 'She is your *sister* –'

'And Tynstar's daughter, do not forget.' That from Finn, still seated in the casement. 'Alix – *before* you seek Carillon's knife to throw at me – make yourself think clearly a moment.' He swung his foot again idly. 'She is Tynstar's daughter. Ihlini as well as Cheysuli, no matter what you have done to hide it from her and everybody else. Who can say what Bronwyn is capable of if the Ihlini in her seeks to dominate?'

'No,' Alix said tautly. 'Not Bronwyn, how could she? She is at the Keep.'

'Not *Aislinn*,' Carillon said. 'Look to another culprit.'

'Aislinn tried to slay me in Hondarth,' Donal reminded him deliberately, and saw the shock in his mother's face. 'Aye – I did not tell you. It was Electra's ensorcelment. But who is to say she has not tried it yet again?'

Carillon thrust a hand in Finn's direction. 'You said he *tested* her!'

'I tested her.' Finn slid out of the casement and stood before his Mujhar. 'I swear – I tested her. There was an echo – a resonance – I thought I had rid her of it.'

Donal grimly picked up the fallen goblet and set it straight again. 'And if you did not?'

'If I did not, and she *is* Tynstar's weapon, there is yet another test,' Finn said simply. 'Let her try again.'

Donal opened his mouth to protest vehemently, but his intention was overriden by a thin voice raised on the other side of the door. 'My lord! My lord! A message for you from the Keep!'

'Sef,' Donal said, and went to tug open the heavy door.

Sef nearly fell into the room. His hair was blown back from his face and he breathed as if he had run all the way up three flights of spiraling stairs. 'My lord – a message from the Keep. From your *meijha*.' He paused, caught his breath. 'She says your sister is missing. Bronwyn is not at the Keep.'

Donal heard the swift, indrawn breath from Alix standing behind him. 'What else does Sorcha say?' he asked the boy.

'She says you had better come home to look for Bronwyn. She has been gone since yesterday.'

'Oh – gods . . . was all Donal could manage in the face of his mother's fear.

But it was Finn who had the answer. '*Lir*-shape,' was all he said. 'It will be faster than going by horse.'

'Wolf-shape, then,' from Alix. 'You have no recourse to wings.'

Lir, Donal called, and led the way out of the solar.

And behind them, as they left the old man with the boy, Carillon cursed his infirmities.

Five wolves and a falcon fled through sunlight into the shadows of the sunset. Silver Storr and ruddy Finn; ruddy Lorn and greyish Donal ran shoulder to shoulder with Alix, the pale silver wolf-bitch with black-tipped tail. And above them all flew a fleet golden falcon.

In *lir*-shape, Donal was aware of an edge to his apprehension. He was frightened for what they might find once they found her; he was worried that they would not find her at all. And if they did not, and she had come at last into a share of her father's powers, only the gods could say what Bronwyn might do to them all.

But the edge began to creep out from under his fear and express a new emotion. Anger. Frustration. Impatience and helplessness. And they drove him to the edge of infinity.

What if I stayed in wolf-shape? he wondered. *What happens if a warrior chooses to give up his human form for the other shape he claims?*

Inwardly, he flinched away from the questions. All Cheysuli, male and female alike, were taught that *lir*-shape was only a temporary guise, borrowed from the earth. *In borrowing, the borrower must return that form which is borrowed.* Donal had always believed the statement redundant; borrowing something meant it *had* to be returned, or it was stealing. Even as a child, he had understood the concepts very well.

But now, so lost within the essence of the shape, he wondered how it could be considered stealing when what he wore was an integral part of his *self*.

A lirless Cheysuli is not a man, but a shadow. He dwells in darkness of mind and body. He is driven mad by the loss, and gives himself over to death.

There was a ritual, of course, because there had to be. Otherwise, the giving over of a life to the gods would be considered suicide, and that was taboo.

Vines and creepers slashed Donal's face. A thorn tore at his muzzle, drawing beads of blood. Curving nails dug deeply into the damp, cool soil, gouging furrows and leaving tracks. But the tracks were spoor of the wolf, not the trail of a man.

He heard himself panting. But how could he be weary? In this shape he had almost endless endurance, because he knew how to pace himself.

Can a warrior maintain lir-shape as long as he desires it?

As a child, he had asked his father. Duncan had told him a warrior probably could retain *lir*-shape for as long as he desired; perhaps *longer* than he desired.

The last had frightened him. Intuitively, he had understood. A man left too long in *lir*-shape might never turn back into a man.

But would that be so bad?

No. But what if he were ever to change his mind again, and found himself locked inside the body of a wolf or falcon forever?

No, he decided. *No.*

Weary. So weary. His left foreleg arched. And then he recalled how it had been burned, broken, in human form; the healing could not give back that which had been lost. The magic was not absolute. He had not given the injured limb enough time to recover.

Through the *lir*-link, he passed the message to Lorn. He must stop. Stop. It was dark now, but the moon, full, had risen and they were nearly there. They could walk the rest of the way.

Donal stopped running. He panted, head hanging; he tucked his tail between his legs. Slowly, so slowly, the shapechange altered his body. He faced them as a man again.

Man-shaped, he leaned against the nearest tree. '– Sorry,' he said. 'Too tired – can we rest?'

Alix put a hand upon his arm. A hand, not a paw. 'We should have ridden at least half the way.'

Donal shook his head. 'No. We needed to get home as quickly as possible.'

Finn's smile was very faint. 'Sorcha should not worry; you will always be Cheysuli.'

'Because I call the Keep home?' Donal laughed breathlessly. 'Aye – I could not become a Mujharan if the prophecy commanded it.'

Alix glanced around. 'We are almost there. Oh gods, let the girl simply be *lost* . . .'

'Unlikely.' But Finn's tone was gentle. 'She is *your* daughter, Alix . . . with all your stubbornness. Perhaps –'

'Perhaps *what,* Finn?' Alix scraped fallen hair away from her face. 'Perhaps she decided to visit another Keep? No. She was helping Sorcha with the baby.'

Finn's hand clasped her shoulder gently. '*Meijha*, do not fret so –'

Donal nearly smiled at Finn's use of the inaccurate term. Alix had never been Finn's *meijha*, but that had not stopped him from wishing she would someday change her mind.

'Do you not fret about Meghan from time to time?' Alix asked in irritation. 'You are a *jehan,* Finn, as much as I am a *jehana*. Tell me you do not know what that entails.'

Looking at them, Donal saw two worried people. More worried than they intended him to know. For only a moment, he saw the possibilities through their eyes; *Bronwyn, Ihlini, attempting to use her burgeoning powers . . . or instinctively seeking her father.*

'But she thinks *Duncan* is her *jehan*.' He said it aloud, distinctly; Alix and Finn looked at him in surprise.

'Aye, of course, but –'

Finn's hand across Alix's mouth cut her sentence off. He made a quieting gesture with his other hand and they instantly obeyed.

In silence, they waited. And in silence, they heard the other approach.

183

Because in the forest, at night, absolute silence betokens a *presence* coming.

Bronwyn –? Donal wondered briefly. *She knows how to move as quietly as any –*

But it was not Bronwyn. It was not a woman. It was a man. A man who had once been Cheysuli.

He was a shadow within shadows, a wraith among the trees. There was no sound, only silence; the silence born of the passing of a spirit on its way to the afterworld. Insubstantiality, Donal thought; yet it had substance. It was not a wraith, but a man. Not a shadow: a man who was once a warrior.

A warrior without a *lir.*

Out of the shadows a man stepped into the luminescence of the moon, and they saw his face clearly: old/young; human/inhuman; of sorrow and bittersweet joy. And his face, in the moonlight, was Donal's, but carved of older, harder wood.

'Forgive me,' he said; two words, but filled with an agony of need.

Donal felt his senses waver. For an instant, the ground seemed to move beneath his feet. He put out a hand to steady himself, and when his fingers touched the trunk of the nearest tree he found himself turning to press against it. Clinging to it. *Clinging,* as if he could not stand up.

And he knew, as he clung, he could not. He could only press his face against the bark and let it bite into his flesh.

Jehan? Jehan? But he could not ask it aloud. He no longer had a voice. No tongue. No teeth. No mouth. He had lost the means to speak.

He shut his eyes. Tightly. So tightly he saw crimson and yellow and white. When he opened them again he blinked against the shock of sight once more, and realized the impossible remained.

It is *my Jehan –* And yet he knew it could not be.

It was Alix who moved first. Donal expected her to run to Duncan. To grab him, kiss him, hold him. To cry out his name and her love. But she did none of those things.

184

Instead, she turned her back.

Her face, Donal saw, was ravaged. 'If I look – *if I look* – he will be gone . . . gone . . . *again*. If I look – he will be *gone*.'

Gone . . . Donal echoed. *But how can he be* here?

The bark of the tree bit into his face. But he welcomed the pain; it kept him from losing possession of his senses.

Slowly Finn reached out and closed a hand around one of Alix's arms. Donal saw how the fingers pressed against the fabric of her gown – pressing, *pressing* – until Donal thought she would cry out because of the pain.

But Alix did not.

It was Finn.

'No,' Duncan said. 'Oh no . . .'

'*You*.' Finn's voice was ragged. '*You* stoop to apostasy –'

'*No* –' Alix, wrenching free of Finn's hand, spun around to face Duncan again. 'How can you call a miracle *apostasy* –?'

'He can,' Duncan said. 'He must. Because it is the truth.'

'Because you are *alive?*' Alix shook her head. Donal saw how she trembled. 'I begged you not to go. Why waste a life? But you denied me. You said you had to go because your *lir* was slain.' She tried to steady her voice. 'How can you come back now? Why did you stay *away* – if the death-ritual could be left unheeded?'

Finn stopped her from going to the man. 'Wait.'

'Wait?' She tried to wrench free again. '*Wait?* Have you gone mad? That is *Duncan* –'

'Is it?'

Duncan moved a single step closer to all of them. And his face was free of shadow, open to them all.

It was in the eyes. Donal saw it even as Finn and Alix did. Emptiness, aye. Sorrow: an abundance of it. Such pain as a man, left sane, could never know.

But there was no sanity left in Duncan.

Oh gods . . . oh gods –! Donal shut his eyes. He felt the

trembling start up in his limbs; the roiling in his belly. *He is back – he is back – and yet he is not my jehan –*

Finn jerked Alix back beside him. 'Rujho,' he said, 'stop.'

Duncan stopped. His head twisted quickly, faintly, oddly to one side, jerking his chin toward his shoulder. Twice; no more. A nervous tic, Donal thought dazedly. He knew other men who had them. But – this was something more.

'I need you,' Duncan said. '*I need you all.*'

'Why?' Finn asked flatly. 'Why does a dead warrior need help from any man?'

'*Finn –*' That from Alix, in horror, but he cut her off again.

'A *lirless* man is a dead man, of no value to his clan. He is half a man, and empty, lacking spirit, lacking soul.' Finn's chant sounded almost bitter. 'Is that not what we believe?'

We believe – we believe – Donal bared his teeth. *But how do we believe? My jehan has come back to us –*

Duncan twitched again. Briefly, so briefly; Donal almost did not see it. But he found himself, in fascinated horror, anticipating yet another.

'I need your help.' Duncan's hair was silver in the moonlight. 'I need your help. I need to find the magic to make me whole again.'

'Whole? You are *lirless*. How can you be whole?'

'Finn!' Duncan cried. 'Would you have me *beg* for this?'

Do not beg, do not beg – not you – not Duncan of the Cheysuli – that man does not beg –

Without waiting for an answer, Duncan dropped to his knees. His head, tilted up, exposed the look of mute appeal. He was a supplicant to his brother. To his wife. And to his son. 'Can you not *see* why I come to be here?'

Now, they could. Clearly. It showed in the eyes; in altered pupils, altered shape. It showed in the set of his shoulders, almost hunched upon themselves. It showed in

the mottled skin of his arms, bare and naked of *lir*-gold. It showed in the bones of his hands: fragile, brittle bones, rising up beneath the flesh to fuse themselves together and turn the fingers into talons.

Not a man. But neither a hawk. Some place between the two.

'Cai was *dead*!' Finn cried. 'How is this possible?'

'I am abomination,' Duncan said. 'Can you make me whole again?'

'But – you are *lirless*.' In Finn, the cracks began to show. '*Rujho*, you are lirless . . .'

'You can make me whole again.'

Alix, trembling, went down on her knees before the kneeling man. She put out her arms and drew him in until his face was against her breasts. '*Shansu*,' she said. '*peace*. We can make you whole again.'

'He is *lirless*!' It burst out of Donal's mouth in something near incoherence.

Alix did not hear. 'I promise. I promise. We will make you whole again.'

'Tynstar took the body. Tynstar took the body,' Duncan said against her breasts. 'I could not give my *lir* proper passage to the gods.'

'Oh gods,' Finn said. 'Oh – *gods*. . . .'

'I could not die,' Duncan said. 'There was no ritual. Tynstar had the body, and there was no ritual.'

'*Shansu*,' Alix said. 'We will make you whole again.'

'Not without Cai's body,' Finn said. 'Oh *rujho*, surely you must see!'

Duncan's head twitched against Alix arms. The taloned fingers came up in a twisted gesture of supplication.

Donal at last wrenched himself from the tree and faced them all. 'The earth magic!' he cried. 'There are three of us, and the *lir*. More than enough, is there not? We can summon up the healing and make him whole again!'

Alix stroked Duncan's silver hair. 'Do you see? Your son is much like you. He will be a wise Mujhar.'

'Donal –' Finn began, and then he shut his eyes.

187

'Make me *whole* again,' Duncan begged.

Lir. For the first time, Lorn spoke. *Lir, what he requests is dangerous.*

But it can be done?

There is much power in the earth, Taj said from a nearby tree. *With three of you to summon it, augmented by three lir, you can call upon powerful sources. But there is danger in it.*

And worth it, Donal said. *This man is my jehan!*

Slowly, Finn knelt down. He bowed his head in acquiescence.

Dangerous, Lorn said.

Shakily, Donal went to the kneeling triad. There were so many things he wanted to say to his father, whom he had not seen in fifteen years. So many, *many* things; he thought none of them would get said.

'Join hands,' Finn said. 'The link must be physical as well as emotional and mental. What we do now will stretch the boundaries of the power; if those boundaries break, all will be unleashed. The magic will be wild.'

Donal, kneeling between father and uncle, looked at Finn sharply. 'Wild –?'

'Before there were men and women in the world, there was magic in abundance. And all of it was wild. It made the world what it is. But it must be held in check if *we* are to live in the world.'

'Then – *this* could destroy the world. . . .'

'Duncan would never risk that,' Alix said suddenly. She looked at the silver-haired man. '*Would* you? That much risk?'

His malformed hands trembled in hers; in Donal's. 'I am abomination. Make me whole again.'

'*Duncan* would not risk it,' Finn said quietly. 'But this man is not Duncan.'

White-faced in the moonlight, Alix looked at Finn. 'Then – what we do is *wrong*.'

'Is it?' Finn looked at Donal. 'is it wrong to do this, *harani?*'

Deliberately, Donal looked into the eyes of the raptor who had once been his father. 'It is not wrong if we can control the magic. Stretching the boundaries is not evil, if we learn from what we do. A risk not taken means nothing of consequence is ever learned.' Donal drew in an unsteady breath. 'I say it must be done.'

'Down,' Finn whispered. 'Down . . . and down . . . and down. . . .'

Drifting.

– drifting –

– *down* –

He sank through layers of earth, of rock, of *rock*, drifting, drifting down, until he was a speck of sentience in the midst of omniscient infinity, aware only of his insignificance in the ordering of things.

Alone?

No. There were other specks, all black and glassy grey, as if they had burned themselves out. As if the infinity had become, all at once, finite, and the sentience emptied out.

Down.

– down –

– *down* –

Jehan, he asked, *are you here?*

Down.

He felt the void reach out for him. Reaching, it caught him. Catching, it tugged him in; tugging, tugging, until he was a fish on a line; a cat in a trap; a man at the end of a sword –

– with the hilt in another man's hands.

Pain.

The sword pierced flesh, muscle; scraped across rib bone. And entered the cage around his heart.

– *pain* –

He cried out. The speck, in the midst of the void, cried out to the other specks that he was in pain, *in pain,* and he knew it should not be so.

The line was cut; the trap was sprung; the sword was

shattered. And Donal, hurled back through infinity to know finiteness once more, heard the words screamed from his mother's mouth: '*Ihlini trap-link –*'

And then he knew the truth.

Not my jehan after all?

Pain.

He lay on his face. His mouth was filled with dirt and leaves. He spat. The sound reverberated in his skull.

Lir. Lorn, whose muzzle was planted solidly in Donal's neck, shoving. Donal felt the tip of a tooth against the flesh of his neck. Lorn's nose was cold.

Lir. Taj, who stirred dirt and debris into Donal's face with the force of his flapping wings. The falcon was on the ground, but his wings continued to flap.

He felt a hand on his arm. 'Donal. *Donal!*'

Finn's voice. Hoarse. Donal allowed the hand to drag him up from the ground. He flopped over onto his back.

Through slitted lids and merging lashes he saw Finn's face. In the moonlight the scar was a black ditch dug into the flesh; the other side of his face was dirty. Scraped. As if he had been hurled bodily against the ground. His leathers were littered with dirt and leaves.

'*Gods* –' Donal shoved himself up from the dirt. He wavered on his knees, pressing one hand against the ground. And then he saw his mother. '*Jehana* –?' Stiffly, he crawled across the clearing. '*Jehana?*'

Finn sat down suddenly in the dirt as if he could no longer stand. One hand threaded rigid fingers through his silver-speckled hair; he stripped it back from his eyes. He bared the face of his grief to his nephew, who still could not believe. Storr sat down next to Finn, leaning a little against him, as if he knew without his support Finn would surely fall.

'He was *sent*,' Finn said. 'That was not my *rujho*. Not your *jehan*. Not my *rujholla's cheysul*. That was Ihlini *retribution*.' He lifted his head and looked at Donal. 'He was *saved*, and he was *sent*. We are alive because of Alix.'

190

Donal could only stare at his mother's body.

Finn's voice droned on. 'We are alive because when she saw how the trap-link would swallow us all, she threw us out of it. There was power enough in the trap to slay four *hundred* Cheysuli, *four hundred* . . . not just *four* . . . but – she threw us out of the link . . . and let it swallow her.'

Donal's vision wavered. He blinked. He could not say if it were tears or the aftermath. He thought it might be both.

Alix was clearly dead. She lay sprawled on her back, arms and legs awry, spilling awkwardly from her clothing in the obscenity of death. Blood still crawled sluggishly from nose, ears, mouth. Her amber eyes were closed.

Transfixed, Donal looked slowly from mother to father. Like Alix, Duncan was sprawled in the dirt. The silent shadows lay across him, hiding malformed hands, hunching shoulders, the predatory eyes.

But not the fact that Duncan was not – *quite* – dead.

Donal twitched in shock as life spilled back into his body. Awkwardly he scrambled across to his father. He saw the blood in Duncan's nostrils. He felt it in his own.

'*Jehan*?' His voice was a ragged whisper as he hunched beside the form. '*Jehan* – have we made you whole again?'

'A toy,' Duncan said thickly, and there was – briefly – sanity in his eyes; his human, Cheysuli eyes. 'Tynstar – made me – *a toy* –'

'*Jehan* –?'

'For fifteen years – a *toy* –'

Almost frenziedly, Donal dragged Duncan's head and shoulders into his lap. Tentative hands stroked his father's silvered hair. '*Jehan*,' he begged. 'do not *go* – I have only just *found* you again –'

And in his arms, his father died.

14

Donal sat in his mother's pavilion. Around him were her belongings, waiting for her return: wooden chests filled with clothing and trinkets; the tapestry she had painstakingly worked for his father so many years before; cook pots and utensils; the jewelry his father had given her; many other things. And all of them spoke of Alix.

She had, over the years, made Duncan's things hers, though she had given many to her son. The pavilion no longer was the clan-leader's pavilion; that was Finn's. But once, this pavilion had known the laughter the three of them had shared; the tears; the evenings of stories and future plans. Once it had known fullness. Now it knew emptiness.

He had spent the long night with Sorcha, trying to ease his grief in her words and her womanhood. She had soothed him as only she could, and yet he had found himself longing for another woman entirely. The one Sorcha could not be.

They had spoken of his father; of what Duncan had once been, and who, but not what Tynstar had made him. For Donal, the memory of the night before was too vivid. Too real. He needed time to understand it and put it in its place. If he could ever find a place for what he had experienced.

In the morning he had left Sorcha, his children, his *lir*. He came alone to his mother's pavilion and sat upon the ragged bear pelt she had kept long past its usefulness, saying Duncan had given it to her and she would never be rid of it. He had sat on it as a child, and now he sat on it

192

again; a man grown, but knowing himself helpless as the child he had once been.

A slim hand slid inside the doorflap and pulled it aside. Donal heard the sibilant scrape of fabric against fabric. He watched in silence, waiting, as Bronwyn slipped into the pavilion. Her black hair was mussed, pulled loose from its single braid. Some hung into her face, veiling much of it from Donal. She was smiling a little, as if she knew a secret. Her amber eyes were alight with inner knowledge. But she was different. Very different. Aside from the fact she wore the leathers of a warrior in place of traditional skirts, he thought she looked more alive than he had ever seen her.

She saw him and stopped short. 'Donal!'

He waited.

The flap, half-closed, was caught on Bronwyn's shoulder. But she did not slide it free or step away. She stood in the shadows of the entrance and stared at her silent brother.

'Are you healed?' she asked. 'Your arm?'

'Healed,' Donal said. 'Bronwyn. Where have you been?'

She looked away from him, staring at the pelted floor. Color came and went in her face. And then she seemed to make up her mind to face him down. She lifted her head again. 'I wanted to see if I could do it. And I *can*. I have the Old Blood, too.'

He stared at her blankly. He was full of his mother's death and the ruination of his father; he could not comprehend anything Bronwyn said. 'Old Blood?' He thought only of Tynstar's blood.

'Aye,' she said firmly. '*Jehana* said perhaps someday I might be able to learn as *she* had learned. And so I made up my mind to do it.'

'Do what?' His response was sluggish. The aftereffects of Alix's throwing him out of the trap-link had not entirely dissipated. He still felt weak. Disoriented.

'Take *lir*-shape,' Bronwyn answered 'I went away to try.'

Awareness returned at once. '*Lir*-shape! *You?*'

Color surged into Bronwyn's face. 'Aye! Do you think I am not worthy because I am a woman?'

Donal thrust himself to his feet. 'Do not mouth such foolishness when our *jehana* is dead!'

He had not meant it to come out so badly; so cruelly. But all he could think of was his mother dying to save them all while Bronwyn played her games.

But perhaps they were not games. Not if she could shapechange. And he could not discount the possibility; Alix had claimed the gift. If her daughter did as well, perhaps the Old Blood might yet counteract the Ihlini in her.

'*Dead*.' Bronwyn gaped at him. 'Our *jehana* –?'

'Last night.' He saw the twitch of shock in her face; the beginnings of comprehension. 'It was an Ihlini trap-link.'

Bronwyn flinched visibly. 'Ihlini! But – *how?*'

He could not tell her how. That meant he must also tell her of his father; he could not do it. It was too private. Too personal. The pain was his alone.

'*Donal* –'

'Tynstar laid a trap. He wanted Finn and me as well . . . all he got was our *jehana*.'

'*Tynstar* –' Bronwyn's amber eyes were full of tears. '*Tynstar* slew our *jehana* –?'

'She has been given passage to the gods.' With Duncan, but Donal did not say it.

Disjointedly, Bronwyn fell down upon her knees. She stared blankly at the unlighted firecairn. Donal, still looking for some indication of guilt, some telltale sign she dissembled, saw only grief and bewilderment. 'Why would he want our *jehana*? What would he want with her? Why would he slay our *jehana* –?'

He knew she would not hear him. And so he did not try. He simply went to his sister, knelt down, and pulled her against his chest so she would not have to grieve alone.

'*Rujho*,' Bronwyn begged, 'why would he slay our *jehana?*'

'Retribution,' he answered unevenly. 'The *Ihlini* require no reason.'

'Dead,' she whispered. 'Dead? But – I wanted to tell her about it. I wanted to say what I did. I wanted her to know how her blood is in me, too. The *Old* Blood . . . as much as in her son.' Bronwyn pressed her face against his shoulder. 'I wanted to have importance . . . I wanted to be someone who *counted* . . . I wanted to be *different* . . .'

Oh Bronwyn, he mourned, *you are more different than you can know.*

Her tangled hair was soft beneath his chin. He smoothed the knots against her scalp as if she were a child, and in his heart he knew she was, regardless of her age. As much as he himself was, in his bitter grief.

'I wanted her to know,' Bronwyn sobbed, 'and now she never will.'

'*Shansu,*' he said, '*shansu.* Be certain that she knows.'

After a moment, Bronwyn drew away from him. 'Donal – what happens to *me,* now? What becomes of me?'

One last time he pushed a lock of hair out of her face. 'You may stay here, if it suits. The Keep is your home. Finn and Meghan are here; so is Sorcha and the children, and all your clan-mates. But – if you prefer – you may come to Homana-Mujhar. Aislinn could use the company. There is a wedding she must prepare for – in less time than I care to acknowledge.' He felt the twist of reluctance in his belly. Fifteen days. But he knew better than to ask Carillon for a delay, even in light of the circumstances. Homana was at stake.

'Wedding,' Bronwyn echoed. 'I do not feel much like a wedding. Even a royal one. Not without my *jehana* –' But she shut her mouth on anything more, as if she could not dare to say what she felt.

Slowly he stood, pulling her up as well. 'I am sorry, but I must go back –'

'*Now?*' She stared at him. 'After what has happened?'

Donal sighed, wanting refuge from the bewildered pain

195

in her voice. He did not blame her; he wanted to stay as well. 'Much as I would prefer to remain, Carillon would have my head. There are responsibilities –' But he did not explain them to her. In her grief, she would never understand. '*Rujholla* . . . do not forget our *su'fali*. You may find comfort in comforting him.'

After a moment, Bronwyn nodded. 'Tell Aislinn I will come. But – not just yet. I think I could not bear it.'

He bent and kissed her forehead, hoping to offer solace. But what he found was doubt. *Oh gods . . . what if I am wrong? What if the Old Blood in her is tainted by the other?*

And yet he knew he might be doing his sister a grave injustice. He had no proof it had been Bronwyn in the Womb. None at all. The possibility seemed remote, now that he knew where Bronwyn had been.

And Aislinn? Where was she?

He said nothing more to Bronwyn. He left her to grieve in private, according to Cheysuli tradition.

The guests had gathered. The vows had been said. The acclamation was made. In the space of an hour Donal went from unnamed Prince of Homana to the actual thing itself; there was an instantaneous change. He could feel it in the air. A tension. A vibrating urgency. No more was it a *someday* thing; Homana would have a Cheysuli Mujhar.

When the feasting was done and the hall was prepared for celebratory dancing, Donal discovered he was now the prey of many courtiers. In his years as informal heir, the men who inhabited Carillon's court had mostly tried to ignore him. No doubt they had thought – or, more likely, *hoped* – the Mujhar might elevate a bastard son to legitimacy and send Donal back to the Keep. But the Mujhar had not; Donal was not certain there *were* any bastard sons, though there had been rumors of one or two. And so now the circle was halfway complete; the shapechanger was Prince of Homana.

They oppressed him, the noblemen of Homana. They stifled him with their insincere sudden change of regard,

expressing condolences for his mother's death as an opening gambit. He stood his ground for as long as he could, using the Homanan courtesy traditions Alix had taught him as well as what diplomacy he had learned in his years within the palace walls. But courtesy and diplomacy ran out; he retreated. And at last, tiring of his evasiveness, they left him alone.

They do not know me, though all have known me for years. They realize they must deal with me one day, and would rather gain sway with me now, so they may lay the groundwork to make me a puppet-prince, and a Mujhar – when it comes to that – in their pockets.

He knew also that the freedom he had just won would never last; soon enough they would learn his moods and his habits, and would play him like a harp.

Donal stood well back from the dancing and laughing and drinking. He leaned against the tapestried wall and watched in silence, considering his newly won rank. And against his will he touched the golden circlet on his brow.

Carillon had put it there during the ceremony. It represented his princely status; it represented the future of Homana. A simple circlet of plain, unworked gold, lacking significant weight. But it was enough to bind him eternally to his *tahlmorra*.

Donal smiled. *But if they expected me to be a Homanan prince, no doubt my leathers shocked them. Good.*

As a concession to Homana, he wore the royal colors. His jerkin was crimson suede, his leggings were black; black boots were stitched in scarlet. A belt of filigreed gold set with rubies the size of his thumbnail clasped his waist. But for that and his *lir*-gold and newly gained circlet, he was a conservative Cheysuli. Other warriors were not so subdued.

He leaned against the wall. But this time he watched Aislinn as she left her women to dance. He watched as she swayed to and fro with a glittering young Homanan nobleman, touching fingertips and dancing flirtatiously.

She moved with a grace almost foreign to her. Aislinn

197

had, growing up, been a coltish girl, even when attempting regal dignity. Since her sojourn on the Crystal Isle with Electra, she had learned a new and supple grace that was almost sheer seductiveness. There was nothing coltish about her now.

The bright, rich hair swung at her hips as she moved. Unbound, as was proper for a maiden, it flowed loosely over her shoulders, cloaking the pale blue gown. At ears and throat and waist glowed sapphires set in silver.

Electra's wedding jewels from Carillon long ago. It is no wonder he nearly made Aislinn take them off. But even a Mujhar cannot take back what is given freely, and so she has a legacy from her jehana.

He looked more closely at her as she danced with the nobleman. In the weeks since Finn had healed his burned and broken arm, Aislinn had been busy with wedding preparations. They had hardly seen one another. Seeing her now, he thought the preparations were well-made; she was lovely. She was almost a woman, with girlhood nearly banished completely.

What is mine is also Tynstar's.

He heard the words clearly, as if spoken into his ears. He snapped upright, free of the wall, and sought Electra in the throng.

But all he saw was Aislinn spinning slowly in the dance.

He stared. Her hair, a rich red-gold, seemed to fade before his eyes. He saw how it blurred, running into a duller color, until the red was replaced with silver-grey. And then the silver turned to white.

But not the white of age. The pure white-blond of youth; Electra's ensorceled youth.

Aislinn's eyes caught his. She stared at him as she stepped lightly through the pattern. He did not know what she thought; he was aware only of her eyes. Electra's eyes, pale as water and full of subtle promises. But the dreams she promised were nightmares.

The heavy girdle spun out from her twisting skirts. He saw how the silver tangled; heard how it chimed, the dull

198

clink of interlocked links. A rattle of stones as the sapphires clattered. And then the laughter was in his head.

What is undone shall remain undone . . . what is mine is also Tynstar's.

Donal flinched as a winecup was pressed into his hand. 'Drink deep,' Finn advised. 'It will be a long night before you can bed your bride.'

He looked up again at Aislinn, shaken to the core. *Gods – is Electra somewhere* here?

'I must kiss you for luck!' It was Bronwyn, coming up to clasp his arms. 'Bend down, Donal – you are too tall for me!'

He saw how the blue-enameled torque and earrings glittered against her skin. She had none of the dark coloring of the Cheysuli, showing the Homanan in her instead.

Or the Ihlini? He bent slowly, still lost in what he had heard inside his head. 'You are certain this will work?'

'Everyone says it will. It must be done, you know.' She kissed him soundly on one cheek, then laughed up at him. 'Every woman who wants a *cheysul* must kiss the most recent bridegroom.'

'*Every* woman –?' He recoiled in exaggerated horror.

'Every single one.' She twisted her head to seek someone in the crowd. 'There – Meghan will undoubtedly be next.'

'Meghan! Meghan is too young to think of marriage – and so, for that matter, are you.'

Bronwyn laughed. 'I am only a year younger than Aislinn. Perhaps by the time *I* am sixteen, I will have found a *cheysul*.' Her amber eyes glinted. 'After all, I am dancing with *men*, not boys. I have danced with Gryffth, and Rowan *himself* has already asked me twice.'

'Rowan is being polite.' Donal unthreaded his arm from hers. 'Then go dance, *rujholla*. Do not keep your partners waiting.'

Laughing, she whirled in a swirl of sky-blue skirts and hastened back to the throng of young women.

'She is nearly grown,' Finn said quietly. 'She has the

199

right of it – by next year she may be wed.'

A twinge of unease unsettled Donal's belly. 'It may be best we do not let her wed. We – do not know what powers she might claim in the coming years.'

Finn looked at him squarely. 'If you stifle her, Donal – if you seek to keep her leashed, no matter how light the chain – you will surely twist her spirit. Right now, there is nothing of Tynstar in her.'

'And when there is?'

'*If* there is . . . we will deal with it then.'

'As we must deal with her ability to assume *lir*-shape?'

Finn looked sharply at Donal. '*Bronwyn*? Are you certain?'

'She says so. Did she not tell *you*?'

'No.' Finn frowned into his wine. 'She – has kept very apart since Alix's death. Oh – she spends time with Meghan, but not much with me. I have tried. . . .' He stopped speaking. His dark face was stark, as if he deeply regretted his inability to deal with Alix's daughter. 'She spends more time with Storr than with me, but if she has learned how to take *lir*-shape, that is why.'

'Storr said nothing to you?'

'Storr said nothing to me when *Alix* learned to shape-change.' Finn's tone was wry, but Donal saw the trace of remembered pain in his uncle's eyes. 'The *lir* protect those with the Old Blood. More so, I sometimes think, than they protect those without.'

Donal frowned. 'Then could they protect her against herself?'

'If she began to show signs of Ihlini powers?' Finn shrugged a little. 'Who can say? All we know is the *lir* are constrained against attacking the Ihlini, no matter what the odds.'

'Gods,' Donal said, 'what my poor *rujholla* faces –'

'We do not know,' Finn said deliberately. 'She may be free of the evil, even *with* the blood.'

Donal swirled wine within the confines of the goblet. 'Aye, but –' He broke it off. A stranger approached, and

he had no wish to share Bronwyn's parentage with anyone but Finn.

'May I join you?' the stranger asked.

Finn turned to face him, then fell back a step. For a moment there was blatant shock in his eyes. 'Carillon did not tell me *you* were coming.'

'I was not certain I could.' The man – tall, very blond, with a silver circlet banding his head – smiled at Donal. 'I think your nephew does not recall who I am. But why should he? – it was nearly sixteen years ago when last he saw me, and he was only a boy.'

Donal released a breath of laughter. 'I remember you, Lachlan! How could I *not*? It was your *Song of Homana* so many of us sang the summer when you had gone.' He shook his head. 'No more the humble harper, are you, with all your fine clothes and jewels.' An eloquent flip of his hand indicated the blue velvets and flashing diamonds. 'No more hiding your identity, but the High Prince of Ellas in all your power and grace.'

'Eloquent, is he not?' Finn observed lightly. 'I think he gets it from me.'

Lachlan's smile was warm and nostalgic. 'Does he get anything from *you*, Finn, it would surely be your gift for inspiring – trust.' The jibe was gentle, but the sting was clearly present. And then it faded. 'I have just come from Carillon. Donal – I am sorry for Alix's death. I admired and respected her greatly. But – as for *Carillon*. . . .' Briefly, he glanced over his shoulder. Near one of the trestle tables Carillon stood head and shoulders above the men who clustered around him; Homanans, mostly, but a few Solindish guests. 'In his letters, Carillon said Tynstar had stolen away his youth, but I did not realize he meant as much as *that*.' Lachlan's voice was even, but Donal heard the undertone of concern. 'Is there nothing to be done?'

Finn shrugged. 'He ages. All men age. Tynstar has merely given it to him sooner.'

Lachlan regarded Finn's expressionless face closely. 'And have you tried to reverse it with your magic?'

'It cannot be done,' Finn said flatly. 'Ihlini powers and Cheysuli gifts are in direct opposition. We cannot undo what an Ihlini has done when it is of such magnitude as *that*.' Briefly, he looked at the Mujhar. His eyes belied his tone. 'I think he has accepted it.'

'Perhaps I, with Lodhi's aid –'

'No.' Finn's voice was flat and inflexible. 'It is a part of his *tahlmorra*.'

'Lodhi,' Lachlan muttered, 'you and your *destiny* –!'

Donal cleared his throat. 'Lachlan – where is your harp? Have you left your Lady behind?'

The Ellasian's blond hair shone in the candlelit room. Unlike Carillon or Finn, he seemed not to have aged at all, save for a fine tracery of lines at the corners of his blue eyes and faint brackets at his mouth. Blond, he was a stranger; Donal recalled him from a time when he had dyed the fair hair dark.

'No. She is in my chambers. Why? – do you want a lesson?' Lachlan smiled. 'When you asked me once before, as a boy, I said you had the hands of a warrior instead of a harper.' He glanced at his own supple hands. 'And, as for tonight – surely there will be *other* things for you to master.'

Finn's tone was subtly mocking. 'And what have *you* mastered since last we saw one another?'

'I?' Lachlan's handsome face smoothed into a hospitable blankness, while diplomacy ruled his tongue. 'I have mastered happiness, Finn . . . and you?' The tone altered a little. 'How is it with *you* – now that Tourmaline is dead?'

Donal saw the taut muscles of Finn's jaw relax just a little. It was shock, he knew; Finn, with most things, was imperturbable. But then no one mentioned his dead *cheysula* to his face.

Finn's face remained expressionless, but only the habitual solemnity of a Cheysuli gave him the control. Donal saw through it quite easily.

But then the control was released. Donal saw his uncle's

eyes naked for the first time in his life, and the intensity of the pain stunned him.

Finn looked directly at Lachlan. 'Had I to do it over again, I would give her up to you.'

The High Prince of Ellas was clearly shocked. 'Lodhi – *why?* Torry wanted *you.* She went with you willingly.'

The tone of Finn's voice was hollowed. '*You* could have kept her alive.'

Color drained out of Lachlan's face. His hand, holding a goblet of gold filled with rich red wine, shook enough to make the metal glitter. 'But – it was you she wanted. All along. Carillon made it quite clear.'

'And you she should have taken.' Finn glanced at Donal. 'It is – hard to admit it when one has made a mistake. I was too selfish, too proud. Duncan had won Alix – I would not allow Torry *also* to go to another man when I wanted her for myself. I was – wrong. But the price was exacted from her.'

'I am sorry,' Lachlan said finally. 'I had no right to bring it up. This is not the time for recriminations – I banished those long ago.' Briefly, he smiled. 'And I am wed now myself – a lovely woman. She loves me well, and I am content with her.'

Finn smiled ironically. 'Where would you find such a fool as *that?*'

Lachlan grinned back, unoffended. 'In Caledon, of course, since our realms have made a peace at last. We have two sons.'

Finn's mouth hooked down sourly. 'Aye, your House runs to boys. How many brothers have you?'

'Five. And five sisters.' Lachlan laughed at Donal's startled glance. 'Speaking of that: would you care to meet another of Rhodri's sons?'

'Who?' Finn asked suspiciously. 'Is this one a harper, too?'

'No. Not even a priest of Lodhi, though he does, when he must, admit to calling upon the All-Wise. Usually when he is in dire need of assistance.' Lachlan turned and

gestured. A young man approached: blue-eyed, dark-haired, well-dressed in quiet brown with little jewelry. He moved with Lachlan's fluid grace. He was not as tall and did not claim the same purity of features, as if they had blurred in him somehow, but he was handsome enough and his mouth was expressively mobile.

He looked at his brother quizzically; there was a glint in his sleepy eyes. 'Aye, my lord High Prince?'

Lachlan sighed. 'This is Evan, my youngest brother. Twenty years divide us, but we are closer than the rest. All the others are dutiful sons; Evan and I are the rebels.' He smiled at his brother. 'He decided to come to Homana because he had heard all the lays I sang of Carillon's exploits. He said he must meet these Cheysuli warriors, to see if the stories were true.'

Evan executed a graceful bow before a startled Donal. 'I must admit I expected something other than *civilized* behavior from you, my lord. I thought Cheysuli were spawned with tails and fangs.'

For a moment, Donal thought he meant it. Then he heard the ironic humor in Evan's tone. He smiled. 'Beware your back – when the moon is whole we seek the souls of such men as you.'

Evan grinned and took the goblet from his brother's hand, swallowing most of the wine before Lachlan could protest. He handed it back with a challenging smile. Then he nodded at Donal. 'She is a lovely bride, my lord.'

'My name is Donal, and aye – she is.'

Evan appraised him briefly. 'I would drink to your future gladly – had I some wine.'

Donal lifted his own winecup. 'Then we shall go and find some. My cup is drunk quite dry.'

'And I have none at all,' Evan pointed out.

They went directly to the nearest trestle table holding all manner of liquor. Donal judiciously stayed with the vintage he had already tasted; Evan, methodically precise, tried four cups before he found the wine he preferred.

204

Then he offered several elaborate toasts in honor of the Prince of Homana and his bride, all spoken in the husky unintelligible language of Homana's eastern neighbor. Having scorched his throat with the words, Evan returned to Homanan and his wine.

The Ellasian prince was full of good spirits, sweet wine and dry wit. He was patently unimpressed by Donal's rank or warrior status; he was too obsessed with having a good time. Donal, accustomed to wary dealings with Homanans disturbed by his shapechanging or turned obsequious because of his rank, found it a novel experience. He relaxed with Evan as he only rarely relaxed with others. They were, he decided, *kinspirits*, drawn together by mutual liking, respect and circumstances.

Evan watched the dancers. Donal watched Evan. 'Will you inherit the Ellasian throne?'

Evan burst into laughter, nearly spraying wine all over himself. 'I? *Never!* There are four brothers between Lachlan and myself, and *he* has two sons. And his wife has conceived again; likely *it* will be a boy, and I will be farther away from the throne even yet.' He grinned. 'Only if war, famine or plague slew all of *them*, leaving only me, would I inherit Ellas.' He shrugged, sounding insufferably content-ed with his lot. 'I am insignificant within my House. I find I prefer it that way.'

'Why?' Donal was fascinated.

'As Lachlan said – I am somewhat a rebel son. Being insignificant leaves me the freedom to be whom I wish and to do what I wish. Within the bounds of reason. Of course, there are times my father forgets the order of my birth – was it fourth? No? Fifth? – but all in all I like it better this way.' His sleepy blue eyes were shrewd behind dark lashes. 'Lachlan is the heir – you have only to look at him to see what the title means. He far preferred being a priest of Lodhi the All-Father and a simple wandering harper, but he was firstborn, and therefore High Prince of Ellas. Those years he spent with Carillon were his free-dom. Now he must be a proper son to our father.'

205

Donal looked at Lachlan still in conversation with Finn. 'And does he resent it?'

Evan laughed and quaffed more wine. 'Lachlan resents nothing. He has not the darkness in him for that. None of us do.' He grinned and arched an eyebrow. 'That is Ellas for you, Donal: a land of laughter and happy people.' His eyes followed the pattern of the dance. 'Your wife enjoys herself with countless Homanan nobles. Is it not time *you* partnered her?'

'It is customary for the bride to dance with all the men before she dances with her husband.' He shrugged. 'Or so I have been told. Dancing is a Homanan custom. I learned because I had to.'

Evan watched as Aislinn slipped through the pattern. 'But she should not have so much freedom just after you have wed. She will think to seek it much too often.'

Donal regarded him in amusement. 'What do *you* know of women, Evan? You are younger than I.'

'Twenty,' he said, unoffended. 'I know more than you think. Now *there* is a lady I would care to know better than I do at the moment.'

Donal looked. He shook his head at once. 'Never Meghan.'

'Why not?' Evan demanded archly. 'Do you think I could not win her?'

'To win *her* you would have to win her father . . . and that you could never do.'

Evan tossed back a gulp of wine. 'In Ellas, I have frequent experiences with fathers. When they know who I am, the thing is always settled.'

'Finn, I fear, would be less impressed by your rank than with your intentions toward his daughter.'

Evan's head turned sharply. 'Finn? The Cheysuli?'

'My *su'fali* –' Donal smiled. '*Uncle*, in Homanan.'

'Then – she is Carillon's niece –' Evan frowned. 'Perhaps I looked too high. Still, she is a pretty thing . . . no, I think not. Why antagonize Cheysuli or Mujhar?' He tapped his silver cup against his teeth. 'What of *her*?'

Again, Donal looked. And again, he shook his head. 'No.'

Evan's brows shot up beneath his dark brown hair. 'No? Why say you no? Is *she* close to the Mujhar?'

'Closer to *me*, Ellasian. Bronwyn is my sister.'

Evan swore in disgust. 'Are there *no* women here who are not kin to royalty?'

'Very few.' Donal grinned and pushed his cup into Evan's hands. 'I think I will do as you suggest and dance with Aislinn . . . before you look to *her*.'

15

Before Donal could reach Aislinn, Carillon intercepted him. 'Donal – come with me. There are men you should meet.'

Politics, of course. 'I mean to dance with Aislinn.' He thought perhaps an appeal to Carillon's parental prejudice would delay the need for such discussions.

Carillon smiled, seeing through the tactic at once. 'Aislinn can wait a few moments. These are men you will need to know.' The Mujhar's hand was on Donal's arm as he turned him away from the dance floor. 'I know, this is your wedding celebration – but you will soon learn that such occasions offer opportunities other times do not.'

Reluctantly, Donal went with him to the knot of noblemen. Two of them he knew, having seen them year in and year out in Homana-Mujhar while they danced attendance on Carillon. Three others were strangers to him, but their accents were Solindish.

Carillon conducted the introductions smoothly with light-headed authority. The nuances told Donal the Mujhar meant to emphasize that this Cheysuli was now the Prince of Homana; did the Solindish seek to discount him, they discounted the man who would one day rule their realm.

But it was the Homanans Donal watched more closely. He expected hostility from the Solindish; it came as no shock when he perceived it, however veiled. But the two Homanans, watching him silently, seemed tense, expectant.

208

Gods – it is worse than I thought it might be. Surely Carillon can see it. These men and others like them will never accept me as Mujhar.

Carillon's hand was on Donal's shoulder. 'Of course we all realize the alliance between our two realms precludes any more war –' his smile was eloquently bland '– so I doubt Donal will ever see it. No doubt he will value the ongoing peace as highly as I do.' Carillon inclined his head at the Solindish nobles. 'It will be a mark of Donal's tenure as Mujhar that his reign will know only peace, and will no longer need petty squabbling.' The hand tightened. 'It would please me well to know I am succeeded by a man who can hold the peace so truly.'

'Peace is indeed something all of us desire,' murmured one vermillion-clad Solindishman.

'Of course, I do not doubt the people of Solinde will be somewhat alarmed by the ascension of a Cheysuli in place of their own Solindish House –' Carillon's smile, once more, held the faintest touch of irony '– but perhaps by the time it comes to that, they will be reconciled to Donal.'

There was a quick exchange of glances among the Solindishmen *and* the Homanans, Donal noted.

'Perhaps it is time I sent for Duke Royce to come home from Lestra,' Carillon mused. 'He has been regent of Solinde for more than fifteen years – he is no longer young. I think Solinde might benefit from another, younger man.' He did not smile as he looked at the Solindishmen. 'How better to accustom a realm to its future Mujhar than to send that man there now?'

Gods – is he serious? But Donal dared not show his surprise at Carillon's intentions.

One of the Homanans stared. 'You send him there *now?*'

It was not, Donal knew, the reaction Carillon wanted. At least, not from the Homanans.

The Mujhar shrugged. 'First he and my daughter shall spend some time together as befits those newly married. At Joyenne, I think, before they go to Lestra.' Carillon's

hand tightened yet again on Donal's shoulder, as if he meant to pull him closer in a brief hug of parental approval.

And then the woman screamed.

Donal spun even as Carillon did. He saw a mass of colors, staring eyes and open mouths, all clustered within the hall, all running into another in a collage of shock and stillness. And then he saw the man with the sword in his hand.

His thoughts were disjointed. – *coming at Carillon . . . a sword – at a wedding –? But – no man may bear a sword into the Mujhar's presence . . . and all the guards are in the corridor –*

His own hand flashed down to clasp his long-knife and came up filled with steel and gold. Next to him, Carillon too had armed himself. But the enemy's sword, even as it sliced through the air in a blaze of shining steel, fell free of the assailant's hand. And the man himself, so close to the Mujhar, dropped a moment later to join his weapon on the floor.

A knife, hilt-deep, stood up from the dead man's back in the very center of his spine. Donal knew the blade at once: a royal Homanan knife, with rampant lion and ruby eye. And he knew what man had thrown it.

Carillon stood over the body. But he did not look at it. Instead, he looked at the warrior who had thrown the royal knife.

Finn's bare arms were folded across his chest. 'It does appear, my lord, you lack a proper liege man.'

'Aye,' Carillon agreed. His tone, though light, sounded hoarse in the silent hall. 'Since I lost the one I had for so many years, I have been unable to find another.'

The question was implicit in his tone. Donal, staring at Finn, felt a strange wild hope build up in his breast.

Gods – did Finn return to Carillon . . . . things would be as they were before – Except he knew they would not. Time had altered them both.

Finn smiled faintly, darkly. 'Aye,' he agreed. 'It is

210

difficult to find a man well-suited to the post. I have always understood a liege man to be – irreplaceable.'

'Unless replaced with the original warrior.' Carillon's face was perfectly blank.

Donal looked not at Finn but at Rowan. The most loyal and dedicated of all Carillon's generals wore, as Donal did, the colors of the realm. But Rowan's garb, rather than Cheysuli leathers, was the silks and velvets of Homana.

Yet it was not the clothing Donal looked at, but the face. The sunbronzed Cheysuli face which had abruptly lost its color, gone ash-grey in shock. Rowan's hand was on the hilt of his long-knife, as if he had intended to draw it in Carillon's defense. And yet – he did not look at Carillon. He looked instead at Finn.

He waits, Donal realized abruptly. *He waits for Finn's answer. Though he is no proper liege man, he is everything else to Carillon. He has served him so well for all these years. I do not doubt he felt he could take Finn's place in some small measure – perhaps more – and now he realizes Finn might return to Carillon's side.* Donal blew out a breath. *I would not wish to live like that, ever on the edge. Ever wondering.*

But at last the wondering could stop.

Finn looked down at the dead man. The golden hilt glittered in the torchlight. 'No,' he said finally, with the faintest note of regret underscoring his tone. 'I think those times are done. I have a clan to lead. Warriors to train.' He looked up and met Carillon's eyes. For a long moment they seemed to share an unspoken communication. Briefly, Finn looked at the twisted hands and the hunching of Carillon's shoulders. 'There *is* something I can offer you. If you will let me do it.'

'Aye,' Carillon agreed, 'when I have cleared my hall of vermin.' He replaced his own knife – a wolf's-head Cheysuli long-knife – then bent and pulled the bloodied knife from the assailant's back. He gave the royal blade over to Finn, then motioned to the guards who had come

in at the woman's scream. Quickly and efficiently two of them gathered up the body, the sword, and took both from the hall. The other six waited for Carillon's command.

He did not look at the Solindish noblemen who clustered near the center of the crowd. 'Take them –' a wave of his hand indicted all six '– and escort them to their quarters. They will return home in the morning.'

'But – my lord Mujhar –!' The grey-haired lord in vermillion velvet spread his jeweled hands wide. 'My lord – *we* had nothing to do with this –!'

'On the day of my daughter's wedding, I have been attacked in my own hall,' Carillon said inflexibly. 'Let there be no more diplomacy between us, Voile – our two realms will soon be at war. This assassination attempt might have won it for Solinde before the thing was begun, had it succeeded. But it failed, and you are uncovered – like a grub beneath a rock – your plan has gone awry.' He signaled his guards to surround the Solindish nobles.

Donal watched the guards take the Solindishmen away. In a flurry of low-voiced commands Carillon ordered the music and dancing begun again; the celebration would continue. Then he and Finn took their leave from the hall, and Donal slowly put his knife back into its sheath.

He turned, meaning to find a servant with wine, and nearly stumbled over Bronwyn who stood directly in his path. He caught her arms and steadied her, marking how pale she was.

Her hand went out to touch him. 'Donal – how do you fare?'

'Well,' he told her. 'Bronwyn – the thing is over now.'

Fingers locked on the blue enameled torque around her neck. 'The sword came so *close* –'

'I am well,' he repeated. 'Come, you had best go back to our *jehana*.'

But Bronwyn stood in place. 'Why does Carillon think it was *him* the assassin wanted?'

Donal frowned. 'It *was*, Bronwyn. Who else would such a man want?'

'You,' she said distinctly. 'Oh Donal . . . I saw how the man looked at you. Not at the Mujhar.' Her amber eyes began to fill with tears. 'It was *you* he wanted, *rujho*. I swear – I saw it in his face.'

'Bronwyn –' He glanced past her toward the door through which Finn and Carillon had gone. 'Bronwyn – are you quite certain?'

'Aye.' Earrings flashed as she nodded her head. 'I danced with him, *rujho*. He asked me questions about you. I thought nothing of it – most people do not know you. But then he left me. He left the hall. And when he came back, he had a sword.'

Donal frowned. 'Were you not made suspicious by all the Solindishman's questions?'

She stared up into his face. 'But – Donal . . . he was a Homanan.'

He felt his blood turn to ice in his veins. The flesh rose up on his bones. 'Bronwyn – *are you certain?*'

'Aye,' she said. 'Oh Donal, I am *afraid* –'

No more than I am, rujholla. But he did not say it aloud. Instead, he looked for his new wife. 'Where is Aislinn?'

Bronwyn gestured. 'There – do you see her? Over in the corner.'

He saw her. He saw how she stood away from the crowd, as if she could not bear to be a part of it. Sapphires and silver glittered. In both hands she held a hammered goblet and raised it to her mouth. He saw her grimace of distaste once she had swallowed. But he could not say if it was the wine that caused it, or the failure of the assassin.

Aislinn . . . I think there are things between us to be settled.

Donal looked down at Bronwyn. 'Stay here, with the others. I think it is time I took my *cheysula* from the crowd.'

'But – what of the bedding ceremony?'

He smiled grimly. 'I think, tonight, it would be better Aislinn did without it.' But he did not say he intended more for Aislinn than a simple nuptial bedding.

213

He left his sister behind and smoothly worked his way through the crowd. The thought of dancing had fled his mind completely, though it was expected of the Prince and his princess. Somehow, the assassination attempt had ruined his taste for celebration.

As he reached her, Donal put out his hand and took the goblet out of hers. Aislinn stared at him in surprise. 'Do you want it? Or do you *need* it?' Suspicion made him cruel.

'What?'

He looked into her face. He saw pale pink underlying the pallor of her cheeks; the hectic glitter in her grey eyes. Sensuous eyes; he knew, for all she was still young, she had learned something of a woman's seductive ways from her incredibly seductive mother.

He reached out and caught one slender wrist. 'You tremble, Aislinn. For me or for your *jehan*?'

'I thought he could slay my father –'

'He did not want Carillon. The assassin was after *me*.'

'*You!* Why would he want *you*?'

Her surprise was sincere. He could not doubt it. It was less than flattering, perhaps – in an odd sort of way – that she would think him so insignificant a target, but he was relieved. He did not think the emotion was feigned.

'There are some men who might desire me dead,' he told her evenly; still appraising her reactions. 'Undoubtedly some women, as well; Electra, perhaps?' He saw how her color faded. 'Carillon ages. He will not hold the Lion forever. How better to wrest the throne from the proper line than by slaying the man who will inherit from the Mujhar?'

'Oh *gods*,' she said. 'Will it always be like this?'

That was not precisely the reaction he had expected, not if she were a part of the plot against him. 'I hope not,' he answered fervently. 'If *this* is what the rank entails –'

'You do not think you are up to it?' Her tone was very cool. In her silver and sapphires, she was more like her mother each moment.

214

'Well,' he said, 'I think Carillon will rule for years yet. By the time he is ready to relinquish the Lion, I *ought* to be up to the task.' He smiled at her blandly. 'You are hiding in the corner, Aislinn. Are you avoiding me?'

Color rushed into her face. Her wrist went stiff in his hand.

'Are you?' he asked in surprise.

'A – little. I have been told what to expect of the bedding ceremony.'

She sounded faintly disgusted as well as uncomfortable. He smiled. 'Aye. They will do all they can to discomfit bride and groom. A Homanan custom, I am told; in the clans, a woman moves into a warrior's pavilion, and that is that.'

'That is *all*?' Her grey eyes were huge. 'At this moment, I would prefer this were a Cheysuli ceremony.'

'Then we shall make it one.' He closed her hand within his own. 'Come with me. We will escape the predators.'

Arrangements had been made for them to share royal apartments on the floor above their separate personal chambers. No one attended them; even the corridor was deserted. Privacy was absolute. But Donal took care to lock the door anyway.

Aislinn stood at one of the narrow, glassless casements. He wondered what she saw, staring so fixedly out of the opening. Her back was to him, and he clearly saw the rigidness of tension in her spine.

She turned. The heavy girdle clashed. He heard the rattle of the sapphires in the thickness of her skirts.

The room was made of shadows. The draperied bed was a cavern full of promises. He could almost hear the whispered endearments, the sighs of lovers pleased.

Aislinn faced him in silence. The wash of light from a single candle touched her hair with gold. At her throat shone the silver torque with its weight of brilliant sapphire. 'I am – a little afraid.'

He leaned against the door so that the carved wood

215

pressed into his spine. He watched her, saying nothing. He could not, for the moment. He was taken too much by surprise. Somehow he had not expected the strong desire he was suddenly feeling.

For Aislinn? When there is Sorcha, who is everything to me?

Everything, perhaps. But for the moment there was also Aislinn.

Slowly, Aislinn moved away from the blackened casement. She went to a table. There was a flagon of wine and two gleaming goblets; a gift from the Atvian king. The bowls of the goblets were glass. The stems were wrought silver, flowing up around the bottom of each bowl in the shape of raven's wings. In the decanter, the wine was red as blood.

Aislinn filled the goblets, then offered one to Donal. 'Will you share the nuptial cup?'

He pressed himself off the door. He approached. He saw how her long nails curved around the wine-filled crystal. When he reached her, he put out his hands and closed them over hers.

'*Shansu*,' he said. 'Do you think I would hurt you, Aislinn?'

'You would never hurt me,' she answered clearly. 'I have seen the look in your eyes.' Unexpectedly, she smiled.

Donal, still clasping her hands and the goblet, lifted it toward her mouth. 'I hope the vintage is good.'

The rim was at her lips. Luminance flowed across her face. 'The cask was a gift from my mother.'

Abruptly, he jerked the goblet away. Wine splashed across them both, staining the pale blue silk of Aislinn's gown in a vivid blood-red gout. He felt the splatter on his arms, against his face. The wine was tepid, warm as blood; he nearly gagged on the heavy scent.

The goblet fell. It struck the carpet and shattered.

'Do you risk yourself as well?' he demanded.

'Risk? What risk? It was a *gift* –'

216

'To you? Or meant for me?'

Color flowed out of her face. Wine droplets glittered against the smooth flesh of one perfect cheek, then rolled down to splash against the gown. 'Do you forget, *husband*, that *I* was to drink as well?'

'No more than I forget you spent two years with that witch on the Crystal Isle,' he answered. 'How am I to know she did not dose you with the poison bit by bit each day, until you grew immune?'

'You *fool*!' she snapped. 'Do you think I would wish for your death?'

'I accuse you of nothing.' He could not, yet; there was no proof of complicity.

'Finn *tested* me!' she cried. 'You yourself were there. Am I not free of the taint of sorcery?'

'You have been tested.' That much he could give her.

'But you still distrust me.' The vivid hair curtained her face on either side. 'Do you not? Do you think the assassin was also my doing? Do you really believe I desire to slay you when all I *desire* is *you*?'

He took three steps, reached out, caught her wrist. He looked at the slim, delicate hand. He could see it again before his eyes: the creamy, gold-veined vault with all its marble *lir*, and the hands that held the torch meant to thrust him to his death.

'Aislinn,' he said, 'you frighten me. I know not what you will do.'

'You are a fool.' She said it without heat. 'A fool, to be afraid, when I would never slay you. I would slay anyone who *tried*. I love you, Donal.'

He believed her. In that moment, he was certain she told the truth. And Finn *had* tested her.

Silently, he unfastened torque and girdle. He left both in a spill of silver and sapphire across the dark wood of the table. And then he took her to the bed.

Slowly he untied the lacings of her gown, baring her smooth, pale, delicate back. As he touched her, her flesh responded.

Naked, she lay against the bedclothes. She watched him with the eyes of a woman desiring a man. And so he divested himself of his clothing and slipped into bed beside her. *Perhaps it will not be so ill-matched a union after all* . . .

But as he put a hand upon her breast, Aislinn screamed.

All he could think to do was clamp a hand over her mouth. But she lunged away from him before he could, scrambling to the farthest corner of the bed.

'*Aislinn* –' He got out of the bed at once, afraid he might frighten her further.

'Wolf.' She said it with cold precision. 'Your blood is the blood of a wolf – your hands the claws of a wolf – your face the *face* of a wolf – *do you think I will lie with you* –?'

He stared at her in horror and his flesh crawled.

Aislinn twitched. He saw an alteration in her eyes. Briefly, a cessation of hostility, replaced with bewilderment. But as he opened his mouth to say her name, she twitched again and the words spilled out of her mouth.

'Beast, not man . . . not a *human* man . . . she has told me – she has told me . . . she has said it would be like –'

'Aislinn, *no* –'

'She said you will take me as a wolf because you can take me no other way.' A shudder wracked her body. 'Donal? Donal? What is wrong? Donal?' One trembling hand covered her mouth. 'What is *wrong*?'

'Aislinn –' slowly he moved one step closer to the bed '– she has filled your head with lies –'

Aislinn's eyes were black. 'Wolf – *wolf* – no man . . . no man . . . demon *instead* – to take me as a *wolf* –'

'Aislinn, I *promise* you –'

'Donal –' She twitched. 'Do you think I will breed with *you*?'

He felt the trembling begin in himself. Facing her, he could not help it. She crouched, beastlike, against the tester of the bed, knees thrust up beneath her chin and one hand twisted into her brilliant hair. But her other hand

218

came up sharply and made the gesture against Cheysuli evil.

'*Beasssst*,' she hissed. '*I will bear you no demon children*!'

Before such fear and hatred, he was totally unmanned. All thoughts of bedding her, no matter how tender, fell utterly out of his mind. Staring at her, all he could see was Electra. Electra on the dais of the palace on the Crystal Isle, facing him defiantly:

'*No marriage is binding if it is not consummated*.'

'Aislinn,' he said, 'oh Aislinn, do you see what she has done?'

Tears were running down her face. 'Donal –? What is wrong? *What has she done to me* –?'

'She has *twisted* you –' But he stopped. Aislinn was beyond comprehension.

Sickened, Donal put on his leathers again. And then he turned back to her. 'Aislinn –'

'*I will not lie with a wolf!*'

Clumsily, Donal unlocked the door and went out. In the darkened corridor he stood, sickened and bereft, wanting only to lick the pain of injured pride. He thought at once of Sorcha, longing for the comfort of her arms. But he could not go to the Keep. Not on his wedding night.

A sound. He looked up sharply and saw movement in the shadows. He heard the sibilance of silk against the stone. His hand went at once to his knife. He half-drew it, then saw the shadows take on the form of a man and woman embracing. The sound became a feminine giggle.

After a moment, the couple moved closer yet, into the spill of torchlight. The man glanced up as he heard the slide and click of knife going back in its sheath. 'What – is it Donal? Have we disturbed the bride and groom?' Closer yet, and the man's identity was revealed.

'Evan.' Donal found he could say nothing more.

The Ellasian came onward, one arm slung around the woman. Donal did not know her, save to know she was Homanan. Evan apparently had given up his attraction to

women who were kin to royalty and had found a willing girl of noble birth. 'Do you tarry out *here* while your bride awaits? Or has she sent you away while she divests herself of her clothing.' Evan kissed the girl quickly, then grinned archly at Donal. And then the grin faded.

Evan kissed the girl again, more soundly, then patted her silken skirts. 'Go back,' he said, with only a hint of regret in his tone. 'I have business with the prince.'

Her protest died. She slewed her dark eyes in Donal's direction, then gathered up her skirts and hastened back along the corridor.

Evan faced Donal squarely. 'There is no need to speak. I have only to look at your face.' His sleepy blue eyes held nothing of humor in them. 'I know a remedy, my lord, if you will accompany me.'

Donal stirred at last. 'There is no remedy for this.'

'Ah, but there is. I promise you, there is.' Evan smiled. 'Will you show me the taverns of Mujhara?'

'*All* of them, Ellasian?'

Evan merely shrugged. 'As many as you can . . . and before the break of dawn.'

Slowly, Donal smiled. 'Let us set this city afire.'

16

The Cheysuli were not brawlers ordinarily. They were warriors, bred in adversity and trained to slay quickly and effortlessly in order to protect kin, clan and king. To fight for the sheer enjoyment of such things seemed utter foolishness. Yet Donal, who had imbibed so much harsh wine he no longer saw anything without a blurred halo surrounding it, found himself embroiled in the midst of a tavern brawl.

He did not precisely recall how it began. Merely that somehow he had discerned an insult to his person and his race, and that redress was necessary. He dimly recalled the offending man had gone down easily enough – and then everyone else in the common room joined in the affray.

He felt himself waver on his feet. Then a shoulder came against his spine and braced him. Without looking he knew, it was Evan, giving him what aid he could.

And I need it –

The tavern was a shambles. Groaning bodies sprawled under tables and fallen benches, counting bruises and fingering cuts. Other bodies, still limply strewn in corners of the room, did not move at all. Donal was dimly aware he and Evan had accounted for all the wreckage; the knowledge made him groggily happy. He was upholding the honor of his race.

The Ellasian fights like a Cheysuli . . . pity he must go home with Lachlan, now the marriage is made –

A great weight landed on him from behind. He folded beneath it, experiencing mild surprise as his face scraped

against the wine-stained boards of the plankwood floor. He struggled briefly, felt an arm wrenched behind his back and grunted with unexpected pain. Then he was jerked to his feet and held quite still by a powerful arm thrust around his throat.

Evan, he saw, was in a similar position. The foreign prince was bruised and bloodied, his face battered, but he was smiling. He did not appear unduly perturbed by the sudden cessation of the fight or that he was so easily contained.

'I will pay the damages,' he announced. 'There is no need to hold us for the watch.'

A short, squat man wearing the rough woolen tunic and breeches of a dalesman pushed his way through the wreckage and stopped before Donal. He was thickset, a common sort, with small brown eyes and a small, pursed mouth. The mouth formed his words oddly, twisted by his thick dalesman's dialect.

He stared up into Donal's battered face. 'Shapechangers be not welcome here.' He spat on Donal's boot.

Donal swallowed. 'I was,' he said, 'before the Homanans began to lose.'

Small brown piglet eyes, malignant and unblinking. 'Shaine the Mujhar put purge on your sort, shapechanger. Years ago, 'twas . . . and those of us'n here still be holdin' with't.'

Donal was dizzy and disoriented, but the mists were clearing from his head. He stared at the pig-eyed man in dazed amazement. 'Shaine is dead. *Carillon* is the Mujhar.'

'Demon-spawn,' the short man said clearly. 'Your kind'll be burnin' in the name of good an' clean Homanan gods, unspoiled by the foulness of shapechanger demons.'

Donal heard stunned disbelief in Evan's voice. 'You would slay a man because of *his race*?'

'Demons,' the man repeated, and spat again against the floor. Mucous fouled Donal's boot. 'I be Harbin, leader of these men. We all of us'n here be servin' the memory of the *rightful* Mujhar of Homana.'

222

'Shaine is *dead!*' Donal repeated. 'Carillon is in his place.'

'Carillon be a weaklin' king, bespelled by Cheysuli magic. We don't be followin' him.'

Donal became aware of the tension in the tavern. This was not some simple disagreement or mere displeasure over the outcome of the fight. Carefully he took a breath, feeling the arm press more tightly against his throat cutting off the indrawn breath. 'Carillon has declared the *qu'mahlin* ended. Do you slay me, you slay a man sworn to the Mujhar.'

Harbin stared up at him. Thick arms were crossed against his wool-clad chest; his heavy boots were planted firmly against the plankwood floor. 'Carillon be bespelled. He holds Homana because of that. Because of his masters, the shapechangers. E'en now he plots to be givin' the throne back into the hands – the *paws!* – of demon-spawn. Us'n be helpless to reach Carillon himsel', but can reach the Cheysuli.' His eyes shone in the candlelight. 'One at a time, us'n be slayin' them. Us'n begin with you.'

'No!' Evan cried. 'You know not whom you threaten!'

Harbin ignored him, staring fixedly at Donal. Then his lips stretched wide over strong yellowed teeth as his eyes took in the *lir*-bands, belt and circlet; the earring shining in black hair. 'You be, for all, a *wealthy* demon.' He jerked his head. 'Strip him of his gold!'

Donal struggled briefly, was contained, and had to stand stiffly as hands grabbed for belt and knife and circlet. But when they sought to pull the *lir*-gold from his arms and ears, it was Evan who shouted to them.

'*Look* at him! He is the Prince of Homana!'

Harbin's head snapped around on his neck. 'What folly you be speakin' at me, stranger?'

'He is Carillon's heir –' Evan grimaced as an arm nearly shut off his voice. 'He is your prince, you fool – he is *Donal of Homana* –'

Harbin looked back at Donal sharply. He motioned the

223

others away, save for the men that held him captive.

'Is it true?' a voice asked in belated discovery.

'Hold yon tongue!' Harbin snapped. He moved closer to Donal. His broad, stubbled face wore a scowl of consideration. 'Is't true? Be claimin' yersel our prince, you be? Carillon's own heir? You wear enow *gold* for it!' He laughed suddenly, harshly. 'Donal o' Homana, is't? Us'n caught us a prize *worth* the burnin'!'

'If he *is* the prince –' one man began.

'Hush'ee!' Harbin shouted. 'He be a shapechanger. See that beast-gold on his arms and in his ear? The mark of *demons* on him.' Harbin's breath came quickly and noisily. 'Must be burned for it. Must be sacrificed.'

'We can't burn him *here* –' another protested weakly.

The dalesman's piglet eyes narrowed as he picked at his yellowed teeth. 'No. But he can still be cut here, and the body taken away for proper offerin'.' He nodded. 'Aye, aye – no one be takin' notice of a drunken man carried out of a tavern in the middle of the night.' He spun around suddenly and faced Evan. 'You be fearin' for your *own* life, stranger? Nay. We be not *evil* men. We be burnin' only demons.'

Evan's mobile face was darkening with bruises. His mouth twisted as he sought to speak clearly. 'He is your *prince* –'

'There bein' the greater offerin'.' Harbin turned back, indicating a long wooden table still upright in the center of the common room. 'Lay him there, and pin him down. On his back, barin' his throat to the gods. We be makin' this sacrifice as our old'uns did.'

Donal felt fingers dig into his arms, broken and grimy nails scoring bare, vulnerable flesh. He bared his teeth at the closest man and saw him fall back in terror. But the others bore him to the table.

Fingers hooked into the heavy bands on either arm. He felt the nails cut as they twisted into his flesh. The *lir*-gold was forcibly dragged from his arms until he was naked without either band. But when a man set hand to the earring, Donal tried to jerk away.

224

'Lay him down!' Harbin shouted. 'Pin him to the wood!'

They threw him down and stretched him flat on his back. His shoulders smashed against the table as they pinned him with countless hands, forcing his head back so that it hung off the end of the tabletop.

His senses reeled. He heard Evan shouting. Frenziedly he lashed out with a booted foot, smashing at any flesh and bone he could reach, but they caught and held him, jerking his legs apart until he was spread-eagled and utterly helpless. Hands grasped at his hair and yanked down his head, baring his throat to the blackened roof beams.

Donal cried out hoarsely, unconsciously reverting to the Old Tongue of his race. He writhed on the table, straining to break free, but he was held too firmly.

Lir! he screamed. *Why did I leave you behind?* Blood welled into his mouth as he bit the inside of his cheek. *By the gods . . . I have slain* myself –

Harbin drew a shearing knife from his belt and approached, eyes fixed on the bared column of Donal's throat. Viewing the dalesman upside down, Donal saw only a face twisted by madness and the rising of the blade.

Gods . . . I should have stayed with Aislinn –

He opened his mouth to cry out a denial –

– *a wailing howl curled around the corners of the common room and echoed within the timbers of the roof.*

Then another came, closer still, and no man dared move.

The horn window smashed as the ruddy wolf leaped through and drove straight at Harbin, taking him in the throat. The knife fell as Harbin fell and the gurgling cry breaking out of his throat was the last sound he ever made.

A second man screamed as a striking bird of prey streaked in through the broken window and stooped, slicing with upraised talons at wide-open, staring eyes.

Rigid hands released rigid flesh. Donal, freed, came up from the table in a writhing twist. He stood atop the wood,

balanced above them all, breath hissing between his tight-locked teeth. He felt a terrific upsurge of rage and the tremendous backlash of fear. He loosed himself, summoning up the magic, and blurred before them all.

Men ran screaming from the tavern, stumbling over others as they fought to escape the nightmare. Some did not make it, for Evan had caught up a fallen sword and cut off several fleeing men, driving them into a corner where he held them.

Lorn, blood-spattered and ablaze with fury, released his third kill. He turned, seeking other prey. Taj, having raked the eyes from one man and sliced open the face of another, screamed from the rafters.

'Hold!' Evan shouted. 'Donal – it is *done*!'

Donal, locked in wolf-shape, heard the shout as a blur of sound, meaningless to him. He was caught up in the sheer lust for blood, snarling in ferocious joy as he stalked a man already bloodied from the encounter. Nails scratched against stained wood. Tail bristled. Hackles raised. Ears went flat against the sleek, savage, silver head.

'Donal,' Evan gasped breathlessly. 'There is no more need to fight. Look around you!'

The wolf moved away from the man who huddled pitifully against an overturned bench, crying and shaking. For a moment the wolf stared fixedly at the Ellasian, yellow man-eyes eerie and half-mad. But then he seemed to understand. The animal shape slid out of focus, blurring to leave a void in the air. Then Donal stood in its place. Blood ran from his mouth and painted his naked arms, but he was whole, and wholly human.

Four men had escaped. Evan held three against the wall. Five lay dead and two more badly wounded. Donal, standing in the middle of the tavern, shuddered once, and was still.

'Were I a vindictive man –' he said hoarsely: '– were I a man such as Harbin, I would order my *lir* to slay you all.'

Evan stared at him. 'Donal – don't. Do not besmirch your race and name.'

Donal pushed a forearm across his sweat-damp brow, shoving sticky hair aside. He left behind a smear of blood. 'Should I not? Should I let them go?' For a moment, he shut his burning eyes. 'Gods – what has happened here?' He opened his eyes again and looked around the tavern blankly. 'What madness infects Homana?'

'Donal,' Evan said.

He shook his head. 'No. I will not slay them. I will not besmirch my race and name.' Again, he pushed dampened hair from his battered face. 'But I will let them see what it is to be Cheysuli.' He moved toward the three men Evan held in the corner. 'Step away from them, Ellasian. This does not concern you.'

Evan, dropping the sword in a gesture of distaste, did as he was ordered. He moved to the broken window and watched as Donal paced slowly closer to the men. He held them with only his eyes, pinning them to the wall.

'We claim three gifts,' he told them clearly. 'One is the gift of *lir*-shape, which you call the shapechange. A second is that of healing, which you refuse to believe, believing instead we are demon-spawn and evil. And the third, the final gift, is truly terrible.' Donal drew in an unsteady breath. 'It gives us the power to force a man's will, to replace it with our own. It is the gift of *compulsion*.' His voice was a whiplash of sound. '*Look at me.*'

They looked. They could do nothing else.

Donal held them all. 'Take your wounded and care for them. Tell your women and children what you have done this night, and what you meant to do, and what both things have earned you. And know that you will never again lay hands upon a Cheysuli with ill intent.' He stared at their blank, slack faces; their empty eyes. He had taken will and initiative from them, putting his own in the places left empty by his magic. The surge of anger within him was so powerful he wanted only to break them all, destroying their minds with a single, savage thought, but he did not. 'Go from here,' he said thickly, and turned away to lean against the table that had nearly been his bier.

227

The men gathered up their dead, their wounded. one by one, and carried them from the tavern. When they were done, leaving Donal alone with Evan and the *lir*, he set a hand to his aching head. 'Now – you have seen what it is to be Cheysuli.'

Evan, slowly sitting down on a righted stool, nodded. 'I have seen it.'

'And do Lachlan's lays exaggerate?'

'No.' Evan smiled faintly. 'I think even Lachlan cannot capture what it is to see a man shift his shape into that of an animal. But I think also the magic exacts a price from the men who know it fully.'

Donal bent down. He gathered up the fallen *lir*-bands. In his hands, the gold seemed to recapture its luster. 'It – exacts a price,' Donal agreed. Carefully he slid both bands over his hands and up his forearms, until they rested in place above his elbows. 'I walked too close to the edge of madness.' Again he bent. He scooped up his belt, his knife, the golden circlet of his rank. And then, too weary to rise again, he sat down and leaned against the table.

Lorn came to him at once, pressing his muzzle against Donal's chest. Donal hung one bruised arm around the wolf's neck and hugged him briefly, putting his bloodied face against Lorn's ruddy head. Taj fluttered down from the rafter and settled on the table, pipping at Donal quietly.

'What do they say?' Evan asked.

'They wish me well,' Donal told him. 'They wish I might have kept myself from the encounter. They wish I had not seen fit to go out with an Ellasian princeling when I might have remained at Homana-Mujhar instead, and safe from such violence.' He smiled. 'They wish me nothing I do not already wish for myself.'

'*I* could not have said the evening would end like this!' Evan was clearly affronted. 'In Ellas, we do not have madmen out to sacrifice others for their blood.'

Donal draped the filigreed belt across one forearm as he propped the elbow across his knee. The rubies glowed

dully in the torch-lit room. Like blood. Like all the blood on his arms. Absently, he smeared it across his flesh and dulled the gold as well.'

'In Homana,' he said, 'we have two races vying for a single throne. A Cheysuli throne, once – we gave it up to the Homanans four hundred years ago. For peace. Because they feared our magic. And now, because of Shaine, they fear us again, and seek to usurp us.'

'You *will* be the king of Homana.'

Donal looked at the Ellasian. 'One day. One day, when Carillon is dead . . . and if *I* am still alive.'

'There will always be fools in the world, and madmen.' Evan indicated Harbin's body. 'You will have to cull them, Donal. Before they cull you.'

Donal rubbed the heel of his hand across his gritty eyes. 'Evan,' he said. 'Gods – I am weary unto death. What I have done this night is not lightly undertaken. I will pay the price for such sorcery.' He stared blearily at the Ellasian. 'Will you see to it I am brought safely home?'

'Of course,' Evan agreed, surprised. 'But why do you ask?'

Donal managed a final, sickly smile. Then he toppled sideways to the floor.

On the first day, he built a shelter out of saplings. He wove them together with vines. He took stones from the ground and made a firecairn in the center of the shelter. He lighted a fire and put herbs into the flames, until smoke rose up to fill the tiny shelter.

He stripped out of his leathers and folded them into a pile outside the shelter. He took off armbands and earrings, setting them on top of the piled clothing. Naked, lirless, alone, he entered and sat down, cross-legged, and allowed the smoke to cloak his body.

It grew warm within the shelter. Too warm. What flesh had first shrunk from the twilight chill now exuded sweat that formed in droplets and ran down sun-bronzed flesh to the earth. Breathing grew labored, and husky.

He did not close his eyes. Smoke entered them. Burned; burning, his eyes began to water. Tears coursed down his face to drip against his chest, where it joined the sheen of sweat that bathed his flesh.

He sat. He waited. When the herbs and wood burned away and the rocks of the cairn grew cool, still he waited. He did not eat. He did not sleep. He did not move at all.

On the second day, he stalked and slew a silver wolf. He drained the blood from the body, and then he smeared it onto his flesh from head to toe. It dried. Itched. Flaked. But he ignored it.

He ate raw the wolf's warm heart.

The taste was vile.

But he disregarded it.

On the third day, he bathed in a glass-black pool. He scraped blood and grime and smoke-stench from his flesh with heavy sand. Blood speckled up where he scraped too hard; his blood; that which was now cleansed as the flesh was cleansed, as the spirit was cleansed; that which made him Cheysuli.

He had sweated out the impurities from within.

He had slain his other self; devoured that which had nearly devoured him; renewed the self he had slain in the bloody christening ritual.

He was cleansed.

I'toshaa-ni.

'Five days,' Rowan said. 'You might have told the Myhar.'

Donal, holding Ian in his arms as he stood before his pavilion, met Rowan's eyes levelly. 'There was a thing I had to do.'

A muscle ticked in Rowan's jaw. 'You might have told the Mujhar,' he repeated implacably. 'The Ellasian prince came back telling a tale of near-murder and violence . . . and yet *you* see fit to leave the city without a word to anyone.'

'I saw fit.' As Ian squirmed, Donal set him down. The boy steadied himself against his father's leather-clad leg, then ran off to chase a new-fledged hawk as it tried to ride the wind.

Rowan held the reins of two horses. One of them was Donal's chestnut stallion. 'You have no choice,' he said.

'There is ever a choice, for me.' Donal did not smile. 'I did not flee, general. I did not run from Carillon's wrath. I came home to my Keep because there was a thing I had to do. A form of expiation.' His face still bore traces of the tavern beating, though most of the soreness had passed. '*I'toshaa-ni*, Rowan . . . or do your Homanan ways preclude you from comprehension?'

Dull color darkened Rowan's taut brown skin. For the briefest of moments Donal saw the general's tight-shut white teeth when his lips peeled back as if he could speak. But he did not. He merely pressed his lips together again tensely and held out the reins to the chestnut horse.

'I might prefer *lir*-shape,' Donal said quietly.

'Do you challenge me?' Rowan's voice gained emotion. There was anger in it, raw, rising anger. 'Do you challenge *me*?' He cut off the beginnings of Donal's answer with a sharp gesture. A Cheysuli gesture, quite rude, demanding the silence of another. 'Aye, I know what you do, *my lord*. You look down from your Cheysuli pride and arrogance and count me an ignorant man. Unblessed, am I? – a man without a *lir*? Do you think I do not know? Do you think I do not *feel* your opinion of me?' Rowan stared at Donal with a predator's challenge; with the unwavering stare of a dominant wolf facing a younger cub wishing to fight for the rule of the pack. '*Lirless* I may be, Donal, but – *by the gods!*– I am Carillon's man! What I do, I do for Homana. You would be better to think of me as someone who means you well, rather than your keeper.'

Resentment rose up in Donal's belly. But also guilt, and a tinge of honest regret. Mutely, he took the reins from Rowan's hands. 'I was in need of cleansing,' he said in low voice. 'Rowan – I needed *i'toshaa-ni*.'

'No doubt you will need it twice or thrice before this war is done.' Rowan swung up on his horse, pulling his crimson cloak into place across the glossy rump of his tall white stallion. He looked down upon Donal, and his face was very grim. 'Carillon has no more time for the follies of youth in his heir. And neither, I think, do I.'

'*You!*' Donal mounted and spun his horse to face Rowan squarely. 'You are not of my clan – my kin – you are not even a proper warrior. Aye, I look down on you from Cheysuli arrogance – how can I not? You are a *lirless* man, and yet you live. You live, while the *lir* you might have had is dead all these long, long years.'

'Would you rather have *me* dead?' Rowan's hand caught the reins of Donal's horse. 'By the gods, boy, you may be Duncan's son, but you have none of his sensitivity. I hear more of *Finn* in you – too quick to judge another man by what feelings are in yourself.' Still he held the fretting stallion. Dust rose into the air. 'Do you think I feel nothing? Do you consider me little more than Carillon's puppet, titled out of courtesy?' Rowan's lips drew back. '*Ku'reshtin!* – you should know better. I *earned* what rank I hold, which is more than you can claim. *No* –' Again, the sharp gesture cut Donal off. 'I was born, as you were, to the clan. But Shaine's *qu'mahlin* raged, and my life was endangered the moment I drew breath. My kin, in running, were slain, and I was left to the Ellasians who found me. Am I less a man for that? Am I less a man because I claim no *lir*?' His eyes held Donal's without flinching. 'Less a *warrior*, aye, as you would count a warrior – but not less a *man* than you. I am what I have made myself. And I am content with that.' For a moment, his hand tightened on the reins of Donal's horse. 'Homanan puppet, some men call me. But what will they call you? *You* claim the Homanan blood . . . while I am *all* Cheysuli.'

Donal glared. 'I claim nothing but the favor of the gods.'

Rowan laughed. The sound rang out raucously, and he

threw the leather rein back at Donal. 'Do you, now? Are you better, then, than others?' But he stopped laughing. The ironic humor left his voice. Donal saw the tautness in Rowan's mouth and heard the too-smooth note of elaborate condescension in his tone. 'And does your divinity preclude you from lying with your wife?'

Donal felt his breath flow out of his chest. He stared back and saw minute disgust in Rowan's eyes.

Disgust . . . with me . . . 'What has Aislinn said?'

Rowan shrugged with studied negligence and gathered in his reins. 'You will have to ask *that* of Carillon.'

'Then let us do it.' Donal set heels to his horse. 'By the gods, *let us do it –*'

17

Carillon sat in his favorite private solar, soft-booted feet propped up on a three-legged footstool and torso slumped back into the depths of a padded velvet chair. In his hands he cradled a goblet of pale yellow wine; he nursed it, sipping almost absently. A fresh flagon sat on the table beside the chair.

Donal, facing him, felt impatience rise. He had sought out the Mujhar and confronted him, demanding to know what Aislinn had said of their failed wedding night. Carillon had said nothing, merely waving him into silence as if he must think things over. And so Donal waited.

Taj perched atop the high back of a second chair; Lorn, sleepy-eyed, slumped loosely against the stones in front of the fireplace. Neither offered comment: Donal thought they, like he, waited.

Carillon stared fixedly into the half-gone goblet of pale sweet wine, as if he dreamed. Donal thought he looked lost somehow, elsewhere entirely; there was a slackness about his spirit, a lessening of the intensity Donal had always known in him. But after a moment he stirred. 'I am told you left Aislinn to seek entertainments with Lachlan's brother; that you embroiled yourself in a brawl that quickly became more than a misunderstanding. Evan says you are fortunate to be alive.'

'Aye.' Donal controlled his voice with effort. 'I am – fortunate. But I left Aislinn because she would not have me lie with her. There were – impediments.'

'Impediments?' Carillon straightened in his chair. One

hand gripped the goblet, the other clenched on the knobbed end of the wooden chair arm. 'If you speak of a young bride's natural modesty, you should know that a caring husband can overcome *impediments* such as that.' He did not smile. 'You and Sorcha were quite young when first you lay together. And yet you managed it. Why could you not manage this?'

Donal felt the coil of distaste and embarrassment tighten within his belly. 'She would not have it,' he said quietly. 'She swore she would not have it. There were – words of insult. Words meant to hurt, to unman me – and they did.' Donal looked straight at the Mujhar. 'What I heard were Electra's thoughts, Electra's words in Aislinn's mouth, and I refuse to lie with *her*.'

Carillon sat forward in the chair, hunching, both hands clutching the goblet. 'Electra,' he said hoarsely. '*By the gods,* I wish that woman were dead!'

Donal moved forward. 'But she is not,' he said evenly. 'She is alive, and well, and no doubt abetting Tynstar as he seeks to attack Homana.' He paused before the Mujhar, a man grown old before his time, and aging too quickly even now. 'But – she is also here, my lord . . . within your daughter's mind. And while she dwells there, there will be no heirs to the Lion Throne.'

For just a moment, the twisted hands on the goblet shook. Wine spilled, splashing against the soft leather of Carillon's boots. 'And so they shall win this realm because there are no children of my daughter and her husband,' he said. 'War becomes – incidental. Unnecessary, somehow. Because they can destroy us another way.' Carillon drank. He tossed back the wine as if it were water, then poured a second goblet. But this time he only stared into it, his face lined with bitterness and regret.

And then he looked at Donal. 'Can you not shut her away? Shut her out of Aislinn's mind?'

Donal shrugged. 'She is the parasite and Aislinn is the host. A rapacious parasite . . . and a fragile, erratic host.'

Carillon sighed and shut his eyes. For a long moment he

235

kept himself in silence. Then, 'Name me a monster, if you will, but I must bid you to use force. Use the power I know you have.'

Donal stared at him in shock. 'You would have me force your daughter?'

'Not *rape*.' Carillon shook his head. 'No, never that. Use the third gift. *Compel* her to lie with you. I know you will not harm her.' He pushed himelf out of the chair. 'Poor Aislinn – it is not her choosing, what Electra has done to her. She has become a valuable gamepiece, a gamepiece which Electra can use to raze the House of Homana. She *infests* Aislinn now, so that against her will Aislinn heeds what Electra intends, even to attempting murder.' He ran twisted fingers through the heavily silvered hair. 'But one way of making certain Electra does not succeed is to overcome her with magic stronger than what she has learned from Tynstar.'

'It is *force*,' Donal said. 'Kin to rape, or worse – you ask me to take her will from her and replace it with my own.'

Carillon set the goblet down on the table and moved slowly to one of the sun-drenched casements. He stared out, but Donal thought he saw nothing. 'It is not force if it be replaced with willingness.'

Donal crossed to the table and picked up Carillon's goblet, meaning to wash the foul taste from his mouth with a swallow of sweetened wine. But the Mujhar, turning back, saw it. 'No!' he said sharply, crossing to catch the goblet from Donal's hand. 'No – I am sorry . . . it is my favorite, and the cask is nearly empty. Until more is delivered, I am limited to a single goblet each night . . . and I am a selfish man.' Carillon smiled. 'I think you might do better to keep yourself from wine this night and think of what awaits you in your bed.'

Donal shook his head. 'I have no taste for this.'

'I do not ask you to *have taste*,' Carillon said raggedly. 'I ask only that you perform a service any man should be ready and willing to perform.'

236

'Ready and willing!' Donal threw at him. 'This is your *daughter*, Carillon . . . not some silly chambermaid!'

'Do you think I do not know?' Carillon shouted back. His voice shook a little, and Donal saw the anguish in the depths of the fading blue eyes. 'Ah gods, would that I had never married the woman, so this would not be necessary. *Would that I had wed someone else* –' He broke off. Tears shone in his eyes. 'They warned me. Finn, mostly. And Duncan. Even Alix and my sister. *Do not wed Electra,* they said, *she is Tynstar's meijha and will only seek to slay you.* Oh, aye, they had the right of it . . . and now I pay the price.'

Donal drew in a deep breath, knowing somehow he had to offer comfort to the man. 'You took her for the alliance between Homana and Solinde. You have spent these past fifteen years teaching me the rudiments of kingcraft – I think I understand at least a little of it. You wed her because you had to.'

'Had to?' Carillon's twisted smile was bittersweet. 'Oh, aye – I had to. For the alliance . . . but something else as well.' He stared into the goblet. 'Aye . . . there was sorcery and witchcraft, but much more to the woman than that. She was – unlike any other I had ever known. Even now. And – I think I even loved her . . . for a little while.' Slowly, he lifted the recaptured goblet and drank down what remained of the pale, sweet wine. 'Do what you must,' he said at last. 'But be gentle with her, Donal.'

Looking at him, Donal felt a chill of apprehension run down the length of his spine. *Gods . . . grant me health, grant me the kindness of* never *putting such choices before me.*

He waited until it was very late and most of the servants were abed. Then, telling his *lir* to remain in his chamber, he went down the corridor to Aislinn's suite of apartments, and pushed open the heavy door.

He had half expected it to be locked. But perhaps Aislinn, knowing her actions had driven him into the city

streets and then to Sorcha in the Keep, thought he would not return to her. And so his way was unimpeded as he entered the darkened chamber.

One candle burned in the far corner. Donal had never understood the Homana penchant for leaving candles lit when sleep was sought; if there were demons sent to catch a man, a candle would not stop them. And if it were meant to ward off mortal enemies, the light destroyed night vision and left the victim more vulnerable than ever.

But he did not blow it out. He wanted Aislinn to know him when she saw him.

Noiselessly he walked to her draperied bed. He could see nothing through the sheen of silk and gauze. But he could hear her breathing.

Gods . . . does Carillon know what he asks? But he knew the Mujhar did.

Quickly Donal shed boots and leathers. Naked, he stripped aside the draperies, prepared to slip into the bed –

– and found Aislinn waiting for him, kneeling amid the folds of the coverlet.

In the shadows of the curtained bed, her eyes were blackened hollows. Dim candlelight threaded its way through the draperies and burnished bronze her red-gold hair. She wore a thin silken nightshift; nothing else, except her pride.

'You knew,' he said.

'I knew. No one told me, but – I knew.' She drew in an uneven breath. 'All my life I have been brought up to know my task in this world is to bear children for my lord. All my life I have known my first-born son would become Mujhar in his father's place, as *you* will when mine is dead. Well . . . there will be no son if I do not lie with you.'

She was frightened even as she smiled a wry little smile, stating the obvious; that much he could tell. But frightened of *herself*, not of him. 'It is not *you*, Aislinn,' he told her. 'It is what that witch has done to you.'

She swallowed visibly. 'I know it. But – knowing it does not undo what she has done.'

Gently, he asked, 'You know what *I* must do?'

Aislinn briefly shut her eyes. '*Gods,* Donal – I would trade almost anything to make this bedding pleasurable for us both! Do you think I *wish* to spew such vileness from my mouth?' Her fingers were locked into the neckline of her nightshift, twisting at the fabric. 'For as long as I can remember, you were the man I wanted. Even as children. I knew I could go to you for anything. And now – *now*, when I can have you – I drive you instead to *her*.'

Her. Aislinn knew very well what competition Sorcha offered. And yet he did not, for the moment, see jealousy in her face. Only dashed hopes and forlorn self-hatred, because Aislinn blamed herself.

He nearly put out his hands to reach for her, to touch her hair, to stroke her shoulders, but he stopped himself. 'Aislinn,' he said gently, 'if there were another way I would seek it. I have no taste for this.'

She nodded. And then her eyes beseeched him. 'Do you think – it is possible whatever my mother did to me has faded? Perhaps – perhaps it was meant only for the wedding night.'

'Perhaps.' He knew better – she grasped at straws – but said nothing of it. 'Aislinn – come and sit beside me.' He himself sat down on the edge of the bed, knowing the posture was unthreatening. And after a moment, she did as he had bidden.

She laughed an odd little laugh. 'I feel like a fool. Like an untried girl, nervous before her lord.'

'Are you not?'

She sighed. 'I am. Donal –' She stopped short, glancing sideways at his nudity, her eyes dark with passion and fear. Tentatively, she put up a hand and touched the *lir*-gold on his arm. 'Do you never take it off?'

'Rarely. It is a part of me.' He let her touch the gold, knowing the motion took more than a little courage.

Her fingers explored the armband. 'I see Taj and Lorn in the patterns,' Aislinn said. 'The crafsmanship is superb – I have seen many fine gifts offered to my father,

239

but none, I think, so fine as Cheysuli *lir*-gold. The knife he wears –'

'Finn's, once. They exchanged knives when they swore the oath of liege man and Mujhar.'

'And broke it.' Aislinn shook her head a little. 'What I know of Finn and what I am *told* are two different things. All those stories . . . and yet, he is different from what is said. It seems odd, to know a man, and yet realize others know him differently from the years before I was born.'

Donal thought of his father. He had been told countless stories of Alix, Finn, Carillon and others about Duncan. So many of those stories dated from before his birth, even before his mother and father had married, Cheysuli-fashion. For many years he had treasured the tales, storing them away in the sacred trunk of memory, cherishing all the contents. And now Tynstar had smashed that trunk, destroying the memories.

'I remember when you were born.' He did, though not well. But perhaps it was time they began to fashion their own memories for the future. 'There was rejoicing throughout Homana, that the Queen had been delivered to a healthy child.' He did not say how that rejoicing had been tempered with disappointment; Homana had needed a son.

Her fingers had left the gold to touch his arm. Now she withdrew them. 'The *Queen*.' Aislinn's mouth twisted. 'When men speak of the Queen, they link her name with Tynstar. Not with Carillon, who wed her and *made* her Queen of Homana. *No.* With that vile, wretched Ihlini!' Bitterness balled her hands into fists. 'I wish – I wish he were dead! I wish someone would slay him!'

'Someone will, someday.' No longer did she seem intimidated by his nudity. 'Aislinn –'

She did not let him finish, turning instead to face him squarely. Hesitantly, she reached out both hands to touch his shoulders, closing fingers on the muscles. 'I want it. I want *you* – I have *always* wanted you.'

Donal did what he had desired since he first pulled back

the draperies. He set his hands into her hair and threaded persuasive fingers, tugging her closer to him. For him, at that moment, Sorcha receded; his present was only Aislinn.

'Gods . . .' She breathed it against his mouth. 'No one said I would feel like *this* –'

'Who could?' he asked. 'Electra? You see what she has done.

'My mother is a fool –' Aislinn was in his arms, twisting shoulders free of her garment to press her bare flesh against his. 'My mother –'

He felt her body abruptly go rigid beneath his hands. 'Aislinn –?' But even as he said her name, he knew what was happening.

'No!' she cried. 'No, *no* –' The shudder wracked her body. Donal saw her head arch back, back, until her throat was bared to him and her hair spilled down against the tangled sheets. The sound she made was one of terror mixed with madness.

'No more!' he hissed. 'By all the gods of the Firstborn, I will *not* let Electra win –!'

A physical link was not necessary, but he sought it anyway. Aislinn, utterly limp in his arms, lay on her back against the bed. He knelt over her, sinking hands through her hair to cup each delicate temple. He felt the pulse-beat beneath the flesh, against the palm of his hands.

'Not this time,' he said grimly. 'Not *this* time, Solindish witch –'

But what Electra had done was not easily broken. Donal met resistence as he sought a way through the barriers to Aislinn's subconscious. Something battered back at him, trying to throw him away. Instantly he threw up his own shields and advanced, gritting his teeth against the intensity of Electra's spell.

'Aislinn . . . *fight* her . . . fight *Electra* – not me!'

But Aislinn was too lost within the ensorcelment. She fought him mentally and physically, sweating and crying in her efforts.

241

He would lose. And by losing, lose Aislinn entirely. He could not see any way to win without risking Aislinn's welfare.

The witch set her trap very well indeed . . . if she does not catch me in it, she may well catch her daugher –

And then he realized there *was* a way to win. It was not fair. He risked Aislinn even as Electra risked her, but if he did not try, she was lost without a fight of any sort. Donal thought she was worth more than that. And so he sought the essence of the shapechange.

He would not change before the girl – did not *dare* to, when that was Electra's key – but he could use a measure of the concentration *lir*-shape required. It was honed sharp as any blade, but offering danger to Aislinn as well as himself. It was a matter of balance again. In such circumstances as these, he could tip over the edge so easily.

Donal summoned up the strength. And without warning the helpless girl, he tore through her mental barriers and forced his will upon hers.

He had told Carillon it was tantamount to rape. Donal knew only that as he forced his will upon the girl, he forced more than mental persuasion.

And yet, even as he fought to win Aislinn back from her mother and the Ihlini, Donal became dimly aware of a part of himself that *understood* the need for compulsion. A part of him knew physical release as well as mental was required, since he sought consummation as a result of forcing her will, and not just persuasion. With a man, there was no question it was merely a mental rape. The compulsion was never sexual. But with a woman, with *Aislinn*, whom he desired anyway, the compulsion was linked with intensifying need.

Perversion? He thought not. But – would he think it *was* while lost in the power of such overwhelming desire?

Man, not wolf . . . man, not falcon . . . And yet he knew, as he slid closer to the edge, it would not be difficult to shift into either form. It was possible he might mimic the being his father had been, neither one nor the other; a *thing* caught between.

242

He felt a wild rage building up inside of him. Not at Aislinn. But at Electra. At Tynstar. For using an innocent, vulnerable girl as bait to trap a Cheysuli. For setting up the obscene circumstances that required such violence.

For turning him into an animal, even in human form.

Will they never stop? Will they never give up their abuse of human beings?

Distantly, he heard Aislinn crying out. So near the edge, *too* near the edge; he silenced her with the only gag he had left; his mouth.

Aislinn, I swear . . . I never wanted it this way. . . . And until the night of their wedding, Donal had not believed he wanted it at all.

Now he knew he had wanted it longer than he cared to acknowledge. He recalled clearly the young woman who had met him on the Crystal Isle: haughty, defiant princess; later, vulnerable, frightened girl. An assassin as well, but it was yet another facet of her being. She was neither the complaisant, spiritless woman so many Homanans were, nor the cold, powerful sorceress Electra had made of herself. Aislinn was merely – Aislinn. And in their mutual battle against her mother, each sought release whatever way they could find it.

Sul'harai. He did not know the Homanan word for the concept. He only knew that with Sorcha, the experience was familiar. The simultaneous sharing of the magic in their union. Not one-sided. That was easy enough for a woman; easier for a man. Simultaneous. And now, he found he wanted it as much with Aislinn.

'I *will* win, Electra –' And with the strength of the *lir*-bond, Donal smashed all of Aislinn's barriers and left nothing in his wake, emptying her resistance like a seedbag spilling grain.

And as she lay empty before him physically and emotionally, he replaced the abhorrence Electra had put there with a terrible need for him.

Not rape . . . not rape, if she wants me as I want her –

But he realized, as she roused to his hands and his

mouth, the compromise was a curse as well as a blessing. Because if the time came Aislinn ever turned to him out of *genuine* affection, he would never know it.

At dawn, Donal stood at the edge of the oubliette. One torch roared against the silences of the vault. Light rushed across the creamy, gold-veined marble, and the *lir* leaped out at him.

He teetered. Closed his eyes. *Oh gods, what have I done – what have I done to the girl –?*

The torch roared. Everything else was silence.

Except for his screaming conscience.

Remorse? That, and worse. Yet he welcomed the guilt, the anger, the horror; the sickness that turned his belly. It meant he was a man after all, not a beast; not a *thing* who took and was pleased by the taking, not caring *how* it was taken or who was hurt. When she awakened Aislinn would recall only a part of what had happened, because the compulsion worked that way, but *he* would know it all. He would remember everything.

See what I have become?

He stared down into the void. It was not death he sought; not suicide. Not a form of expiation, to pay for the loss of his soul. He had no wish to die regardless of the reason. Suicide was taboo; he was too much a warrior to consider denying himself the afterworld. But he wanted a way of assuaging some of the *pain*.

'My lord –?'

Donal spun at the brink of the void. He was reminded suddenly of the other time he had visited the Womb, and how someone had tried to push him in. Memory flared; he threw up an arm against the assassin.

'*My lord*!' Sef's voice, and shocked. Memory faded; Donal saw the boy standing just inside the open door. His odd eyes were stretched wide in fear. 'You do not mean to *jump* –'

'No.' The weight of the Womb was at his back, begging him to give himself to the *Jehana*. 'No, Sef – I do not

mean to jump.' Donal felt sweat sting his armpits; he smelled the fear on himself. No, he had not meant to jump, and yet he had come close to it regardless. 'What are you doing here?'

He said it more sharply than he intended. Sef's face blanched white. 'I – couldn't sleep. Bevin had a girl with him, and –' He broke off, plainly embarrassed. Sharing a room with Bevin meant sharing a room with many women as well. 'I – went out to walk. I – went to the Great Hall, to see the Lion sleeping.' Color washed back into his face. 'There was a stairway in the firepit, and so I came down to see where it went.' He looked sidelong at the walls with their leaping *lir*. 'What *is* this place, my lord?'

'The Womb of the Earth.' Donal saw no sense in secrecy, not when the boy had seen it himself. 'Cheysuli made it long, long ago. Legends say a man who will be Mujhar must go back into the Womb to be reborn a king.'

'Have *you*?'

'Gone in? – no. For me, I think there is no need.' He did not pursue it further. For Carillon, the rebirth had been required; for a man born to the clans with the gifts of the Old Blood, there were other initiations.

Sef stared around the vault. 'So many animals . . . they look so alive.'

'They are not. At least – not now,' Donal frowned a little. Who was to say the *lir* had never been alive? Perhaps they only waited for the Firstborn to come again before they broke free of the stone.

Donal shivered. And Sef, staring at the oubliette again, mimicked him unconsciously. 'My lord – this place frightens me.'

'Then let us leave it together. There is nothing more for me here.' Donal took the torch from the bracket. 'Come, Sef. I think it is time you learned some geography.'

'My lord?' Sef stared.

'Maps. If you cannot sleep, look at maps. It is better than counting trees.'

He led Sef out of the vault and back up the one hundred

and two steps to the Great Hall with its sleeping Lion. Donal shut the hinged plate and kicked ash and logs back over the iron to hide it. Then he took Sef to one of Carillon's council chambers. Donal set the torch into an empty bracket, selected the appropriate map and spread it out on the table, then lighted the fat white candle. He touched a blue-shaded portion of the map. 'There. That is Solinde.'

'*All* of that?' Sef stood next to the stool upon which Donal sat. The boy stared avidly at the map, hands clasped behind his back, afraid to touch the valuable hide.

'All of this, aye.' Donal's finger swept around the blue borders of the realm. 'Lestra is here, you see . . . the city, at the moment, is loyal; but much of the aristocracy is not – these men want to sever the alliance between Homana and Solinde, to claim the land their own.'

'But – don't they also want Homana?'

Donal glanced at the boy as he hung over the map. '*Tynstar* wants Homana. The Mujhar believes the Solindish aristocracy would be content enough to ignore Homana, given Solinde again – but under Tynstar's dominion, they give tacit approval to the war. The armies will ride against us while Tynstar, as ever, watches from a distance.'

'Then – Solinde isn't really your enemy,' Sef said. 'It's the sorcerer, isn't it?'

Donal sighed, smiling wryly. 'You ask things I am not fit to answer. These are questions with historical implications – being clan-born and bred, I know more of the Cheysuli than the Homanans. But I can tell you this much: for years upon years, Solinde – under Bellam – fought to take Homana. Bellam, being an acquisitive man, wanted Homana for himself. But I do not doubt Tynstar blew a fire from the embers with exceedingly careful breaths.' Idly, Donal rested his chin in the palm of one hand. 'Bellam is dead now and Carillon holds both realms – but I doubt the Ihlini will ever give up entirely. They will ever be our bane.'

Sef frowned, screwing his pale face into an expression of concentration. 'Then – if you slew the demon, Tynstar – we would be free of this war?'

'Perhaps not entirely, but I do not doubt Tynstar's death would have great effect on Solinde. In time, did he die, the traditional enemies might make a lasting peace.'

Sef straightened from his hunched position over the table. 'Then – why not send someone to slay him?'

'Tynstar?' A wry smile that twisted Donal's mouth. 'Could *that* be done, it would have been long ago.'

'But – he's a *man*, isn't he? A sorcerer, aye – but a man. Can't he die like others?'

Donal regarded the boy's intensity. 'Tynstar is a man, of course, and no doubt he can die. But he has escaped death for three hundred years – it will never be easily done.'

Self blanched. '*Three hundred years* –?'

'He has the gift of immortal life from Asar-Suti himself.'

'*Gods* –' Sef whispered. 'How will we ever win?'

'With my help, it will hardly prove so difficult.' Evan of Ellas, striding through the open door, grinned at them both. 'I am coming with you.'

Donal stared at him in shock. 'I thought you had gone home to Ellas! After that tavern brawl –'

'*That* brawl?' Evan asked nonchalantly. 'I have seen worse in a brothel. No, I have not gone home to Ellas. Not yet. I prefer to stay here a bit.'

'To come to war.' Donal shook his head. 'A foolish way to pass the time, Evan. Ellas has no stake in this. If she lost a prince –'

'She has seven others, if you count Lachlan's sons.' Sleepy eyes alight, Evan shrugged negligently. 'I have neither wife nor sons – that I know of – with which to concern myself. I will come with you.'

Sef spoke up before Donal could. 'But what would the Crown Prince say?'

'Lachlan?' Evan's brows rose, though he looked a bit

surprised at Sef's presumption. But it was Donal he answered, not the boy. 'Lachlan knows he cannot gainsay me when I put my mind to a thing.' He grinned. 'You need my help, Donal. You may as well admit it.'

'It isn't Ellas's war,' Sef said.

Donal glanced sharply at the boy. Sef stood stiffly by the table, facing Evan squarely. His chin was thrust upward, as if he prepared to do battle. 'Sef. This is better left to the Prince of Ellas and me. You may go.'

Sef stared fiercely at Evan a moment, then abruptly turned to Donal. 'Aye, my lord. But –' He broke off and shrugged. 'I just – I just want to come with you.'

'And you think I will not take you if the Prince of Ellas comes?' Donal shook his head. 'Sef, I have already said you may go to war with me – though I do not understand why you would *want* to, any more than I understand *him*.' His glance included Evan. 'You may come. *Now* – you may go.'

Sef went. Donal shook his head and Evan, staring after the boy, merely sighed a little and shrugged. 'He worships you, Donal. I think he would give his life for you.'

'So long as he does not have to.' Donal looked at Evan and began to smile. With the Ellasian prince he felt a weight lifting from his soul. Before Evan, he was free to be the man he so seldom had been able to be. 'I think we will show Solinde how two princes can force a realm to its knees.'

Evan raised one dark eyebrow. 'If we can destroy a single tavern, we should surely have no difficulty with an entire kingdom.'

18

When the Homanan army marched at last across the western borders into Solinde, it met with little resistance. Carillon took care to distinguish between Solindish crofters and citizens who had no stake in the battle beyond trying to survive while their realm was battered by war, and those who supported Tynstar. Much of the realm still served Carillon's interests, albeit reluctantly. Still, the tension was apparent from the moment they crossed the border.

The Cheysuli moved within the ranks independently, under the command of their clan-leaders who dealt directly with Carillon. Donal, who had grown up in the aftermath of Shaine's *qu'mahlin*, had known only a grudging peace between the two races. The incident in the tavern – compounded by recollections of his reception in Hondarth and the reaction to his wedding – served to remind him that the restoration of his race was hardly completed.

He found that most of the soldiers accepted the Cheysuli readily enough – the races had fought together to help win Carillon his throne – but there was uneasiness within the ranks. It was Carillon who kept the peace. And Rowan, whose Homanan ways and Cheysuli appearance made him a man of both and neither races.

Evan proved an easy companion for Donal. Together they argued and debated and discussed all manner of strategy in all varieties of emotions, but always recognizing the bond of true friendship. A bond Donal

had never experienced before, being caught between his Homanan rank and Cheysuli warrior status, and he found it was one he valued greatly. It was not the same as the link with his *lir*, but it was very satisfying nonetheless.

Now, seated across the table from Carillon in the Mujhar's crimson field pavilion, Donal realized his present companion was somewhere else in spirit if not in body. Carillon, done with eating, sat back on his three-legged campstool. One hand cupped the footed silver goblet filled with his favorite wine.

It was mid-summer and temperate. An evening breeze rippled the brilliant fabric of the pavilion. Light from the setting sun crept through the weave of the fabric and splashed color into the interior, so that the blood wood of table and chairs was dyed a rich ocher-bronze. The silver shone golden in the light.

Donal smelled roasting boar, spitted in the center of the camp. He smelled the bouquet of Carillon's wine and a faint tinge of bitterness he ascribed to the coals in the brazier. He smelled the aroma of war, though they had barely met a soul in battle. He smelled death and futility, and the strivings of men who would spend their lives in defense of a throne they would never see, a throne that one day would be his.

Carillon slowly turned his goblet in circles on the wood. 'Where is Evan tonight? I invited both of you.'

Donal smiled. 'You recall those Solindish crofters' daughters who felt compelled to follow us? Evan found several more than willing to share their favors with him. He sends his regrets.'

Carillon laughed. 'I am glad one of us can lose his cares in a woman's flesh tonight.' Abruptly, he sat upright on his stool. 'Gods – I have forgotten! A message for you from Aislinn came earlier today – I put it aside and forgot it. There – in the small chest by my cot.'

Donal pushed back from the table and rose, going at once to the teak casket near the bed. Inside it he found a parchment scroll sealed with wax, stamped with the royal Homanan crest.

He broke the seal. He was afraid as well as curious; in the two months since the army had marched into Solinde, there had been no letters from Aislinn. There had been nothing but silence between them.

Donal read the message, then stared blankly at the lettering. 'She has – conceived.'

Carillon rose slowly to his feet. 'She is certain?'

'There has been confirmation.' Donal sucked in a deep breath. 'Well, my lord . . . forced or not, it seems to have succeeded.'

'Thank the gods,' Carillon said fervently 'the throne is secured at last.'

Donal shook his head. 'Only if the child is a boy.'

'You have already sired one – is it so foolish to think there may be another?' But Carillon turned away to pour more wine in his goblet, not bothering to wait for a response, though Donal offered none.

He watched Carillon drink. Of late the Mujhar drank more and more, no doubt to ease his pain. Even in the dry warmth of a Solindish summer, his swollen joints ached.

I could not bear it, Donal knew. *I swear – I could not bear it . . . and he leads us all to battle.*

He looked again at the message, penned in a wavering hand. From Aislinn herself, he did not doubt; a scribe would do it more carefully.

Gods, what is she thinking . . . what does she think of me? 'She says she is well,' he told Carillon. 'But – first births are often hard. With Sorcha –' He broke off abruptly, knowing it was not the time to speak of his *meijha*. But then he turned sharply to Carillon. Of late there had been a bond between them of mutual affection and circumstances. Donal recalled how Carillon had taught him to read a map and explained the battles he had fought with Finn at his side. But now, with the specter of Sorcha suddenly between them, he felt the faint tension rise up to mock them both. 'You hate me for that, do you not?' Donal asked. 'For keeping Sorcha when Aislinn is my *cheysula*.'

251

Carillon moved to one of the supple leather chairs and sat down slowly, lowering himself carefully into the seat. 'I have learned, over the years, to respect many Cheysuli customs. I admit I do not understand most of them, but I have learned what integrity there is in your race. Though, given a choice, I would prefer you set aside your *meijha* – for my daughter's sake – I will not ask it of you.'

'You did not answer my question.'

Carillon smiled. 'No, I did not. Well enough.' He shifted in the chair and drank more wine; the pale, sweet wine with its acidic bouquet, that Carillon allowed no one else to touch. 'I do not hate you, Donal. I kept myself to Electra when we were together because I desired no other – she would inspire fidelity in any man, regardless of his tastes . . . but it does not mean I cannot comprehend your ability to wed one woman and keep another as well.' He gazed into the brazier coals. 'For all that, I am the *last* to speak of such things as a man desiring only one woman when there is another one he cares for. The gods know I wanted your mother badly enough, even when both of us were wed to other people.' There was pain in his voice as he said it, immense pain; he had taken the news of Alix's death very badly.

Donal's hand closed spasmodically on the parchment, crumpling it into ruin. 'My *jehana* –?'

Carillon turned. In his eyes was an arrested expression. 'Did she never tell you?'

'My *jehana*?' It was all Donal could manage.

Carillon sighed heavily and rubbed his eyes. 'An old story, Donal. . . . I thought surely you must know it by now.' Twisted fingers scraped silver hair back from his pain-wracked face. 'Gods – I cannot believe she is *gone*. Not *Alix*. After all she has been to me . . . after all she has done. . . .'

And my jehan? Donal wanted to ask. *You say nothing of my jehan. Is it that even in death you compete?*

Aloud, Donal said, 'What old story, my lord?'

Carillon shook his head after a moment. 'I never stopped

caring for her, Donal, even after she wed your father. Even after she had borne you.' He swirled wine in his goblet. 'I wed Electra. And when that marriage was finished, I turned again to your mother.'

Possessiveness overruled Donal's empathy. 'Even while she was Duncan's *cheysula* –?'

'No.' Carillon looked at him. 'Your father was already *lirless*. Dead – or so we believed.' Carillon's brow furrowed a little, as if reflecting a measure of his grief. 'The day I took you and your mother back to the Keep, I asked her to marry me. I would have made her Queen.'

My jehana, the Queen of Homana – But the wonderment did not last. 'She wanted no one but my *jehan*.' He said it a trifle cruelly, but he felt threatened by Carillon's admission. For so many years he had known how deeply his parents had loved one another, and how deeply Alix grieved for Duncan. Now, to think of her wed to Carillon – 'No,' Donal said. 'She was Cheysuli.' He thought it was enough.

Carillon lifted his head and looked directly at Donal. There was no hesitation in his tone, no tact. Just raw, clean emotion. 'It would have made you my son . . . as much as if you were my own.'

Donal stared at the aging face; at the lines and creases and brackets put there by Tynstar's sorcery. He saw sorrow and regret and anguish in that face, and an almost inhuman strength of will coupled with unexpected vulnerability.

Donal drew in a breath. 'I never knew, my lord.'

Carillon smiled a little. 'She would not have me. She would not put another man in Duncan's place. And so we did not wed –' He broke off a moment. When he resumed, it was with careful intonations so as not to display the magnitude of his grief. But Donal heard it regardless. 'Together, they died. And you are still Duncan's son.'

'My lord!' The urgent voice came from outside the pavilion.

'Rowan –' Carillon straightened in his chair. 'Come in at once!'

253

Rowan pulled aside the flap and came through part way, so that the crimson fabric hung over one shoulder like a cloak. 'Carillon – you had best come. There is something you should see.'

The Mujhar pushed himself up from his chair awkwardly and moved at once to pick up his sword and sheathe it. The black ruby glittered in the candlelight; Donal, seeing it again, felt guilty that he had not yet accepted it from Carillon. But somehow he *could* not.

'Come.' Carillon went with Rowan out of the pavilion. Donal, waiting for his *lir*, threw down the crumpled parchment and followed a moment later.

Outside, Donal frowned. Something was – different. Something was – not right. There was a tension in the air, a sensation that set the hairs to rising on the back of his neck. A prickle ran down his spine.

Sorcery. That from Taj, flying above in the darkness.

Ihlini, Lorn agreed as he paced next to Donal's left leg.

The light was wrong. Instead of normal deepening twilight, it was nearly black as pitch. Torchlight illuminated the encampment, but the flames seemed almost muted, swallowed by the darkness. Something muffled sight, sound, smell, as if the camp had been swept beneath a carpet.

Rowan took them westward to a line of gentle hills that rolled out to ring the camp. He gestured briefly to the moon hanging so low against the starless sky: its face was filled with darkness. A thick, viscid darkness. The color was deepest purple.

Carillon stopped at the crest of a grassy hill where another man waited with his wolf. In the light from the dying moon, the slender stalks of grass glowed a luminous lavender.

'Ihlini,' Finn said.

Donal frowned. Wreaths of cloying mist rose up from the flatlands below the hills: bog steaming in a storm. There was the faintest of hisses, almost lost in the heavy darkness. 'Some form of spell?'

'More like a warning – or a greeting.' Carillon's hand was on his sword. 'Who can say what Tynstar means by anything he does?'

Rowan, next to them, frowned. 'How can he summon sorcery before so many Cheysuli?'

Carillon's eyes did not stop moving as he studied the lay of the land and the mist that rose to obscure it. 'Here, there are four times as many Homanans. Tynstar strikes at *them*.'

Finn's expression was stark in the purpled moonlight. 'Even face to face with a Cheysuli, the Ihlini still have recourse to simple tricks and illusions. With so many Homanans present, he need not concern himself with us. He need only play upon the superstitions of the Homanans, as he has done in the past.'

Lir, Donal said. *I wish you could do something.*

Nothing, Lorn answered. *You know the law. We cannot fight Ihlini.*

And yet Ihlini fight us.

I did not say the law was fair. Lorn's tone was ironic. *I only know we of the lir honor what the gods have given us.*

If I die, you and Taj are dead.

It is all a part of the price.

Too high, Donal retorted. *You should tell the gods.*

Why not do it yourself?

Ground fog rolled. Within the violet wreaths flashed tiny sparks of deepest purple, as if fireflies danced in the mist.

'The men are understandably – *concerned*,' Rowan said pointedly.

'They are afraid.' Finn had no time for wordplay. 'As Tynstar means them to be.'

Donal glanced around. Behind the rim in the shallow bowl gathered all of the Homanan army. He heard whispers and mutters and curses as the river of fog flowed over the hill and downward. The muffled silence of the night was palpable.

Donal shivered. *Lir – call me a coward. I do not like this at all.*

Taj still hung in the air. *Then all of us are cowards.*

Carillon gestured sharply to Rowan. 'Go and speak to the captains. I will not have my men fleeing Ihlini *illusions.*'

'Aye, my lord, at once.' Rowan departed with alacrity, wading through rolling fog.

'Donal? Donal?' It was Evan's voice, as the Ellasian climbed the hill. 'Is this what you meant when you told me about Ihlini magic?'

Donal waited until Evan had reached the top of the hill. 'Somewhat,' he answered tersely. 'Evan – it is not a joking matter.'

The Ellasian prince frowned as he looked out across the blackened land. 'No,' he said after a moment. 'It is not. *Lodhi*! – but what a coil!'

Donal looked at his uncle worriedly. 'You think he intends no harm, then – if he uses only illusion?'

Finn shook his head. 'It is not Tynstar's way to join in battle without first seeking to fill men's minds with fear.' His mouth hooked down. 'What better than to win before blood is shed?'

'That would never stop him,' Carillon answered. 'He will spill all the blood he must.'

'*Look*!' Evan cried.

The mist parted, sliced neatly as if cloven with an ax. In the wound stood a fountain of purple flame with a heart so brilliant it burned a pristine white. The illumination pouring from the fountain filled the world up with light, bathing each face with a starkness from which there was no hiding. Men squinted, holding up their arms to shield their eyes. Picketed horses screamed and tried to bolt. Cries of fear rose from the clustered mass of men.

Carillon spun around to face them all, thrusting up a belaying hand. '*No!* It is only Ihlini *illusion.* Do not fear what is not real!'

But Donal watched the burning fountain. It cracked open and spilled out a sinuous gout of flame that crept across the grass. Blackness spread out around it; what it

touched it consumed, and anything else nearby.

'*Lodhi!*' Evan whispered dazedly.

A serpent, Donal thought. *Tynstar's serpent, sent to do his slaying for him –*

'Carillon,' Finn warned.

The Majhar turned. Ten feet from them all, on the crest of the hill, the writhing serpent halted. It coiled, rose upward, stretched itself toward the sky. It thickened, as if it had been fed. It swelled, as if heavy with child.

And then the swollen belly split open, and the serpent gave birth to a man.

He was wrapped in a purple cloak so dark it was nearly black. A silver brooch glinted at one shoulder; silver earrings flashed in his robes; a ring was on one hand. But it was the eyes, not the jewelry, that Donal saw more than anything else; the eyes, black and beguiling, set in the smooth flesh of eternal youth. The smile, framed by black and silver beard, was singularly sweet.

For the first time Donal faced the man who had done so much to destroy his life, and he found he was afraid.

Gods – I am not fit to hold the throne – I can barely look *at the man –*

'I bid you farewell, Carillon.' The voice was warmly affectionate, lacking the hostility Donal had expected. 'We have been good enemies, you and I, but I am done with you at last. The time for your death has come.'

Donal looked quickly at Carillon. He could not conceive of what *he* might say, did Tynstar speak to him. But Carillon was more accustomed to facing the man.

The Mujhar laughed aloud. 'Tynstar, you *fool* – what makes you think you will succeed *this* time? Have you not failed repeatedly before? Even the last time we met, nearly sixteen years ago, you could not end my life. Oh, aye, you *shortened* it – but I am still alive to thwart you.'

Donal was more than a little amazed by Carillon's composure *and* the audacity of his answer. But then, the Mujhar had had years in which to refine his courage.

Tynstar's smile was genuinely amused. 'It is true you

257

have guarded yourself well. The Cheysuli ever serve their Mujhar.' He looked at Finn. Then at Donal. 'But now there is one of their *own* who waits to take the throne – and you are no longer needed.'

Carillon shook his head. 'You will not put me in fear of the warriors who serve me so well. I am not Shaine, Ihlini. I do not succumb to such transparent tricks as these.'

The flame around Tynstar rippled, as if the serpent writhed. 'Shaine succumbed to his own fears and inner madness. You will succumb to something else.' Light glinted off his silver ornaments. 'Carillon, you have played out your part in the prophecy. You are toothless now, like an old lion – useless and merely a bore. There is another who serves the prophecy now, even as it serves him.' One hand rose to point directly at them. 'Do you see him? You have only to look at the warrior who wards your left side, so solemn and silent beside you.' The sorcerer smiled. 'A man at last, Donal . . . no more the boy I sought to make my own so many years ago.'

Unconsciously, Donal put one hand to the flesh of his throat. He could feel the kiss of the iron collar, the weight of his vulnerability. Then he forced his hand away. 'You are a fool indeed if you think I will turn against Carillon.'

Tynstar smiled. 'No. I am quite aware of the folly in trying that. You are not so pliant as I could wish. No, you will not turn against Carillon . . . but you will not have to. He will be dead within a year.'

'And the throne?' Carillon rasped.

'Mine,' Tynstar said simply. 'As it was ever meant to be.'

'*Mine,*' Donal retorted. 'The Lion will never accept an Ihlini. The gods intend it for *us.*'

Tynstar, cloaked in purple shroud and brilliant flame, merely shook his haloed head. 'Your *shar tahl* has failed your clan, Donal. You know nothing of the histories.'

'*Ku'reshtin!*' Donal swore.

'*Resh'ta-ni,*' Tynstar returned equably, clearly fluent in the language.

Donal stared. But he told himself anyone could learn the Old Tongue – including an Ihlini – if there were reason enough to do it.

Casually, Tynstar made the gesture of *tahlmorra*. 'I shall have to instruct you, I see, to reduce your alarming ignorance.'

Finn laughed. 'An amusing idea, Ihlini. *You* instructing *us*?'

'I know the truth of the histories,' Tynstar said. 'And I will willingly share them with you.'

'I will not listen,' Donal told him flatly. 'Do you think I would heed *your* words?'

'Take them to the Keep with you and question your *shar tahl*,' Tynstar challenged. 'See then who lies. See then who speaks the truth.' He put up a silencing hand. 'Have you never wondered why the Firstborn left Homana to the Cheysuli? Have you never wondered precisely *how* an entire race died out?'

'You are an unlikely tutor,' Carillon told him. 'I think you had better go – or do what you came to do, so we may end this travesty.'

'I come, I go – I do as I wish.' Tynstar did not smile. 'Heed me well, all of you – I give you insight into a truth you have never encountered.' Again, the hand was raised. He looked directly at Donal. 'Cheysuli warrior, you are – with a little Homanan blood. Because the shape-changers serve the prophecy of the Firstborn, who gave it to them before the race died out. Do you know why?'

'A legacy,' Donal answered. 'We are the children of the Firstborn –'

'– who were the children of the gods.' The flame burned more brightly around Tynstar, as if it answered some secret bidding. 'But are you so proud, so insular, so *arrogant*, as to believe they sired no others?'

A blurt of sound escaped Donal. He felt Lorn go rigid beside him.

'What are you trying to *say* –' But Finn was interrupted.

'They sired a second race,' the sorcerer said. 'They sired

the Ihlini . . . who bred with the Cheysuli.'

'*No!*' burst simultaneously from Finn and Donal.

A rasp. Metal sliding. It hissed, almost like the serpent cloaking Tynstar. Carillon drew forth his Cheysuli sword.

Tynstar laughed. 'That cannot slay me, Carillon. Have you not tried with it before? Have you not seen the blackened stone?'

'Aye,' Carillon agreed evenly, 'and would you care to see it again?' Before the image in the flames could answer, Carillon turned and thrust the sword into Donal's reluctant hands. 'Show him. *Show him the blackened stone!*'

Donal held the edged blade in one hand, clasping it beneath the hilt. He could feel the runes against his palm. Slowly he raised the sword, thrusting outward with a stiffened arm as if to ward off evil. Against the flame the sword was a silhouette, lacking all colors save the blackness of the night. As if Tynstar had leached it of life.

But then the ruby turned brilliant crimson and set the hill afire.

The fog evaporated at once. The ruby blazed, and as its magic burned away the Ihlini mist Donal felt the thrumming of power in his hand. He thought at first he might drop the sword, so startled was he by the growing strength, but he found he could not. From him the sword took life; from the sword he took strength. A perfect exchange of power.

Tynstar's smooth face exhibited mild surprise, but very little concern. 'So – Hale's sword at last finds its master. I feared it might happen one day. I thought perhaps I might gainsay him in time when I slew him in the forest, but obviously not.'

'*You* slew him!' Finn took a single step forward. 'It was *Shaine's men* who slew my *jehan* –'

'Was it?' Tynstar smiled. 'Do not be such a fool. I sought Hale because I knew his was the seed that could destroy the Ihlini race. Think you I could let him live?' A

dismissive wave of a graceful, negligent hand. 'Lindir I intended to slay as well, before she could bear the child – but she escaped me and fled to Homana-Mujhar. So I slew Hale after I slew his *lir* – I meant to take the sword. But he had given it to Shaine.' For a moment his beautiful, bearded face altered into something less sanguine, much more malevolent. 'I should have known it would be Alix's child for whom it was meant. I felt it in her, before she lay with Duncan. I should have slain her too, as I took Duncan's hawk. It would have gainsaid the propecy and saved me the trouble of meeting you here.'

Donal lowered the sword. The ruby had dimmed a little, as if knowing much of its job was done; only Tynstar remained, surrounded by his cocoon of living flame. The fog and the serpent were gone. 'You slew her anyway. And my *jehan*. When you sent him to trap us.'

'That was not my idea,' Tynstar said. 'It was my – *apprentice's* suggestion.' He smiled. 'Was it not a good one? Nearly successful, as well.'

Donal drew in an unsteady breath, recalling how his mother and father had died. 'I do not believe your *lesson*.'

Tynstar's shrug was slight. 'I know your prophecy very well, Donal. I helped *make* it, merely by being born three centuries ago. I understand what a *tahlmorra* is much better than you or any other Cheysuli, for I have known the gods much longer than any of you.'

'Dare you speak of *gods* when you worship that filth of the netherworld?' Carillon demanded.

'I worship nothing,' Tynstar retorted. 'I *serve*, even as you pretend to serve. The Seker does not require the non-sense of obeisance and ritualistic loyalty. He *knows* what lies in a man's true soul.' He touched the brooch at his left shoulder. 'Aye, I am an integral part of the same prophecy that orders Donal's life – but I serve it not. I seek only to break its power, before the Ihlini are destroyed.' For a moment, there was a touch of humanity in his eyes. 'Can you not see? I do this for the *salvation of my race*.'

No one answered. Donal stood with Finn, Evan and Carillon as the *lir* locked themselves in silence, and looked at the Ihlini. The sword was heavy in his hand.

'Salvation.' After a moment, Donal shook his head. 'I do not believe you. Were the Ihlini truly children of the Firstborn, we would not be mortal enemies.'

'Ask the *lir* why they will never attack an Ihlini,' Tynstar suggested.

Donal could not answer. Neither did Taj or Lorn.

Tynstar smiled. 'You are idealistic, Donal – or perhaps merely young. Comprehension will come with age. You see, we Ihlini desired more gifts than those the Firstborn gave us. More – power. We turned to the only source that would heed us when the Firstborn would not –'

'– Asar-Suti,' Carillon finished.

'The god of the netherworld, who made and dwells in darkness.' That from Finn.

'Aye,' Tynstar agreed. 'A generous lord, in fact. He did not stint what powers he gave those who wished to serve him.' His eyes were on the sword still clasped limply in Donal's hand. 'But the Firstborn sought to destroy us when they learned of our oath to serve the Seker. Knowing they would die before this destruction could be accomplished, they fashioned a prophecy instead, and left the destruction to the Cheysuli –'

'*No,*' Donal said.

Tynstar did not allow the interruption to interfere. 'They instilled within you all a perfect and blind obedience that even now binds your soul. They gave each warrior a fate and called it a *tahlmorra,* to make certain the task would be fulfilled. They turned you into *soldiers for the gods,* as dedicated to preserving and fulfilling the prophecy as we are to its downfall. Because that fulfillment, once achieved, means the annihilation of my race.' Tynstar's voice was harsh. 'An Ihlini *qu'mahlin,* Donal – instituted by the Cheysuli.'

Donal shook his head. 'The prophecy says *nothing* of annihilation. It speaks of a Mujhar of all blood uniting

four warring realms and two magic races. Is *that* so horrible a fate?'

Tynstar's teeth showed briefly. 'It means the mingling of Cheysuli blood and Ihlini, Donal. It means the swallowing of our races and a merging of the power. No more independence. No more – apartness. The Ihlini and Cheysuli will die out, drowned in each other's blood.'

Gods . . . tell me he is wrong . . . Donal felt as if he had been walking in darkness all of his life. Blind. Deaf. Mute. Yet now he could see and hear and speak. Tynstar had given him sight and hearing: Tynstar had loosed his tongue.

But he did not speak. He lifted the sword and hurled it at the image as if the blade were a spear.

The ruby blazed a trail of incarnadine fire as it arced downward toward the column of flame that housed Tynstar's image. The sword fell, slicing through the fire like a scythe; a ringed hand flashed up and slapped the blade aside. The sword fell, point first, and stuck into the ground. There it stood, sheathed in flame, like a headpiece to a grave.

'No –' Finn caught Donal's arm as he started forward blindly.

'Wait you –' Carillon whispered.

The ruby flickered. Tynstar, smiling, reached down to touch the stone with a single finger. Again, it flickered. Then it turned to black.

Tynstar laughed. 'Shall I make it *mine*? I have only to shut my hand around the hilt. I will take it into my hands and caress the shining blade – until the runes are wiped away. And then Hale's sword will be nothing but a sword, intended for any man, even a common soldier.' He reached down, threatening languidly; one finger touched it, another; the palm slid down to rest against the grip.

'*No!*' Donal cried.

And then, as Tynstar sought to shut his hand upon the hilt, the ruby blazed up again.

The Ihlini cried out. He snatched back his hand

instantly; Donal heard his breath hissing in startled comprehension.

But the hand stretched out again. It lifted. Paused. Considered. The silver ring winked in the sorcerous flames.

Tynstar scribed a rune in the air and split the darkness apart.

19

'My lord . . . *my lord* –'

Hands caught at his shoulders, urging him to rise. Donal, mouth tasting of dirt and flame, realized it was Sef.

'My lord – *please* . . . are you hurt?'

He thought perhaps he was. His head was filled with a darkness rimmed by colored light. Sef's voice was distant, fogged, distorted by the humming in Donal's ears. Even the hands on his clothing did not seem real.

'*My lord!*' Sef cried in desperation. 'Please – get *up* –'

Slowly, Donal rolled onto his side, then pressed himself upward. He sat on one hip, braced against a stiffened arm. Squinting against the brilliance in his head, he tried to see Sef's face.

Abruptly, he recalled what had caused his present condition. He jerked around, drawing his legs beneath him as if preparing to leap. Splayed fingers pressed against the ground; the other hand half drew the long-knife at his belt.

But there was no enemy. Where Tynstar had been was only a charred patch of smoking ground, and the sword.

The sword. Still it stood upright, though tilted, sheathed in the earth from which it drew power. The moon, clean and unobscured once more, flooded the hilltop with silvered light. The rune-kissed blade shone with an eerie luminance. The ruby, cradled in its golden prongs, was a crimson beacon in the night.'

'My lord?' Sef whispered.

Donal came out of his crouch. He rose slowly, aware of a faint tingling numbness in his bones. But he did not approach the sword. He looked instead for the others.

Lorn stood but two or three paces away, legs spraddled as he shook his coat free of dirt and debris. Taj still spiraled in the air. Evan was sitting upright, spitting out dirt and muttering of Lodhi and sorcerers. Finn stood even as Donal rose. He went at once to Carillon and put down a hand to him just as Rowan arrived.

'Carillon –!' In his urgency, Rowan nearly shouldered Finn out of the way. 'My lord?'

Finn did not give ground. His very silence transmitted itself to Rowan, who – bending down to aid Carillon – glanced up at him in irritated impatience.

Watching them both as Carillon sat up and brushed his clothing, Donal was struck by their eerie resemblance. In the moonlight the differences in their faces were set aside. All Cheysuli resembled one another, but some more than others.

They are alike in more than appearance, Donal thought. *Both of them serve the Mujhar. Finn may have given up his rank as liege man to Carillon, but the loyalty is still there.*

He saw the momentary flash of possessiveness in Rowan's eyes. No, he had not taken Finn's place when the oath had been broken; no man could. But he had made a new place at Carillon's side, and Donal knew he was indispensible. Facing Finn, it would be difficult for Rowan to give way.

'Get me up from here!' Carillon said testily, and caught Rowan's outstretched hand. Donal saw how Finn remained very still a moment, and then moved a single step away.

Relinquishing the service yet again . . . Donal saw the pain graven deeply in Carillon's face; the taut starkness of his expression and the incredibly tight set of his jaw. Like Donal's; like everyone else's, his face was smeared with traces of ash. Moisture glittered on Carillon's brow, and

Donal realized it was the sweat of unbearable pain.

And yet he bears it . . . Donal moved to him at once. 'My lord – Carillon . . . how do you fare?'

Briefly, Rowan's teeth were bared in a feral, possessive snarl. 'How does he fare? *Look* at him, Donal! How do *you* fare after what Tynstar did?'

'Enough.' The word issued hoarsely from Carillon. He stood nearly erect as they surrounded him, allowing the pain no opportunity to swallow him whole. One hand rested on Rowan's shoulder as if in placation; Donal saw how the sinews stood up against the flesh of Carillon's hand and knew he clutched the shoulder for support. 'Tynstar is – gone. Let us go as well: down from this hill to our pavilions. Tomorrow, I do not doubt, we will be tested by the Solindish.'

'He sought to slay us,' Donal said. 'Who is to say he will not do it again?'

Carillon's eyes were couched in brackets of strain. 'That was not an attempt to slay us. That was his manner of leave-taking. No doubt he *might* have tried to slay us, but the sword prevented that.' A fleeting grimace crossed his face as he glanced back at the shining sword. 'Hale's blade begins to serve its master.'

Donal shivered once. 'No. That sword is *yours*.'

Sef, standing between Donal and Evan, wrenched his head around to stare. '*That's* the magic sword?'

Donal looked at him sharply. 'What are you saying, Sef?'

The boy shrugged self-consciously. 'I – I've heard it's got magic in it. There's a story around Homana-Mujhar that it'll be *your* sword, and when it is –'

'Enough!' Donal cut him off with the sharp Cheysuli gesture. 'There are better things to do with your time than listen to stories. Go on, Sef – go back to camp. Is there nothing for you to do?'

Color moved through the boy's face. For a moment his vitality dimmed, then came rushing back. He flicked a glance at the Mujhar with his odd, uncanny eyes, then

looked directly at Donal. 'But they say the sword was made for *you*.'

Donal's bones tingled. His head ached. He glared at Sef through eyes that burned from smoke and flame. He pointed at the sword. 'Then go and fetch it, Sef, and see what nonsense you mouth.'

Sef shrank back. 'No! *I* can't touch it!'

'Do not be foolish, Sef.' Donal, still somewhat disoriented, felt his patience slipping. 'What is to keep you from touching the sword?'

'It – it might stop me.' He shrugged. 'Somehow. It *might*. You don't know it *wouldn't*.' Furtively he looked at the sword. 'It's a magic sword, my lord. It isn't meant for a boy like *me*.'

'Donal.' Carillon's voice, with the snap of command in it. 'Fetch the sword yourself. I have no more time to waste on Tynstar and his tricks.'

The Mujhar turned away. With Rowan's aid he made his way down from the crest of the scorched hill and walked through his gathered army, speaking quietly to frightened men. Finn and Evan were silhouetted against the horizon, lighted only by the moonlight. Lorn waited as well, and Taj, still drifting in the heavens.

Donal turned from Sef to fetch the sword. The blade was half-buried in charred earth. He reached down, clasped the hilt and tugged.

At once he felt again the thrumming of life in bones and muscles; the promise of power and strength. *Gods . . . is this what has kept Carillon strong all these years as his body decayed? A sword –?*

He pulled it free of the earth. The blade was perfectly clean, unblemished by ash or dirt. The runes seemed to writhe upon the steel.

In the silvered darkness, Sef's pale face was almost translucent. 'Hale's sword,' he said, 'is not meant for such as me.'

'This sword,' Donal said deliberately, 'is meant for any man who can wield it.'

'Oh?' Finn's voice held a familiar undertone of irony. 'Is that why it warded us against Tynstar?'

Evan shook his head. 'In Ellas, magic is limited to such things as simple tricks and potions, or to the harpers of Lodhi. You have seen Lachlan's power. But – I have never seen *anything* like this.'

Donal looked down at the sword. In his hand, the grip was warm. The ruby blazed bright red. 'Nor have I.' He could deny the sword no longer. And so he turned and left the hill.

The pavilion held two cots, two stools, one chair, a tiny three-legged table. Tripod braziers stood in two of the corners. The fabric was pale saffron. The candlelight, thrown against the sides, painted the interior burnt gold, pale cream and ivory. It reminded Donal of the Womb with all its marble *lir*.

He sat in the chair. Beside him slumped Lorn, sleepy-eyed in the glow of fat white candles. Taj perched precariously on Donal's chairback; he could feel the meticulous balance of the falcon. In front of him stood the table, and set on the knife-scarred wood was the sword. No more did the ruby blaze, but neither was it black. It was the rich blood-red of a Cheysuli ruby, no more, no less – yet full of significance.

'In the clans, it is held a Cheysuli-made sword has a life of its own when matched with the proper master. I have heard of others made for foreign kings and princes because of all the legends . . . but this one – *this* one Hale made for Shaine. I know the story. It was Shaine who gave it to Carillon when he became Prince of Homana . . . it has been his weapon for years and years. It is a part of the tales they tell about him. And now he thrusts it upon me, says it is mine –'

Evan, sprawled inelegantly across the cot, shrugged. He held a cup of wine in his hand. 'Perhaps it is. Does it matter so much?'

'Aye. Cheysuli do not use swords.'

269

Evan snorted. 'Then what is the use of *making* them?'

'We do not, now. When the *qu'mahlin* was declared, no longer did we make weapons with which to arm the Homanans.' Faintly, he frowned. 'If – *if* it is true Hale made that sword for me – *why*? I am Cheysuli.'

'And Homanan, are you not?'

Donal shifted in his chair, disturbing the falcon. Taj reprimanded him gently. 'Aye,' he said grimly. 'But none of me wants that sword.'

'And if Carillon leaves it to you?'

'I will not use it,' Donal declared. 'Never will I fight with it. There is my knife, my bow – even *lir*-shape. Why would I want a sword?'

Evan smiled. 'Just because you don't *want* it, does not mean it wasn't *meant* for you.'

Donal's smile was wryly crooked. 'You sound almost like a warrior discussing his *tahlmorra*.'

Evan drank for a moment, then shifted his posture to sit more upright. 'Well, every man has a fate. Some men make theirs. I may not be Cheysuli, but I am a son of Lodhi – for all I may not seem so.'

'The All-Father,' Donal said wryly. 'Is it true you Ellasians believe he sired *all* of you?'

'Well, He did not precisely lie with my lady mother, if *that* is what you mean.' Evan grinned and drank again. 'But aye, in a way, He did. You see, Lodhi lay with a single mortal woman, and from that union sprang Ellas.'

Donal, losing interest, looked again at the sword. He rubbed absently at his chin. 'This sword is Carillon's –' Abruptly, he rose. He snatched up the sword and went out of the pavilion, ignoring Sef's startled question as the boy rose up from his mat outside the doorflap. Donal ignored everyone as he strode through the encampment; he was intent upon his mission.

Carillon's crimson tent stood apart from the others. Tall wooden stave torches had been thrust into the earth around the pavilion to bathe it with light. Shadows flickered against the crimson fabric; Donal saw there were no guards.

No guards –?

And then he heard the Mujhar's startled cry of pain.

Donal ran. He felt the grip settle more comfortably into his palm. His fingers found ridges meant to cradle his bones; the remaining space beckoned his other hand. The metal was warm, alive; he could feel the power rising. It bled into his body and spread to fill the very marrow of his bones. He almost *wanted* to fight.

His free hand ripped aside the crimson doorflap. Automatically it dropped the fabric and went unerringly to the hilt, closing around the gold. He felt the blade rising, rising, incredibly light in his hands and yet substantially weighted as well. The balance was perfect. The sword was a part of his body, an extension of his hands, his arms, his mind –

'*No!*' he shouted as he saw the man bending over Carillon's body in the cot.

Candlelight flashed off the blade. The reflection struck full across the man's face as he turned; Donal saw a haze of gold and black and bronze. And eyes. Yellow eyes, staring back at Donal.

The blow faltered. His arms sagged. Donal let the weight drop down, releasing his left hand so that the sword dangled limply from his right. 'By the gods, *su'fali* . . . I might have had your head –'

'And regretted it later, no doubt.' Finn straightened. His hands were empty. But he stood at Carillon's bedside, and the Mujhar was clearly unconscious.

'What are you doing?' Donal demanded in alarm. 'What is wrong with Carillon?' He moved closer to the cot, fingers clenching the sword hilt. 'Gods – he is not *dead* –'

'No.' Finn glanced down at the Mujhar's slack face. 'No, not yet.'

'*Yet*?' Donal stopped beside the cot, but he did not look at Carillon. He stared instead at Finn. 'You do not mean –'

'– I mean he has little time,' Finn said flatly. 'Are you

blind, Donal, to say you do not know it?'

'But – but he is so strong –' Donal gestured with his empty left hand. 'He *rules* –'

'– stolen time,' Finn said, and his voice had roughened a little. 'Tynstar took it from him – I have stolen it back. A little. Not enough. But – as with all things, it carries a price.' He looked down at Carillon. 'Donal – are you prepared to be Mujhar?'

'*No!*' It burst out of him instantly. 'No, *su'fali* – no.'

'Have you learned nothing from Carillon?'

At last, Donal looked down at the man who ruled Homana. He saw how the flames overlay the face and emphasized the slackness of the flesh, the banishment of the strength inherent in Carillon's bones. The beard had silvered, thinning, so that the line of the jaw was visible. The hair, fallen back from his face, no longer hid the fragility of his temples; Donal saw clearly the hollows of age, the upstanding threading of veins, the prominent bones of the nose.

But it was not the face that shocked Donal. It was the leather that had been wrapped around Carillon's naked torso. Stiff leather, laced together; it held his spine perfectly straight, almost too straight. Straps ran over both broad shoulders. The leather bracers, which Donal had always believed were mere cuffs providing some measure of support, were reinforced with metal.

'Years ago, when the disease began to twist his spine and shoulders, he had that made.' Finn's tone was expressionless. 'It allows him to resemble a man instead of a blighted tree. It allows him to hold the sword you have just returned.'

He is dying. I see it, now – 'Gods!' Donal whispered, 'Oh, *su'fali* – say it is not true.'

'I will not lie to you.'

Donal felt pain knot up his belly, rising to fill chest and throat. 'Is there *nothing* you can do?'

'I have done it.' The tone was minutely unsteady, yet tight, controlled. 'I gave him *tetsu* root.'

Donal blanched. '*How much?*'

Finn's smile lacked humor. 'Enough to do some good. And it has. He has been – better – since the wedding.'

Donal felt a chill. '*Su'fali* – *tetsu* root is deadly.'

'So is growing old.' Finn looked down at Carillon's unconscious body. 'It was his choice, Donal. I did not force him. I did not hide it in his wine. I simply told him about *tetsu* and what it could do for him. He said he would take the risk.'

'Risk? There is no risk! *Tetsu* always kills.' Donal gestured emptily again. 'Have you known a man to set it aside once he has begun drinking it regularly? *I* have not. Every warrior who desires it has taken it once, then twice, and soon enough there is no stopping it, not until the root slays. By the gods, *su'fali*, you have given him over to death!'

'I have lessened some of his pain,' Finn declared. 'For him, I could do no less.'

Donal stared at the Mujhar. All the grief welled up and made him feel helpless. Carillon was dying more quickly than was natural. Tynstar had seen to that. But Finn, in a final obscene service performed by a loyal liege man, had made it more immediate.

'How long?' he whispered.

'A month. Two. Perhaps a little longer.' Finn looked down at his friend. 'What Tynstar did tonight destroyed many of Carillon's defenses. His will has been such that he would not give in to disease or drug. But now – time is running out.'

Donal tried to swallow down the swelling in his throat. 'Does – does he know it?'

'He knows it.'

Donal looked down. He would not cry before his uncle, who would have no tolerance for such things. Instead, he stared hard at the sword. In his hands the ruby glowed, catching the candlelight; the rampant lion seemed to move upon the hilt.

'Do not tell him I know,' he said, barely above a whisper. 'Do not tell him I came.' Mutely, he held out the blade

273

to Finn. 'Say I sent a servant with the sword.'

Finn relieved him of the weapon. '*Ja'hai*,' he said. '*Ja'hai, cheysu, Mujhar*.'

'Not yet,' Donal said. 'Oh, no . . . not yet. Not while Carillon breathes.'

'He will breathe a little longer,' Finn said, 'but one day he will stop. And you will hold the throne.'

' *'Su'fali* – do not.'

'Do not what? Speak the truth?' Finn did not smile. 'You will have to accept it, Donal. It is for this you were born.'

Donal looked at Carillon. And then he turned away.

20

Donal gasped at the impact of bodies meeting. The Solindish soldier weighed more heavily on him than he had expected. He reached in, thrusting a forearm against the man's sword hilt, and drove the blade off course. The tip of the sword hovered, then drifted back near his ribs; he leaned away, pivoting from the hips, and took a firmer grasp on the long-knife in his right hand.

He thrust. The tip struck leather-and-ringmail, catching in steel circles linked together. The blade scraped; a screech of subtle protest. Donal wrenched it away and thrust yet again. Upward this time, beneath the Solindishman's arm. He sought the vulnerable, unmailed flesh of the armpit.

The gap – there!

The blade slid in. He felt it catch on leather, slowing, then digging deeper into flesh, where there was less resistance. The entire length of the blade sank in; he twisted.

The Solindish soldier cried out. His sword wavered in his hand, then fell free altogether. Blood pumped out of the man, flooding his side and painting his ringmail red. Donal felt the warm wetness flow down to wash across his hand, his arm, dripping from his elbow.

As the man sagged, the knife went with him. The hilt slipped out of Donal's blood-smeared hand. He followed it down, bending to regain the weapon; as he caught the hilt once more, he heard Evan's warning cry.

'Donal! *'ware sword!*'

He dropped to one knee, ducking instantly. The whistle

of a blade near one ear told him how close he had come to losing his head. A wrench freed the knife at last; he twisted, spinning on the knee, and came up offensively, slipping beneath the swinging sword. One hand caught the soldier's wrist, the other thrust again with Cheysuli long-knife.

Again, blade met ringmail. Cursing inwardly, Donal tried to draw back and thrust again. But his man brought up a knee in an attempt to catch him in the groin.

He twisted and caught the blow on the thigh. He grunted as the impact nearly knocked him down; grimly, he stood his ground and leveled a vicious knife swipe, at the Solindish soldier. The swordsman's reach was greater, but the maneuver nonetheless took him by surprise. He jumped back instinctively and left Donal free of the sword.

Donal backed away. First one step, then another. And then, as the soldier prepared to follow, he flipped the knife in his hand and threw it with a snap of his wrist that sent the blade slicing through the tough leather collar at the man's throat and through it, into the flesh beneath.

He turned. Evan, he saw, had engaged yet another soldier. The field was filled with men: Homanans, Cheysuli, Solindish. Those of the clans he knew by their *lir*-gold and yellow eyes; the Homanans and Solindish, save for blazons on their tunics, he could not tell apart. In the midst of battle, one grimy, blood-stained face looked very much like another.

From the corner of his eye he saw a flash of muted gold, feathers blurred in flight. Taj, swooping, scythed through the air. Donal watched him choose his target: the swordsman who confronted Evan. The Solindishman, intent upon his Ellasian prey, never saw the bird. Taj closed talons on leather gauntlets, slicing through to rend flesh and muscle.

'Hah!' Evan cried as the man staggered back, sword falling from wounded hands. 'My thanks, Donal!'

'Not my doing,' Donal returned. But the conversation

went no further. A dying Solindishman, falling at Donal's feet, struck a final blow. Knife blade flashed in the sunlight of midafternoon; tip bit through the leather of Donal's left boot and into flesh, cutting to the bone. Donal, staggering back, wrenched himself free of the knife. But not before he realized he had lost most of his mobility.

He hopped back again, favoring the wounded leg. Curses filled up his mind and mouth; teeth gritted, he hobbled away from the dying man.

Lir, It was Lorn, shoring up his side. *Lir, seek help.*

Not yet, he answered, testing the leg. *I can still stand well enough.*

He sheathed his bloodied knife. Quickly he unstrapped his compact Cheysuli warbow, pulled an arrow from the quiver and nocked it, seeking out a target. But even as he raised the bow, preparing to let fly, he smelled the stink of sorcery.

Tynstar –? he wondered vaguely.

But there had been no sign of the Ihlini since the battle had begun.

Fog. Fingers of it, violet, drifting along the ground. And then, almost instantly, the fog thickened. Stretched. Swallowed up the field.

He could see nothing. His eyes were filled with haze. The smell of it, sickly sweet and cloying, coated his tongue, and he bent to spit it out. Damp, malodorous arms seemed to twine around his neck, putting fingers into his ears. He was cold, wet, nauseatingly sickened by the smell.

'Donal! *Lodhi* – there are *demons* –'

Evan's voice, raised in honest horror. Donal turned, staggering on one leg, and tried to locate his friend. But the vapor was like clay, sealing up his eyes. They burned. They teared. He cursed.

Lir? Lir –?

Here, Lorn's voice sounded distant, swallowed up by the fog. *Lir – this is the Ihlini's doing.*

Donal put away his arrow and the bow. Neither could help him now. *Taj?* he asked.

Above, the falcon answered. *Lir – it is everywhere – I can see no sky –*

'Evan!' Donal shouted. 'Tell me where you are!'

There was no answer. In the depths of the heavy fog Donal could hear other voices, all muffled, all indecipherable. But the tones were clear enough. Fear. Horror. Blind, unreasoning terror.

'*Evan!*'

'Demons!' Evan shouted. And then the Ellasian screamed.

Lir, go to Evan, Donal ordered, hobbling through the choking mist.

I cannot even find you, Lorn retorted. But then the wolf loomed up through the fog, a solid ruddy shape in the pervasive violet shroud. *Lir, you are limping.*

Aye, Donal agreed. He felt safer with the warmth of the wolf against one knee. *Gods – where is Evan –?*

Here, sent Taj. *To your right by seven steps.*

Seven steps. Donal hobbled. It took him more than seven steps. But at last he saw the body, belly down, sprawled against the ground.

'Evan!' Fear shot through him. He dropped to both knees, ignoring the pain in his leg, and put one hand on Evan's shoulder.

The Ellasian prince came up from the ground in a twisting, convulsive lunge. His blue eyes were wide in a pale face, his mouth agape in fear. But a knife in his hand, and he nearly thrust with it.

Donal fell back, sprawling on his rump against the earth. 'Evan – *wait* you –'

Breath rasped in Evan's throat. He stopped hunched, legs spread, nearly swaying on his feet. 'Donal?' He peered uncertainly. 'Lodhi – is it *you*?'

'I,' Donal agreed. It felt better to sit than to stand. 'What demons do you mean?'

The knife shook a little. 'There was one. There was. It

came at me out of the fog . . . *Lodhi!* – but what a vile, horrid *stinking* thing it was! It had no mouth – no eyes . . . it was a slimy, foul, wretched *tentacled* thing –' Evan shuddered. 'It wrapped itself around my head and nearly smothered me –' He turned his head and spat upon the ground. '*Lodhi* – I can still *taste* the horrid thing!'

'But now it is gone?' Donal had seen nothing. He thought it likely the demons were illusion called up by the Ihlini for those of the enemy who were not Cheysuli.

Evan sucked in a steadying breath. 'Gone, I thought – when you touched me – I thought it had come again. But now even the fog is clearing.' Evan looked down at Donal. 'You are hurt.'

Donal glanced down at the torn, bloodied leather of his boot. 'A slice. Nothing more.'

Evan knelt, putting away his knife, and peeled aside the leather. In the flesh of Donal's shin, not far above the ankle, was a deep, clean-edged cut. 'To the bone, and beyond. You are fortunate the bone is whole.' He reached out and caught Donal's elbow. 'Come up. I will see you to a chirurgeon's tent.'

Donal glanced around as he fought to regain his balance. 'The battle seems to be ended. I see both sides withdrawing.'

'But no victory, I will wager.' Evan steadied Donal's progress. 'How much longer will this Solindish folly continue?'

'In two months, we have got nowhere,' Donal said. 'Neither side has won. Who is to say how much longer this will go on?'

'Aye,' Evan agreed grimly as Lorn trailed Donal. '*We* have the Cheysuli, but the Solindish have Tynstar and his minions. The advantages are cancelled.'

Donal sighed, wincing as movement jarred his aching leg. 'We *will* win, Evan . . . the gods are on our side.'

The Ellasian snorted. 'Aye. And no doubt the Solindish claim the same thing – just that *their* gods are different.'

Donal gritted his teeth. 'Let us cease discussing war.'

'Aye!' Evan agreed. 'Why speak of war when there are *women* in the world?'

Regardless of his pain, Donal had to smile.

Carillon came in as the army chirurgeon tied the last silken knot of the stitches in Donal's leg. Donal himself was too intent on locking his teeth against the pain to pay much attention to the Mujhar, but he was aware of Carillon's entry.

'Not serious, then?' the Mujhar asked.

The chirurgeon shook his head. 'Hardly, my lord. It will hamper him a little, but should heal well enough.'

'Good.' Carillon's bulk blocked most of the sunlight from the open doorflap. 'Rumors said you had nearly lost the leg.'

'No – though it feels like it *now*.' Donal scowled at the chirurgeon as he bound the calf with tight linen bandages.

'Do you think you will need a crutch?' inquired Evan in mock solicitude.

Knots tied off, Donal brushed the chirurgeon aside with a muttered word of thanks. Then he glanced up at Carillon. 'My lord –'

His words trailed off. He was faced again with the advancing age of the Mujhar; with the knowledge of what Finn had done to him. And Carillon's willingness.

'Aye?' Carillon waited.

'No,' Donal muttered, looking away. 'Nothing.'

'Courier!' called a voice. 'Courier for the Mujhar!'

Carillon turned back toward the entrance. 'Here!'

A moment later a young man in royal livery bowed before the Mujhar. 'My lord – messages for you and the Prince of Homana.'

Carillon accepted them. Like Donal and Evan, he was obviously weary, clothing torn and bloodied. Hands soiled by the dirt of sweat and boiled leather closed around the scrolls, and Donal saw again the leather bracers at his wrists.

'Yours.' Carillon passed one over.

Donal, frowning, broke the crimson seal. He read the two brief lines and the signature, and felt the cot shift beneath his weight.

He became aware, suddenly, that Carillon was demanding to know what was wrong. His face must show what he felt. When he could, Donal looked up and met the anticipatory eyes. 'Aislinn, my lord. She has miscarried of a son.'

For a long moment Carillon stood unmoving in the sunlight as it slanted inside the tent. But then he reached out and caught the parchment from Donal's hand, nearly tearing it in half. He read it, and then he shut his eyes.

Slowly, so slowly, one hand crumpled the message. The parchment crackled in the silence. Donal saw how the fingers spasmed, shutting, and how the callused, grimy hands took on the aspect of a corpse's.

The Mujhar expelled a breath that hissed upon the air. His eyes, when he opened them again, were filled with a quiet desperation. 'I am sorry,' he said at last. 'The loss of an unborn son . . .' He did not finish the sentence.

Donal felt the kindling of distant grief into something very real. *A son unborn* . . . It had happened once before, when Sorcha had miscarried his first child. Ian and Isolde had come into the world safely, and he had grown complacent. He had thought Aislinn would bear him a healthy child; he had not considered a loss. He had not thought of what it meant to lose an heir.

'My lord –' Donal stopped and cleared his throat. 'My lord – Aislinn says she is recovered. She says she does well enough.'

'Aye. For which I thank the gods.' Carillon looked at the scroll given to him. 'Perhaps this is from Aislinn as well – perhaps there was something more she wished to say –' He broke the seal, read the message, then stared blindly at them all.

'My lord –?' Donal nearly rose.

Carillon turned away from them. He stepped into the opening and shouted for Rowan. He said nothing at all

until the general came, and then his words lacked all cere-mony. 'Osric,' he said clearly. 'Osric of Atvia invades through the port of Hondarth.'

'*Osric* –!' Donal blurted.

Rowan hardly glanced at him. 'He means, then, to march on Mujhara while we dally here with Tynstar.'

'Aye.' Carillon sighed in utter weariness. 'To protect one we risk the other.'

'There is no other way,' Rowan said flatly. 'You must, my lord.'

The Mujhar nodded. 'He has been stopped a week out of Hondarth, on his way to Mujhara – just this side of the fenlands. The domestic troops hold him for now, but for how long?'

Rowan's tunic was stained and torn. The rampant lion hung in tatters. 'We are a month's march out of Mujhara. Osric is only a week away from the city. My lord – we must go *now*.'

'And lose Solinde entirely.' Carillon grimly crumpled the message. 'That may be Tynstar's plan. Can you not see him, Rowan? He suggests to Osric the time is now – the Atvian sails to Hondarth while we wrestle here with Tynstar. Faced with no army to gainsay him, Osric takes Hondarth and marches toward Mujhara. Once he over-comes what few domestic troops there are, he has trapped us between Tynstar and himself: a grub between two stones.' He turned to Donal. 'Do you understand what we must do?'

Donal felt a hollowness in his belly. 'We must stop them both, somehow – Tynstar as well as Osric.'

Evan frowned. 'My lord – if you were to shift your warhost from Solinde to Homana, would you lose this realm entirely?'

'With Tynstar here? – of course.' Carillon looked at Donal. 'Tell me what we should do.'

Donal stared down at the earthen floor of the infirmary tent. 'We fight on two fronts, my lord. We split the army in half.'

'Our only chance, and a desperate one.' Carillon turned back to Rowan. 'Speak to the other officers and the clan-leaders as well. We will leave half the army here – I want the Cheysuli here to fight the Ihlini – while the rest of us go to Osric. Rowan, you will come with me to Mujhara.' He cast Donal a level glance. 'And you. But you will remain in Mujhara only a week or two, and then return here to command the army.'

'Carillon – *no* –' That from Rowan, even as Donal thought to echo the identical words. 'He is unschooled in warefare *and* the leading of men. Leave *me* here instead.'

'You I take with me.' The tone was inflexible.

'Rowan has the right of it.' Donal pushed himself up from the cot and rose, suppressing a grimace of pain. 'What do I know of leading men into battle?'

'These are veterans.' Carillon's voice was harsh. 'These men do not require you to hold their hands. They will teach you what there is to know – it is time you learned how to conduct yourself as a soldier must in order to survive – and to keep others alive as well.'

'Then why send me to Mjuhara?' Donal demanded. 'Why not leave me here?'

'Because Aislinn is in Mujhara.' Carillon's face was completely expressionless. 'It is difficult to conceive a child when man and wife are so many leagues apart.'

'*By the gods* –' Donal said raggedly. 'She has only just recovered! There is no *decency* to this –'

'There is not time for such things as *decency* in war,' Carillon said baldly. 'I have an heir; you do not. It is necessary for you to make one.' He turned back to Rowan again. 'Make certain my half of the army is prepared to leave in the morning.'

'Ay, my lord Mujhar.' Rowan stepped aside as Carillon brushed past him.

'He is gone mad,' Donal said hoarsely. 'By the gods – I think he *has* –'

Rowan raised his brows. 'What madness is there in trying to hold Homana – and in serving the prophecy?'

'Like *this* –?'

'If this is what it takes.' Rowan did not smile. 'Be ready to ride in the morning.'

The borderlands of Solinde did not have the varied beauty of Homana. The land was flat, and low, scrubby trees barely broke the straight line of the horizon; to Donal it looked as though it stretched forever.

A barren, dismal place . . . fitting for the Ihlini.

He and Carillon rode out ahead of the army bound for Homana. Not far. Just barely out of eyesight. Rowan had protested the lack of escort regardless, but Carillon had over-ruled him.

The Mujhar rode in silence. Donal, watching him with subtle, sidelong glances, saw how the morning sun glinted off the silver of his hair. He wore few ornaments to mark his rank: his ring and a collar brooch of gold and emerald. His clothing was exceedingly simple: ringmail over a boiled leather hauberk. Black breeches. Thighboots. Bracers banded with slender ribs of steel.

Gods, what a man he is – what a warrior still . . . would that I could have known him before Tynstar stole his youth –

And what will they say of you? Taj asked, wheeling idly in the air.

Of me? Inwardly, Donal grimaced. *That I could never be Carillon's equal.*

Is that truly what you desire? Lorn asked from beside the stallion. *Did he not make his own way in the world – just as you yourself will?*

Aye. Donal sighed. *What they say, I will know in time. And perhaps they will have the right of it after all.*

On the crest of a rise, Carillon halted his horse. Still he sat in silence, staring eastward toward Homana. Donal, waiting beside him, heard the buzz of a bee in the air.

'I thank you for coming with me to this place,' Carillon said at last. 'You might have refused.'

'Refused *you* –?'

284

Carillon rubbed his beard thoughtfully. 'Aye. You may refuse me, Donal. I have not stripped you of your freedom *entirely* – it only seems that way.'

The chestnut stallion stomped to discourage a bothersome fly. Dust rose. Donal smelled the pungent tang of freshly crushed plains grass. Absently, he tapped his mount with a heel and reprimanded him gently, urging him into stillness. 'It is – difficult to refuse you.'

'Because that is what I wanted.' Still Carillon stared eastward. 'But I am done telling you what you must be, what you must say, how you must behave. I am done locking the shackles around your wrists.' At last, he looked at Donal. 'I have brought you here so I may ask your forgiveness.'

Donal started, frowning. 'Forgiveness –? From me?'

'Aye,' Carillon said gently. 'Duncan left me a chunk of naked metal and I did my best to shape it into a sword – even to tempering it to my liking, knowing what weight and balance I desired. But I am no arms-master, and I may have unwittingly set blemishes in the steel.' His mouth hooked down in a brief ironic twist. 'Now I seek to blood the blade after keeping it sheathed for nearly sixteen years.'

'My lord –'

'I am sorry, Donal. I could offer you countless reasons and excuses for what I have become – and what I have done to you – but I am finished with that. I am finished with – much.' His brows twisted briefly; Donal heard the undertone of despair in the steady voice. 'I am sorry. I am sorry. For you . . . for Aislinn . . . for the child that must come of this.' He looked at his ruined hands as they clasped the saddlebow. 'Last night I said there was no time for decency in war. Perhaps I meant it then, but it is not true. War may be obscene, but it is also necessary. So is decency, if you are to retain a measure of humanity.' His faded blue eyes met and held Donal's. 'My wars are nearly over. It is you who will fight them for me, and eventually for yourself. I pray you do it with the decency I denied . . . and the humanity you will need.'

'*Ru'shalla-tu*,' Donal said thickly. *I pray the gods it may be so.*

Slowly Carillon smiled. '*Ja'hai*, Donal. *Cheysuli i'halla shansu.*'

After a moment, Donal put out his arm. Their hands met and locked in the firm Cheysuli clasp. 'Accepted,' he said. 'May there be Cheysuli peace upon *you*.'

Carillon at last broke the clasp. 'We had best go back to the army. Rowan will be worried.'

'As well he should be,' agreed a sinuous voice. 'Have I caught you two alone?'

Donal spun his horse even as Carillon mimicked him. Before them, unmounted, stood Tynstar. And with him was Electra.

She laughed. 'We have taken them by surprise.'

Tynstar smiled. 'I think we have made them mute.'

'No,' Carillon said. 'Hardly that. But I *am* surprised you come to us here. The army is not so far.'

'What I mean to do will not take much time.' Tynstar said benignly, 'and whenever has an army been able to gainsay *me*?'

Electra's cool grey eyes watched Donal. He felt the power of her gaze. 'You wanted Carillon, and now we have the wolfling as well. Will you give him to me, my love?'

Donal felt a frisson slip down his spine. Apprehension filled his belly. *Lir* –

What is there to do? Lorn asked wretchedly.

Taj circled in agitation. *It is law, lir, our law, given by the gods. We do not attack the Ihlini.*

Because we are bloodkin? For the first time, Donal wondered if Tynstar's falsehood might hold some truth after all. *Is that why you keep the law?*

Neither bird nor wolf answered.

Tynstar smiled sweetly. 'If you want him, Electra, I will give him to you when I am done with Carillon.'

Donal straightened in his saddle. 'If you think I will sit idly by while you attack Carillon, you are a fool indeed.'

'Not a fool,' Tynstar answered. 'Merely – patient.' He raised a hand noncommittally. 'For now, I do not desire your meddling.'

The Ihlini flicked a single finger. A blow knocked Donal off his horse and into nothingness. He floated, bodiless and mindless, knowing only fear and helplessness and a strange, wild grief. Then he landed against the ground and all such fleeting sensations were knocked utterly from his head, along with the breath from his lungs.

He struggled up to one elbow, trying to catch his banished breath, and saw the tableau take life before him. Taj flew in circles, shrieking in desperation; Lorn tipped back his head and howled in despair.

Donal's leg throbbed. He sank his teeth into his lip, tried to rise, and found himself fastened to the ground. He could not move at all.

'You sent Osric to Hondarth,' Carillon challenged.

'I take Homana how I can,' the sorcerer agreed. 'Would you not do the same? You have learned what it is to be ruthless in order to get what you desire.'

Carillon glanced back at Donal. Indecision and concern showed briefly in his eyes. But the indecision faded; Donal saw him smile –

– and set spurs to the flanks of his stallion.

Carillon rode at Tynstar. The Ihlini, unmounted, was prey to a galloping horse. He was prey to the sword the Mujhar drew.

But he merely lifted a languid hand and split the air with flame.

Concussion knocked Carillon from the saddle. Donal saw the Mujhar crash against the ground, sword dropping free of his hand.

Another gesture brought a bolt of lightning lancing out of the sky. It blasted the ground around Carillon's sprawling body, splattering him with dirt.

'Slowly,' Electra said. 'Let him know he dies.'

'Old man,' Tynstar said, 'shall I release you from your pain?'

Slowly, Carillon pushed himself to his knees. Donal saw how his body trembled, how the chest heaved in complete exhaustion. Dust filmed his face; part of his beard was burned away.

He slumped. Slumping, his hands went to the ground. Fingers splayed. Elbows stiffened. He braced himself with every ounce of his waning strength.

Gods – Donal begged, *do not let it end like this!*

Failing, Carillon's body curled forward, slumping –

– but did not fall. Instead, he jerked the knife from his belt and hurled it through the air.

'*No* –!' Electra screamed.

The knife went home high in Tynstar's chest.

Carillon laughed. 'Whose death today, Ihlini? Mine – or is it *yours*?'

Tynstar's right hand clawed at the hilt. A hissing exhalation poured from between his lips. 'Seker –' he said, 'Seker – I call upon the Seker –'

'What?' Carillon asked, still kneeling on the ground. 'Do your powers begin to fade? Do you call upon your god?'

'Seker –' Tynstar hissed. 'I call upon the Seker –'

'Before a Cheysuli warrior?' Carillon climbed unsteadily to his feet. 'I think the petition will fail.'

Tynstar thrust his right hand upward into the air. The fingers shook. 'Asar-Suti!' he shouted. '*I summon you to me!*'

Carillon did not wait. He hurled himself forward and came down near the forgotten sword. He rolled rapidly and thrust his failing body upward, leveling the blade in a vicious, scything sweep.

Electra screamed. Tynstar's upthrust hand dropped limply back at his side. He stood a moment longer, then buckled at the knees.

But his head struck the ground before his body did.

The scream went on and on. It sliced through Donal's head like a blade, and then it stopped. Abruptly.

Electra simply stared.

Donal slowly got up. He looked at the severed neck. The blow had been quite clean, no wasted effort.

Blood, thick and viscid, oozed slowly from the trunk. But the color was not red, but deepest black.

Carillon turned to Donal. 'How do you fare?'

'He did not harm me, but – *Carillon, look to Electra* –'

The Mujhar spun round. But Electra made no move to attack. Instead, she walked unsteadily toward the decapitated body and knelt beside it.

White-blond hair spilled down her breasts and trailed into the blood. Slowly, the blackness benighted the shining strands. It stained the pale lilac of her gown.

'Electra.' Carillon walked slowly toward his wife. 'Electra – he is dead.'

She leaned forward. She moaned. She put her hands on the bloodied shoulders of the body. She slid them down across the torso in a morbid caress.

She jerked the knife from the chest –

– and came up, spinning, aiming for Carillon's belly –

– in time to spit herself to the hilt of Carillon's waiting sword.

'Such beauty . . .' he whispered in a ragged, helpless voice.

The knife dropped from her hand. Knees buckled. She fell, and Carillon caught her.

Carefully, he pulled the blade from her body. He set the sword upon the ground. Then he shut the lids of her grey-pale eyes and straightened her silken skirts. her hands, still stained with Tynstar's blood, he folded beneath her breasts. The glorious hair, half-black, half-blond, he smoothed away from her flawless face.

Carillon knelt. Donal saw the bloodstain spreading beneath Electra's folded hands. Black. Black and thick and viscid.

With Tynstar dead – with Electra dead . . . is Aislinn free at last?

The Mujhar rose. He took up the sword again. He turned to face his heir. 'You must go back. Return to the

encampment. I must go on to vanquish Osric – I will send your regrets to my daughter.'

Donal stared. 'But – I thought you wished me to go to her.'

'I was wrong.' He looked down at the body of his wife. 'Once, she must have been a woman. A woman . . . not a witch.' Slowly he sheathed his sword. He clasped Donal's shoulder, squeezing firmly, as if he were young again. 'Go, my lord. Win back Solinde for me.'

Donal turned away. He mounted his chestnut stallion and eased his throbbing leg into the stirrup. Taj perched on the saddlebow; Lorn stood by his side. He turned westward, toward the camp that lay so many miles behind them.

But when he looked back he saw Carillon standing over the bodies of his wife and the Ihlini.

As if he mourns them both –

21

Sef's odd eyes were stretched wide in shock. 'The demon is
dead?'

Donal sat on the edge of his cot and worried at his boot,
trying to strip it off without causing more pain to the
injured leg. Sef stood stock still in front of his master, not
helping.

'Aye.' Donal caught heel and toe and pulled, gritting his
teeth. 'At last, we are free of Tynstar's plotting . . . it may
be this war will end sooner than we hoped.' His foot
moved in the boot. He tugged harder, grunting with
effort. 'Sef – help me with this. Stop gaping at me like a
fish.'

Sef's usually efficient hands caught the boot clumsily
and pulled it off. 'But *you* did not slay him –?'

'No. The Mujhar did.' Donal, frowning, felt at his bandaged leg. 'But it was Electra who slew herself. Had she
not tried to slay Carillon, she would not now be dead.' He
wiggled his toes experimentally. 'So we are rid of them
both.'

'And now?' Sef asked. 'What happens to all the other
Ihlini – the ones who still fight here?'

'The race is still powerful,' Donal told him. 'All of them
claim some measure of the dark arts. But without Tynstar
to lead them, I think perhaps we will have less trouble with
them all. Carillon cut the head from the serpent – it may
be all the little snakelets will wriggle about in confusion,
with no knowledge of how to strike.' He stretched out
carefully and lay back on his cot. '*Ru'shalla-tu.*'

Sef, moving to the table to pour a cup of wine, twisted his head to stare over his shoulder. 'What do you say?'

'*May it be so*. Old Tongue saying.' Donal scrubbed the heel of his hand across his forehead.. 'Gods, but when I recall the sight of Tynstar's head falling from his body –' For a moment, he shut his eyes and summoned the vision again. 'And all the blackened blood –'

Sef spun around, nearly spilling the wine. 'Blackened blood! Tynstar's blood was *black*?'

'Black and thick and heavy.' Donal levered himself up on one arm and accepted the cup of wine. 'Electra's too –' He grimaced. 'It is enough to give one nightmares.' Abruptly, he looked at Sef with his pale face and staring eyes. 'Gods, I am sorry. I should not have spoken so plainly.'

Sef shrugged. 'No. No, better I know the truth . . .' He shrugged again, as if to ward off the gooseflesh of fright. 'But – what will happen now? Here – to us?'

Donal sipped. 'We continue to battle. The Mujhar and his portion of the army will try to stop Osric before he reaches Mujhara – here, we must put a stop to the Solindish-Ihlini uprising.'

'Then – we will stay here until this war is done – and *then* return to Homana?'

Donal nodded as he swallowed down the wine. 'Aye. Carillon has left me a task. I am to lead these men while *he* confronts the Atvian.'

'Then – Osric doesn't know the demon has been slain.' Sef frowned. 'Does he?'

'No. Perhaps it will aid Carillon's campaign – he will go against Osric knowing the sorcerer is dead, while Osric anticipates Tynstar's help.' Donal smiled. 'A surprise for the Atvian – one that should help our cause.'

Sef's voice was tentative. 'Then – *these* are politics?'

Donal laughed. 'More like strategies. But often enough they appear to be one and the same.'

It was gloomy inside the tent. Night had fallen; candles illuminated the saffron interior of the pavilion and turned

it pale ocher and dull gold. Evan had absented himself to spend time with one of his women; most of the encampment celebrated Tynstar's downfall. Donal had passed on the news calmly enough, then retired to rest his throbbing leg.

'I will rest, Sef. If you wish to go out and celebrate with the other boys, please yourself.'

'My thanks.' Sef had grown a little since joining Donal's service, but he was still thin, still almost delicate. The sleeves of his tunic and shirt were too short now; bony wrists protruded.

Inwardly, Donal smiled. *More clothing, yet again.* 'You may go, Sef. I will not need you again until the morning.'

The boy grinned crookedly. 'I will drink the cider, my lord – I will drink a toast to the victory over Tynstar!'

'Go.' Donal waved a hand, and the boy ran out of the tent.

He sipped his wine. He stared into the shadows and thought of how he had come to be the victim of circumstance. Nearly twenty-four years before a child had been born to a warrior and his woman. Their freedom, like the child's, did not exist. The gods had seen fit to give them all another fate.

Taj perched upon the chairback. He piped softly, preening his feathers into perfection, hardly aware of Donal's presence. On the floor, next to the cot, lay Lorn, curled upon rough matting, nose covered by the tip of his ruddy tail. He twitched, and Donal knew he dreamed.

He sighed. He stretched out to set the cup of wine upon the table, and then he lay back, head pillowed on arms thrust beneath his neck. He shut his eyes, and slept.

He dreamed. He saw a palace and a dais and a woman upon the dais. She was beautiful. She was deadly. She had the power to twist his soul.

Beside her stood a man. Cloaked in black with a silver sword hanging at one hip. In his outstretched hand glowed a violet rune. It danced. Subtly. Seductively. Promising many things.

From behind them came a girl. Half-woman, half-child, trapped between youth and adulthood. Like her mother, she was lovely, but her beauty was unfulfilled. Like her father, she was strong, but without a will the strength was blunted.

'*Donal,*' someone said, '*Donal, you must come.*'

He frowned. None of the mouths had moved. The rune still danced in the sorcerer's hand.

'*Donal – rouse yourself –*'

A hand on his shoulder, and he was suddenly awake. *Awake* – the dream was banished. He blinked dazedly at Evan and saw how the sleepy eyes were filled with grave concern.

He bent at once and picked up his boot, pulled it on with effort. Evan waited, solemn-faced and silent. There was no frivolity in his face; no hint of celebration.

Donal rose, suppressing a grimace of pain. 'Is it better told or shown?'

'Shown,' Evan said. 'Words would not describe it.'

Lir, Donal summoned, and they went with him out of the tent.

Evan led him through the encampment to a hollow in the hills ringing the huddled tents. Not far. But away from the bonfires and clustered soldiers who still celebrated Carillon's victory over Tynstar.

The night was cool. The light had changed; it was nearing dawn. He had slept longer than he intended.

He saw three men standing at the edges of the hollow. Two Homanan sentries. The other a Cheysuli.

Finn turned as Donal came up with Evan. His face, like the others, was solemn, etched with tension. But there was something more in the eyes. Something that spoke of a hope destroyed.

He put out a hand and halted Donal. 'There is grief in it for you.'

Both sentries held flaming torches. Light hissed and flared, shedding faulty illumination. In the hollow, Donal saw shapes huddled on the ground, sprawled awkwardly

294

in the macabre dance of death. Outflung arms, legs; limp, questioning hands. Faces, stricken with amazement and terror. Open eyes, staring into the heavens.

Boys, all of them.

One of the sentries stirred. 'My lord – the others would not have them at the fires. They said it was for men to do, without the company of boys. And so they came here to celebrate on their own.'

Donal counted the bodies. Fourteen that he could differentiate from others. Fourteen boys who had run messages between the captains and tended their noble lords.

As Sef had.

His head snapped around as he stared at Finn. 'Is he here?'

Mutely, Finn gestured to one of the sprawled bodies. It was mostly hidden by another.

Donal went to the body and knelt. The flickering torchlight showed him shadowed, ghostly faces; slack, childish mouths. He gently moved the body off Sef's legs, then beckoned one of the sentries over.

The torch was unmerciful. Sef's head was twisted slightly, so that his face was turned away. But his neck was bared, and the cut in his throat showed plainly. From ear to ear it stretched. The ground was sodden with his blood.

Red blood, Donal thought. *None of the blackened Ihlini ichor* – 'Fourteen boys,' he said aloud. 'Surely *one* of them must have heard the Solindish coming.'

'This was Ihlini-done,' Finn told him grimly.

Donal snapped his head around. 'Are you certain? This smells of raiders to me.'

'It is meant to. But see you this?' Finn held something out.

Donal, frowning, took it from his uncle's hand. It was a stone, a round, dull grey stone with a vein of black running through it.

'An Ihlini ward-stone,' Finn explained. 'Apart from the other four, it is worthless. But it tells us who was here.'

'Dropped?' Donal rolled the stone in his hand. 'Used to

295

make them helpless – silencing their cries . . .' He looked again at Sef. Near one bent knee lay a flaccid wineskin. Donal smelled the tang. Wine, not cider; boys had tried to mimic men.

Carefully, Donal closed the staring odd-colored eyes. He recalled Carillon performing the same service for Electra. And then such grief welled up as to nearly unman him before the others. 'Gods –' he choked '– why did it have to be *boys* –?'

'Because they knew what it would do.' Briefly, Finn touched Donal's rigid shoulder. 'I know what he was to you. I am sorry for what has happened.'

'To *me* –?' Donal stared up at his uncle. 'What of you? What if he was your son – or kin of some other kind? What *then, su'fali*?'

The scar jumped once. 'It changes nothing,' Finn said evenly. 'The boy is dead.'

'Dead,' Donal echoed. Gently, he touched Sef's right wrist. He felt the feathered band. He recalled how it was meant to be a charm against sorcery.

Cheysuli sorcery.

Deftly, Donal untied the knot in the leather lace on the underside of the cool, limp wrist. He took the band and tucked it into his belt-purse.

Not strong enough, he told the murdered boy. *Was I not charm enough against the sorcery you feared*?

But then, looking again at the fourteen bodies, he knew he had not been.

Donal rose stiffly. He could not look at Finn. 'We need a burial detail.'

The other sentry inclined his head. 'My lord – I will see to it.' With the torch smoking in his wake, the Homanan went away.

Part 2

1

Donal stared gloomily out at the drowning world from the open flaps of his saffron pavilion. It was late evening, just past supper. It was cold. Summer was gone; fall had settled in. In Solinde, it rained during the fall. He was bored, restless and weary, and heartily wishing Carillon had left someone else to lead the army.

He had led it, now, for two months. Occasional word came from Carillon that Osric of Atvia still pressed them on the plains between Hondarth and Mujhara. Worse, it seemed unlikely there would be any immediate resolution. Osric, Carillon claimed, was a master strategist. The two armies were utterly deadlocked.

Donal sighed and turned away from the rainy darkness to watch Evan rattle a small wooden casket. It held ivory dice and slender sticks of rune-carved wood. The Homanans called it the fortune-game. There were two levels of play: a straightforward dicing game for unimaginative gamblers, and the more elaborate rune-stick portion involving portents and prophecies.

I weary of prophecies. Let Evan play at being Seer – I have enough to concern myself with.

The Ellasian prince had unmatched skill with both dice and rune-sticks. Dice and sticks fell his way repeatedly, but Donal knew he did not cheat. The game itself was not Evan's, but won from a Homanan soldier in an unconnected wager.

Evan rattled the casket. 'Come, my lord of Homana – let us see what your fortune says.'

Donal smiled wryly. 'Have you wearied of taking my coin? *Now* you wish to steal my fortune also?'

Evan raised dark brows in feigned indignation, one hand touching his heart. '*I*, my lord? Do you mistrust me, then? But here – I will show you. . . . . *I* shall throw and read you what I see.'

Donal watched idly as Evan chanted over the rune-sticks and dice as he rattled them in their casket. Boredom settled more deeply in his bones.

Solinde, of late, had been peaceful. The Ihlini, perhaps stunned by Tynstar's death, were quiet. The Solindish did not attack. The most recent encampment had stood safely for three weeks. It was possible the rebellion was over; also possible the Solindish meant to trap the Homanans into leaving prematurely. And so the warhost waited.

Evan spilled out the dice and rune-sticks across the wooden table. Ivory rattled; rune-sticks rolled, then settled. Evan frowned in concentration. 'Ah!' he cried in discovery. 'Fortune looks kindly on you, my lord. See here the rune signifying the *Wanderer*? And the die here for modification? It means within days you shall find yourself traveling on a journey filled with adventure and discovery – see you here? *Jester* and *Charlatan*.' Evan's grin was sly. 'A *Woman* as well, Donal – see you this rune here?'

'I see the folly of idleness.' Donal retorted. Before Evan could speak, he scooped up dice and rune-sticks without dropping them into the casket, and threw them across the table. 'There. Read them for me now.'

Evan stared at the pattern. After a moment he lifted his head and met Donal's eyes squarely. 'You mock the game, my friend. Not wise. Now what you see is genuine destiny.'

Donal snorted. 'I was promised a *destiny* long ago, Ellasian – all Cheysuli are. Read me my fortune.'

Evan looked back at the tumbled dice and rune-sticks. He touched none of them, but he pointed to the indicators. 'There. A minor rune, representing *Youth*. But, coupled with a Major one, *so* –' he pointed to another rune on

the same stick '– that is the *Magician*, Donal, and a very powerful rune.'

Donal, still smiling, nodded. 'Say on, Seer.'

Evan's habitual sleepy expression was gone. 'Here – this is the *Prisoner*. This die signifies time spent – months. And this rune is another Major – it is the *Executioner*.' He met Donal's eyes again. 'Conjoined with what I threw just before you did, the fortune is a powerful one.'

'Aye?' Donal waited.

Evan sighed. '*Wanderer*: you will embark upon a journey. *Charlatan* and *Jester*: you will meet those who are more than what they seem. *Woman* is obvious – perhaps she is also the *Magician*. And at the end of the journey there is imprisonment and potential death – there is an *Executioner*.' Evan gestured. 'There, my friend, is your fortune.'

'A full one,' Donal said lightly. 'You do not underplay the moment, Evan.'

'I underplay *nothing* –' Evan began, but his words were drowned out in a shout from outside the pavilion. Donal heard his own name called.

He turned to the doorflap at once. Framed in the opening was a cloaked and hooded man, nearly indistinguishable from the rain and darkness. 'My lord.' The voice was raised to reach above the downpour. One hand came up to move the hood and the shadows shifted.

'Rowan! Come in.' Donal stepped aside at once and gestured the general in. 'Word from Carillon?'

Rowan moved past him into the pavilion. Rain ran down the muddied cloak and splattered against the hard-packed floor; he threw it back from his shoulders. He wore leather-and-ringmail, and his rumpled crimson tunic was stained with blood and grime. The brazier cast harsh shadows across his face and limned his weariness.

'My lord,' he said without ceremony. 'Carillon is dead.'

Donal stared at him. For a moment he felt nothing, as if the words were syllables of nonsense. But then they came together into a sentence he understood. Shock reared up in

his soul. 'Carillon . . .' he whispered.

Rowan reached into his belt-pouch. From it he took an object and placed it on the table. In the candlelight, the bloodstains shone dark red.

A ring. A gold ring, set with a black stone, and into the stone was carved the rampant lion of Homana.

Rowan bent his head. Silver shone in his hair. And then, with a gracelessness that emphasized his grief and utter weariness, he knelt upon the floor. 'My lord,' he said. 'You are Mujhar of Homana.'

Donal looked down at him. Rowan knelt stiffly and his head was bowed. The wet cloak molded itself to his body and tangled on his spurs. He was wet, wet and weary, and stark pain was in his voice.

For a moment Donal shut his eyes. Beneath his lids he saw Carillon as he had seen him last. Standing over the bodies of Tynstar and Electra, knowing he too would be dead before the year was out.

He knew. He knew – I knew . . . and still I am unprepared.

He looked blankly at Rowan again. No. It was not right. The posture was incorrect. He was not the man for whom the homage was intended. 'Get up from there,' he said unsteadily. 'You do not kneel to *me*.'

Rowan raised his head. 'I kneel to the Mujhar.'

Again, the words were unconnected. He heard them, but he could not acknowledge them. Slowly he shook his head. '*Carillon* is your Mujhar.'

The older man's face did not change expression. It was a mask, a blank, weary mask, hiding what he felt. 'You are in his place, my lord. And I must offer my fealty.'

'Get up from there!' Donal shouted. 'You do this purposely!' His voice cracked. He stopped speaking. He felt the trembling in his body. And then, only then, did he see the tears in Rowan's eyes.

He nearly turned away. He could not face the man's grief, or it would swallow up his own. Instead he stared blankly at the ring.

Now it is meant for me. He looked down at his right hand. On his forefinger the ruby signet ring meant for the Prince of Homana. No longer was it his. He must replace it with the other. *Gods . . . I am not worthy.*

'Donal.' It was Evan, speaking softly. 'Donal – will you keep him on his knees the length of the night?'

Abruptly, Donal looked back at the general. He saw how the sun-bronzed skin had lost much of its color. It was stretched taut over the strong, prominent bones, shadowed in the light. Rowan looked almost old.

He has lost so much . . . Donal bent. He caught Rowan's left arm and raised him up. 'Do you think I would not accept you?' His voice was steadier now. 'Did you think I would *dismiss* you?'

'I am Carillon's man,' Rowan said clearly. 'I can never be anyone's else's.'

Donal did not answer at once. He lacked a voice; the words. Somehow, he had always known it. Rowan was Carillon's man, as he himself had claimed. For more years than Donal had been alive, Rowan had served his lord. He had dedicated his life to Carillon utterly. And now the task was finished.

He will never serve me. To him, I am a makeshift man, not fit to assume the Lion. I can never take Carillon's place.

He looked at the older man. 'Surely you will aid me. My task will not be easy.'

'Nor was his.' The tears were gone from Rowan's eyes. His face was a mask again.

Gods – he will never *acknowledge me.* Donal looked at the ring again. He felt empty and full all at once. Empty in spirit because Carillon was gone; full of the grief it brought. 'Rowan,' he said softly, 'I will need your help.'

The other Cheysuli drew in a deep, uneven breath. 'Years ago, Carillon gave me an estate as a reward for my services. I have had it administered for me through all the years I remained at Homana-Mujhar . . . but I intended, when this time arrived, to leave royal service.'

303

'Leave.' Donal felt the apprehension spill into his belly. 'Do you think I can do this alone?'

'I doubt you can do it at all.' The tone was uninflected. It made the words more cruel.

'Oh, *gods*,' Donal said. 'Do you hate me so much?'

'I do not hate you at all.' Neither tone nor expression changed. 'You are not – Carillon. That is all. It is not fair, I know . . . but then nothing is fair. Is it?' Rowan's eyes were filled with bittersweet empathy. 'You are resented by the Homanans because Carillon made you his heir. Oh, aye – they begin to accept the prophecy, but they would prefer to accept it *later*. With you, that time is now.' Rowan sighed and closed his eyes briefly. 'There are foreign realms who view the succession with alarm and distaste: *they must deal with a man who shifts his shape.* And, of course, there are the Cheysuli, who view you as something like unto an avatar of all the ancient gods. How can I hate a man as swallowed up as *you*?'

Swallowed up – Aye, he was, or would be. The Lion would regurgitate a different man.

Fear lodged in his throat. 'Rowan – *I will* need *your help*.'

After a moment, Rowan nodded. 'And I will see that you have it.'

Donal turned to the table and poured a cup of wine. He offered it to Rowan. 'Here. You are in need of food and rest. But for now . . . will you tell me how it was? Supposedly it is a painless ending.'

Rowan, accepting the wine, looked at him sharply. 'Painless? His *death*?'

Donal gestured emptily. 'I am told the root is – gentle. That at the last a man simply slips away in his sleep. I had hoped it would be so for Carillon.'

Rowan stared, the wine forgotten. 'Root? What do you say?' Then his mouth dropped open. 'Are you speaking of *tetsu*?'

'Aye,' Donal answered. Then, in shock, 'Did you not know? I thought he told you everything.'

304

Color drained from Rowan's face. 'Gods – was *that* it? I knew he was in pain – the disease was eating his bones. But not once – *never* did I think he would resort to such as *tetsu*.' His mask had slipped. There was bewilderment in his face. 'But where would he get it? It is a Cheysuli thing, and kept hidden from Homanans.' He looked at Donal questioningly. 'How would he know of *tetsu*, and who would give it to him?'

Donal felt his jaw clench. 'It was Finn who gave it to him.'

Shock flared in Rowan's eyes. '*Finn!*' He caught his breath. 'Aye – *it would be!* Leave it to Finn to give poison to Carillon!'

'For the pain,' Donal protested. 'He said Carillon desired it.'

'And so he stole more time!' Rowan said bitterly. 'Did he tell him what it would do? Did Finn say to him he would lose what little time was left?' His hands shook in his anger.

Donal's fingers curled against his palms until the nails bit in. 'I am certain Finn told him everything. He is not a murderer, Rowan.'

'He has been that, and worse.' Rowan's tone was harsh, the words clipped. 'Most of the stories of him are true.'

An answering spark of anger flared in Donal's chest. 'Finn was loyal to the Mujhar! What he did was because Carillon desired it! Do you dare intimate to me that Finn *wanted* him to die?'

Rowan shut his eyes. 'No . . . no . . . I – do not. No. Forgive me, I am not myself. But – *tetsu* root? *Why*?'

'He was in pain,' Donal answered. 'Did *you* not tell me that often enough?'

The older visage was haggard in the candlelight. Rowan passed a hand across his face and rubbed at his circled eyes. 'Gods – he meant to rule until the end . . . he meant not to give himself over into imbecility from the pain . . . aye, I see it. A man such as Carillon would take *tetsu* and give up quantity for quality. It was his way.' Suddenly a

breath of ironic laughter issued hollowly from his mouth. 'And then, for all that, it was Osric who took his life.'

Breath spilled out of Donal's body. 'Osric! *Osric?*'

Rowan nodded. 'Three weeks ago we rode into battle against Osric. And it was done with. We had won the day. We had only to gather our dead and wounded.' He drew in a heavy breath. 'I saw him. Carillon was mounted, standing on a hilltop. Just – looking. Looking across the battlefield as we went out to gather our dead. I saw him sitting there, watching . . . I wondered why he was so still. Now, I think it might have been the root. It – affects a man's perceptions.' His brows twisted together in a spasm of grief. 'I – saw him fall.'

'*Fall –*'

Jerkily, Rowan nodded. 'He fell.' The words spilled out. 'He went down by the hooves of his horse. For a moment I could not understand – Carillon would never fall! – and then I saw the arrow in his chest.' He stopped talking. 'I was – too far . . . *too far* – I could not reach him in time. But – I saw the Atvian archer – I saw him ride up to my lord. Even as I ran across the hill, I saw him kneel down by my Mujhar. I shouted – *gods, how I shouted!* – but the archer did not listen. And by the time I reached my lord, the Atvian was gone.'

Silence. Donal heard the sibilance of the rain. It ran off the pavilion and splattered against the ground. 'More?' he asked raggedly.

Tears ran unchecked down Rowan's Cheysuli face. 'He knew it was done.' he said. 'He said I must not trouble myself to send for a chirurgeon. He said – he said he wished Finn were with him, or Duncan, so they could take away the pain.' For an instant, his voice shook. 'He told me it was Osric himself – the Atvian archer was Osric . . . that he named himself to Carillon as he knelt down beside him. And then – then he said I was to carry the sword to you, because now you would accept it.'

'The sword . . .' Donal echoed. 'Gods – now it *is* mine.'

Rowan's face was grey. 'My lord – Osric has the sword.'

'*Osric!*'

'I could not tell Carillon,' Rowan whispered wretchedly. 'That is what the Atvian took.'

Donal recalled the sparring match he had had with Carillon so many months before. How they had discovered that, in his hand, the blade knew its true master. Not Carillon's sword at all, for all it served him. Meant for another man.

Donal looked down on Rowan. 'Then I will have to get it back.'

Rowan's voice shook. 'I served him for twenty-five years.' He spoke with a dry factuality, as if that would somehow hide his grief. 'I was twelve. Did you know that? Twelve. He was only eighteen himself, but he was so far above me I could hardly see him for the brightness of his spirit. And he saw to it I was saved . . . he saw to it I was rescued, while he remained in iron.' His smile was bittersweet. 'I swore then I would do what I could to serve him. Even while he and Finn kept themselves in exile, I did what I could to serve him. I kept his memory alive.' The smile faded away. 'And when he came home, he took me into his service – my *tahlmorra*, if you will –' He smiled no longer. 'And now it comes to *this*.' He nearly crushed the silver cup. 'That service is ended by Osric's arrow.'

And that arrow makes me king – Donal turned away from Rowan. He could not bear to look at his face.

On the table he saw the ring, still stained with Carillon's blood. *His* ring, now. Slowly, with a dreadful fascination, he drew off the one on his forefinger and set it down beside the other. His son's, if Aislinn ever bore one.

And I pray the gods she will . . . I am in need of an heir, am I to be Mujhar. His inward smile was ragged with irony.

Donal took up the heavy black ring with its incised rampant lion. Carefully he pushed it onto his naked forefinger and felt his flesh form itself to the metal.

He turned to Evan. 'See to it the general has food and rest. Then find Finn and have him wait for me here. I will come to him when I can.'

'But – how long should he wait?'

'Until I have come back.' Without picking up his woolen cloak he went out into the rain.

He ran. He thought it might ease the pain. But it only deepened it. He felt it fill up his belly until he wanted to vomit onto the ground. But he was empty. He was empty of all save grief and fear.

He ran –

– and when he stopped, it was because he knew he had to. Because his lungs burned and his belly ached and his soul had shrunk up within his chest. There was nothing left but breathlessness and sorrow, and a wild, wild rage.

He stood upon an escarpment. Below him lay the valley and the encampment. The sky was brackish with clouds; neither moon nor stars shone against the darkness.

He clenched his right fist and felt the heavy ring bite into his finger. 'You take them all,' he said aloud. 'My *jehan*, my *jehana* – the boy . . . now Carillon as well. You take them *all* from me – and you thrust this upon me too soon!'

Do you think yourself unworthy? Taj, spiralling in the misty drizzle.

I am unworthy.

You are a Cheysuli warrior. You are worthy of anything. Lorn's tone was inflexible. It sounded like Carillon's.

Donal shook his head. 'I am afraid,' he said clearly. 'Do you understand that? *Afraid.* Because I cannot begin to rule as he has ruled. I cannot be Carillon. I cannot take his place!'

Lorn's eyes glinted. *You are not meant to take his place. You are meant to make a new one..*

Taj circled closer. *In death, as in life, he served the prophecy.*

'He was Homanan, not Cheysuli! Why did *he* have to take the risk?'

A life without risk is empty, Lorn retorted. *A life not risked for something as high as the prophecy of the Firstborn is not a life at all.*

'And mine?' Donal demanded. 'What is mine to be?'

Lorn pressed against his leg. *Why not have the Ellasian dice you your destiny?*

Donal's laugh was bitter.

Taj circled more closely. *Who is to say he will be wrong?*

Donal stared across the soaked plains. He saw the guttering sparks of reluctant firecairns built beneath fabric rainbreaks. His army – *his* army – spread across the land like a silent tide.

And it was time he returned to it.

When he ripped aside the doorflap on his pavilion he found it empty save for Finn. For a moment he thought perhaps his uncle did not know, but then he saw past the subtle control.

The scarred face was perfectly blank. But the fury and grief in his posture was such that it struck Donal like a blow.

Donal drew in a slow, even breath. 'I go to Homana in the morning.'

Finn, half-hidden in the shadows, did not move at all. 'You have an army here.'

The flat impersonality of the tone shocked Donal. Their eyes met across the pavilion. Then Donal made a dismissive gesture with his hand. 'Solinde, for the moment, is quiet. I will go to Homana.'

'Why?' Finn demanded.

Rain ran from Donal's soaked leathers and spilled across the floor. 'You were his liege man for nearly ten years. You commanded Cheysuli and Homanan alike in the wars that won Homana back from Bellam's tyranny. I need you to command this army while I fetch home my sword.'

Finn smiled tightly. 'The Homanans will never suffer a Cheysuli in command.'

'They have suffered *me* these past months!'

'At Carillon's behest.'

'What of Rowan?'

'*At Carillon's behest!*'

Donal brought his right hand up into the light so that the ring was clearly visible. '*At their Mujhar's behest*, surely they will accept you as temporary commander.'

Finn moved forward until he stood no more than two paces away from Donal. His breath hissed through his teeth as he spoke. '*I* will go to Homana and slay the Atvian serpent. *I* will take his life. Not you. *I* am owed this death!'

'Are you?' Donal held his eyes. 'You said once I must choose my own path. I have done it. You will remain here and command the army, *as once you did for Carillon*, and I will go to Homana.'

Finn bared his teeth. '*I* am owed that death!'

'I,' Donal said. 'I am his heir. I will do it. Osric will die by my hand, and I will bring home the sword again.'

Finn spat out something in the Old Tongue that set the hairs to rising on the nape of Donal's neck. He felt color drain out of his face. 'Insult?' he asked, and heard the waver in his voice. He fought to steady it. 'I am your bloodkin, *su'fali!* I have spent my life honoring you for wisdom, strength, and power, and now you offer *insult* –'

'Aye!' Finn snapped. 'And will again, do you mean to deny me this.'

'*I am your Mujhar!*' Donal's voice was hoarse with the effort of swallowing the shout. 'Do *you* fail me in this, think you the *Homanans* will accept me?'

Finn's hand spasmed as he closed it on his knife. 'I want only the life of a *single Atvian lordling* –'

'*Shansu, su'fali,*' Donal said gently. 'Do you think I do not grieve at least half as much as you?'

The scar writhed on Finn's dark face. For a moment there was such grief and anguish in his eyes Donal feared he might go mad. But Finn contained his emotions.

When he could, he drew in a slow breath and released it carefully. 'Duncan would say I am a fool . . . too

impetuous for my own good – he told me so often enough – and perhaps it is the truth.' Finn's voice was hoarse. 'Perhaps I am. Perhaps I must recall all the good advice he gave me and let his son offer it as well.' The sigh was ragged around the edges. 'I suppose – so long as Osric is slain – it matters little who has the doing of it.'

Donal reached out his arms and waited, and at last Finn accepted the brief clasp that sealed their bond again. 'Osric will be slain,' Donal told him clearly. 'That I promise you.'

[faint text from previous page bleeding through at top]

2

He thought it a little like the Womb of the Earth. The walls were intaglioed with marble carvings, but the stone was pale pink and the shapes were not *lir* but men instead: the sarcophogi of kings.

Effigies and marble coffins filled the shadowed vault. Donal stood in the half-open doorway and looked in on the silent dead. It was a Homanan thing to carve likenesses of the dead into polished stone. A Homanan thing to hide them away in privacy. A Homanan thing to store them all together in the bowels of Homana-Mujhar, which was a Cheysuli place. To Donal, the practice was abhorrent.

Aislinn was within. She was alone, unaware of his presence. Grieving by herself. Of all the candleracks only one was lighted, throwing the intaglios and effigies into stark relief. The illumination emphasized the sepulchral silence of the mausoleum. But Aislinn did not seem to care. She held a single candle over a plain, undressed marble coffin.

Donal moved through the doorway. His step sounded, loud in the vault; Aislinn spun around with a gasp and dropped the candle onto the coffin. It rolled, snuffed out; spilled hot wax across the stone. A curl of smoke drifted upward and filled Donal's nose with the odor of scented beeswax.

'*Donal!*' Aislinn gasped, one hand clutching at her robe.

He moved into the vault, a fat candle clenched in his hand. The flame flared and guttered as he moved, striking odd shadows across the pinched face before him. He saw

the glint of tears and the lines of bitter grief.

'They have put him here?' he asked. 'Why here? Why not above the ground, in freedom?'

Her eyes were black in the muted light. 'This – this is where all the kings are placed.'

'Shaine too?'

'Sh-shaine?' She stared at him in amazement, as if she could not believe he would speak of such inconsequential things in the face of her father's death. 'No. When Bellam took the palace, Shaine was already dead. He was not entombed with honor. Bellam disposed of the body; no one knows where those bones lie.'

'Good,' he said quietly. 'Shaine was not deserving of any honor.'

'Donal –!'

He looked at her levelly. 'Shaine was a madman and a fool. Carillon deserves better company.'

She turned from him then, lurching back to face the marble coffin. Her hands went flat against the undressed lid. Fingers splayed out. She bent her head, and Donal saw how her shoulders trembled. 'I saw him,' she whispered. 'I *saw* him. They told me I had to see him while they prepared him for entombment – so that no one could claim the Mujhar yet lived, and use that for some purpose.'

He heard the note of horror mixed with anguish. 'But he does,' Donal told her. 'The Mujhar *does* yet live.'

She spun, pressing her back against the coffin. '*What* –'

He overrode her unfinished question. 'I am Carillon's heir, Aislinn . . . *I* am Mujhar of Homana.'

Color drained from her face, but her voice was surprisingly steady. 'You do not waste time.'

'I have none.' The light from his candle played on the red of her heavy braid, turning it to gold. 'Do I falter now, the war may well be lost. There is no time for a leisurely expression of royal grief. Not even for Carillon.'

'Then why do you come *here*?' She was wrapped in a robe of cerulean velvet. It slid off one shoulder and displayed the linen of her nightshift; he had thought to spend

his time in the vault alone, since his arrival was quite late, but Aislinn did not look as if she had slept at all.

'I came to see how you fared,' he told her, 'and to bid my good-bye to Carillon.'

Tears glittered in her eyes. 'I fare well enough – for a woman who has lost both unborn son and father.'

He wanted to go to her, to take her into his arms and offer the comfort she needed. But he was afraid. Cheysuli honored the dead with deep respect and solemnity, and the keening of women was abhorrent. He dared not sacrifice his own tenuous control to acknowledging Aislinn's need.

'I am alone,' she said. 'I have no one in all the world.'

He held himself very still. He felt the pain blossom in his chest, then slowly rise to fill up his throat. He found he could hardly breathe.

Slowly, he set his candle down on the coffin. Then he touched her fingertips. When he felt their trembling he knew he was undone.

Aislinn moved into his arms. She clung but she did not break down. She cried but it was silently, with a sort of dignity he had not expected. Somehow, it made the moment more poignant.

'How long do you stay?' she asked at last, when the tears had dried on her cheeks.

'I do not stay,' he answered. 'I must go on to the Keep.'

Aislinn stiffened, 'You go to *her*?'

'Aye, there is Sorcha,' he admitted, 'but also there are my children.'

She stepped back from him, leaving his arms empty again. 'Then – you will not spend the night with me?' He saw how she twisted the fabric of her robe. 'You – forgo a husband's responsibilities?'

'Aislinn,' he said gently, 'you recall how it was last time. Are you prepared for that again?'

'I think – I think there will be no need.' Color flared in her face. 'I think you will find me a willing wife instead of a lunatic girl.'

He looked at her. It was true there was greater awareness

in her eyes. Save for a natural embarrassment and proper modesty, she appeared to lack the fear she had shown before.

Perhaps – now that Tynstar and Electra are dead – she is free of the link entirely.

After a moment, he shook his head. 'Aislinn – I am sorry. But tonight there is no time, I must go on to the Keep, and then I will join the army. There is a death I must mete out.'

'Osric's?'

He nodded.

'I thought it might be that. Well then, I will not keep you. It is not my place to reprove you for avenging my father's death.' She turned, reaching for his candle. 'Will you sup with me? You look weary. After that, I will not gainsay you.'

Somberly, she led him from the vault.

He ate. He drank. He told her what he could of the battles in Solinde. She listened attentively, and he found she had gained a new maturity in the months since he had left her. The shape of her face seemed different. Excess flesh had faded so that he saw the line of her bones clearly, as he had seen them in Electra. No more the young woman who only hinted at adulthood; conceiving the child and then losing it had done much to banish her girlhood.

They were alone. His *lir* were in his apartments in another wing. They dined in her chambers; the servants she had dismissed, saying they would tend to themselves in privacy.

Now, as she set her goblet down, she regarded him more closely. 'You look so weary, Donal.'

He leaned against one elbow. 'I came directly from Solinde. It is taxing to hold *lir*-shape so long without proper rest, but – I felt the circumstances warranted the sacrifice.' He sipped from his cup of wine. 'That is partly why I am out of sorts. If I was cruel to you in the vault, I am sorry for it.'

315

'You are unhappy.' She poured more wine for him. 'I see it clearly. The heirship has been a long one, and now that it has ended and the throne is truly yours, you find you do not like it.'

'I never wanted it,' he said wearily. 'I told you that, once. But – Carillon needed an heir, and I have a drop or two of royal blood.'

'More than a drop,' she retorted. 'For all you flaunt your Cheysuli blood, there is Homanan in you as well. And, as for heirs – we should make some of our own.' Her long-lidded eyes flicked a slanting glance at him. 'Do you not agree?'

He smiled. 'I agree. And when I am done with this war, I shall do my best to sire some.'

'Will the war take so long.' Reddish brows knitted together over her lambent gaze.

Donal scratched an eyelid thoughtfully. 'Osric has entrenched himself in the plains just north of the fenlands. Mujhara is not precisely *threatened* . . . but it might be if we do not continue to hold him. While our strength is split, there is little we can do. Carillon meant to stop him permanently – now it is up to me.'

She reached across the table and caught his hand before he could withdraw. 'Donal – stay with me this night. Delay a day or two.'

Her flesh was warm against his. 'I have said why I cannot. And you agreed you would not gainsay me.'

'I lied.' Her single braid had loosened so that her bright hair tumbled around her face. Deftly she undid the lacing until the hair fell free of its confinement. The robe slid off her shoulders; through the thin fabric of her nightshift he could see the lines of her breasts.

'Aislinn,' he said, 'enough.'

'No.' she rose, pressing her hands against the table. She shook back her hair and smiled. 'I am free, Donal. No more Ihlini magic. I can be what you wish me to be.'

He was not indifferent to her. But in his weariness, in his single-mindedness, he thought he could refuse her.

'Aislinn, please be *patient*. We will have our time.'

Slowly, she rounded the table and stood behind his back. Her hands settled on his neck. 'That time is *now*.'

'Aislinn –'

'Do you think I play a game?' She bent forward and pressed herself against his rigid back. Her hair hung down to fall across his shoulders. 'This is not a game. This is my *retribution*.' Abruptly she caught two handfuls of his hair. '*Do you know what it was like?*' she demanded. 'Can you *conceive* of what it was like? Can you *consider* what it is to know such utter helplessness as what you gave to me?'

He caught her hands and rose, stepping free of the stool beside the table. 'Aislinn – this is nonsense –'

'Is it?' Her wrists were trapped in his hands. '*I* say it is retribution.'

He shook his head, baffled. 'Aislinn – are you mad –?'

'You will stay the night with me.' He saw the intensity in her clear grey eyes. 'I want you to know what it is like. *I want you to feel the helplessness*, as I did, knowing I could *do nothing!*'

He wavered. A shudder coursed through his body. His tongue felt thick in his mouth. 'Aislinn – what have you done?'

'Sought power where I can get it.' Her long eyes were wide and watchful. 'You have drunk much wine, my lord. You are weary. You require rest. But when a husband is stubborn, a wife must make shift where she can.'

'By the gods – *you are your* jehana*'s daughter* –'

'I am what I must be.' Her image wavered before him. She retreated. He followed, trying to catch a hand so he could hold her still.

She said nothing as he fell against the bed. He struggled to push himself upright, clinging to the carved tester and heavy tapestries. His clawing hand pulled down the silken folds.

'You *will* know what it is like,' she said in a hard, brittle voice. 'I want you to *feel* what it is like. I want –'

But he did not hear what else she wanted.

He dreamed of Sorcha. And sought release in her supple body.

Donal sat bolt upright in the bed, shocked into full wakefulness so quickly his heart lurched within his chest and his head pounded. He thought he might be ill.

He stared at the woman blindly. He swallowed twice, tasting a flat foulness on his tongue. 'Aislinn, *what have you done?*'

She turned from her belly to her back. Languorously, she stretched, then pulled silken sheets up demurely to cover her nakedness. 'I took your will away.'

He rubbed at his face with one hand, trying to vanquish the tingling numbness. His body told him he had lain with a woman last night; his mind recalled nothing of it. 'I did not intend to spend the night – I was going to the Keep, and then on to the army.'

'I know.' Aislinn's smile reminded him of Electra's. 'What was it like, my lord, to know yourself so helpless?'

He swore violently and got out of the bed, but clutched one of the testers for support. 'Witch. No better than your *jehana.* –'

'We will not speak of her.' Aislinn hitched herself upright in bed and wrapped herself more tightly in the sheets. 'I did not *bewitch* you, Donal . . . I merely drugged your wine.'

Dizzy, he sat back down on the edge of the bed. 'But – why did you not simply *slay* me? The gods know you have tried before. Unless you have a different plan, now that Electra and Tynstar are dead.'

'Plan?' Aislinn frowned. 'What do you say? Why would I try to slay you? What do you mean – I have done it before?'

He glared at her sourly. 'In Hondarth, Aislinn. Do you not recall? That is a fine example.'

Color rushed into her face and one hand flew to cover her mouth. 'But *that* was my mother's doing!'

318

'And last night was yours.' He rubbed at his head again, suppressing a groan of pain.

She shifted closer to him, kneeling at his side. 'I did not mean for you to feel ill. But you drank more wine than usual – you swallowed more of the drug than I intended.' Her hand, reaching out to his shoulder, fell away. 'By the gods, Donal! – what do you expect me to do? Last time you took my will from me with your magic and forced me to lie with you. I only wanted you to know what it was like! Can you blame me? And – and – it is true we need an heir. We cannot put off such need.'

'We can.' – *And now we will*.

'We *cannot*! Do you think I am blind to the requirements of a queen?' Her eyes were blazing at him. 'You seek your light woman, my lord – what *else* am I to do when I am in need of a son?'

'Aislinn –'

'I want a baby,' she said with a desperate dignity. 'to replace the one I lost.'

He opened his mouth to answer harshly, then shut it again. He had never thought what it was to be a woman, waiting only to bear sons to inherit a throne. And in Aislinn's case it was imperative she bear them soon; sooner, now Carillon was dead.

He slumped on the bed and stared at her; at her pale eyes and paler face. She had much of her mother's beauty and all of her father's pride.

Slowly, he rose from the bed and dressed. He said nothing until he was done, and then he walked to the door. 'Perhaps a woman must do a thing she dislikes for a reason that demands it – but I cannot *forgive* you for it. No more than you have forgiven me.'

'I do not want *forgiveness!*' She rose up on her knees before him. 'If you cannot bring yourself to get sons on me I will do what I have to do.' Her voice shook with tears. 'Go back to your light woman, Donal – go back to your shapechanger whore!'

It was all he could do not to cross the room and take her

throat into his hands. But he did not. 'You have delayed me long enough,' he told her curtly. 'Now I must ride directly to the army, without stopping at the Keep.' He looked at her angry face and felt his own anger intensify. 'You had best hope for a son from this travesty . . . you will get no more children from me.'

Her anger fell away. 'But – Homana must have an *heir*!'

'I have a son already.'

Aislinn scrambled out of the bed. She stood before him, perfectly nude, but her fury was unimpaired. 'You would not claim *her* child Prince of Homana!'

'If there is no other, what else could I do?'

Pale fists clenched. 'The Homanan Council would *never* accept a bastard by your Cheysuli whore,' she said flatly. 'Never.'

Donal smiled grimly. 'I am Mujhar. In the end, they will do as I tell them.'

Aislinn glared back at him. But the quality of her anger had undergone a change. Her tears were dry. He saw a new awareness in her eyes. A cool guardedness in her appraisal.

She smiled Electra's smile.

Donal took a horse from Homana-Mujhar, knowing if he went straight to the army in *lir*-shape he would be too weary to go direct into battle. He sent Taj on to the Keep to pass word to Sorcha that he would not be home after all. He did not relish the confrontation when at last they *did* meet. She would claim the Homanans turned him from his Cheysuli heritage, and in a way, he thought perhaps she was right.

As the fleet bird disappeared Donal felt a twinge of regret. Without Taj he felt half naked. A part of himself was missing, and would be, for a while. He had told Taj to fly ahead to the army when he had finished his business at the Keep. Still, he was more fortunate than other warriors. He would lack the ability to assume falcon-shape while separated by such distance, but his link to Lorn remained intact.

Donal slowed the horse as the forest grew more dense. The track narrowed to little more than a footpath, but hoofprints marked the ground. Branches slapped at his head. Fighting the vines grew tedious.

Lorn, trotting ahead, glanced over one shoulder. *Catch me if you can.* With a flick of his tail he was gone.

The wolf was at home in the forests of Homana; the horse was not. But Donal gave it a try.

He bent low in the saddle, hugging with his legs while his heels urged the stallion faster. He rode high on the chestnut withers, shifting his weight unobtrusively. Hands gave the bit to the horse. Flying mane whipped against his face and he tasted the acrid salt of horsehair.

Lir – lir – lir –

Lorn's agonized scream scythed through Donal's mind as the path before the horse fell away into a pit. He felt weightless and a sudden blaze of fear.

Donal threw himself free of saddle and stirrups.

He caught a twisted, buried root in one hand. Gnarled and whiplike, the root dropped him three more feet before jerking him to a halt. He felt shoulder muscles tear.

He swung in perfect silence, eyes shut tightly against the pain as he reached out with his other hand. As he grasped the root he pulled himself upward, taking the weight from his injured shoulder. Sweat ran down his face as he tried to detach himself from the link with Lorn, for the wolf's pain compounded his own. Taj was too far; there was no hope of flying out

He swung himself gently against the earthen wall of the pit, clinging with both hands. Slowly he forced himself upward, hand-over-hand, boot toes digging into the crumbling sides. Inch by inch he rose. dragging himself upward to the rim. For a moment he hung suspended, gathering his strength, then lurched upward and clawed at the tangled roots that fringed the pit.

He grunted with effort; tasted the salt-copper tang of blood against his teeth; smelled the sweat of his effort and the stench of his growing fear. The link with Lorn vibrated

with the intensity of the wolf's pain. But he dragged himself over the edge of the pit and fell down against the ground.

He coughed. His breath whistled in his throat. His belly heaved as it tried to draw in breath. *Lorn!* he shouted silently, and received no answer through the link. Only pain. Pain and emptiness.

Donal struggled to his knees, nursing his aching shoulder. Dazedly he pushed himself to his feet and staggered toward the trees, trying to follow the thin threat of contact with his *lir*.

– *bind a* lir *and a Cheysuli is bound* . . . *harm a* lir *and a Cheysuli is harmed* . . . *trap a* lir *and a Cheysuli is trapped* –

The litany clamored inside his skull. His *jehan* had explained it once in terms a boy could understand; a boy who had received his *lir* too soon, sooner than anyone else. He had never forgotten the lesson.

He fell against a tree, jarring his sore chest and aching shoulder. He stumbled on, responding to the desperate compulsion in his body.

Lir – lir – lir –

He tripped. He fell to hands and knees.

A figure stepped out of the trees and stood before him. Donal, half-blinded by pain, saw the boots first, then slowly looked up.

He saw a slender figure in dark, unremarkable clothing. Pale, delicate hands. And in those hands was clasped the sword with the rampant lion on its hilt.

Donal's head rose. He saw the smooth, youthful face; the parti-colored eyes.

Sef smiled. 'My lord Mujhar, this is well-met. Though you seem discomfited at the moment.'

'You – you are *dead* –'

'Am I? No. That was another boy. But I am glad the illusion held. I lost one of my ward-stones, you see.'

Donal gasped. '*You* are Ihlini –?'

'My name is Strahan,' he said, 'not Sef. I am the son of Tynstar and Electra.'

Donal sat back on his heels. 'Electra *lost* that child! In

322

Hondarth – on the way to the Crystal Isle – my *jehan* said she *lost* the child –'

Sef – Strahan – smiled. 'So she wanted him to think. But – when you are Electra of Solinde and you have loyal women by you – there are many secrets you may keep . . . many illusions you may hold.'

'Not before a Cheysuli.'

'Look at me, Mujhar. Tell me if I lie.'

Donal looked. No more did the boy give him humility and innocence. He gave him truth. He smiled the pure, beguiling smile of his father, with all the lambent beauty of his mother.

Donal grasped at his knife with his left hand, knowing his right arm too numb, too weak and sore to accomplish the task. But the boy set the tip of the sword against his throat, and Donal did not move.

'I hold your wolf, warrior, and therefore I hold you. Do you wish him to live, do nothing to gainsay me.'

Donal spat blood from his bitten lip. 'It was *you* in the Womb of the Earth. It was *you* all those times.'

'Of course. *I* gave the poison to my mother so she could escape imprisonment. *I* hired the Homanan to attack you in the hall, knowing he would fail. I wanted you afraid. I wanted you uncertain. I wanted you in a place special to the Cheysuli, so I could slay you there.'

'Not Aislinn,' Donal said. 'And – not *Bronwyn*, either.'

Strahan smiled. 'Not Aislinn. Not Bronwyn – *this* time.' The smile widened. 'What is it like to know your wife and sister are bloodkin to the enemy? They are, do not forget. Aislinn through her mother, Bronwyn through her father. What is it like, *Cheysuli*, to know you are kin to Ihlini?'

He echoes Tynstar's words . . . Donal swallowed heavily and looked at the rune-worked sword. In Sef's – *Strahan's* – hands, the weapon was huge. The ruby was half the size of his fist. 'How did you come by Carillon's sword?'

'Carillon's? Or yours?' Strahan laughed. 'Osric brought it to me. I had joined him by then – in the aftermath of my "death" – and I asked for it. As proof of the murderer of my mother and father was dead.' Fierce anger and a powerful hatred burned deeply in the un-matched eyes. 'He *should* have left Carillon to me. He *should* have let me slay him. *I* would have given him a much more fitting death.' His teeth showed briefly in a smile echoing that of his father. 'Do you wonder why I touch the sword now? Do you wonder how I *can*? Because of you, *my lord* – you have been so remiss in your responsibilities. Oh, aye, this sword knows you – a little. But you have not had the ritual performed. You have not held it long enough in your possession for it to know an enemy's hand each time one is laid upon it. It knew me on the hilltop – knew me for what I was – but it has been too long now since you touched it. And without the ritual, the power is reduced.'

No one has spoken of a ritual to me – But Donal shook his head. '*I* should have known you. Through my *lir* . . . an Ihlini is ever known.'

'No,' Strahan said gently. 'Not while I wore the feathered band.'

Donal's left hand went at once to his belt-pouch. But he did not try to open it.

The boy laughed. 'Look upon it, Donal. See what has helped me so well.'

Unwillingly, Donal unfastened the pouch and took out the feathered bracelet. He looked at it mutely. Such a simple thing. A slender band of braided feather: black and gold and brown.

He met Strahan's eyes. 'How could *this* gainsay my *lir*?'

'They are from your father's hawk.'

Breath rushed out of Donal's body. He stared blindly at the feathers in his hand, and recalled his father's body in his arms. *How could I not have known* –?

'A token, but powerful,' the boy explained cheerfully. 'My father took the hawk's body. And then he took

Duncan. With them both, dead *lir* and live warrior, my father fashioned a powerful spell. It hid my identity. It allowed me to come to you. It even made Finn wonder if I were *kin*!' Strahan laughed. 'And it made it an easy thing to infiltrate the palace.'

I kept this to recall Sef's murder . . . but it is a tool of my own. He looked up at the boy again. 'What do you intend to do with me?'

'Make you a *toy*,' Strahan said. 'The way I made one of your father.'

3

Inside his head, the memories were at war.

He recalled his father from his childhood, when Duncan had been clan-leader and responsible for people other than his son. But he had still made time for that son, teaching him what he could.

He remembered Duncan in his madness, with empty eyes and taloned hands.

He recalled the first time his father had taken him hunting, to teach him what he must know about tracking animals and slaying them to help feed the clan.

He remembered Duncan begging for their help, begging to be made whole again; a man.

He recalled how his mother had taken care to keep his father alive in his memories when Duncan was gone because all too often memories faded into nothingness.

He remembered how Alix had saved them all by sacrificing herself.

But mostly he remembered how his father had died in his arms, knowing himself a toy in the hands of Tynstar's son.

And Donal knew *he* was, also.

No! he cried. *I – am –*

'– not!'

He jerked awake. He heard his breathing rasping in the confines of the cabin. The echo of his shout. The clank of heavy iron as it rattled at wrists and ankles, bolting him to the bunk aboard the ship.

Oh gods . . . He remembered it *all*, now. How Strahan

had captured him and thrown him into irons, abusing Lorn to keep Donal a subdued, well-mannered prisoner.

'Tell me something.' The boy's voice; Donal opened his eyes. 'Tell me something, Donal . . . why was it so easy?' Strahan stood in the cabin just inside the door. He wore dark blue tunic and trews of the finest wool, belted with leather and silver.

Donal swallowed. He had no intention of answering Strahan, but his throat was very dry.

'All my life my father taught me the Cheysuli were not men to be taken without expending great effort . . . yet you fell easily into my hands and make no effort to break free.' Black brows knitted over hooded eyes. 'Is this an example of the power of the *lir*-bond? I have heard how consuming it is – how a warrior gives up his life when the life of a *lir* is taken . . . but Lorn is not yet *dead*. Merely – *confined*.'

Strahan did not elaborate on the confinement, but Donal knew very well what the wolf had undergone. He could feel it in himself as he lay chained to the bunk. Weakness. Hunger. Disorientation. Great thirst. Fever. And while Lorn suffered, so did he. So *would* he, until the wolf was free and well.

The boy moved closer to the bunk. 'I expected more from you. In all our months together, you led me to believe you were a warrior. But I see no warrior. Just a *man* – a *human* man, caught within my trap.' Yet another step closer. '*Where is the falcon, Donal?*'

Donal heard the change in tone. Strahan was a boy, but a boy with recourse to all the arcane arts of the netherworld. It made him old though young. It made him seem a man when he was not.

He is not a fool . . . and I dare not treat him as one. 'Taj is dead.' His voice was mostly a croak.

Strahan laughed. 'Do you expect me to believe *that*? I *know* what that death entails, Donal. I know about the madness.'

'Taj is dead.'

'Do not undervalue me!' Color stood high in Strahan's face. 'I will paint you a picture, *my lord*. Let us say the falcon is dead. Because you have the wolf, you need not concern yourself with the death-ritual; you are released from the responsibility. But I hold Lorn. Lorn is – ill. The wolf is not himself. And while neither are *you* yourself, precisely, I would hardly claim you mad.' Strahan shook his head. 'With Taj dead and Lorn so close, you would not be sane.'

'What lies has Tynstar told you?'

'None at all,' the boy said gently. 'It is no secret to me. A *lirless* Cheysuli, left alive, loses what mind he has left. But because your race is so proud, so strong, so *arrogant*, you cannot bear to see any warrior lose his mind along with his *lir*. And so you created a ceremony. Glorified suicide.' Strahan smiled. 'Oh, aye, I know about the taboo. A Cheysuli would never stoop to suicide. But what else does a warrior do when his *lir* is dead? He gives himself over to whatever force will slay him.'

'No –'

'*Aye*. I know it, Donal. Do you forget I held your father?'

Donal lunged up against his chains. 'Get out of my sight!'

'No.'

'He was not – a *toy* . . . he was a man . . . a *man* – you did not defeat the warrior! Therefore you did not defeat the man! You did not defeat my *jehan* –'

'Oh, but I think I did.' Strahan stared at Donal. The faintest underscore of comprehension edged his tone. 'And, in doing it – I think I defeated *you* –'

'He was a *man* . . . not a beast, not a bird, not a *thing* –' Donal sucked in a breath. 'He was Duncan of the Cheysuli, from the line of the Old Mujhars . . . in the days when the Lion of Homana still belonged to *us* –'

Strahan looked down upon him. 'Us,' he echoed. 'Aye. My father has taught me, too. How the Lion belonged to us all.'

'*No*!' Donal shut his teeth into his lip. *No more – give*

this boy no more words to twist around – 'The Lion was ever ours. *Cheysuli* – never Ihlini. Tynstar spun a tale –'

'Tynstar spun *nothing*,' Strahan retorted. 'My father told the truth.'

'The old gods take you,' Donal said weakly. 'There are nothing but lies in your head.'

'And nothing but truth on my tongue.' Strahan stood next to the bunk. 'Even *if* my father lied, do you think he would ever claim kinship to you? Would he admit to a taint so willingly if there were no need for it?'

'*Taint*.' Donal nearly spat. 'Cheysuli blood would be his saving grace.'

Strahan's lips peeled back from his teeth in a smile full of spite. 'Then consider us nearly *saved*, my lord. Consider us full of grace.'

'*Ku'reshtin*,' Donal swore weakly, but the boy had left the cabin.

He did not know where Lorn was. He had wakened on board a ship in heavy iron, half senseless from the blast of power Strahan had leveled against him. He knew Lorn still lived for the link was intact. His Old Blood gave him the ability to converse with his *lir* regardless of the presence of Ihlini, but he could not break through the wolf's pain. He was, more or less, alone.

Yet again he entered the link in search of Taj, knowing it likely the falcon was still too distant to hear his pattern; knowing also it was worth trying. With Taj free, he had a chance. The falcon could rouse the others and warn of Strahan's purpose.

But there was no answer from Taj. All Donal could do was detach himself from the links and hope Lorn would recover in time.

He hung in his chains and sweated into the thin blanket on his bunk.

Donal was brought on deck under close guard. He squinted against the sunlight and nearly fell. Confinement

in irons had stiffened his muscles and slowed his reflexes. He caught himself against the taffrail and wrenched himself upright, then realized where Strahan had brought him.

By the gods – does he think he can hold the Crystal Isle? This is a Cheysuli *place!*

The mist still clouded the island, closing down over the ship. It settled into his furred leathers. He looked past the dock to the beaches and saw the fine white sand; the forests that lay beyond.

Strahan stood nearby. He was wrapped in a crimson, fur-lined cloak as fine as any Donal had known in Homana-Mujhar. 'When last we were here you brought me as a servant, thinking to elevate a homeless orphan from the degradation of the streets.' He laughed. 'All my talk of demons – all my talk of fear! Enough to lull you to my purpose.' He gestured. 'I have made the island mine. I have Atvians and Ihlini to serve me. Fitting, is it not, after you so eloquently told me how the Firstborn came from here?' His odd eyes were fixed on Donal's face. 'How does it feel, warrior, to know I have made this an Ihlini place?'

Donal, clinging grimly to the rail with manacled hands, did not choose to answer. What he saw and what he knew conflicted in his mind, for before him stood a slender, delicate boy who had yet to reach proper manhood, and yet claimed all the burgeoning power of the Ihlini.

Tynstar spent more than three centuries learning his arts. Strahan is a boy – those centuries stretch ahead. What will he be in a hundred, two *hundred years from now?*

The Atvian guards took him from the deck and led him off the ship. Donal stood silently on the dock, watching how Strahan ordered the unloading. He tried to get some glimmer, some indication from the gods that they watched what Strahan did, but there was nothing. The wind was empty of omniscience.

Strahan turned to him and laughed. 'Where are your old gods *now*, shapechanger? How could this have happened?' Silver glinted in his ears. No more was he the

urchin but a well-dressed young man instead, clothed in fine woolens and glittering ornamentation.

It was useless to remonstrate, to offer Strahan worthless threats and promises. If Lorn recovered, there was a chance Donal could escape. If Taj at last heard his seeking pattern, the falcon could carry warning to Finn and the others as well. But there was no certainty of either.

'Your wolf, Donal.'

He swung around, taking an involuntary step forward. He saw a crate, a wooden crate, rolled end over end down the plank, from the ship to the dock below. He heard a muted yelp.

Pain blazed through his mind. *What has Strahan done? Lorn – what has he done to you?*

Guards held him back. He was helpless to aid the wolf. All he could do was mouth incoherent appeals, but he voiced none of them to Strahan.

The boy gestured. 'Release him. I want him to understand what it is to confront a dying *lir*.'

Donal jerked free of the loosening hands and stumbled across to the chest. He fell to his knees, seeking to work stiff fingers through the single narrow opening admitting air to the wolf. He touched a crusted nose.

Lorn! You must not fail!

The wolf's pattern was very weak. *No water – no food – little air –*

You cannot die . . . Lorn, I beg you –

You have another, Lorn answered weakly. *You will not be lirless. You will not face the death-ritual.*

Donal tried to thrust his fingers more deeply but the wood compressed his flesh. *Lorn – I will not let you die –*

It is better so. I grow weaker. Were I an unblessed wolf of the pack, the others would slay me to protect themselves. The crusted nose pressed briefly against his bruised fingers. *Lir – there is also another reason.*

There is no reason worthy of giving in! Donal said angrily. *Have you gone mad? I need you!*

As I weaken, so do you, Lorn told him. *Do not deny*

it – I can feel it in the link. Do you lose strength because of me, the Ihlini will have his victory.

Donal could not deny it. In the days since Strahan had taken them both he had known a steady lessening of his strength; a gnawing weakness in his spirit. While Lorn was so ill from his injuries and captivity, Donal was affected as well.

Lir – I will not allow *you to die*.

'Come,' Strahan said. 'It is time you saw your quarters.'

Hands on his arms dragged Donal from the chest. Donal lashed out in fury with manacled hands and booted feet, seeking to slay what he could reach, but the guards were well-prepared. He struck out again, then froze as he heard a low wail of pain from Lorn.

Lir –?

He turned. He saw the sword in Strahan's hands. The tip of the blade protruded into the crate through the narrow opening. 'Do as I say,' Strahan ordered. 'Accompany my servants.'

'And if he dies?' Donal challenged. 'How will you make me obey you then?'

'If he dies, so does your will.' Strahan smiled. 'You will live a while longer because there is still the falcon, but when I am done with you the madness will be a *blessing*.'

One of the Atvians thrust an arm into the air. 'My lord – *look*!'

A fleet falcon swept through the air toward the ship. It circled neatly over them all and dipped toward the dock, screaming its agitation.

Taj! Donal cried within the link. *Go! Seek Finn and the Cheysuli. Tell them it is Tynstar's brat who holds me – the boy we thought was Sef –*

'By the Seker, it is the falcon!' Strahan shouted. 'I will slay *both* of them.'

'Taj,' Donal shouted. 'Go!'

Strahan took two steps to Donal and set the tip of the sword against his spine. 'I know you. I know your heritage. Alix's son, are you not? – and she with all the Old

Blood. Seek you the shapechange? Do not. Or I will slay you here.'

'Slay me, and you lose your tame Mujhar.' Donal bared his teeth, feigning a smile.

'I plan to replace you one day,' Strahan pointed out. 'It can be sooner rather than later.' He raised one hand. In the other, the sword wavered, tilted downward, too heavy for him to hold up. The tip bit into the wood of the dock.

Fingers stiffened, snapped apart. From the tips came a blinding stream of brilliant light. Deepest purple, tinged with sparks. An echo of the power Donal had seen in Tynstar.

He aims for Taj – Donal turned on the Ihlini, striking out with shackles and chains. He struck through the flame streaming from Strahan's fingers and felt it spark and burn against his skin, raising crimson weals. Then the fire abruptly died, for the boy lay gasping and blue-faced beneath Donal's weight and throttling fingers.

Hands were on him, jerking him from the boy. Donal teetered at the dock's edge as they thrust him roughly away. He saw that Taj still flew unmolested toward the mainland and released a sigh of relief.

Strahan got unsteadily to his feet. The sword lay on the dock, but he ignored it. 'Punishment,' he promised hoarsely. 'You will be sorry for that.'

He thrust both arms into the air as if he invoked a deity. Donal, recalling how Tynstar had tried to summon Asar-Suti, thought Strahan intended the same. He saw the air darken around the pale hands; smoke rolled out of the mist. It wreathed the hands in flame.

Strahan laughed. 'Would you care to meet my *lir*?'

Donal's flesh rose up on his bones. 'The Ihlini *have* no *lir* –'

'No? Well, perhaps she is not a *lir* precisely – but she is made of the same blood and bone.' Crimson sparks shot out of the smoke as it spun around his hands. 'She comes from the netherworld, from the Gate of Asar-Suti. And such a lovely, lovely demon –' the flame and smoke

exploded '– shall I fly her for you, Donal?'

Black smoke and flame took substance. Donal saw talons, wings, a wickedly curving beak. And a pair of golden eyes that watched him with a malicious intensity.

'Sakti –' Strahan hissed, '*take* the falcon for me!'

Donal spun. '*Fly!*' he shouted at Taj.

The falcon dipped and dove, streaking from the hawk, but Sakti was relentless. She gained, caught up, struck out with raking talons.

'Taj . . . *fly!*'

Taj flew, but the demon-hawk flew faster. Sakti rose, stooped, struck down with curving talons. One pierced the falcon's breast.

'Taj!' Donal screamed.

The falcon fell out of the sky.

Taj –

– Taj –

Taj?

He drifted, he dreamed. He cried. He knew himself half mad.

Lir –

– lir –

Lir?

He slept. He wakened. He cried.

He could not help himself.

– '*Wanderer,*' Evan said, '*you will embark upon a journey.*' *The dice and rune-sticks fell, rattling on the wood –*

– '*Jester and Charlatan: those who are not what they seem –*'

– *Youth –*

– *Imprisonment –*

– *Executioner –*

– *Why not have the Ellasian dice you your destiny?*

– *Who is to say he will be wrong? –*

– *wrong –*

Wrong.

He slept.
Dreamed.
Drifted.

*– Your shar tahl has failed your clan. You know nothing
of the histories –*
   – They sired also a second race –
   – They sired the Ihlini –
   – who bred with the Cheysuli –
'No!'
   – who bred with the Cheysuli –

He wakened shouting *No*. But there was no one there to
hear.

For a long time he forgot who he was or why Strahan held
him. And then he remembered.
   He remembered *why*.

He was alone. He was locked within a room that held a
comfortable bed, a bench, a table and high narrow casements that let in the mist and muted sun. The iron remained
on his wrists, but he had the freedom of the chamber.
   Freedom.
   It almost made him laugh.

Lorn he could not reach. There was a barrier in the link.
But not utter emptiness that would signify Lorn's death.
The wolf lived, but Donal could not touch him.

He tried to follow the days by scratching runes into the
bedpost with the buckle of his belt, but he knew he had lost
track. The light was somehow wrong. The fog occluded
the sun. He could not judge the season or the time.
   But it was cold. One brazier was not enough.

He ate.

He drank.

He was left entirely alone.

The door crashed open. Donal spun around.

Strahan stood within the chamber –

– and so did Finn and Evan.

The boy laughed. 'It pleases me to reunite you, now that I have you all.'

Donal's breath rattled in his throat as he stared at Finn. 'He – took – *you*?'

'Evan and I came to rescue you.' The tone was wry, reproving.

The Ellasian grinned. 'You might at least give us your gratitude.'

'*Why?*' Donal demanded. 'How could you come *alone* –?'

'It seemed the best idea.' Finn and Evan seemed well enough. Unharmed, and certainly less than horrified by the presence of Tynstar's son.

Donal glared at Evan. 'What will High King Rhodri say when he learns his youngest son has fallen prisoner to Strahan?'

'Probably that I am a fool, and no loss,' Evan said lightly. 'Perhaps I am, and it is not . . . but I thought to aid a friend.'

Donal thrust out his hands, displaying the heavy shackles. '*How?*' he demanded. 'By wearing Ihlini iron?'

The scar twisted on Finn's cheek as he laughed. 'I see a lengthy confinement has not improved your temper.'

Donal stared at him. He felt his mouth dry up. 'How long?' he asked. 'How long have I been here?'

No one answered at once. And then Strahan laughed. 'Have you lost count? Did you not see the season change? It worked – *it worked* – I made you forget *everything*, even the time of year!'

Donal recalled how he had made marks in the bedpost to keep track of time. One day, he had stopped. And then

the time was lost, and *he* was lost, and now he could not recall how long he had been a prisoner of Strahan.

Gods . . . is this how the madness begins?

'It *worked*!' Strahan exulted. 'Do you not recall all the times you begged me for your name? How you begged me for a polished plate so you could see yourself? You believed yourself a hawk – a *hawk*, not a falcon. Mimicking your father?'

'Six months,' Donal whispered in horror.

'Winter has come and gone,' Finn said gently. 'Donal – let it go.'

He looked at his hands. Hands only. The fingers were fingers, not talons. But he recalled it, a little; he recalled how he had feared the shapechange as he slept. As Strahan teased him with his power. *By the gods . . . I think we have all gone mad –*

He stared at Finn and Evan. 'You are fools.' His tone was inflectionless. 'Fools, both of you . . . you have given Homana over to Tynstar's son.'

'I think not,' Finn answered. 'You see, the boy is just a boy – still learning about his power. He may be Tynstar's son, but can he lead his race? He is young. *Young* – and youth has a way of tripping over hardships before the highest goal is won.' He turned to Strahan. 'Did you think we *fell* into your hands when we made certain you would take us?'

Color shot into Strahan's face. 'What do you say to me?' he demanded. '*What do you say to me?*'

'That it is time for us to go.'

'You *cannot!* I hold you! You are my prisoners!'

Finn's hand was in his belt-pouch. 'It is time for us to go.'

The boy stretched out his hand. At his fingertips danced a rune of brilliant purple. 'I am Tynstar's son. *I am the Ihlini!*'

'And you have lost one of your ward-stones.' Finn held it up so all could see it: a small round rock, dull grey, with a single streak of black. 'Boy,' Finn said, 'do you know enough to be frightened?'

Clearly, Strahan did. He backed away, clutching at the crimson robe he wore over dark grey winter leathers. His thin face turned white, then splotchy red; the rune snuffed out in his hand.

Finn smiled. 'I do not suppose you have the other four somewhere upon your person –?'

Strahan turned and ran.

'Apparently he does not.' Finn returned the stone to his belt-pouch. 'I think it is time to go, before he fetches the rest of the stones.'

Donal stared at his uncle. 'Why? What would happen if he did?'

'Together, the ward-stones augment his power. Apart, they can be used against the sorcerer who made them.' Finn gestured toward the door. 'Do you tarry, I will think you wish to *stay*.'

'I need Lorn.'

'We will find him.' Finn preceded him through the door.

They ran down a corridor. 'What of the other Ihlini?' Evan asked.

'They die like other men.' Finn led them down a staircase and through an airy chamber. 'You have a knife, Ellasian – surely you can use it.'

They went down. Down and down, into the bowels of the palace.

'*Su'fali!*' Donal cried. 'I can touch him . . . *there* – Lorn is there!' He gestured at a narrow wooden door half hidden by an arras.

Finn tore it aside and jerked open the unlocked door. 'Storr,' he said in satisfaction. The wolf held a guard at bay.

'Lorn –?' Donal asked.

'Through there, I would hazard.' Finn indicated a second door. 'And now, Ihlini – safe journey to your god –'

Donal's chains clashed as he shouldered open the door. He stumbled inside, ducking his head, and nearly fell over his *lir*.

338

'Lorn!' He dropped to his knees beside the wolf.

Lorn lay on his side in soiled straw. The visible eye was rolled back in his head. The tongue, protruding from between his jaws, was dry and crusted. But he breathed. Barely, but he breathed.

Donal touched the lusterless, matted fur. *Lir – I will not allow you to die – I order you to live –*

He felt the faintest flicker of amusement from the tattered edges of the link. *But it is the lir who have the ordering of the Cheysuli.*

Fingers spasmed, then dug more deeply into the pelt. He felt the ladder of Lorn's protruding ribs. *Will you live?*

You still have need of me.

Donal wavered in relief, then bent and set his face against Lorn's shoulder. *I could not bear it if you died.* Then he smiled up at his uncle. 'I think he will be all right.'

Finn knelt and gathered the wolf into his arms. 'I will take him. You are not much stronger than he.' He rose and jerked his head at Evan. 'See he comes, Ellasian. We have gone to too much trouble to lose him so easily now.'

Evan grinned and grasped Donal's arm. 'Come, my lord – we must steal ourselves a boat.'

339

They won free of the palace proper without coming to harm – Evan slew three Atvian guards – but the high white walls of the bailey proved a greater foe than man. Locked and attended gates denied them an exit as easy as their entrance.

They ducked down into the darkness of full night, hiding themselves in shadows and vegetation. Finn tended Lorn while Evan watched for guards. Donal knelt against the wall and pushed a trembling forearm through sweat-dampened hair, aware the six months of captivity had leached him of grace and quickness. He rested his head against one doubled knee, trying to catch his breath, and felt the hard cold iron of Strahan's shackles on his arms.

Gods – is this what it was for Carillon when he wore Atvian iron? Inwardly, he shuddered. *It is a perfect humiliation.*

'Donal –?' It was Evan, hunching down beside him. One hand touched Donal's leather-clad shoulder.

Donal lifted his head. 'I am well enough, Evan . . . see to yourself.'

Evan, laughing softly, withdrew the hand. 'Without me, my proud Mujhar, you might still be Strahan's prisoner. Do I get no thanks from you?'

Donal smiled into the darkness. 'Would a prince accept *payment* for the aid he rendered a fellow prince?'

'Mujhar,' Evan corrected. 'Aye, he might . . . could he win it in a fortune-game.' Slanting shadow across the Ellasian's face hid his eyes and nose, but not his mobile

mouth. He grinned. 'But there may be a better reward than that. There was a young woman I admired at your wedding celebration. Could you give her good word of me, it might be payment enough.'

'Which one?' Donal asked dryly. 'I cannot recall them all.'

'You said her name was Meghan.'

Chains clashed as Donal glanced at Evan sharply. 'And do you forget? – I also told you who sired her.' He indicated Finn crouching not far from them with Lorn still cradled in his arms. 'Say to *him* you wish to know his daughter better.'

'Were you to give *him* good word of me –'

'I think he knows you better than most.' But the levity quickly faded. Donal moved over to kneel beside his wolf. *Lorn?*

I have not died yet, lir.

Donal smiled. Then he glanced up at Finn's face. 'He requires proper healing.'

'And will have it . . . but not just here.'

Donal peered through the bushes at the wall. Absently, he chewed at a broken thumbnail. 'We can hardly scale the walls with an injured wolf –'

'Scale them? Why not fly over them?'

Donal looked back at him sharply. 'Taj is – lost. I have no recourse to falcon-shape.'

'Do you not?' Finn's mouth hooked down as he shook his head. 'Can you not even trust your own senses, Donal? Or your own *sense*. Were Taj truly lost, how could Evan and I have found you?'

'But – I thought you somehow knew Strahan had come here –'

'How?' Finn's voice was underscored with contempt. 'Am I omniscient? Did Evan throw the rune-sticks? And how were we to know the boy was Tynstar's get?' Grimly he shook his head. 'Imprisonment has not improved your sense anymore than your temper.'

Donal hunched forward, trying to keep the chains from

clinking. '*I saw* it, *su'fali*! Strahan summoned a demon-bird from Asar-Suti, and she slew Taj. I saw him fall!'

'The hawk injured him, aye, and he fell. But he was not slain.' Finn indicated the wall with his head. 'Do you think that is Strahan's hawk? Or is it more likely a falcon?'

Donal's head snapped around. Now that Finn pointed him out, the bird was visible. But only as a shape in the shadows. There was no light to give the bird name or color.

Hope and longing leaped up to fill Donal's chest. 'Taj?'

I am here, the falcon said. *Why do you tarry, lir? Do you come, or do you stay?*

'*Leijhana tu'sai*,' he muttered aloud in a prayer of thanksgiving to the gods. Then, within the link again: *Finn says I must fly over the walls.*

You have done such things before.

Donal laughed to himself wryly. *I am somewhat weary, lir – this has not been an easy imprisonment.*

Then why not leave it behind?

Donal shook his head in resignation. *How many guardsmen, Taj? Ihlini or Atvians?* If they were Ihlini, he had no recourse to *lir*-shape. And Taj could not help him attack them.

Six Atvians.

'Six,' Donal said glumly. 'And I am only one –'

'Are you?' Finn asked. 'I thought you were Cheysuli.'

Donal scowled at him, then turned to Evan. 'There is something you must do for me. When a warrior assumes *lir*-shape, that which he touches also changes. I would prefer *not* to take the shackles with me; I need you to hold them, and as I change from man to falcon you must pull them free of my wings. Can you do that?'

Evan shrugged. 'It does not sound particularly difficult.'

Donal smiled a little. 'And if the change encompassed *you*?'

The Ellasian's blue eyes widened a trifle. '*Could* it?'

'Who can say?' Donal, grinning inwardly, held out his shackled arms. 'Catch hold, Evan, and we shall find out.'

The Ellasian, after only a momentary hesitation,

reached out and closed his hands around the heavy chains at wrists and ankles. Donal, doubled up in a sitting position, drew in a deep breath and shut his eyes. The shape-change required extreme concentration, and of late the concept had become an alien one.

He felt the peace come rushing in to fill him up with a marvelous sense of well-being. All the pain and anguish of the past six months melted away into nothingness. He was at peace within himself, and from the center of that calm he reached out to tap the power that gave him the gift of the shapechange.

Donal froze. Even as he tapped the power and felt it run up from the earth to encompass flesh and bones, he thought of the *thing* his father had been. And he could not face himself.

'Donal!' Finn's voice sounding oddly frightened. 'Donal – *go one way or the other –*'

So, he *was* a halfway thing. Even Finn saw the difference.

Instinctively he reached out to his falcon. *Taj?*

Trust me. Trust yourself. What Strahan did was Ihlini-wrought, and not of good, clean earth magic. Do you think the gods would allow the magic to fail when it is you who asks it?

No. And he reached out again, let the power enfold him utterly, and took flight as the shackles and chains crashed against the ground.

Two falcons drove out of the darkness at the guardsmen, striking with deadly talons and hooked, sharp beaks. They were not large birds, not as dangerous as eagle or hawk in full attack, but in darkness – and unexpected – even a small creature can prove powerfully effective.

Men screamed and fell to their knees, arms flailing at the birds. When three of them groveled in the dirt, clutching bleeding faces, three others drew swords and slashed viciously at the attacking falcons. One sought safety in a tree. The other flew to the ground and became a man.

A blade dipped as the hand that held it clenched in spasmodic fear; the tip bit into dirt. Donal stepped close and broke the man's neck with a single blow, then caught up the sword and turned to face the other two.

He smiled. *Leijhana tu'sai, Carillon . . . the skill will not go unused after all* –

He spun, whirling, as one man sought his unprotected back. He swung, felt blade bite through leathers and wool, then more deeply, splintering ribs and sundering flesh. But his hands were ungloved in the nighttime chill, and the gush of warm blood slicked the grip of the blade. It slipped in his hands, and as the man crumpled to the ground he took the sword with him.

The last guard came at him as he turned, lacking knife, sword or bow. Donal's arms rose slowly as he lifted them away from his body, hands spreading in the air. He saw the faintest flicker of the sword in the torchlight near the wall; he leaped back, nearly tripped over the dead man's body, then lunged backward yet again.

Lir – he began.

I am coming, Taj replied. *You require my help after all*.

The falcon swept down out of the tree and dug his talons into the guardsman's hands upon the hilt. He bit out a startled oath and dropped the sword. Taj veered away, but as he did the guardsman drew his long-knife.

Donal watched the knife blade. But the guardsman was no fool; he swung with his other arm and smashed it into Donal's face. Ringmail bit in and scored his cheek, Donal swore viciously and jerked his head away. The knife sought his abdomen even as he held the ringmailed wrist.

The Atvian slammed him against the gate. The left arm slid up to crush Donal's vulnerable throat.

Thank the gods he is not Ihlini – Donal took *lir*-shape instantly and left the guardsman staggering against the gate. He darted up, then flew down again and took back his human form.

The Atvian plunged forward with his knife. Donal slid easily aside. He caught the man's slashing arm as it drove

past him and snapped it against his upraised thigh.

He caught the knife as it fell from spasming fingers. He allowed the man to fall –

– he spun –

– threw –

– the knife was buried in the back of the Atvian's unprotected neck.

Three more – Donal turned, prepared, but the Atvians provided no threat to him. All three still groveled in the dirt, hands thrust up before their bleeding faces. One man had lost both eyes; the other two bled badly from mouth and nose.

All cried piteously for help from their gods and Strahan. And the man who faced them.

Donal turned away. Grimly he unbarred the gate and thrust open one of the leaves, whistling for Finn and Evan. They came, accompanied by Storr, and Lorn clasped in Finn's strong arms.

'Six,' Finn remarked as he passed by Donal into the darkness. 'A warrior after all.'

'I slew only three,' Donal retorted.

'Ah,' said Evan, nodding as he slipped by. 'That does somewhat diminish your accomplishment.'

Donal departed the gate and followed them to the dock. 'Which boat?' he asked.

'The closest!' Evan answered.

They ran –

– and Strahan's black hawk exploded out of darkness.

Donal was hurled to his knees as the tremendous weight drove into back and shoulders. Talons closed. Leather tore open; so did flesh and muscle.

He arched, straining upward in an effort to catch the hawk in his hands. Pain vibrated through his body until he thought he would scream with it. But his fingers could not touch the bird.

Evan thrust with his knife. But Sakti drove upward, avoiding the blade with a snap of her powerful wings. She shrieked, wheeled, stooped. Talons slashed past Evan's

desperate defense and drove again into Donal's back. She hurled him onto his face.

Donal was half-blind with pain. He tasted blood in his mouth from having bitten his tongue. His face pressed into sand and seashell; he dug handfuls of fine-grained sand. '*Su'fali!*' he cried. Sand and shell crept into his mouth as Satki's weight ground his face into the beach. 'By the gods, *su'fali – gainsay this demon-bird –*'

'No warbow!' Finn raged. '*Had I my bow –!*'

'Do something!' Evan shouted, diving at the hawk. 'Lodhi! – how can we stop this thing –?'

Finn set Lorn down upon the beach. Hastily he sought stones. Those few he found he caught up in his hands, and searched for the hawk. She spiraled over their heads, drifting in apparent idleness; her cries were malevolence given tongue.

One by one, Finn hurled the stones at the hawk. His aim was good, but Sakti was too swift. Strahan's borrowed demon began to play with them all.

Donal pressed himself upward, biting his lip to keep back his cry of pain. His back and shoulders were afire, but he thrust himself to his knees. 'She – seeks to delay us – for Strahan –' he said breathlessly. 'We must ignore her – go on – get away from here –'

'How?' Evan demanded. 'That *thing* is more than hawk!'

'Demon –' Donal gasped. 'Strahan summoned her from the god of the netherworld –'

Sakti wheeled. Stooped. But her target was Evan now.

His breath exploded from his chest as the hawk drove into his ribs, talons closed, knocking him to the ground. But this time Finn was prepared. He waited as she rose, preparing to stoop again, and as her wings snapped closed he drew his knife and hurled it into the air.

The blade glinted in the moonlight. It sliced upward toward the hawk. Sakti, screeching, turned aside. But one foot shot out and talons grasped, closing on the hilt. Wings snapped shut. She stooped. Now she drove at Finn.

He dropped to the ground, rolling as the hawk came at him. One lone talon slashed across his shoulder, tearing fur-lined leather. But she released the knife, and as she hurled herself upward to stoop again, Finn thrust himself to his feet and caught the hilt as it fell.

Sakti soared, wings extended against the stars. Finn waited. And when she snapped her wings shut he hurled the knife again.

Taj darted out of the darkness directly at the hawk. Sakti's size dwarfed the falcon, but Taj did not give in. He flew straight at her and turned her from her course into the path of the oncoming knife.

The blade struck home in Sakti's chest. She screamed; screaming, she fell. But her talons were still extended.

Donal, head tipped back to stare upward into the sky, cried out as the talons sank into the side of his neck. Sakti's weight threw him over onto his back; the talons dug deeper still.

He clawed at his neck, seeking escape. Sakti quivered and was still, but even death did not loosen the clutching talons. It was Evan who at last pried them free and clamped a hand over the wound in Donal's neck.

'*Lodhi!* – how he bleeds!'

'– to death, do we not stanch it.' Finn pressed Evan's hand more tightly against the wound. 'You must keep it shut – I will take Lorn . . . Ellasian, get him *up* from there! We must take him into the forest.'

Donal was half-senseless. He felt Evan urging him to his feet, but his limbs would not obey him. He thought it would be easier and far less painful did he simply remain lying on the beach with the cool sand under his twitching body.

Up – get you *up* –' Evan panted. '*Lodhi*, Donal – do you wish to bleed to death?'

Evan's hand was clamped to Donal's neck. The pressure hurt. Donal's own hand rose up to peel the Ellasian's fingers away, but Evan withstood his feeble attempt.

'Finn – can you not compel him? Can you not use a little of your magic?'

'Not here; not I. Too many Ihlini present. *Donal* might have the ability –' his voice broke off a moment '– *carry* him, if you have to!'

Evan dragged him from the ground. Donal stumbled, staggered, nearly fell again. His neck was bound up in pain. 'Gods –' he said hoarsely, '– *gods* –'

'Bring him,' Finn said harshly, and carried Lorn from the beach into the forest.

– pain –

He stumbled. Evan held him up. He staggered. Evan kept him from falling. He nearly vomited. Evan merely held on more tightly and gave him what words he could of encouragement. But most of them were in Ellasian.

– pain –

His left shoulder was wet with warm blood. It soaked through his leathers and dampened the fur lining, until he could feel it running down his arm in rivulets. It dripped from his fingers to the forest floor, splattering onto his boots.

– so much pain . . . pain and blood –

He staggered. But Evan held him up and mumbled Ellasian encouragement.

'Here!' The call came from Finn, hidden by trees and shadow, 'Hurry, Ellasian –'

Evan hurried. Donal could not. But at last they broke from the trees into a clearing, and saw the tumbled ruin.

Finn came out of the crooked doorway, lacking Lorn, and helped Evan carry Donal. 'Bring him inside. It is cold, damp – offering little enough shelter – but perhaps Strahan will forget this place exists.'

'What *is* it?' Evan asked.

Donal, half-dragged, peered through slitted eyes. He saw huddled green-grey stones taller than Carillon, set in a haphazard circle. Slotted darkness lay between them; they had lost their uniformity, the perfection of their edges. They gaped apart, like a man missing most of his teeth.

'This place was once used as a place of worship by the Firstborn,' Finn said grimly, half-carrying his nephew. 'There are a few remaining in corners of Homana. . . . I do not doubt this is the first, the oldest. Perhaps it will be our protection against the boy. Here – let us settle him here, against the wall.'

Donal moaned as they put him down on the cold, damp ground. The stone was hard and cruel against his torn back.

'Lay a fire,' Finn told Evan.

'With what, my *will*?' Evan demanded. 'I have no flint.'

Finn dug into his belt-pouch. 'Here. Use your knife and your wits. This calls for cautery.'

Evan caught the flint as Finn tossed it. 'Can you not use your healing powers?'

'I am one man. I have not the strength to seal so deep a wound. And you are not your *rujholli* with his magic harp.'

Evan turned and went out. He brought back chips of wood and broken branches and piled them carefully. Sparks flew from the flint as he used his knife upon it, but none caught in the kindling.

'Princeling.' The twisted title, from Finn, was an insult. 'Too gently raised in Rhodri's hall.'

Evan said nothing, but Donal could see the grim line of his mouth. Finn, kneeling next to his nephew with one hand shutting off the blood, watched impatiently as Evan worked the flint.

'*Su'fali* –' Donal's voice was little more than a broken whisper. 'Is this how you treated Carillon?'

Finn stared down at him. His yellow eyes were black in the dimness of the chapel. Starlight shone in through the broken beamwork, but not enough to illuminate the place. 'When he was deserving of it,' he said at last. Donal saw the crooked smile. 'That was most of the time.'

The kindling caught at last and began to smolder. Carefully Evan coaxed it into a flame, fed it more wood, then set the knife blade in the fire.

349

'Patience, Donal,' Finn said softly. '*Shansu, shansu* – I will not let the boy prevail.'

Blood still coursed from beneath Finn's pressing hand.

Donal felt weakness and lethargy seep into his flesh and spirit. Could he sleep, the pain would go away –

'Donal!' Finn said sharply. 'Do you forget your *lir*? He needs your aid. When the wound is closed, we will heal him. But I need you for that – do not give in now!'

Donal reached instinctively for Lorn, but his own pain and Lorn's weakness threw up a barrier in the link. He could sense the wolf's presence – or was it Storr's? – but nothing more. Taj as well was denied to him.

Evan sighed and rubbed an arm across his eyes. The knife blade glowed crimson at the tip; heat slowly spread up the steel. When it had reached the hilt, Evan took off his fur-lined velvet doublet and folded it into a wrap to protect his hand as he held the knife. He took it out of the fire and carried it back to Finn.

Donal, transfixed by the glowing blade that danced against the darkness, opened his mouth to tell them no.

Finn nodded. 'I will take my hand away. You must sear it quickly; I may not be able to hold him.'

'Aye,' Evan said roughly. 'I am sorry, Donal –'

Finn released the wound. Blood welled up afresh, spilling down Donal's chest. But Finn caught his shoulders and pressed his back against the wall. '*Now* –'

Blood hissed as the blade came down. Fluids popped; flesh was seared together. Donal's body spasmed and arched like a man in the clutches of death. Finn held him, spoke to him, but Donal heard nothing. He was eaten alive with pain.

'Enough,' Finn said. He shut his fingers in the leather of Donal's winter shirt. 'Rouse yourself! Lorn has need of you.'

Donal's hand clawed at the cauterized wound, then spasmed away as the pain renewed itself. 'Gods – have you *slain* me?'

'Rouse yourself,' Finn repeated. 'Do you deny your *lir*?'

Sense crept back. With Finn's aid, Donal got up onto his knees. At Lorn's side he shut his eyes and waited for weakness to pass, then set his hands against the dry, staring coat. 'Help me, *su'fali*. . . . I have not the strength to do it alone.'

'Nor I.' Finn's tone was uncommonly gentle. 'Let yourself go, Donal. Give yourself over to the earth.'

Donal's head bowed down. The puckered seam in his neck blazed up as if newly cauterized. Donal shut his eyes.

Give myself over . . . give myself over to the earth. But – what am I to do if the earth does not wish to give me up when the healing has been completed?

But he could not wait for an answer he knew would not come. Instead, he sank his awareness into the warmth of the earth and sought Finn's presence in the darkness. He found it. They linked at once, then sought the healing magic.

A spring, bubbling up from underground. It flowed. It encapsulated their spirits, examined them, understood their need, and went onward to the wolf. It flowed, bathing him in its strength, until the wounds were healed and the bright burning of his spirit was renewed. And then it flowed away.

'Done,' Donal mumbled. 'See how he sleeps?'

'Done,' Finn agreed. '*Shansu*, Donal . . . it is your turn now.'

Donal opened his mouth to answer. Nothing issued from his mouth, not even a final sigh. He felt himself slump sideways and struggled to halt his fall, knowing the landing would hurt his wounds, but his body did not obey.

He felt Finn catch him, and then he sank down into a sleep as deep as any he had known.

5

Donal roused to pain. It burned in neck and shoulders, down his back. He felt as if someone had flayed him alive and left the bones to molder in the ruins.

He lay perfectly still, still wrapped around the warmth of Lorn's furred body. He felt the regular lifting of Lorn's side; heard the subtle thumping of his heart. He lay relieved, with weary exultation: he was free of Strahan, and the wolf would recover fully.

Slowly, he pushed himself into a sitting position. He grunted against his will; torn flesh and muscles protested. An exploratory hand told him someone had bandaged the talon wounds in his back and shoulders. Finn, most likely – and with Evan's velvet doublet. He felt terribly weak, battered.

He scowled, trying to clear his vision. He saw grey-green stones surrounding them in a tumbled circle. Some stones stood upright, sentinels in the dawn; others tilted against neighbors; a few lay on the ground. Broken beamwork littered the center of the chapel; a ruined altar stood farthest from the fire Evan had built.

Finn squatted by the makeshift cairn. 'Well?'

Donal turned his head carefully. The flesh pulled; he touched a puckered seam half a man's hand in length in the hollow where neck and shoulder met. 'You have butchered me, *su'fali*.'

'We did not touch your face,' Finn retorted. 'When the marks of battle have faded, no doubt Sorcha will find you just as pretty as before.'

352

Donal scowled.

Finn stood, stretching elborately. Mist drifted in the chapel and dew beaded on the stones. 'I will fetch us something to eat. I go no farther until my belly is full again.'

'Make it plump game,' Donal advised. 'If Evan is as hungry as *I* am, we shall need a sizable breakfast.'

Finn loosened the Homanan knife in its sheath. Donal, looking at the heavy hilt with its rampant royal lion, thought again how bitter it must be for Finn to know Carillon was dead.

For so many years his task was to keep him alive . . . yet in the end, he aided his death.

Finn glanced over at Evan, still curled up on a pile of leaves. 'The Ellasian sleeps like the dead,' he said scathingly, and then he went out of the chapel with Storr trotting at his side.

'I am neither asleep nor dead.' Evan rolled over and sat up. 'I was merely trying to get warm.'

'Then move to the fire.' Donal did so himself, albeit slowly, and put more wood on the flames.

Evan got up, twisted to unkink his neck and spine, then moved to the fire and squatted down. 'What is Finn about?'

'Hunting breakfast.' Donal saw how Evan's beard had come in, forming dark stubble along his jaw. He scratched at it, grimacing, and Donal blessed the gods for seeing to it the Cheysuli could not grow beards. *Too much trouble to take it off every morning.* He was amused by the transformation in his Ellasian friend. Evan's normally immaculate appearance had undergone a decided change. He was dirty, grimy; his clothing was soiled and torn.

Evan put his hands out over the flames. His fingers were scraped. Nails were broken. There was not much remaining of the prince who had come to Donal's wedding. 'I am sorry for the pain,' Evan said, looking at the bright red weal in Donal's neck. 'Finn said it was the only way.'

'It was.' Donal did not finger the puckered seam. 'But I

do not see why you did not simply sever the rest of my neck.'

Evan's mobile mouth hooked down wryly. 'I considered it seriously – but I thought Homana might wish to see her new Mujhar. She has not, you know. . . . Strahan took you too soon. There are rumors you are dead.'

'And if I am?' Donal looked at him squarely. 'You are the son of a king and know of such things. In Ellas, what would happen if the High King were slain?'

Evan shrugged. 'Lachlan would become High King. There would be no great stirring among the subjects – do you forget Rhodri has so many sons? And Lachlan himself has two – by now, perhaps three. There would be an unremarkable passing of the throne from one man to another.'

Donal stared into the fire. 'Not here. No, not here. Without me, Homana is Homanan again.' He bit at a torn flap of skin on one thumb. 'Perhaps that is what all of this is about.'

Evan frowned and added more wood. 'What do you say? This is Strahan's doing.'

'Strahan's, aye – but who else's? There could even be Homanans. Not all are reconciled to Carillon's heir.' He stood up for the first time, collected his senses, and glanced around. 'Gods – this place – it makes a man feel humble.'

He moved around the chapel slowly, looking more closely at tumbled stone and broken beamwork, fallen altar and vine-choked foundation pedestals. It was sunrise, but only the faintest tinge of orange got through the mist. It filled up the place with bronze and gold.

Donal picked his way through the debris to the altar. It leaned haphazardly sideways, propped up by another stone. Its pedestal was shattered. But on the face of the altar were runes, velveted with lichen, corroded by dampness and time.

He bent, picking at the runes with a broken nail. Pensively, he frowned. And then, when he could piece

354

together a portion of the inscription, he let out an involuntary blurt of sound.

Evan left the fire. 'What is it?'

'It is no wonder we were not disturbed last night by Strahan or his minions. This is a holy place.'

'Finn said it is a chapel.'

'*Was*. Look at the inscriptions – see how they border the altar?' Another gesture indicated the other stones. 'Each one is inscribed, I will wager, though time had hidden the runes. See you here? *These* runes – see how they are cut so deeply into the stone?' He tapped with the broken nail. 'This place offers the guardianship of the gods to any who would seek it of Cheysuli or Firstborn blood. Sanctuary, Evan. Even the Ihlini cannot touch us here.'

Taj's scream cut through the mist like a scythe.

Donal spun around and felt the scabbing of his wounds tear apart. 'Evan – *come*!'

He ran. He felt the fire in his neck and back and shoulders, but he did not pay attention. He ran.

Thorns snagged at his flesh and leathers as he leaped over fallen trees and skipped across tumbled boulders with the borrowed energy of fear. He heard Evan coming behind him, cursing the briers, but Donal had no time for oaths. Only prayers.

He broke from dense undergrowth into a tiny clearing. He stopped. He stopped so quickly Evan ran into him from behind. But he said nothing to Evan's irritated question. He could not. He could not speak at all.

Finn lay on his back in the clearing. His limbs were sprawled in an obscene parody of his normal fluid grace. He stared upward into the misted sky and blood ran from his mouth.

The sword stood up from his ribs like a royal standard. The hilt was gold, lion-shaped; the pommel stone was baleful black.

Su'fali – Slowly, jerkily, Donal moved across the clearing until he stood at Finn's side. He knelt, knowing shock

355

and pain and a tremendous, blossoming grief. '*Su'fali!*' he shouted.

Finn's left hand lay loosely clasped around the blade. Fingers were stained with his blood. Already his furred leather shirt was sodden.

As if it had been twisted in his body . . . Donal felt the wild grief break free. He swore softly in the Old Tongue, repeatedly, with all the pain and rage he felt.

Finn's mouth moved in a tiny smile. 'You have, at least, learned enough of the Old Tongue for *that*.'

'*Su'fali . . . su'fali . . . what can I do?*'

'Do not grieve, kinsman. It is a warrior's death.'

'Who?' Donal heard his voice quaver. 'Who has done this to you?'

'The boy. Retribution, he said, for the loss of *jehan* and *jehana*.' Finn's face twisted briefly with immense pain; the scar writhed upon his cheek. 'He – wanted the sword back when he was done with me. He tried to take it back. But – I am Hale's son and perhaps the sword knew me – the magic came, the sword-magic – Strahan was denied even as he put his hands upon the hilt –' Muscles in his jaw stood up. 'He wanted you as well, *harani* – he wanted to slay you with the sword Hale made for you – to prove the legend false –'

'Say no more,' Donal begged. 'Waste none of what strength is left –'

'He said you had denied the sword time and time again, diluting the magic – but *he* was willing to claim it –' A trickle of blood overspilled Finn's lips. 'You must claim it, *harani*. The sword is yours.' He swallowed heavily. 'It begins . . . it begins again . . . with yet another generation –'

'Say nothing,' Donal ordered desperately. 'Be silent, *su'fali* – I will seek the magic –'

'There is nothing you can do,' Finn said clearly but as from a great distance, 'Release my spirit when I am dead. You know the custom, Donal. The rite for a warrior slain in battle.'

'Aye.' The word rasped in Donal's swelling throat.

Finn's fingers traced the shining blade and left a smear of blood. 'Strahan sought to hurt you by slaying me, but he has given you back the sword that will, in the end, defeat him. Justice from the gods.'

Justice? No, I think not – not when it slays my su'fali –

'Say you will take it . . .' Finn's voice was just barely above a whisper. 'Say you will take it and slay Osric of Atvia with it – to avenge Carillon's death –'

'What of *yours* –?' Donal cried.

'My death does not matter. It was ever my *tahlmorra* to die in the service of the Mujhar. And – I have served them both –' Briefly he shut his eyes as pain spasmed across his face. 'Donal –'

'Aye?'

Finn struggled to tap the last of his reserves.

'You never . . . never understood Carillon . . . his reasons for doing things the way he did them. Oh I know – you are young, and youth lacks compassion and comprehension . . . but – he did what needed doing in the best way he knew how.' Again pain twisted his face. 'I – did not always agree – but I cannot dispute results. He took Homana out of the flames of war and oppression and made her whole again. He restored our race to freedom –'

'*Su'fali*' Donal begged '– speak not of Carillon *now* –'

'Should I not? But you are so much alike, Donal – when I speak of him I speak of you.' Faintly, Finn smiled. 'There are differences, of course . . . but you claim the same pride and strength and determination. I pray the gods you use them as well as he did.'

Donal swallowed painfully. 'I swear – I will see to Osric's death.'

Finn caught Donal's hand in his own. The firm grip was weak now, like a baby's tentative grasp. 'I do not – do not go into death without having done a portion of my service . . . the boy – the boy lacks an ear –'

'*Su'fali* –'

The bloody hand closed more tightly on Donal's flesh.

357

'I bequeath Homana to you, kinsman. . . . Answer your *tahlmorra*.'

Donal could not speak.

Finn's eyes were nearly shut. 'I would ask – one more thing –'

Donal closed his own.

'*Claim the sword*,' Finn whispered. 'Make it yours from this moment forth.'

'*Su'fali* –'

'Do as I command.' The voice was little more than a sound. 'I am clan-leader of the Cheysuli. . . . You may be Mujhar, but you are still a warrior of the clan.'

Donal heaved himself to his feet. He stood over the dying man. '*Su'fali* . . . I am honored.'

'*Ja'hai, cheysu, Mujhar*,' Finn whispered. '*Cheysuli i'halla shansu*.'

'Accepted.' The Homanan word hurt his throat. '*Shansu, su'fali*. Peace.'

Donal put out both hands and touched the hilt. The ruby blazed brilliant red. He shut his hands in a stiff-fingered, unsteady grasp.

And pulled.

'*Ja'hai-na*,' Finn whispered as blood ran out of his body. 'Oh, Alix . . . you would be so proud of your son –'

Donal stood over the dead warrior with Hale's sword grasped tightly in one hand. He felt the silent keening begin to well up in his soul. He dared not let it become audible; such things were not done. Such things dishonored the code of his clan. But as his face twisted with the pain he could not help but wish he were a small child again, unknowing, and free to cry out his fear and anguish.

When he could, he looked from the warrior's face and stared blindly at Evan. Tears ran down his face. 'I am King,' he said hoarsely. 'Mujhar of Homana and Solinde. And I would trade it all *could I have him back again*!'

Evan's face was still and white as he slowly pointed.

Donal turned. He dropped the sword instantly when he

saw Storr. Storr, who stood silently by a huge spreading oak.

Donal fell to his knees and gathered Finn's beloved *lir* into his arms. *Wolf, O wolf . . . he is gone . . . everyone is taken from me –*

You are not left alone, Storr said gently but with a frightening hollowness, *You have your lir – the Ellasian – Rowan – the women who care for you so.*

Donal pressed his face against the silver pelt. *But I lose them, one by one . . . I lose them all . . . my jehan and jehana – Carillon – Finn – now you –*

And one day you will lose more.

Donal drew back. Storr was wiser then anyone he knew. *You are in pain*, he said in alarm as he saw how heavily the wolf panted.

It does not matter. It is time for me to go.

You will die *if I do not heal you!*

You cannot heal a shattered lir-bond. The wolf pressed his muzzle against Donal's arm. *I am too old. My time is used up. And – I have no wish to survive, now my lir is gone.*

Storr – wait – do not leave me alone –

The magic has ended, kin of my lir . . . it is time for me to go.

Donal shut his eyes. *I will miss you badly, old wolf.*

No more than I shall miss you. Storr's tone was bitter-sweet. *I had much of the raising of you.*

Donal smiled. He passed a gentle hand through Storr's pelt once more, caressed the grizzled muzzle, and knew he could not gainsay him. *I will tend him, Storr. I will tend your lir as he is due.*

He is deserving of honor – The wolf's sigh was heavy, ragged; the sound of a life used up. *He is deserving of much.*

'Safe journey, old wolf,' Donal whispered aloud.

And in his arms there was nothing but dust.

6

Donal and Evan stole a boat on a night with no moon and sailed to Hondarth, where they shed their heavy boots and slipped overboard near the docks, swimming the rest of the way so as not to give warning to the Atvian fleet. Lorn swam strongly, apparently fully recovered, though still a little thin; Taj flew ahead and waited, perching on the seawall.

They splashed out of the harbor under cover of a dark night sky, wrung water from their clothing and headed up toward a seaside tavern. Donal clenched the sword in his left hand, for he had no belt or scabbard. The blade gleamed in the infrequent wash of torchlight; the ruby, black in Strahan's grasp, glowed blood-red in his.

'I am trusting my life to you,' Evan whispered as they crept into the shadow of an alley by the tavern.

Donal raised his brows and slanted a curious glance. 'To me? What of yourself? I thought you ever claimed yourself a valiant fighter.'

'Oh, aye, I am, I am . . . but certainly not as accomplished as *you*. After all, you have wolf and falcon by you and the ability to shapechange – what have I?' He grinned. 'And you carry that sorcerous sword.'

Donal looked down at the sword. He thought perhaps it *was* ensorceled somehow; he recalled how it had warded them against Tynstar; how it had felt like a living thing in his hands when he had nearly beheaded his uncle.

Briefly, he shut his eyes. *Su'fali, oh su'fali* –

A sound. His eyes snapped open. He saw two men

passing in the darkness, on their way to the tavern. Donal looked down at his bare feet and wiggled icy toes. 'I could use a pair of boots. My feet grow weary of this abuse.'

Evan grinned. 'Shall we relieve those two sailors of theirs, then?'

'Aye, But quietly . . . *quietly.*'

Evan ran lightly through the darkness from the alley with Donal at his side. A moment later they dumped two unconscious bodies into the shadows, stripped them of their scuffed, fish-oiled boots and tugged the footwear on.

Donal winced. 'Too small.'

'Mine will do well enough – and no, I will not trade with you.' Evan pushed a forearm across his grimy face. 'What do we do now. Mujhar?'

Donal chewed a ragged fingernail. 'I have already turned thief with the acquisition of these boots . . . I think I shall have to worsen my lot and steal a horse as well.'

'No,' Evan said. 'These horses broke loose of their tethers. We only seek out their owners.'

'Ah.' Donal smiled. 'And where might we *look* for these owners?'

'The army might do,' Evan said thoughtfully. 'Rowan is there – doubtless he could use two more horses.'

'And two more men –?' Donal went softly after the two horses tied to the tavern's front wall. He released one animal and handed the reins to Evan, then took a mount for himself.

Hooves clopped against the cobbles. Donal bared his teeth and cursed, wishing he could somehow muffle the iron shoes. But at last he and Evan reached another deep pocket of darkness in the rabbit-warren of seaside buildings. They mounted and headed north.

'I should have made *you* steal them.' Donal said. 'It is you who requires a mount. I can always *fly.*'

'The proof of a real king lies in his humanity.'

Donal scoffed. 'What nonsense do you mouth?'

'A man who will rule others must learn to treat them as he himself would wish to be treated.'

Donal laughed. 'Such wisdom from a renegade prince!'

'Well, my father said those things. Rhodri grows pompous at times.' Evan plucked his torn linen shirt, still wet and grime-stained, from his skin. 'I fear I no longer resemble a prince, my lord Mujhar . . . nor do you much resemble a king.'

Donal unsheathed the old sword attached to his saddle. It was hardly worthy of the name; likely the sailor had carried it for appearances in port. He leaned out of the saddle and dropped it into a running gutter, hearing the splash and clank of poorly tempered steel.

Carefully, he slid the Cheysuli sword into the sheath and slid it home. The old leather scabbard was too short; the blade extended a handspan from the lip. But it would do. 'I am not yet a king,' he said absently, settling the blade.

'You are Mujhar. The difference lies only in the name.'

'First I must slay Osric.' Donal wished for a cloak against the cold; winter had passed into the edge of spring, but nights were still quite cool. 'Only then will I be worthy of assuming the Lion Throne in Carillon's place.'

'Well,' said Evan, 'I think it is worth the doing. And I think you will succeed.'

Donal smiled grimly and rode on, one hand resting on the glowing Mujhar's Eye. Beside him ran the ruddy wolf; above him flew the falcon.

They crept around the outskirts of the Atvian host and found the Homanan army settled upon a wide plain. It was patently obvious the plain had been the site of repeated battles. The ground had been churned into a fine, pale feathering of dirt. No grass grew. There was no vegetation, but the miasma of too much death.

Donal slipped through the Homanan lines like a wraith, with Evan close behind. He spoke quietly to the guards who challenged him. When they saw clearly who it was, all men fell to their knees and swore allegiance. It was a forcible reminder of Carillon's death. Donal – accepting

the fealty offered wholeheartedly – nonetheless felt the weight of the burden usurping any pride he might have felt by the reception.

Rowan's vermillion field pavilion was separate from the others, perched atop a swell of a hill overlooking the spreading plain. The moon was nonexistent; Donal could see the tiny fires of Osric's host on the other side of the field.

He dismounted, forgetting the sword at his saddle, and handed the reins to a young boy, who bowed his head shyly. Black-haired, he reminded Donal of Sef.

Until he remembered who – and what – Sef was.

Lorn flopped down outside the doorflap. Taj perched upon the ridgepole. Donal took a deep breath and pulled the flap aside.

Rowan glanced up from the map he studied. Black brows drew down in; no doubt he was irritated by the unannounced intruder. But his mouth dropped open as he saw Donal clearly in the candlelight. The map rolled itself back into itself. 'Donal! We had begun to fear you were dead.'

'No.'

Rowan shook his head. 'We received word from Finn a month ago, before he and Evan went in to get you free. But – we had begun to think the attempt had failed.' Rowan's gaze sharpened as he saw the weal burned into Donal's neck. 'By the gods! – What, is *that*?'

'A token from the boy.' Donal moved into the pavilion as Evan came up behind him. 'How fares the army?'

Rowan gestured them to stools and hooked one over for himself. 'Well enough. We do not advance, but neither does Osric. He is a master strategist. He lacks our numbers, but he knows how to make his few work in his favor. It is a long drawn-out affair, my lord. And now – he hangs back. As if waiting for something.'

'He waits for me,' Donal said.

Evan, who had remained standing in the entrance, moved forward. He set the unscabbarded sword down on

363

the table with a thud and folded his arms. 'He waits for *that*.'

Rowan started, staring at the blade. 'Carillon's sword! You have got it back.'

'I said I would,' Donal said grimly. 'Osric gave it to Strahan.'

'And you took it back from the boy –'

Donal looked away. 'No.' His voice shook a little. Slowly he reached out and touched the rune-kissed blade. 'No . . . I did not *take* it. Strahan – left it unintentionally.'

Rowan drew in a breath. 'Have you slain him, then?'

'No,' Donal could hardly look at him. 'He left it because it was not his, but mine. He left it because Finn saw to it he left it. My *su'fali* –' Donal broke off sharply. When he could, he met Rowan's waiting eyes. 'He – is slain, Rowan . . . by the sword made by his own *jehan*.'

'*Finn* –' Rowan's breath ran ragged. 'Not *Finn* . . .' he begged. 'No. Oh . . . no – *no* –'

Donal could find no words to answer Rowan, so he gave him only silence.

After a long moment, Rowan slid awkwardly off his stool and knelt in the dirt of the pavilion floor. 'Forgive me, my lord,' he whispered. 'I did not give you proper honor when you came in.'

Donal stared at the general's bent head. They had ever been at odds, it seemed. Rowan served Carillon, not his heir, and that exacting a service had made him intolerant of Donal's small rebellions. But Carillon was dead. And now Finn. It left him with no one at all.

Save me. Donal bent and clasped Rowan's shoulder. 'I have said I will not have you kneeling to me.'

'It is done.'

'Not this night. Rowan – I need your help.'

Rowan stood up. 'And I have said you will have it.'

Donal tried to ignore the pain in his back. Finn had not had time to heal the talon wounds. 'I am Mujhar,' he said. 'Cheysuli . . . . but I do not suit.'

364

Rowan, turning to pour three cups of wine, frowned. 'Why do you say that?'

'The prophecy speaks of a man of *all blood* who unites four warring realms. Blood of *two* races flows in my veins – not four.'

'Four realms,' Rowan said thoughtfully, pouring the cups full. 'Solinde and Homana, of course – we are ever at war with Solinde, it seems. And Atvia might be the third. But – which realm is the fourth?'

'Ellas?' Donal turned to Evan.

The Ellasian sat down on his stool near the doorflap. 'I think not. Ellas has never fought overmuch. *Never* with Homana or the other realms you name. No . . . when we fight, we fight the Steppes . . . and occasionally Falia and Caledon.' He shrugged. 'It is why we wed their princesses so often – to settle alliances. For a while.'

'It leaves Erinn.' Rowan handed out the wine. 'Erinn of the Idrian Isles. Not much larger than Atvia – but we have never fought with Erinn.'

Donal frowned. 'Shaine's first *cheysula* was Erinnish. The one who bore Lindir, my Homanan granddame.'

'But we have not treated with Erinn since then.' Rowan indicated the map he had been studying. 'There has been no reason to. Erinn and Atvia fight one another like two male dogs over a single bone with each turn of the season – some question of a title and imagined insults – but *Homana* has never been involved.'

Evan shrugged and stretched out his legs, displaying his stolen boots. 'Perhaps that is the key. Perhaps Erinn fights Atvia, and Atvia fights Homana, while Homana battles Solinde.' He held up a fist. One by one he flicked up a finger as he named the names. 'Homana – Solinde – Atvia – Erinn. Four realms.'

'But – I lack the bloodlines.' Donal shook his head. 'I am not the man in the prophecy.'

Rowan's brows lifted a little. 'Perhaps your son will be.'

Donal grimaced. 'I think it *extremely* unlikely Ian

would ever be accepted as my heir. He is a bastard, and the Homanan Council –'

'I do not speak of Ian,' Rowan said steadily. 'Aislinn has conceived.'

Donal let out a rush of sound. '*Aislinn* –'

Rowan nodded. 'The child is due in two months. We pray this one will be full-term.'

Gods . . . she has won . . . that night she drugged me – Donal shut his eyes. *Does she serve Strahan, that child will be a travesty!*

'Donal, there is more.' Rowan's voice was expressionless. 'It concerns your *meijha* and your children.'

Donal's eyes snapped open. 'What do you say?'

Rowan took a breath. 'Aislinn – summoned Sorcha to Homana-Mujhar. What they discussed I cannot say . . . but not long after it was announced the queen would bear a child, Sorcha took the children and left the Keep.'

'*Left* –' Donal was on his feet. 'Aislinn has *sent them away* –?'

'They are well, Donal.' Rowan said it sharply. 'They are well. Aislinn meant them no harm. But Sorcha has taken the children and gone up across the Bluetooth, into the Northern Wastes.'

'To the other Keep –?' Donal slammed down his cup so hard wine slopped over to spill across the table. 'I cannot believe she did it . . . not *Aislinn* – but –' His resolve hardened as he recalled how she had tricked *him*. 'I swear – if she does this out of spite or to serve Strahan, I will do to her what Carillon did to her *jehana*. Send her *away* from me –'

'Donal.' Rowan cut him off in mid-spate. 'She was not harmed, and neither were the children.'

'Sorcha would never do it,' Donal said flatly. 'She would never leave me. She would not take the children away.'

Rowan shrugged, plainly uncomfortable. 'Who can say what happened between Aislinn and Sorcha? They probably argued over you. Sorcha would never give you up.

But neither would Aislinn.' He shook his head. 'Never Aislinn. She is too much like her father.'

'And she is pregnant,' Evan said casually. 'My mother bore twelve of us. I recall how she was with several of my sisters. Breeding women occasionally have – odd notions.'

'I do not care if Aislinn has *odd notions*! I will not allow her to do this to my *meijha* or my children.' He set one forefinger into the spilled wine and tapped the map. 'I will slay Osric – I will *win* this war – and then I will fetch them home.'

'How?' Rowan asked. 'We have been fighting Osric for more than half a year. Half our army remains in Solinde; Osric supplies his men from Hondarth. Do you propose to end this war tomorrow?'

Donal heard the underlying hint of contempt in Rowan's tone. He did not blame him; no doubt it was hard for Rowan to serve another, younger master, who had less knowledge of war than *he* did. It was a bittersweet service. *Like an old dog separated from an older, beloved master.* Donal sighed. 'Not tomorrow. I propose to do it tonight.'

Rowan laughed. But there was nothing of humor in his tone. '*How*?' he repeated.

'I will go to him as a Cheysuli . . . and fight him as a king.' Donal's eyes were on the sword.

Evan snorted. 'How shall you get through the lines?'

'Not through them, Evan – *over* them . . . as a falcon.'

Evan said nothing more. His silence was heavy; he frowned, but swallowed his wine and sat unmoving on his stool.

'When?' Rowan asked.

At least he does not try to gainsay me – 'Later, when darkness is hard upon us. When I have made this sword truly mine.'

Rowan drew in a careful breath. 'Do what you must do. I will not argue with the gods. But Donal – you have no heir.'

Donal caressed the shallow runes in the gleaming steel,

dragging broken nails across the incised edges. 'I can name none now living. But – should aught befall me and Aislinn bears a son, *he* shall be Mujhar.'

'*Executioner*,' Evan said suddenly. 'The rune might have meant the boy for slaying Finn. Or you, for slaying Osric of Atvia.'

'It does not matter,' Donal said calmly. 'I will see to his death regardless.'

With his *lir*, he stood on the field of battle. Behind him stretched the endless leagues of Homana and the endless Homanan army. *His* army. And before him, clear to the dark horizon, lay the massive Atvian warhost.

The moon was a nacreous curving sliver in the blackness of the night. But he could see by the light of the ruby.

Donal had feared, at first, the stoneglow would give him away. But what illuminated the area around him was apparently invisible to Atvians and Homanans alike, for no man came to investigate.

Or else each army believes it something inconsequential. Donal smiled. The ruby – and the sword – was hardly inconsequential. He had come to believe it at last.

The sword was naked in his hands. Unsheathed, the steel was silver in the moonlight. A bright, white silver, wrought with eloquent runes. Oh, aye, he could read them. He could read what was written there. What Hale had put there for him.

Ja'hai, bu'lasa. Homana tahlmorra ru'maii.

Donal nearly laughed. How he had run away. How he had turned his back. How he had repeatedly refused to accept a gift meant for him alone.

'*Ja'hai, bu'lasa. Homana tahlmorra ru'maii.*' Donal spoke the words aloud. First in the Old Tongue, and then in the language of Homana: '*Accept, grandson. In the name of Homana's tahlmorra.*'

He released a tremendous breath. And then slowly he bent and knelt upon the ground. The tip of the blade he set into the powdered dirt, and then pressed downward

against the crossguards. When he let go, the sword stood up of itself.

'*Lir*,' he said aloud. 'I lack the proper words. I do not know the ritual.'

A ritual is what you make it, Lorn said.

Taj flew down and lighted upon the crossguard. *Say what words you will, and they will be enough.*

Donal wet his lips. Tension knotted his belly. When this thing was done, he would have to confront Osric of Atvia. For all he was willing to take on the task, he was not sure he could do it.

He drew in a breath and held it. Slowly he closed both hands around the blade just below the hilt. Below Taj's talons. And then, summoning all his courage, he jerked his hands downward, downward, until they touched the ground, and he felt the pain fill up his palms.

'*Ja'hai-na*!' he cried. '*Ja'hai-na, Homana tahlmorra ru'maii*! I accept in the name of Homana's *tahlmorra*!'

He sat back on his heels. His fingers sprang open rigidly; he saw the blood pour forth. It spilled through his fingers and down his wrists to splatter the ground.

His arms shook. Pain ran the length of his forearms to his elbows, then up into his shoulders. Shock filled his belly with sickness. '*Ja'hai-na*,' he breathed. 'Accepted.'

Still the blood flowed out of his hands to spill against the soil. He saw how the drops soaked in almost immediately, as if the battlefield had not had its fill of the blood of men. And yet he could smell it. He could smell the stench of war; the stink of rotting bodies. All had been burned or buried, but still he could smell the stench.

'More?' he asked. 'Is that what you want, Homana?'

But the earth did not answer him.

Donal looked at the sword. The runes ran red with his blood. But the ruby seemed dull by comparison.

Slowly he reached out his hands. He closed both of them upon the pommel and shut away the ruby from the light of the virgin moon. And then he shut his eyes and emptied himself of the knowledge of who he was.

369

He needed to know *what* he was.

– he was a boy again, so small, and listening to his father. Listening to the man who was clan-leader of the Cheysuli, wiser than everyone save the shar tahl, who kept all the histories.

'*You are a Cheysuli warrior, a child of the Firstborn, and beloved of the gods. You are one among many; a man who is more than a man; a warrior who serves more than war, but the gods and the prophecy. In you lies the seed of prophecy, dormant now, but waiting for the day when you will awaken at last and comprehend the tahlmorra of a kingdom. Not of a boy, of a man, of a clan. Of a kingdom, and you will be its king. You will be what no one has been for nearly four hundred years: a Cheysuli Mujhar of Homana. The man in the prophecy.*'

Donal opened his eyes. Took his hands away from the sword. The blood-bathed ruby glowed more brilliantly than ever. And when he looked at his palms, he saw the wounds had healed.

Osric of Atvia, when Donal finally found him, was ensconced in a huge black field pavilion ringed with smoking torches. He was alone. He sat at his table and pondered his maps, plotting new strategy. Four braziers and two tall candleracks illuminated the interior of the tent. Light flashed off ruddy hair banded by a plain gold circlet; it glinted as he absently smoothed the map with a thick-fingered hand. His broad shoulders threw odd shadows on the fabric behind him: black on black. He scratched idly at his heavy, sun-gilded beard.

He was not old. Perhaps thirty, a year or two more. He was a hardened fighter in his prime; Donal knew he faced harsh odds. But he would not turn from them.

Donal stepped into the glowing light and smiled, carrying the sword. Osric, glancing up at the faintest whisper of sound, froze. His blue eyes widened minutely, then narrowed; he did not otherwise indicate alarm or fear. He appeared more irritated than anything.

'*Hist?*' he asked curtly in his Atvian tongue. But then he saw the sword. He pushed himself to his feet. 'You are Donal.' Now he spoke Homanan, accented heavily.

'I am the Mujhar.'

'How did you come by that sword?'

Donal watched him. 'You took it from Carillon. I got it back from the boy.'

'Strahan gave it to you?'

'After a fashion.'

Osric was very tall, massive as a tree. Donal recalled Carillon's description of Keough, Osric's grandsire, and thought this man must resemble him. He knew himself outweighed badly, outreached as well, and undoubtedly outmatched when it came to deadly swordplay.

'Strahan held you captive, I was told.'

'I was freed. I brought the sword out with me.' He paused. 'It is *mine*, Osric. My grandsire made it for me.'

Osric's blue eyes glittered. He was so vital Donal could sense the strength moving in the man. 'I have heard that sword holds magic. Shapechanger sorcery.' The blue eyes dipped to the sword, then lifted to Donal's face. 'Hale was your grandsire, then?'

'Aye. You see, do you not, I am not an upstart warrior who wishes to grasp at a throne? I have a lawful right to it, Osric. I have blood in me that harks back to the Mujhars of old, and the Cheysuli Mujhars before them.'

'*I* have the right of conquest,' Osric said. Then, 'How did you come through my lines?'

'I flew.'

'*Flew?*'

Donal smiled. 'I am a falcon when need be – or a wolf whenever I choose.' He pulled aside the doorflap. Lorn came into the pavilion silently. 'You have chosen a bad enemy,' Donal told the Atvian lord. 'We Cheysuli do not sit idly by while you try to usurp our homeland.'

Osric still stared at Lorn. 'My grandsire died because of a wolf,' he said slowly. 'In Homana, it was – inside Homana-Mujhar. It was whim – a *wolf's* whim. It did not

slay with tooth or claw – it slew by using fear.'

Donal laughed aloud. 'That wolf, *ku'reshtin*, was my mother.'

Osric's teeth showed briefly. 'No matter. I know the truth of you. Hold that sword if you wish – I know the truth. The Cheysuli have no sword-skill. I do not mind slaying Homana's shapechanger Mujhar, but I would prefer a better match.'

Donal shrugged. 'It was Carillon who taught me. Judge my skill by the reputation of my master's.'

Osric's eyes narrowed. 'Carillon is dead. *I* was the one who slew him – as once he prophesied.' He smiled suddenly as Donal started. 'Did you not know? Aye – Carillon prophesied our meeting. He told it to my brother, Alaric, when I sent him here some sixteen years ago.' He laughed. 'Carillon said – if I recall it right – that if we ever met on the field of battle, one of us would die.' He studied Donal closely. 'Carillon's reputation? Overpraised, I think. As for yours? Let us make one now.' He turned. He caught up his own broadsword from his cot, swung back and advanced on Donal.

The hilt settled comfortably in Donal's hands. He felt the warmth of the metal. The odd, vibrant *life* sprang up again.

Osric was a master swordsman. Donal discovered that very quickly. The Atvian's bulk gave him both superior reach and strength, but slowed down his reactions. Donal was quicker than Osric.

He ducked under two whistling slashes that clove the air near his head. He felt their wind in his hair. Still he ducked away, not yet engaging the man. *I am no swordsman, for all I boasted to him – there is too much I have left to learn –*

Osric needed no lessons. He shattered the edge of the table with one huge swipe of his broadsword and laughed aloud as Donal stumbled back hastily. Teeth gleamed in his sun-gilded beard as he lifted the blade, teasing Donal with its tip. 'You are mine, fool. Homana falls as *you* fall.'

Donal skipped back as Osric's blade flashed by his ribs. He stumbled over a brazier, overturning it; rolled to his feet as he blocked a blow with his blade. Coals burned his legs and feet, charring the leather of his boots, but he ignored that as Osric came on.

'Homana has stood firm against you for over half a year without me,' Donal pointed out, moving constantly. 'What makes you believe the realm will fall do *I* fall?'

'It is the way of battles involving kings.' Osric struck again; Donal ducked. 'Soldiers require leadership, royalty preferred. But slay the king and the army is slain, though most men walk away.' Osric shifted his stance. The sword was a splinter in his tremendous hands. 'Atvia is but a small place. I grow weary of an island. A realm the size of Homana will suit me well enough.'

Donal moved back. 'After Homana – Solinde? Your present ally?'

Teeth gleamed in Osric's beard. 'Too soon to say, Cheysuli.'

The sword seemed to hum in Donal's hands. He felt it protest his poor skill, as if it were disappointed by his lack. Donal set his teeth and set up a fence of steel, trying to maintain his ground as Osric sought to batter him down.

He stepped back, back again. The table pressed against his spine. Donal threw himself onto the table in a bid to roll away and gain his feet, but Osric's sword was in the way. It settled at his throat.

'True,' Osric said. 'The Cheysuli have no sword-skill.'

The ruby blazed up and created a nimbus around them both. Osric, crying out, fell back, eyes popping in their sockets. His own sword shook in his hands, but he was too much a warrior to give over to fear so easily.

Donal pressed up from the table. Osric brought his sword down. Blades clashed. The immense strength of the Atvian drove Donal down again. His torn back pressed against the wood.

The nimbus continued to burn. It splashed blood-red

light across Osric's face until his blue eyes turned Ihlini purple.

Donal felt the numbness beginning in his hands, felt the sword cleave to his grasp as if it was part and parcel of his body. Runes glowed white the length of the blade – he swung –

– Osric's sword broke in a rain of shining steel.

He stood there with nothing in his hands but a useless hilt. His mouth hung open: a tombstoned cavern in red-gilt hair.

Donal, still flat on his back on the table, felt the sword lift him up; felt the power surge through his arms from shoulder to fingertips. He was lifted; he thrust. The blade slid home in Osric's belly.

That for Carillon. That for my su'fali.

7

Donal took back his human form in front of Rowan's pavilion. As he pulled open the doorflap he met Evan in the entrance. 'Osric?' Evan demanded.

'Atvia lacks a lord.' He could still feel a residual warmth and vitality in the sword. The ruby was red against his hand.

'Good.' Evan had shaved; put on fresh clothing worthy of his rank. The stolen boots had been replaced with finer footwear. 'You are unharmed?'

'As you see me.' But Donal thought Evan did not see him clearly. There was a drawn tautness at the corners of his eyes and mouth, as if he spoke automatically with little thought for what he said. 'Evan – what is it?'

Evan stepped aside and gestured limply for Donal to enter. His hand scraped against the fabric as he let the flap down again. 'A messenger came early this morning, just at dawn, while you were still in Osric's encampment.'

The pavilion was empty. The bedclothes on Rowan's cot were rumpled. One cup of wine, half-filled, stood on the table next to a pile of maps. A fly buzzed around the rim.

Donal sat down on a stool, hunching a little; he lay the blade across his thighs and fingered the hilt with its rampant lion. 'This message was for me?'

'No. For me.' Evan frowned a little. He looked almost bewildered. 'My brother is – High King.'

Donal looked at him sharply. 'Rhodri –?'

'Dead of a sudden fever.' Evan combed a hand through

his dark brown hair. 'It took him too quickly – the leeches could do nothing.'

Donal stood up again. He understood the puzzled grief in Evan's eyes better than before, now that he lacked Finn. He reached out and clasped Evan's arm briefly. 'I am sorry. Do you ride for Ellas immediately?'

After a moment Evan shook his head. 'I would have. At once, of course – I should go home and pay my respects. But – Lachlan has said no. He gives me leave to remain here.' He shrugged a little. 'He says – he says all of Ellas knows how I honored my father, and that now I must honor the wishes of her new High King.' His eyes were full of grief and lethargy; his anchor had been taken from him. 'He says I must stay with you.'

Donal stared at his friend. His own emotions were detached, as if Finn's death had drained him of the capacity for grief, but he understood what Evan felt. *He has only just discovered how much his jehan meant to him, for all he has spoken casually of their relationship.* Donal sat down again. 'Why would Lachlan wish you to stay here? I am more than glad of your company, but perhaps you would do better to go home.'

Evan's mouth hooked down on one side. 'He heard of Carillon's death. Out of sorrow and a wish to keep Homana whole, he is sending five thousand men.' Evan smiled. 'The Royal Ellasian Guard . . . which was, I know, dispatched once before to Homana, when Carillon needed aid. Out of respect for Carillon's memory, Lachlan wishes to make certain Homana does not fall. But – I think there is more, though he did not say it. I think he fears for Ellas as well. Does Osric take Homana, there is a good chance he will turn his eyes to Ellas one of these years. Why not gainsay that now by sending aid to Homana? He could not do so before – my father preferred to stay out of Homana's troubles – but now he is High King. He may do what he wishes.'

Donal sighed, staring pensively at the sword. 'Whatever Lachlan's reasons – his gesture is more than welcome.'

Evan nodded. 'Rhodri was a worthy king. Ellas loved him. But Ellas also loves Lachlan, the scapegrace, priest and prince who wandered as a harper for three years, riding with an exiled Homanan lord as he sought to win back his realm. He will be a valuable ally, Donal.'

Thinking deeply, Donal scratched at his forehead beneath the thick black hair that hung nearly into his eyes. 'Five thousand men may be more than enough to swing this battle to a conclusion. Unless, of course, Osric's death is enough. It may be that Lachlan's gift is not necessary. But regardless, I must leave Rowan in charge of the Homanan troops, while you lead the Ellasians.' He frowned. 'It would give me time to go up across the Bluetooth.'

'Still you will go?'

'I will. And I will bring Sorcha and the children home – home to Homana-Mujhar.'

Evan sucked in a whistling breath. 'Not wise, Donal. Aislinn is already jealous – installing your light woman and bastards beneath the same roof may not be for the best.'

'I do not care.' Donal looked up from the sword. 'I am not totally blind to Aislinn's reasons for what she has done. But there are other factors I must consider. She is Electra's daughter. It means I can never view her without suspicion – has she not given me enough reason for that? – because it may be that she has a measure of her *jehana*'s power. For all I know, the Solindish blood in her holds stronger than the Homanan.'

'She bears a child, Donal. Possibly a son, and heir to Homana.'

Donal laughed. 'I have no intention of *slaying* her, Evan! Nor do I wish to beat her. I intend only to put Sorcha and the children where I know they will be safe.'

Evan shook his head. 'Do not put her so close to Aislinn. Donal – this is merely jealousy. Once Aislinn has borne her own, she will not resent Sorcha's children so much.'

Donal shook his head. 'For a man who has neither children nor *cheysula*, you know much about both.'

'I have five sisters,' Evan retorted, 'and – at last count – fourteen nieces and nephews. Perhaps more, by now – my sisters breed like coneys. I speak from experience, Donal.'

Donal sighed. 'Well, nonetheless, I will go to the Northern Keep and tend to my *meijha* and children. *Then* I will see to Aislinn.'

Rowan gave him a new sheath and belt for the sword, since Carillon's was missing, presumably somewhere in the Atvian encampment – unless Strahan still had it. But the new one suited Donal's taste. It was plain dark leather oiled to a smooth sheen, worked with Cheysuli runes from top to bottom.

Donal slid the blade home until the hilt clicked against the lip. He looked at Rowan. 'Your workmanship?'

Rowan's angular face was solemn. 'Aye. My blood showing in me at last. I have the Cheysuli skill.'

Donal looked at him in surprise. 'Then you are finally admitting openly to your heritage.'

Splotches of color formed in Rowan's face, flushing the sunbronzing darker still so that the yellow of his eyes was emphasized. 'I have not had to deny it for many years,' he said with a quiet dignity. 'Not since I acknowledged the truth to Carillon.'

He will judge everything in his life by Carillon. Donal sighed and tried to summon what little he knew of tact. 'I know you have never had a *lir*, but you *are* Cheysuli. You might have sought a clan instead of the Homanans when you were old enough to know the truth.'

Rowan shook his head. 'I did not seek the Homanans, Donal. I was *raised* Homanan. Oh, aye . . . I knew what I was *inside*, but how could I fight Homanan habits that grew to be second nature? A child becomes what he is made . . . and I was made Homanan.'

Donal frowned down at the rune-worked blade. 'We are so different. The races. So – apart. We are different men. And I think you cannot be both.'

'You can.' Rowan smiled a little. 'One day, you may see

it. One day you may *have* to. You yourself are less Cheysuli than *I* am, if we are to speak of blood – and yet you are the one who claims the races are different.' He shook his head. 'You do realize, of course, that even though Homana has a Cheysuli Mujhar once more – that the Cheysuli race will not last forever. We will be swallowed up by the truth of the prophecy.'

Donal looked at him sharply. The words, oddly, echoed what Tynstar had said; what Strahan had emphasized. And Donal did not like it. Somehow, it *threatened* him. 'We have lost nothing in thousands of years. We still claim the *lir* and all that bond entails. The earth magic that heals, the power to compel –'

'Aye.' Rowan interrupted calmly. 'But have you never thought that when the goal of the prophecy is attained and the Firstborn live again, there will be little room left for the Cheysuli?'

'There will *always* be Cheysuli in Homana.' Donal's tone obliterated room for speculation. 'Homanan-raised you may have been, but not Homanan-*born*. Did you not set the runes into the leather of this scabbard?'

'Some things a man never forgets.' Rowan looked at the devices he had tooled. 'I remember – when I was very small – how my *jehan* used to write out the runes with a chunk of coal on a bleached deerskin. It fascinated me. I would sit for hours before the pavilion and watch his hand draw the runes – making magic. And the birthlines, when the *shar tahl* showed me mine.' He smiled reminiscently. 'I remembered all the runes. So I pieced together the prophecy and the runes, and put it all into the leather.'

Donal watched the changes in Rowan's face. In that instant he felt closer to the man than ever before. In that instant, Rowan was Cheysuli, and Donal could understand him. 'What else do you remember?'

The smile fell away. 'I remember the day the Mujhar's men came across my family. How they slew them all, even my small *rujholla*. I remember it all very well, though for years I denied it.'

379

'Because your new kin never said you were Cheysuli.'

'They never knew.' Rowan shrugged. 'They were Ellasian, come to Homana for a new life. They found a small boy wandering dazedly in the forest, unable to speak out of fear for what he had seen, and they took him as their own. They were – good people.'

'But they were not Cheysuli.'

'Half of *you* is not,' Rowan retorted. 'When I look at you, Donal, I see and hear a Cheysuli warrior, because that is what you desire to show to people. You have all the Cheysuli characteristics – including that prickly pride – and you certainly bear the stamp. But you also are Homanan, because of Alix. You should let it temper that pride. Do not become *so* Cheysuli you cannot understand the people you will rule.'

Donal's fingers closed on the leather scabbard. 'I – I would prefer to have nothing but Cheysuli blood in my veins.'

'But you do not. There is Homanan as well. Else you would not be part of the prophecy.' Rowan sighed and shook his head. 'You are what they have made you, your mother and your father. Duncan was all Cheysuli, and Alix – out of a wish to keep alive the husband she had lost – did what she could to make you Duncan come again. It is – not necessarily bad. I could think of worse warriors for you to emulate – including Finn.' Rowan flicked one hand in a silencing gesture as Donal moved to protest. 'Finn was what the prophecy made him. He was what Carillon needed for many years. But – people change. They grow older, they mature. Carillon no longer needed him. And neither, now, do you.'

Donal shook his head in violent disagreement. 'I need him badly, my *su'fali*. There is so much left for me to learn.'

'You will learn it. But first you must learn to acknowledge the Homanan in you as well as the Cheysuli.'

Donal lifted the hilt. 'Do I not wear *this* now? What Cheysuli has ever borne a sword – except, perhaps, for you?'

'It is a beginning,' Rowan agreed.

'It is *more* than a beginning,' Donal muttered. 'It is an alteration of tradition.'

'Perhaps it is necessary.' Rowan smiled. 'You are the first Cheysuli Mujhar to hold the Lion Throne in four hundred years, Donal. *That* is alteration.'

Pensively, Donal nodded. Then he sighed and looked up at Rowan. 'There is a thing I would have you do.'

The general shrugged. 'What I can, I will.'

'Win this war. Win this gods-cursed war, so I can begin my reign in peace.'

Donal rode northward through Homana, bypassing Mujhara entirely, until he reached the Bluetooth River. On the southern bank he pulled in his horse, staring at the river. It had been sixteen years since he had last seen the Bluetooth, when Tynstar's Ihlini servitors had taken him toward the Molon Pass for entry into Solinde. He had been Valgaard-bound, prisoners, he and Alix, but he had escaped because of Taj and Lorn's aid in accelerating his ability to take *lir*-shape. Alix had not. He had left his mother behind, crossing the huge river on his escape to Homana-Mujhar.

Then it had been much colder, for winter had only recently left the land. Now it was spring and the waters were quick, unclogged by ice and slush. He stared at the wooden ferry on the far side and wondered if he should wait for it, or cross Cheysuli-fashion.

Taj, perching in a nearby tree, fixed him with a bright dark eye. *Do you recall it, lir?*

I recall.

You sought the air then. Shall you do it again?

Donal turned to stare over his shoulder, searching for Lorn. A moment later the ruddy wolf broke free of the dense vegetation fringing the riverbank.

No – I will ride. I will have Sorcha and the children with me.

Lorn shook dust from his coat. *Then I must swim this*

381

river, unless you bribe the ferry-master to let me pass with you.

The ferry-master, when he banked his wooden vessel, accepted Donal's gold eagerly. He slanted an apprehensive glance at the wolf, eyed Donal closely, then gestured them both aboard. Donal led the horse onto the thick wooden timbers and waited for Lorn to join him.

The man cast off and began the lengthy process of pulling the ferry back across the wide river. But it did not keep him from watching Donal, or from talking.

He hawked, spat over the side into the water, and jerked his head. 'Na' meanin' to offend ye, but 'tis curious I am. Be ye a halfling, then?'

'Halfling?' Donal was startled by the rough northern dialect. The language seemed hardly Homanan.

'Halfling. Aye. Lookit yersel'. Yon color is Cheysuli, but ne'er I seen one dressit like ye. Leathers, they wear, and gold. Be ye only half, then?'

In shock, Donal realized the Homanan clothing Rowan had lent him after his escape from Strahan robbed him of identity. He had put off the torn and soiled leathers, replacing them with black soldiers' breeches, linen shirt and rich brown velvet doublet, which hid the gold on his arms. His hair, left uncut for too long, hid his earring.

He eyed the ferry-master speculatively. 'Were I to say I was all Cheysuli, what would you do?'

The man laughed, hawked again, spat over the ferry again. 'Indeed, nothin'. On'y curious, master. But ye don't be lookin' like'ee others. Ne'er hae I seen one wear a *sword*.'

Donal's hand dropped to the heavy hilt. Possessively, he shut his fingers upon it. 'A new custom.'

'Yon breed be fierce, master. I seen many of 'em here, crossin' south, bound for the Mujhar's city.' Interest flared up in the man's brown eyes. 'Hae ye been to Mujhara, master?'

Donal smiled. 'Aye.'

'Big as they do say?'

'Bigger.'

'Hae ye seen yon palace, what called Homana-Mujhar?' His dialect – and several missing teeth – ran the syllables together until they were nearly indistinguishable.

'Aye, I have.'

'Ye'll say 'tis grander than I can 'magine, doubtless.'

Donal patted his horse's muzzle. 'Aye, it is.'

'And be he the man they do say he is?'

'Who – the Mujhar?' Donal shrugged. 'Tell me what they say.'

The ferry-master pulled hard upon the ropes. His mouse-brown hair was long, clubbed back with a strip of leather. He wore rough woolen clothing and heavy boots. Brawny muscles played across his back and shoulders as he pulled against the current. 'They do say Carillon chose hi'self a right'un. A man even the 'lini give a wide road to.'

Donal smiled wryly. 'I thought the Ihlini feared no one.'

The man eyed him. 'I dinna say they *feared* 'im. The 'lini, most likely, fear nae man. But up here I carry passengers from all lands and all races, and I do say I hauled a few 'lini sorcerers 'cross this beast.' He shrugged. 'Man doesna say nae to gude gold.'

Donal stared across the swift-running river to the far side. He shivered slightly as the chill wind blasted from the frozen mountains of the Molon Pass, several leagues away from the river, but close enough to wall them in on one side. 'I would have thought,' he said lightly, 'that Ihlini sorcerers had no need of a *ferry* to cross this river.'

The ferry-master laughed. 'Aye, so ye *would* think – but they dinna fly. Nae more than ye do, master.'

Donal smiled. 'But I do.'

'Fly?' The man shook his head. 'Ye be jestin' wi' me, then.'

'No.' *Nae*, he said silently, liking the dialect.

The man eyed him closely. 'Then why be ye takin' my ferry?'

Donal laughed. 'I do not *always* fly. Besides, I will have

383

company on the way back.' He studied the man a moment. 'Do you fear me, ferry-master?'

'I hae heard of yon sorcery. Na' feared to say I 'spect it.'

'Respect and fear are two different things.' Donal leaned idly against the rail. 'You have a Cheysuli Mujhar. Do you fear him?'

'I do fear what it might be meanin'.' The ferry-master's head rose and he met Donal's eyes squarely. 'The legends do say the shapechangers once held Homana, and gi' her oop to men of my race. Now ye hae it back. 'Tis no wonder honest Homanans wonder what it all be meanin'.'

'There is no danger in it for any Homanan,' Donal told him. 'The Mujhar means to keep peace in this realm.'

'That I'll be havin' to see fer mysel', then.'

'So you shall.' Donal gestured. 'We are nearly there.'

The man whipped a quick look at the bank, hauled on the brake ropes and brought the ferry in smoothly. Donal led the horse onto the bank and mounted. As he waited for Lorn he saw the ferry-master watching him in a mixture of curiosity and suspicion. Donal raised his hand in a brief wave, then put his horse to the northernmost track.

The Keep was set in the toothy foothills of the mountains. Like most Keeps, it was ramparted by high stone walls that wound their way up slopes and down again to encircle all the pavilions. It was a harsh blue-grey stone, almost indigo, that greeted his eyes, not the warm greyish-green he was more accustomed to. In the Northern Wastes, many things were different.

He rode up to the entrance and paused. Three warriors guarded it; even now, nearly twenty years after Carillon ended the *qu'mahlin*, the clans knew better than to trust any stranger who rode in. Even one who appeared Cheysuli.

One of the warriors came forward from the wall. His yellow eyes appraised Donal shrewdly, marking the characteristic Cheysuli features; marking also the Homanan clothing. There was calm politeness in his tone as he

offered casual greeting, but Donal saw the slight trace of contempt in the eyes.

Gods – he does not see a warrior . . . he sees a city-bred Cheysuli – It nearly made him cringe.

'I am Kaer,' the warrior said. 'Have you business in our Keep?'

Not quite the ritual greeting of warrior to warrior – well, I can expect no better. Not hiding all my gold, even with *the lir.* Donal looked down upon Kaer. 'My business is with my kin, who shelter here. Sorcha, my *meijha*, and our children, Ian and Isolde. I am Donal, son of Duncan.'

Kaer's expression altered at once. Quickly he made the subtle hand gesture denoting acknowledgment of his rudeness; rarely did a warrior admit to such before another warrior, since Cheysuli were rarely rude, and so an apology was never spoken. The gesture was enough.

'My lord Mujhar.' He reached out to catch the stallion's reins. 'I will escort you to the clan-leader at once.'

It was proper for a visiting warrior to meet first with the keep's clan-leader. Donal badly wanted to see Sorcha and the children, but he forced himself into patience as he dismounted, gave up the reins of his horse to Kaer and went with him across the Keep toward a rust-colored pavilion. On the side a yellow mountain cat was painted.

Kaer paused, called for entrance, was granted it and pulled aside the flap. He spoke quietly to someone inside. A moment later he turned and gestured Donal within, then disappeared with the horse. Donal saw Taj light upon the ridgepole. Lorn flopped down beside the doorflap to exchange greetings with the sleek tawny mountain cat who sprawled upon a rug.

Donal went in. A Cheysuli sat cross-legged before the small pavilion fire, but he rose fluidly as his guest slipped through the doorflap. He smiled. 'Be welcome among us. Do you hunger, you will be fed. Be you weary, safe rest is yours.'

Donal felt the brief flicker of nostalgia rise up, tempered

with a touch of sorrow. So many times, as a boy, he had heard his father say those traditional words to a stranger being welcomed into the Keep. And then Finn. Now they were said to him.

'*Cheysuli i'halla shansu*,' he returned. 'I am Donal, son of Duncan and Alix. My *meijha*, Sorcha, is here.'

The yellow eyes flickered, then assessed him shrewdly, though the warrior's face remained bland. With a flash of insight Donal realized he would be judged more harshly by his own race than by any Homanan. The Cheysuli had waited for four centuries for one of their own to regain the Lion.

Now one has, but they do not know me as well as they would like to.

The clan-leader nodded. 'I am Tarn.' He reached out to clasp Donal's arm in a gesture of welcome, then indicated the thick brown bear pelt spread by the fire. Donal sat down accordingly and accepted the cup of honey brew from Tarn's own hands. 'I have heard of the war you wage against Osric of Atvia.' Tarn poured his own cup full and drank.

Donal nodded, sipping at his portion. It was warm, rich and satisfying; he had drunk too much wine of late, and found he missed the traditional liquor of his race. 'We have left warriors from my clan in Solinde, but I think the rebellion dies. Osric is slain now, and we will soon boast an additional five thousand soldiers from Ellas. The war should be over soon.' He did not ask why Tarn had not sent warriors of his own; it was not the proper time.

Tarn nodded. 'We are isolated here. But we hear many things. Such as Tynstar's death – and the rising power of his son.'

Donal slowly released a silent breath. 'Strahan is yet a boy, but powerful. He has learned well from his *jehan*. I do not doubt Valgaard will soon be inhabited again – if it is not already.'

'We have heard nothing of that.' Tarn set down his cup. 'You have come to see your kin.'

Donal was relieved the casual talk was ended. 'Aye. And to thank you for taking them in. But now I shall have them come home with me.'

'I – think not. Not all of them.' Tarn's voice was steady. 'Donal – it is unhappy news I bear. Shocking news, as well. I wish there were another way –' He broke off, then said it plainly. 'Sorcha has taken her life.'

Donal dropped the cup. It overturned against his knees, spilling hot liquor across the fabric of his breeches to soak into his skin. But he felt nothing. Nothing but total shock.

'Sorcha?' he whispered. '*Sorcha* –?

Tarn nodded. 'I sent a messenger to Homana-Mujhar, not knowing where you were.'

Donal stared blindly at the man. 'I was – I was –' He stopped speaking. He could not form another word. All he could do was stare at the blurred face before his burning eyes.

'*Shansu.*' Tarn said compassionately. 'It grieves me to give my Mujhar such news.'

'Suicide . . .' he whispered. 'Oh – gods – *no* . . . she has forfeited the afterworld –'

'Aye.' Tarn would not meet Donal's eyes so as not to acknowledge a grief that should be private.

'But – *why?* Why would Sorcha *do* such a thing?'

Still Tarn avoided his eyes. 'The women came and spoke to me and told me what Sorcha said before she did the unspeakable. It was – grief and anger and loss, the loss of the warrior with whom she had shared her life.'

'She had not *lost* me –'

'It was anger, much anger; she told them the Queen had sent her here. Banished your *meijha*, to keep her from your sight.' Tarn's voice was carefully modulated; he would not be judge or arbiter, merely a spokesman for what had happened. 'She told them she had lost you to the Homanans and to Homana's queen; that you had turned your back on all your Cheysuli heritage.'

'Aislinn sent them here . . .'

'That is what we were told. Sorcha and your children were banished here, never to go south of the Bluetooth.'

'But – *suicide* –' He could not conceive of the woman doing the unspeakable.

'Sorcha was – half-mad with grief and anger. I spoke to her when she came. Donal – she could not face life without you. Sharing you was bad enough, she said; she could not bear losing you altogether. Not to the *Homanans*. And so she emptied her veins of blood.'

Donal stared blindly at the damp liquor stain on his breeches. *She said she wished to, once. To be rid of the Homanan taint . . . Oh gods – Aislinn is no better than her jehana –* He shut his eyes. *What am I to do?*

'I am sorry.' Tarn said it gently, more gently than Donal expected; Sorcha was not deserving of compassion to a clan-leader's way of thinking. She had done what was never to be done. 'What will you do, my lord?'

Donal heard the rank without surprise. Another time, he might have remarked upon it; Cheysuli rarely gave rank to another man, and never to warriors other than the *shar tahls* and clan-leaders.

But things are different, now. He looked levelly at Tarn. 'I would like to see my children.'

'At once. Wait here – I will send them' Tarn rose and stepped outside, speaking quietly to someone. When the flap was pulled aside again, Donal saw his son.

Ian came in silently and conducted himself with grave correctness, waiting for encouragement before he moved closer yet. He was four now, and Cheysuli pride was apparent in every line of his slender body, from the lifted chin to the squared shoulders. He wore winter jerkin and leggings.

I wonder . . . will he find his lir as young as I did –?

Then a woman came in with Isolde and he banished everything else from his mind. He took the girl from the woman's arms. When the woman went away again, he sat alone with his children.

He snugged Isolde into his lap, settling her against his

chest. She was just over a year now; he realized, with a sense of shock, he had lost too much time. Since Isolde's birth he had wed, gone to war, been held imprisoned for six months – too much, too much time. He cradled her silky-haired head in one hand and felt the uprush of grief and anger.

Oh gods . . . oh gods . . . why do you do this to children? Why do you take so many people? From me . . . and now from my children as well. Why do you do this to us?

He held Isolde there against his chest, eyes closed, softly caressing her wispy raven curls. He felt a child himself, badly in need of comforting . . . but his *jehana* and *meijha* were dead. Even Finn, who might have mocked his grief – while understanding it better than most – could do nothing to help him now.

Donal drew in a ragged breath. He looked over Isolde's head to the face of his son and saw a matching conflict there. Ian was frightened, confused, lost. Badly in need of something he could easily comprehend.

No different from myself . . . 'She loved you.' Donal knew perfectly well he broke Cheysuli custom by even discussing the emotion, but he did not care. Things were different now; he wore a sword at his side. 'She loved you – and so do I.'

Tears welled up into the wide yellow eyes. Trembling, biting his lower lip, Ian came forward and knelt at his father's side. His right hand hesitantly twined itself into the wide sword belt at Donal's waist; the other hastily wiped the fallen tears away.

'*Jehan*,' he began in a small, soft voice, 'where do we go now?'

Donal slid an arm around Ian's slim shoulders. Isolde, cuddled against him contentedly as a kitten, scratched at the nap of his velvet doublet. 'We go to the place that will be your home.'

Ian brightened. 'The other Keep?'

Donal stared into the beseeching eyes of his son and

realized with a sickening wrench that a Cheysuli keep would never again be home to any of his children. His line, and theirs, would come to know only the walled palaces of kings.

Already, it begins. He squeezed the boy's shoulders. 'Ian, you will go to the Keep and see your clan-mates as often as you wish. But you I will have by me.'

Ian's fingers tightened on the sword belt. 'Will she come back?' he whispered. '*Jehana?*'

'No,' Donal told him. '*Jehana* will never come back.'

Silently, his son's face crumpled, and he began to cry.

8

In the bright, cool light of mid-morning three weeks later, Donal rode through the gates of Homana-Mujhar. Isolde he held in one arm, guiding the stallion with the other; Ian sat perched behind him on the broad, smooth rump, clutching his father's sword belt.

Donal was weary unto death. He had refused Tarn's offer of an escort with a woman to care for the children; in some strange, possessive way he felt it better *he* should tend to the children his *meijha* had borne him. And so he had ridden alone with his children and his *lir* and knew somehow it was best.

He halted the stallion by the marble steps leading to the archivolted entrance. Lads came flying from the stables, all vying for the horse. They challenged one another for the loudest greeting, but fell silent soon enough when Donal did not answer.

He swung one leg across the stallion's neck, turning in the saddle so he would not dislodge his son. Isolde was pressed against his chest. He steadied himself against the saddle, then offered an arm to Ian. The boy slid off as well, clutching his father's hand.

For a moment, Donal shut his eyes. He drew again on what little strength he had left. Then he ordered the horse put away and turned to climb the steps.

'*Jehan* –' It was Ian, moving closer to Donal's side. 'This is Homana-Mujhar?'

'Aye.' The tone was flat, lifeless; he was too weary to

summon another. 'Come up, Ian – there will be time later for you to gape.'

He hardly saw the servants who bowed or curtseyed. He saw only endless corridors and marble pillars. And then he saw his sister.

She ran. Both hands clutched at her skirts, pulling them nearly up to her knees as she hastened down the corridor. 'Donal – is it *true*?' She stopped short in front of him, breathless. 'He said Sorcha was *dead* . . . he said he came from across the Bluetooth –'

Black hair tangled on her shoulders. Donal thought she looked genuinely shocked. Well, she would be, she and Sorcha had been close. But looking at her, he remembered Strahan. He remembered how closely their blood was linked.

Even as Aislinn's is linked. He placed his hand on Ian's head. Then he summoned one of the women servants forward. 'Take the children. See they are fed and given rest. They are weary. It has been a brutal journey.'

To his *lir* he said, *Go to my chambers and wait.*

'*Donal* –' Bronwyn began, but he waved her into silence as the woman curtseyed and took Isolde from his arms.

'Go with her, Ian. See how your *rujholla* goes with her?' Without the weight in his arms, he felt empty. Isolde began to cry. 'Ian, do as I have said. And see to your *rujholla*.' He gave Ian a gentle push in the direction of the woman, then turned to face his sister. 'Where is Aislinn?'

Bronwyn reached out and caught the velvet of his doublet. 'Donal – is it true?'

'Where is Aislinn?'

She stared up at him in perplexed disbelief. 'Can you not answer my question? The warrior came down from the north bearing horrible news about how Sorcha had taken her life – can you not even tell me?'

'She is dead.' It hissed between his teeth. '*Tell me where Aislinn is*!' He set her aside deliberately and started down the corridor.

'Donal – *wait* –' Bronwyn hastened after him. The

wind whipped from her passing cast shadows against the walls. 'Donal – she is *resting* –'

'Is she in her chambers?'

Bronwyn caught his arm and tried to hold him back. 'Aye, of course – she wearies quickly now the birth is only a month away – *rujho* – wait . . . you are hardly back, and I heard how Strahan kept you prisoner. Donal – *wait* –'

Again, he forcibly set her aside.

'Donal,' Bronwyn called, 'what are you going to *do* –?'

He did not know. He thought Aislinn might give him the answer.

He said nothing as he entered her chambers. He made no sound. He shut the door. Aislinn looked up and saw him, and terror was in her eyes.

'Donal! *Donal* –' She pushed herself more upright in the bed, scrabbling in satin pillows. 'Donal – *wait you* –'

Still he said nothing. He crossed the room to the bed and stood there, staring down upon her. She looked so young, so *defenseless* –

– and so perfectly willing to drive Sorcha to her death.

'D-Donal –!'

'Should I trouble myself to listen to your lies?'

She shook. Her lips were colorless. 'I knew – *I knew* – when the messenger came, I knew what you would think –'

'You *sent* her there. You banished her from her home.' He saw how her taut belly pushed against the linens of her nightshift. 'Did you think it would mean nothing to her to lose her *home* as well as me?'

'Donal – I did not *send* her! She went of her own accord.'

'Do you say you did not meet with her?'

'We met. We *met* – I called her to the palace. But I never sent her away. I merely *warned* her –'

'Warned her about *what*?'

'That I would never give you up.' Tears ran freely down Aislinn's face. 'Oh gods, all I did was say I would fight her for you. I *never* sent her away. Donal – I *swear* –'

He bent over her and pressed her shoulders against the pillows. '– swear nothing! Let me see for myself instead.'

Her mouth shaped his name in a cry of terror, but by then he was in her mind.

He felt the shock of the contact reverberate through her body. Her head pressed back against the satin, but her eyes were not closed. They stared at the timbers of the roof beams; blind, senseless eyes, filled with emptiness.

Faintly, very faintly, he heard the protests from his distant *lir*, who knew very well what he did. And he deliberately ignored them.

– *barriers* –

Weak. Hardly enough to justify the name. There was no defense as there had been before; no effort to gainsay his entrance. He pushed against her barriers and felt them go down, collapsing, like a castle made of sand.

– *fear* –

That he could deal with easily. For the first time in his life he did not try to soothe her. He did not try to banish the fear from her mind. Instead, he intensified it, letting her see what he could do.

Aislinn moaned.

– *a stirring in her mind* –

Donal smiled grimly.

– *retreat* –

Pursuit.

He allowed his awareness to seek out her own, impinging itself upon her will, until she turned and ran from him. In his arms, limp and twitching, she was helpless; in her mind, chased by his will, she was even more so.

Aislinn moaned. She spasmed once, and was still.

Beware the trap-link, even now – He warded himself quickly with what skill he had, drawing in upon himself. He focused, focused, until he could slash through the web of deceit –

– and then he found there was none.

For a moment, he retreated. Then he touched her awareness again, probing it tentatively. He recalled how he had

made contact with *something* before, something that had caused him to withdraw as quickly as he could. But this time, there was nothing. No shadow of a link. No trace of any meddling. Aislinn was simply *Aislinn*.

– and nothing but innocence –

He touched her emotions then. Fear was uppermost. But he caught also the last fading traces of love and trust, as though she knew, even as he forced her, he would never hurt her.

But I have!

Donal withdrew at once. He fell out of her mind and into his own, aware he had stolen will and wits from her. It was worse, far worse than what Finn had done in his testing. This time it had been much more.

'Aislinn!' His hands still clasped her shoulders. She hung limply in his arms. But her eyes were open. And blank.

'Aislinn – *come back –*' He shook her. *Oh gods – what have I done to her –?*

He heard, dimly, voices outside the door. Bronwyn, calling to ask him what was wrong. But he could not take time to answer.

He pulled Aislinn against his chest, pressing her against it as if she were a child. 'Aislinn – *Aislinn* – oh gods, do you hear me? Aislinn – *I was wrong –*'

Her belly moved. He felt it. It spasmed against his own. In horror, he realized he had brought on her labor too soon.

Carefully, so carefully, he lay her down against the bed. Still her eyes stared blankly at the roof beams. Donal felt bile rise up to fill his mouth, and turned to flee the room.

Bronwyn stood in the open doorway, one hand pressed against her mouth. Behind her stood several others; faces he knew but could not name.

He stopped. He stared at them. And then, as Aislinn cried out in pain, he pushed through them all and ran.

– and ran, until he burst through the hammered silver doors and nearly fell into the Great Hall.

It was empty. Sunlight slanted through the stained glass casements and cast their shapes upon the floor, all tales of

Homanan lore. That, and Cheysuli history. But Donal hardly saw them.

Instead, he saw the Lion. It crouched upon the dais as if it stalked him, hunching in long grass. But there was no grass, only the cold heart of rose-red stone and the ivory, gold-veined marble dais. The Lion was brown and gilt and gold; its shape was static, trapped in aging wood. But Donal could almost see it beckon.

Slowly, he walked the length of the hall. He was surrounded by ornaments of the past, relics other men kept to remind themselves of what they once had been. Tapestries worked by their women to show their feats of strength and glory. Weapons hung up upon the stone, stained dark with forgotten blood. Banners, some faded to dreary monotones; keepsakes of ancient wars. But even without them, even without the banners, weapons and tapestries, and the glowing, brilliant casements, there was yet another monument to the men who had lived before.

And its name is Homana-Mujhar.

Donal stopped before the dais. In the dim, pink light of mid-morning in the hall, he looked upon the Lion. And felt old. Old and *wrong*.

He sat down. But not upon the throne. Instead, he turned his back on the silent Lion and settled upon the dais. He stared into the firepit, empty of coals or logs.

He thought of going to his chambers, but he could not face his *lir*. Even in their silence, Taj and Lorn would make him confront the truth. And so he faced the guilt alone.

His eyes burned. His throat was raw. His chest was heavy with the weight of what he had done. He waited for someone to come.

– to tell me she is dead –

But he was not expecting Evan.

He heard the footsteps. He did not look up. He stared blindly at the fabric of his breeches stretched over his doubled knees. He sat with elbows in his lap; hands dangled between his thighs, hair falling into his face.

Evan walked the length of the hall until he reached the dais. After a moment's hesitation, he joined him on the smooth, cool marble. 'Is there anything I can do?'

'No.' He hardly knew his own voice. 'I think *I* have done enough.'

Evan sighed. For the briefest moment their shared silence was almost companionable, lacking the tension of knowledge. 'I arrived a week ago. There was no need for me to stay – the war with Atvia is over.' He shifted his seat upon the stone. 'When you slew Osric, you took the heart from them. Two days after you left, the Atvians sent an envoy to our camp, offering their surrender.'

'That is something.' Donal ran a hand through his hair and stripped it from his face. 'Evan –'

'Alaric, I think, will also offer fealty,' Evan went on, 'but – he is home in Atvia, fighting Shea of Erinn over a silly, pompous title: Lord of the Idrian Isles.' His tone was underscored with contempt. 'Still, I think he will come. I think he will ask alliance.' Again, he shifted on the dais. 'Rowan has gone on to Solinde. The rebellion there is nearly finished; he should be home in a month or two, with words of victory. I do not know why those fools still fight. . . . They lack Tynstar now. Their cause is no better than it was before. They should give up.'

'They want freedom from Homana,' Donal said dully. 'I might be moved to give it to them – except Carillon was the one who won the realm, and I cannot let go of what he has held. Not if I wish to keep the Homanans satisfied.' He sighed. 'If I could know Solinde would never again invade Homana –' He shook his head, 'But I cannot. Not yet. Perhaps – someday.'

'Perhaps. After more wars.'

Donal thought of the battles he had seen. He thought of how he had slain Osric in retribution for Carillon's death, and because Finn had asked it. He had been proud to know that he had accomplished the task his uncle had set him; now, seated on cool, hard marble with the Lion crouching behind him, he could think only of the young

woman, Carillon's daughter, whom he had effectively slain.

He shut his eyes. 'You know what I have done.'

'I know what you have done.'

'And will you curse me for it? I know the others will. The Homanans –' He broke off. 'Gods – they have every right. I nearly slew the Queen. And if I am exceedingly fortunate, this will not begin a war.'

'Aye,' Evan agreed. Then, gently, 'How could you think it of her, Donal? Aislinn is not the enemy.'

'Not the enemy, no; the victim. Sorcha's victim, as much as Sorcha was victim herself.' He buried his head in his hands, pressing his forehead. 'Oh, gods – how can I believe it? Sorcha – gone . . . and making Aislinn look so guilty!'

'She must have been very unhappy. To love you so much and yet hate you so much –'

'Hate *me*?' Donal's head snapped up. 'It was *Aislinn* she hated, and the Homanans.'

'And you. For leaving her, even briefly.' Evan shook his head. 'I never knew her. I cannot explain much about her, except to say that there are women – and men – whose affection becomes obsession.'

'She said I would turn away from the clans. Turn away from our customs. Seek instead the Homanan way of living.'

'And you did.' Evan put up a silencing hand. 'No, *I* know you did not – but it probably appeared so to her. You were gone for months on end. You wed Aislinn, then went away to war. Returned long enough to get a child on your Homanan wife, then got captured by the Ihlini. Sorcha met with Aislinn, as Rowan said, and undoubtedly the discussion was – *heated*. Aislinn has a powerful pride. No doubt Sorcha thought she had lost you for good, and to the *Homanans*. And so she went away, intending to take her own life, but intending also to make it look as if Aislinn had driven her to it.'

'And succeeded.' He dug fingers into his hair. 'Evan –'

He broke it off. Meghan had come into the hall.

'Donal?' Her call echoed in the timbers. 'Donal?'

She comes with news of Aislinn – Donal shut his eyes. 'Aye?' he said. 'Meghan – I am here.'

She picked up her skirts and hastened toward the dais. 'Donal – you have a son!'

He stared at her as she arrived before them both, a little breathless; gods knew how long she had been looking for him. 'A son?'

Tawny hair tumbled over her shoulders. 'A healthy son, Donal. She has given you an heir.'

He felt the guilt rise up to stab him in the belly. 'Aislinn?' he asked hoarsely.

Meghan raked a hand through her shining hair. 'She is – very weak. Donal . . . you had best go to her.'

He felt cold, cold and empty, sucked dry of all but the knowledge of his guilt. Slowly he pushed himself to his feet. 'Aye . . . I will go.'

When at last he looked upon his wife, he saw a child in the bed; a child whose glorious hair spread across the pillows in rich red disarray. Her fair skin was whiter still with the waxy look of the ill. Gold-tipped lashes lay against the dark circles beneath her eyes. The bedclothes were pulled up under her chin, but one arm lay across the coverlet, blue-veined against the fairness of her flesh.

Oh gods, what have I done to her? How could you let me do it? But he knew, even as he asked it, the question was unfair. He had only himself to blame.

Donal sat down on the edge of her bed. He was alone with her, having dismissed her women, and now all he wanted was to see her looking at him from her great grey, shining eyes.

Electra's eyes – Abruptly he shook his head. *No, her own. I am done laying Electra's machinations at the feet of her innocent daughter.*

He smoothed the strands of fine hair back from her brow. He traced the winged line of her eyebrows and the

399

cool silk of her eyelids. 'Aislinn,' he said. 'She was all I ever wanted. A Cheysuli warrior may take as many women as he chooses, providing the women are willing, but for me – for me it was always Sorcha. Ever since we were young.' He looked down on her pale, still face. 'You yourself are so young – you cannot know what it is to love someone from childhood – ' He broke it off. *By all the gods! – I wrong her again, as I have wronged her all along. I pride myself on knowing I have loved Sorcha all these years – and all the while I was no younger than Aislinn is now when I knew what Sorcha meant to me. She bore me a child when she was not so much younger than Aislinn is now. Gods – I have been such a selfish brute –*

He clasped her hand in his. Then, slowly, he slid off the bed and knelt beside it, setting his forehead against the silk of the counterpane.

He sent the call winging deep into the earth, praying the magic would answer him though he had already used it wrongly. He could not afford another mistake. Not with her life at stake.

Donal drifted. He felt the wispy, tensile strength of the magic in the earth. He abased himself before it, admitting freely his guilt. He did not hide what he had done. He opened himself up to the omniscience of the earth and let it see what manner of man he was.

And at last, when he thought it would not answer, the power flowed up from the earth to bathe Aislinn in its magic.

When Aislinn roused, moving beneath the bedclothes like a fretful child, he released her fingers and rose. He put out his hand and caught the nearest bedpost to steady himself; he was dizzy, disoriented. The healing should not have been done alone. He had nearly lost himself within the overwhelming power of the magic, and he still trembled from the knowledge. But he felt the risk worth it; after what he done *to* her, it was time he did something *for* her.

But Aislinn stared up at him in astonishment. 'No,' she

400

whispered, clearly terrified. 'Oh, gods . . . *no* –'

'It heals,' he said hoarsely. 'All it does is heal. I promise you that –'

'Promise *me*? You will slay me!' Her eyes were blackened by fear. 'As you sought to slay me *before* –'

'No.' He said it as clearly as he could, but his mouth did not work properly. He felt his knees buckle and clung desperately to the bedpost, sliding slowly to the floor. 'I sought – sought only to know the truth. . . . I would *not* have slain you – I swear –'

Aislinn stared at him like a doe cornered by the huntsman. Red-gold hair tumbled over her shoulders; her mouth trembled. 'I loved you,' she said. 'I loved you all my life. But – you already had *her*.' Color crept into her waxen cheeks. 'It was you I wanted, Donal – ever since I was a child. And – I wanted to bear children for you, as many as I could – but even *that* she had already given you!' One shaking hand was touched to her mouth as if she sought to halt her words, but she let them spill out with a ragged dignity. 'There was no gift left I could give you that *she* had not already given – *no gift at all* . . . oh *aye*, I wanted her gone – I *wanted her gone from here*! But I swear I did not send her. Donal, I did *not*!'

'I know.' He held himself up against the post. 'I know it, Aislinn –'

'What have you done to me?' Tears spilled down her face. '*What have you done to me?*'

'Healing,' he mumbled, 'only healing. I want you strong again.'

She recoiled utterly. 'Why? So you may send me away as my father sent my mother?'

Donal felt his last reserve crumble. All the savage grief he had tried to suppress surged up into his chest until he nearly choked on it. He took handfuls of the silken counterpane, clenched it tightly in white-knuckled fists and wept. 'I have no one.' It hissed through a throat nearly sealed by grief. '*I have no one left at all* –' he closed his eyes '– except for you.'

Aislinn said nothing at all.

'*Tahlmorra*,' he said thickly. 'All of it –' And he put his face down against the bed and knelt before her, a supplicant to the gods.

Aislinn's breath was audible. '*Do you expect forgiveness?*'

He heard the savagery in her tone. 'No,' he said, but the word was muffled against the bed.

'Then what *do* you want from me?'

He lifted his head and saw her face. The deathbed pallor was replaced by an angry flush high in her cheeks. Her emotion-darkened eyes glittered balefully.

'I want you to live,' he told her plainly. 'I ask for nothing from you save that.'

'Why? So you may hurt me again?' Her hand shook as she touched her breast. 'So you may hurt my heart again?'

Her broken, vulnerable tone broke the final barriers against emotion. 'What promises can I make you?' he asked in desperation. 'What words would you have me say? After all I have done to you, do you expect me to change with a wave of a hand?' He felt bitterness in his mouth. 'Would you wish to have me beg? I will do it.'

'Beg *me*?' She stared.

He shut his eyes. 'Tell me what you want.'

She swallowed heavily. 'Once – I wanted your love. But that was too much to ask . . . you had given it to her.' Tears ran down her face. One shaking hand tried to hide the quivering of her mouth. 'I only – I only wanted a chance – a *chance* to know what it was –'

He could not answer her. He could only shut his eyes and put his head down on the bed again.

'You do not love me.' The intonation was precise, as if she wished to make it clear.

He looked at her sharply, fearing she sickened again. But he saw high color in her face and a startled recognition in her eyes. 'You do not love me,' she repeated, with wonder in her voice, 'but you *need* me. *You* need *me*.'

The breath slipped out of his throat. 'I need you,' he

admitted. 'By all the gods, *I do*.'

Aislinn stared at him a long moment, all manner of emotion in her face. He saw anger and pain and grief and regret, but he also saw something else. Something akin to *possessiveness*.

'Well,' she said in an intense, peculiar triumph, 'perhaps that will be enough.'

9

Evan raised his goblet. 'To Niall, the Prince of Homana. Four weeks old and thriving.'

Donal smiled. He brought up his goblet to clash against Evan's, then drank down a swallow of wine.

They sat over their cups in Donal's private solar. Sunlight spilled through the casements. Evan sat slumped deeply in a chair; Donal stretched out on a snow bear pelt with Lorn collapsed against his side. Taj perched on a chairback.

Evan put up his feet on a three-legged stool. 'What will you do about Strahan?'

Donal scowled into his cup of wine. 'What *can* I do? He is Ihlini – he has what freedom he can steal.'

'Could you not set a trap for him?'

'He has gone underground. There is no word of him. He could be in Valgaard by now, high in the Molon Mountains. He could be in Solinde, sheltered by those who still serve the Ihlini. He could be almost anywhere, Evan – there is nothing I can do. Except wait.' *And the gods know I will do that, no matter how long it takes.*

Evan sighed and swirled his wine. 'I know, I know – but it seems so futile to do nothing. You know he will do what he can to throw you down from the throne.'

'He is a boy,' Donal said. 'I discount neither his power nor his heritage – but he *is* a boy. I think it likely he will wait until he grows older, old enough to inspire trust in other men. Oh, he will lead the Ihlini on the strength of his blood alone – but how many others will follow? I think he will play at patience.'

'Donal?' It was Aislinn, standing in the open doorway. 'A messenger has just come with word from Alaric of Atvia. It seems he is in Mujhara, intending to see you.'

Donal pressed himself upright. 'Alaric is *here*?'

Evan nodded. 'I said he would come, did I not? He will offer fealty, does he have any sense at all.'

Aislinn, hair braided and threaded with silver cord, pulled her pale green mantle more closely about her shoulders. 'Shall we have his baggage moved into the palace?'

Donal, frowning, nodded. 'Aye. It would transgress all decency did we leave him at an inn. Aye, send servants for his baggage. Gods! – I need a bath!'

Evan laughed. 'Let him see you as you are.'

Donal, draining the rest of his wine, cast Evan a sour glance. 'I intend to – but I also intend to show him what courtesy I can muster . . . can I muster *any*.' He turned to leave the room. 'Aislinn – have Torvald set out fresh clothing.'

'Aye,' she said. 'Cheysuli or Homanan?'

He stopped in the doorway. She faced him squarely, exhibiting no fear. What had passed between them after the healing had fashioned her into another woman.

One I do not know. 'Which would *you* say is more fitting to receive a man who was once an enemy?'

Aislinn smiled. 'The shapechanger, my lord. How can you consider anything else?'

Donal received Alaric in the Great Hall, ensconced in the Lion Throne. He had put on blue-dyed Cheysuli leathers and a torque of gold around his throat to match his heavy belt. To Alaric, he did not doubt, he would resemble nothing more than a crude barbarian. Which was precisely what he desired.

So I may lull him into carelessness? On the throne, Donal smiled.

Alaric was nothing like his brother. His height was average, no better; hair and eyes were dark brown. He dressed well but conservatively, in black breeches and

velvet doublet, showing no ornamentation other than a silver ring set with black stone on one hand and a narrow chain of office – also silver – around his shoulders. He was accompanied by five Atvian nobles, all dressed more richly than himself, but none of them claimed the same intensity or the air of absolute command Alaric held even in silence.

Donal considered the formal greetings he had learned. He discarded them all at once. He disliked Alaric instantly; he disliked diplomacy even more.

He waited.

Alaric stood before the dais. He inclined his head a trifle. 'My lord – I have come to offer fealty – and to tender an alliance.'

'Why?' Donal asked.

A minute frown twitched the arched eyebrows. But Alaric's face retained its bland, cool expression. 'Plainly, my lord, you have overcome my realm. My brother is slain and I am Lord of Atvia in his place . . . but I do recognize the virtue in admitting our defeat. You have – quite effectively proved your competence as a king.'

Donal regarded him appraisingly. 'Have I? Enough to keep you from our borders forever? – or only until you rally an army again?'

A muscle jumped in Alaric's shaven face. 'A king does not offer fealty to another unless he intends to honor it, my lord.'

'Usually.' Donal relaxed in the Lion. 'Not *always*, but –' He waved a hand. 'Enough of this. You offer fealty, which you *owe* me, and an alliance, which undoubtedly *you* need more than I do.'

Alaric's mouth was tight. 'Aye, my lord – like you, I do not doubt it.'

Donal studied him. He knew instinctively Alaric was more than a competent warrior. He was also a strategist. A diplomat. He would give up much to gain more. *But what does he want? And what will he give up in order to*

406

get it? He gestured idly. 'Once before you came here. To Carillon, after he slew Thorne, your *jehan*. Then, you said Atvia would offer fealty to no foreign king.'

Alaric inclined his head. 'I was a boy then. I am a man now – and king in my brother's place – and I must do what is best for my realm.'

'Your fealty I will have – you can hardly refuse me now – but the alliance I must consider. What do you offer me?'

Alaric gestured eloquently. 'My brother died without heirs. He had two sons, but both are dead of fever. I myself am unmarried, without legitimate heirs. What I offer Homana is quite simple: myself. And a binding peace between our realms when children are born of this match.'

Donal frowned. 'You wish to wed a Homanan woman?'

'No. I wish to wed your sister.'

Donal's hands spasmed against the clawed armrests of the throne. 'You wish to wed with *Bronwyn?*'

'Aye, my lord. If that is her name.' Alaric did not smile.

Gods . . . he cannot mean it! But he knew Alaric did. When he could, he asked a single question. 'Why?'

Alaric's smile was very slight. 'My lord, I have said – to settle a peace between our lands.'

'What *else?* We can make a peace without wedding my *rujholla* to you.'

'Perhaps.' Alaric's tone was negligent. 'Perhaps not. But consider it in this light, if you will: a princess of Homana – though she be Cheysuli – is wed to the Lord of Atvia. From that union, provided the gods see fit to bless it, will come children. Sons, of course. And the eldest to rule in my place when I am dead.' Alaric gestured idly. 'He would be your nephew, my lord Mujhar – and never an enemy. How better to insure peace between our realms?'

'How better for you to make yourself a claimant for the Lion!' Donal's fist smacked down on the throne. 'Do not

407

play me for a fool, Atvian – I am no courtier with silken tongue and oiled palms, but – *by the gods!* – neither am I blind. You desire peace between our realms? Then keep your armies from my borders!'

Alaric's dark brown eyes glittered, but only a little. He kept himself under control. 'But of course, my lord – I had intended to. And yet – it seemed such a perfect way to link our realms. As for *me* desiring to claim the Lion Throne, I say no. Of course not. Do you not have a legitimate heir?'

Donal smiled thinly. 'Aye, my lord, I do.'

'Then the continuance of your House is certainly insured.' Alaric smiled. 'I offer this alliance because I desire to insure the continuation of *my* House. And nothing more.'

'Nothing more?'

'Perhaps support against Shea of Erinn.'

Donal sat back again, conforming his back to the crimson cushion. 'What quarrel have you with Shea?'

'He has usurped my brother's title: Lord of the Idrian Isles. It was my father's. It was *his* father's. Shea claimed it when Osric died.' Alaric shrugged. 'I want it back.'

Donal frowned. 'With Homanan help? Why should I offer that? Homana has no quarrel with Erinn.'

'No. Nor do I wish to begin one.' Alaric spread his hands. 'Mere word of this marriage would send Shea back behind the walls of Kilore and keep him from my shores until I can regroup my demoralized army – demoralized because of my brother's death. I would not ask men of you, my lord, merely the *appearance* of support. It would be more than enough.'

Donal frowned at the toes of his soft leather boots. 'I cannot see a single sound reason for agreeing to this. It gets Homana nothing. You say it gets us peace, but that we should have anyway. We have defeated you.'

Alaric shrugged. 'And eventually the Atvian throne. Your nephew will be my heir. There will be Cheysuli princes in Atvia.'

Donal shrugged. 'I am not so certain that would serve

anything –' Abruptly, he stopped speaking. His belly turned in upon itself. *By the gods – it is the prophecy . . . even from the mouth of the enemy!* He stared at Alaric in shock. *Four warring realms –*

He pushed himself back in the throne before he could display his shock to the Atvian. The pattern lay before him as clearly as if Evan had thrown it himself. *If I wed Bronwyn to him, her son will have the throne. Cheysuli in Atvia. Adding one more realm to the prophecy. By the gods, it* will *come true!*

Bronwyn in Ativa. No, he could not see it. She would never agree. The Cheysuli did not barter women or use them for sealing alliances.

And yet, things changed. So many things *had* to change. His own mother had told him how Finn had stolen her from the Homanans because for years the Cheysuli had needed to steal Homanan women, to strengthen the clan again. It was alien to him, but no less alien than the thought of wedding his sister to Alaric.

If I do it – if I do *it – Bronwyn would never forgive me –*

Alaric still watched silently, all politeness, waiting for an answer. He was like a cat ready to spring, elegant in his readiness; Donal did not like him. He did not like him at all.

Give my rujholla to this ku'reshtin of Atvia?

And yet, if he did not and it was part of the prophecy –

I will not decide this now. *There is no need to decide this* now – He steadied his breathing with effort. And then, as he prepared to give Alaric a diplomatic reason to delay the expected answer, realized with blinding clarity the marriage could never take place. Even if the prophecy demanded it.

Slowly, Donal sat back. 'You are guests of Homana,' he said evenly, *'Cheysuli i'halla shansu.'* But he knew he did not mean it.

Alaric frowned as Donal moved to rise. 'My lord – your answer? May I know when you will give it?'

Donal stood. 'I give it now,' he said. 'My *rujholla* may never marry.'

Bronwyn, whom he tracked down in Aislinn's solar, looked on in silence as he banished everyone from the chamber save herself. She stood before an open casement with light falling on her shoulders. She wore a simple indigo gown embroidered with interlocking leaves in silver thread. He looked at her silently, wondering when she had grown up. She had done it without his knowledge; he clearly recalled her girlish laughter at his wedding; her tomboyish way at the Keep. Now she was a woman. Only sixteen and still young, but there was a new maturity in her eyes and grace to her movements.

He gestured her to sit down upon a stool even as he himself did. 'A man is here,' he said. 'He has come to Homana-Mujhar because he wishes to wed the Mujhar's *rujholla*.'

Color blossomed in her cheeks. 'Wed *me?*'

'Aye. He offers you the chance to be a queen.'

'*Queen!*' Bronwyn was clearly shocked. 'Who would wish *me* to be his queen?'

'Alaric of Atvia.'

Bronwyn shot to her feet. '*Alaric of Atvia!*'

Donal rose slowly. He heard the horror in her tone. *At least I may save her that.* 'Bronwyn – Bronwyn, you do not have to wed him. I promise you that. Do not think I will send you away.'

She shut her eyes. A breath of relief hissed out of her mouth. 'Thank the gods – *thank the gods* – I thought it might be a political thing –' She shuddered. 'There are dangers in being *rujholla* to the Mujhar.'

'It *would* be a political thing,' Donal pointed out. 'Alaric offers alliance to Homana. It would also be a dynastic thing, binding the realms together.'

She understood him perfectly. 'It – seems to be sound reasoning – to bind the realms together.' Her tone was very flat.

'Bronwyn, you need fear nothing. There can be no royal marriage. There can be no marriage at all.'

'Not with Alaric.' Relief put life back into her tone. 'But someday –'

'No.' He said it plainly, wishing to have it done with. 'Bronwyn, you will never be able to marry.'

She stared. 'Have you gone mad? Of *course* I will marry! What would keep me from it?'

'I would.' He said it flatly. 'I have no other choice.'

She laughed. The tone was incredulous and perplexed. 'You *have* gone mad. Donal . . . *what are you saying?*'

He reached out and caught her shoulders. 'That because of the blood in you, I can never let you wed. You can never bear any children.'

She went stiff in his hands. He felt the convulsive shiver that shook her limbs. She tore herself from his grasp. 'You are mad – you are *mad* – how can you say such things? How can you tell me this?' Slowly she shook her head. 'Do you think my children would threaten the throne? By the gods, Donal – I am your *rujholla!* Our *jehana* bore us both! Our *jehan* –'

'– sired only me.' He saw the spasm in her face. 'Gods, Bronwyn, I wish I could spare you this. I wish it were not true. But – when you say I fear your children may threaten the throne – you may have the right of it. I cannot shut my eyes to the possibility.'

Her eyes were fixed on his face. 'You said – you said we do not share a *jehan* –'

'No. Another man sired you.'

'*Who?*' she demanded 'Gods, *rujho*, I beg you who I am –'

He felt the tightness in his throat. 'You are *Tynstar's daughter*.'

Silence. Bronwyn stared. He could not look away.

'Oh –' she said. 'Oh – oh – *no* –'

'Aye,' he told her gently, and reached out to steady her. Slowly he guided her to the stool and made her sit down again. 'Bronwyn, you are still my *rujholla*, still our

411

jehana's daughter. Almost half Cheysuli, and bloodkin to the clan. It changes nothing. It changes nothing.'

'It changes *everything*.' The words were dead in her mouth.

'No, Bronwyn, it does not. Do you think I will send you away? There is too much blood between us –'

'– too much *spilled* blood between us.' She looked up blankly to meet his gaze. 'Why was I never told?'

'There was no reason for it. You were raised Cheysuli – it was hoped you would never show Tynstar's power. And – unless you have purposely hidden it – you never have.'

Trembling, she touched the vicinity of her heart. 'I have ever felt Cheysuli . . . Cheysuli and Homanan.'

'You are both. You are. But – there is also Ihlini in you.'

'*How* –?'

Donal sat down again. 'You have heard how Tynstar had our *jehana* taken to Valgaard. I was just a boy. He wanted me as well, but I managed to escape.' He looked down at her shaking hands as she clutched them in her lap. 'He kept our *jehana* captive. And while she was there –'

'– he raped her?' Bronwyn shuddered. 'Gods, oh gods – it makes me feel so *dirty* –'

'No!' He reached out and caught her hands. 'It has nothing to do with you.'

'But I do not *feel* Ihlini!' she cried. 'How do you know it is true?'

He put out his arms as she slid off the stool to kneel on the floor. He soothed her head against his shoulder, as if she were Isolde requiring special comfort. One arm slid around her shoulders. He held her close, knowing he could never share her grief.

A woman told she cannot bear a child – He shut his eyes. He whispered inanities.

Bronwyn clutched at his leather jerkin. 'I begin to see – all the times I sensed a barrier between us . . . something

eeping us apart. That was it, was it not? The knowledge I
was Tynstar's daughter?'

'Oh *rujholla*, I would do anything to lift this grief from
you.'

'*Jehana* never said. *Never* did she say –'

'She told it to no one. Only a few of us knew, and none of
us ever spoke of it to others.'

'Why did you let me live?' The question was hardly a
sound.

'Bronwyn! Oh, *gods*, Bronwyn – do you think we would
ever desire to have you slain? What do you think we are?'

'You are Cheysuli. And – I am the enemy.'

'No enemy. *No enemy*!' And yet he recalled all the times
he had watched her, wondering, and felt the guilt in his
soul. *Not an* intentional *enemy*.

'But you will never let me wed.' The tears welled up
again. 'Do you distrust me so much? Do you think I will
work against you? Do you think I would ever aid the boy
who slew our *su'fali*?' Bronwyn shook her head. 'Gods,
Donal – I would *never* do such a thing! You know I would
not. We are kin. There is blood between us.'

'There is blood between you and Strahan.' He shook his
head. 'It is not *you* I do not trust – it is how your power
might be used. By another, if not by you.'

'Power!' she shook her head. 'I *have* no power, Donal. I
would know it. I swear – I would know it. There is nothing
in me. Do you think I would not know?'

'Bronwyn –'

'Then test me.' She rose and stood before him. '*Test* me,
Donal! See if there is power.'

He shook his head. 'Bronwyn, I could not –'

'You did it to Aislinn!' she snapped.

'*And* I nearly slew her! Gods, Bronwyn, *have sense!* Do
you think I wish to harm you?'

'You harm me now,' she said. 'You tell me I cannot wed,
cannot bear children – you name me Tynstar's daughter.
How can I live with that? You have given me a life of
emptiness!'

He could not answer. He had no answer for her.

'Donal,' she said, 'I beg you.'

He threaded his fingers into hers and pulled her down to kneel against the tapestry rug. He looked into her eyes. 'Do I do this – do I test you, and learn you are Ihlini . . . you must promise never to wed. Never to bear a child.'

Bronwyn shut her eyes. '*Ja'hai-na*,' she said. 'Accepted.'

Tentatively, he parted the curtain of her awareness. He slid through, hardly disturbing the threads of his sister's consciousness. What she felt he could not say; what he felt was a sudden unexpected communion that nearly threw him out of the link. It had been different with Aislinn, who had received him unwillingly. What he had done to her was little different from rape. But Bronwyn understood. Bronwyn desired his presence. She welcomed him willingly, but he sensed a trace of fear. She was not certain what he would find.

Gently. Gently. He left no residue of his passing.

The barriers went down.

In the web of her consciousness he saw the junctions of inner knowledge that buried itself so deeply. He allowed his own awareness to expand, touching the junctions carefully. He feared no trap-link in his sister, but it was possible that Ihlini were born with warding powers. That somehow, unconsciously, she would move to throw him back.

But she did not. He sensed only complete acceptance; a trust that nearly unmanned him. She had seen what he did to Aislinn, yet she did not fear the same for herself.

Gently, he expanded his awareness. And her own surged up to meet him.

Patterns linked. Meshed. Knotted. Everything fell into place.

He knew, without a doubt, Duncan had sired them both.

* * *

Bronwyn sagged. He caught her against his chest and stood up, holding her on her feet. Gently, he said her name, until she opened her eyes. She was dazed, clearly disoriented. But sense moved into her eyes.

'*Rujho?*'

He hugged her as hard as he dared. '*Rujho*, aye – there is no Ihlini in you.' He felt the tears in his eyes. *All those years, all those years . . . oh rujholla, how we all have wronged you –*

Bronwyn's laughter was little more than a breath of sound. 'It was worth it, *rujho* . . . oh, it was! To know I am not that demon's daughter!' She hugged him, laughing against his chest. But then she went stiff in his arms. 'Gods – *oh gods* – there was the boy! *He* told me the truth –'

Donal drew back. 'Bronwyn –'

Her hand was at her mouth. 'He said – oh, I recall it so well! We sat outside *su'fali's* pavilion while he tested Aislinn. He showed me those runes – he asked me to try my own –' Her breath was harsh in her throat. 'None of this was necessary! Sef gave me the answer *then*.'

'Sef! What answer could *he* give –' And then he recalled it also. How he had seen them kneeling in the dust, drawing foreign runes.

Bronwyn nodded. 'Something he said made no sense. I thought nothing of it. But – he said I was not who you thought I was.' She frowned, shaking her head. 'It made no sense: *You are not the woman your brother thinks you are.*' She clutched at his shoulders. 'Oh gods, Donal – he knew – he *knew* I was not Ihlini!'

'He tested you.' The words were bitter in his mouth. 'Even as Finn tested Aislinn, Strahan tested you.'

Bronwyn shuddered. 'How could I have been such a fool –?'

'No more so than any of us.' Donal loosened his arms and turned her toward the door. 'I am no less glad than you are to have it settled at last. But we have no more time for it now, either of us. Bathe and dress yourself as fits a

princess, Bronwyn – we feast the Atvian tonight.'

Bronwyn made a face. 'Could I not plead sickness? I would rather not see this man who thought I would wed him.'

'Let him see *you* – to know what he has lost.'

She laughed. But then she frowned. 'But I have nothing to wear!'

Donal merely sighed.

10

Donal saw Alaric's amazement when first he set eyes on Bronwyn. Undoubtedly he had prepared himself to charm a barbaric Cheysuli woman who hardly understood the niceties of courtship. Instead, he saw a lovely young woman in copper-colored silk with her heavy hair bound up in a mass of looped, shining braids pinned against her head with gold. Garnets glittered at ears and throat; a matching girdle of tiny bells dripped down her heavy skirts.

Donal realized, as he watched her, she knew precisely what she was about. He smiled inwardly. *Does my young rujholla play at being a woman? Well – perhaps she should. No longer is she a girl.*

Bronwyn, during the feast in the Great Hall, was seated next to Alaric. Donal, watching them both, noticed how quickly Alaric saw through his partner's subterfuge. He did not set out to charm her, as he had undoubtedly first intended; instead, he spoke courteously and sparingly. But Bronwyn was not won over.

Throughout the feast Alaric and his countrymen were unceasingly polite to the Homanan nobles. Nowhere was there a sign of hostility or resentment. Nor were there any signs the Atvians considered themselves the vanquished. They moved quickly, smoothly, speaking of unification. More and more Donal saw how members of the Homanan Council looked first at Alaric and then at Bronwyn. More and more he saw consideration in their eyes.

They will *ask*, he knew. *Oh, aye, they* will *ask . . . and I will have to answer them.*

And after the food was taken away, with Donal in an adjoining antechamber, the council members asked.

Donal listened. He heard the arguments for and against the match. Some members said Atvia was too distant, too unknown; the Mujhar could never keep constant watch on political happenings. Others said the match would unify the two realms, much as Carillon's marriage to Electra had, while it lasted, unified Homana and Solinde – save for a few insurgents who fought against the alliance.

But it was an elderly man, Vallis, former counselor to Shaine himself, who spoke most clearly to them all. 'Many of us, my lord Mujhar, understand we are here to serve the gods. Cheysuli, Homanan . . . it does not really matter by what names we call our gods. It merely matters that we serve them.' He was in his eighties, and frail, with a thin, soft voice and thinner hair. The dome of his skull was mottled pink. Only the merest fringe of fine white hair curled around his ears. 'While it is true as Homanans we do not dedicate ourselves to this prophecy of the First-born, we do acknowledge its existence. We do not discount it – or *should* not.' He looked at each of the men with rheumy, pale blue eyes. 'Before the purge, Cheysuli and Homanans intermarried. You yourself, my lord, claim blood from both those races. And does not this prophecy say there must be more?'

Donal agreed warily.

Vallis nodded. 'What I tell you now is by wedding your sister to Alaric of Atvia, you move one step closer to fulfilling that prophecy.'

'I am aware of that.' Donal kept his tone very even, giving nothing away of his private thoughts. 'Say on, Vallis.'

The old man braced himself against a chair. Ropes of veins stood up beneath his flesh. 'Prince Niall bears the blood of Homana and Solinde, as well as the Cheysuli. Do you wed your sister to Alaric, and she bears him a daughter, in time that daughter could be wed to the Prince of Homana.'

Donal raised his brows. 'And does she bear him a son instead?'

Vallis shrugged narrow shoulders. 'Doubtless by *then*, you and the Queen will have daughters enough to wed into every royal House.'

He felt their eyes upon him. Slowly he walked to a casement and stared out, though he could see little in the darkness. Then he turned to face them. 'Bronwyn does not desire it.'

Some of the others smiled. Some faces expressed outright surprise. He knew his statement made no sense to them; Homanans wed their daughters to men most able to advance their rank or wealth.

Like bartering horses. He shook his head. 'Bronwyn does not desire it.'

They knew it was his answer. They had learned that much of him since he had become Mujhar. And so they filed from the antechamber and back into the hall, while Vallis stayed behind.

'My lord,' he said, 'I know you value your sister. Do not lump me in with the others. I am an old, old man . . . I have seen the Cheysuli elevated by Shaine and then destroyed by him – I know your customs well. She is not a broodmare. She is not a ewe. She is not a favorite bitch. She is a woman, a Cheysuli woman . . . but she is also a part of the prophecy.' Slowly, the old man put out a palsied hand. Palm uppermost, with the fingers spreading. '*Tahlmorra lujhala mei wiccan, cheysu.*'

Donal turned and left the chamber, returning to the hall.

Evan came up to him, holding two cups of wine. One he held out. 'So solemn, Donal . . . did they put you into a corner and make you listen to their babble?'

Donal, smiling grimly, accepted the wine. 'You know court habits very well.'

Evan laughed. 'Ellas is no different! Only the language.' But his laughter died away. 'I must go, Donal. It is time I went back to Ellas.'

The taste of the wine turned flat. 'Evan! So soon?'

'Soon?' Evan stared. 'I have been here nearly a year.'

'Stay another.'

He shook his head. 'I cannot. It is time I went home. There are things in Ellas for me.'

Donal drank down the rest of his wine, gave the empty cup to a passing servant and got another to replace it. He saw his sister across the hall, laughing with Aislinn and Meghan. 'Have you told Meghan you intend to leave?'

Evan's mouth turned down wryly. 'No. I dislike tears cried into my velvet doublets.'

'Tears from *Meghan?*' Donal shook his head. 'She is stronger than you think.'

'Oh, aye – strong . . . if you count willfulness as strength.' Evan scowled into his wine. 'No, no tears from Meghan. But I could wish for more complaisance.'

'I warned you,' Donal told him. 'She is not meant for just any man. Not even for Evan of Ellas – does he desire no more than an evening in her bed.'

'Ah, but he does desire more.' Evan ran the rim of the cup across his bottom lip. 'Lodhi protect me – but I invited her home with me.'

'To *Ellas?*' Donal stared at Evan in surprise. 'Did you really think she would go?'

'I – hoped.' Evan shrugged. 'It was useless. She refused me.'

Donal saw the genuine unhappiness in the Ellasian's sleepy eyes. It was not like Evan to exhibit anything other than mild distress when a woman refused him; it did not happen very often, and generally he found another who suited him as well. But Meghan was different. And Donal realized Evan knew it.

He smiled. 'I am sorry. She may be Cheysuli, but there is Homanan in her also. Living so close to Aislinn lately may have given her Homanan sensibilities when it comes to such things as men.'

'Because she would not become my light woman?' Evan shook his head. 'But I asked her to wed me.'

'*You?*'

'Aye,' Evan said gloomily. 'And a waste of time it was.'

Donal sighed. 'I am sorry. I did not know it had gone so far.'

'Oh, it had not. But I thought it was the only way I might get her to lie with me.' Evan grinned. 'Unlike all of the others, she did not believe I meant it.'

Donal laughed and nearly spilled his wine. 'You fool! Do you forget she is Finn's daughter? She will take a man on *her* terms, if she takes a man at all.'

Evan raised his goblet. 'To Meghan,' he said. 'And to the warrior who sired her.'

Donal lifted his cup. And then, abruptly, he told Evan not to go. 'What will I do without you?'

'Learn to govern Homana without me to offer bad advice.' Evan shook his head. 'My time here is done. I am sorry – but I must go.'

'When?'

'Probably in the morning. Or, depending on my head after this celebration, perhaps in the afternoon. But I do have to go.'

Donal reached out and clasped his arm. 'In advance, I will wish you safe journey and good fortune in your games. And – I wish I did not have to lose you.'

'No more than Carillon wished to lose Lachlan.' Evan grinned. 'But I am not so bound by responsibility as my brother, and I think I will come back. At least to bother Meghan once or twice more.'

Donal released Evan's arm and glanced back across the hall. Alaric still lingered near Bronwyn. *Hoping, no doubt, she will have him. But why does he want her? What does he expect her to bring? Peace with Homana? Support for the island wars? Gods – I wish I could read that man.*

But he could not. Grimly, he drank more Falian wine. 'You have heard, of course, that Alaric wishes to wed with Bronwyn.'

Evan's tone was wry. 'Who has not, by now? But – with her Ihlini blood, you dare not allow the match.'

'She has no Ihlini blood. I tested her today.'

'None!' Evan turned sharply to him. 'None at all?'

'She is my full *rujholla*, Evan. She is Duncan's daughter.'

The Ellasian shook his head, frowning perplexedly. 'Then – if you could have tested her all along, why did you wait so long?'

'Because it could not have been done without her knowledge, without her willingness.' Donal sighed. 'It was our *jehana*. She wished to leave Bronwyn in peace. She did not wish to awaken potential powers *or* bring grief to Bronwyn. And so – she was kept in innocence.'

Evan's blue eyes were fixed on the girl as she laughed with her two kinswomen. 'Then – there is nothing preventing this marriage.'

'No,' Donal said. 'There is nothing preventing this marriage.'

Evan looked at him sharply. 'Lodhi! – you *do* intend to honor Alaric's request!'

Donal shut his fingers on the heavy cup. 'All my life I have been told there would be choices placed before me. Choices I would hate. I knew it, of course – but it is so easy to push the knowledge away.' He heard the unevenness in his voice and worked to steady it. 'I remember all the times I wanted to call Carillon a fool because of the choices he made . . . particularly the ones he made regarding *me*. And now – now it will be *Bronwyn's* turn to ask me what I do, and how – in the name of all the gods – can I possibly even *consider* it.'

'I understand what you do.' Evan said. 'Being a prince, I can hardly *mis*understand why you do it. But – I do not envy you.'

'No,' Donal agreed. 'But too many other people do.'

Donal stepped forward. He waited until his stillness silenced them all. And then he beckoned Alaric forward. 'Tonight, in this hall, we feast you, my lord of Atvia. Tonight we give you good welcome and blessings for your health. But you came to us with a purpose, that being to pledge us your fealty.' Donal met Alaric's wary eyes. He

did not smile. 'Then pledge it, my lord. Here in this hall before us all.'

Alaric's lips parted. Briefly, Donal saw the tic of a muscle in his jaw. But he knelt. In elegance, he knelt, making it not an act of submission but of calm willingness to sacrifice anything for his realm.

Donal unsheathed the Cheysuli sword. The ruby blazed in the pommel as he raised the blade toward Alaric's face. 'Swear,' he said, 'by all the gods you have.'

Alaric bent forward. He placed his lips upon the runechased blade and gave it the kiss of fealty. 'I swear by all the gods of Atvia, by my rank and by my birth, that I am vassal to Donal of Homana. My sword, my life, is his. I pledge this in all good faith. I break this oath only upon my death. My liege – will you accept me?'

Unless he were a false man, willingly surrendering birthright and royal holdings, Alaric *would* die before renouncing so binding an oath. Donal did not believe the Atvian would risk his place so casually.

'I accept your oath and do hold you by it,' he agreed. 'Rise, my lord of Atvia.'

Alaric rose. His intense gaze did not move from Donal's face. He waited.

Donal slid home the sword in his sheath. 'By my right as Mujhar of Homana, I enter into willing alliance with this man. Let all know there is peace between our realms.' He inhaled a steadying breath. 'By my right as Mujhar of Homana, I enter into willing agreement with this man: that this oath of fealty be sealed with a wedding. He has asked for my sister in marriage.'

He heard Bronwyn's gasp clearly. 'Donal! Donal – *no!* You said I would not have to!' She thrust herself out of the crowd to face him in the center of the hall. She did not look at Alaric. 'You *said* –'

'I said.' His tone was harsher than he meant it to be. 'I said, aye. But now it must be done.'

'My lord.' It was Alaric, urbane and calmly pleased. 'My lord, you honor me.'

'I do not honor you. I honor the prophecy.' He would not hide the truth, blatant though it was; he would not hide his open dislike of the man. 'Because of *that*, my lord of Atvia, I will give Bronwyn into marriage. But there are agreements you must make.'

Alaric inclined his head and spread his hands. 'Name them, my lord.'

'That should Bronwyn bear you a son and heir, any daughter the Queen of Homana bears *me* shall be wed to him, thus fixing the succession.' He did not smile. 'That should Bronwyn bear you a *daughter*, that daughter will come to Homana and wed Niall, the Prince of Homana.'

Alaric's smile was one of subtle triumph. 'Aye, my lord, I agree.'

'*Ku'reshtin!*' Bronwyn cried. 'You are no *rujholli* of mine!'

'Fetch a priest,' Donal told a servant.

'*How can you do this to me?*'

He looked into her angry face. 'For the prophecy, I will do anything.'

It was quickly done; too quickly. The priest was brought. The ceremony performed in front of everyone present over loud protestations from Bronwyn; so loud Donal doubted anyone else could hear the vows. It did not seem to matter to Alaric. He smiled a cool, satisfied smile. But the priest was clearly offended by her words. And a Homanan priest at that.

At last Donal stepped in and caught her elbow. '*Rujholla*,' he said quietly, 'you lend credence to the belief we are little more than beasts with such noise.'

'Noise!' She stared at him through tear-filled amber eyes. 'I will make more *noise* than *this*, given the chance. I want no part of this!'

'It is done,' he told her. 'You are wife to Alaric of Atvia.'

'And I promise a fine celebration when we have reached Rondule,' Alaric said calmly.

'I want nothing to do with *celebrations!* I want nothing to do with *you*. I want *none* of it, do you hear? And I want none of my *rujholli*, who turns his back on Cheysuli customs!'

'Bronwyn! –'

'You *do!*' she cried. 'You sell me off to a stranger, just to make an *alliance* –'

'Bronwyn, you cheapen your *jehana's* name with such behavior.'

'*You* cheapen it as well, Donal.' Bronwyn shut her eyes a moment, teeth clenched so hard the muscles stood up along her jaw. 'I swear, *I swear*, when I am given the chance I will show you all what gifts I claim. I will *show* you what the Old Blood means –'

'Old Blood,' Alaric frowned. 'I have heard rumors . . . the girl has it, you say?'

'*The girl* is now your *cheysula*, my lord of Atvia, and your queen. You might give her proper rank,' Donal said tightly. 'And aye, she does. Why? Does it make you wish to end the marriage almost as soon as it is made?'

'Not at all,' Alaric said smoothly. 'I welcome the Cheysuli with all their arts. I must. It may be that my children will reflect their mother's gifts –'

'There will *be* no children,' Bronwyn said bitterly. 'I will see to *that* –'

'Enough,' Donal said gently. 'You will send all our guests from here muttering of your intended witchcraft.'

'Let them. *Let them*. Do you think I care?' And then, before he could move, Bronwyn brought the flat of her hand across his face. 'I renounce you. *I renounce you*. You are no *rujholli* of mine!'

For a moment, Donal shut his eyes against the pain and humiliation. Then he swung around to face them all. 'Get you *gone!*' he shouted. 'Can you not see the celebration is done?'

Blindly, he watched them go. Bronwyn. Alaric. Even Aislinn, Meghan, Evan. And then the hall was empty save for a single man.

His hair was disheveled. A smear of dirt marred his face. His clothes were soiled. Mud clotted his boots. He wore no leathers, no gold; there were no *lir* at his side. But as he faced his Mujhar, Donal knew he was a Cheysuli.

'So, the travesty is concluded.'

'Rowan –' He broke it off; the time for defense was past. 'It is done.'

Rowan smiled a little. 'I came to bring news of a final victory in Solinde. Instead, as I make my way through the hordes of departing guests, I am given news of my own: the Mujhar of Homana has wed his *rujholla* to Alaric of Atvia.'

'For the prophecy.' The words came out listlessly.

'Of course. *Everything* is done for the prophecy.' Rowan laughed, and then the laughter died away. 'But I wonder – what would *Alix* say to see her daughter bartered away –'

Donal flinched. 'We do not speak of my *jehana!* I have done this thing!'

'Oh, aye, you have. And now you must live with it.'

Donal wanted to turn away. But he did not. The time for that was also passed. He was Mujhar; he must behave as a Mujhar. 'I will live with it.'

'Am I to assume the Homanan Council also desired this match?'

'Aye. And campaigned most eloquently for it.' Donal stared down at the cup in his hand. He had forgotten to drink. The tang of the wine filled his nose and head.

'So quickly you succumb to the desires of Homanans. Do you think Clan Council would have agreed?'

Sluggishly, anger rose in his defense. 'This was done for Homana – Homana *and* the prophecy! A son of Bronwyn's will one day sit on the Atvian throne.'

Rowan's eyes narrowed. Tiny creases fanned out across his cheeks. 'Do you care *so much* for kingship?'

'Aye,' Donal answered harshly, 'Would you tell me I should *not?* Is it not what Hale left to me when he fashioned a sword and took a Mujhar's daughter as his *meijha?*'

Rowan slowly closed his eyes. 'Ah gods, ah gods . . .

426

you have accepted it at last . . . after so many years.' He opened his eyes and smiled a bittersweet smile. 'Carillon used to despair that you would ever know the cost. The legacy of the thing. And a man, never knowing the *cost* of kingship, is never really a king.'

'Carillon despaired . . .' The pain was worse than he had expected. 'And you as well?'

'From time to time.' Rowan's smile was a little broader, but his tone was still ironic. '*Now* – do you see what it does to others? Do you see what it does to *you?*'

'You do not approve.' Somehow, he wanted Rowan to approve. He needed *someone's* approval.

'It is not my place to approve or disapprove.'

At last Donal succumbed and turned his back on the man. He faced the Lion instead. 'Do I see what it does to others?' he cried. '*Aye*, I see what it does! No doubt it was much the same for Carillon. And now – only *now* – I understand why a man curses his birth if only to escape the demands of his entrance into the world.' He drew in a ragged breath. 'Bronwyn's children will bring us another bloodline. *I do what I must do.*'

He expected Rowan to answer. When he did not, Donal turned. And found himself alone.

He wanted his *meijha*. He wanted his mother. He wanted his father, his uncle, his *lir*. He wanted his *rujholla*. And he could have none of them, because this he must face alone.

Donal turned back to look at the hall. He saw the casements, glowing dimly; the banners, the tapestries, the weapons. The Lion upon the dais.

Slowly, he walked the length of the hall. He stood before the throne. He felt all the pain and grief and fear well up into chest and throat. He could not bear it. He thought he might burst with all the anger and frustration.

Before he could consider the blasphemy of his actions, he hurled the cup of wine against the ancient wood. '*All* of them, gone!' he shouted. '*All* of them you have taken. You have robbed me of even my pride, even the pride in

my *heritage*, because I must be a ruler before I am a Cheysuli. A man before a warrior. And a lion before a man: *The Lion of Homana.*'

Wine spilled down to stain the crimson cushion. The Lion bled. Or cried. He could not tell the difference.

Donal put his hand upon the hilt of his sword and drew it from the scabbard Rowan had made. He heard the steel-song as it slid; the hiss when it rattled free.

By the blade, beneath the crossguard, he held it. He looked at the hilt from gritty, burning eyes, and saw how the weapon shook in his trembling hand.

Gold. Solid gold, with the mark of men's hands upon it. The curving prongs that caged the ruby, brilliant Mujhar's Eye; the avatar of his soul.

And the lion. The royal rampant lion.

Donal laughed. It was a sound of discovery, lacking all humor; the futile sound of a man who knows himself trapped by what he has done and what things he still must do.

He laughed, and the sorrow filled up the hall.

'I am Donal,' he said when the echoes had died. 'Just – Donal. Son of man and woman. Born of the Cheysuli and a dutiful child of the prophecy. But – just once – *just once* – I wish I could turn my back upon it all and be nothing but a *man!*' His challenging stare shifted from sword hilt to crouching Lion, looming on the dais. And then, abruptly, he shut his eyes.

I wish Carillon were here.

After a moment he turned, intending to leave. He stopped. Aislinn stood in the doorway with their child in her arms.

Waiting.

Donal sheathed the sword and went to his wife and son.

THE END

Shapechangers
Chronicles of the Cheysuli: Book 1
by Jennifer Roberson

They were the *Cheysuli,* a race of magical warriors, gifted with the ability to assume animal shape at will. For centuries they had been allies to the King of Homona, treasured champions of the Realm. Until a king's daughter ran away with a Cheysuli liege man and caused a war of annihilation against the Cheysuli race.

Twenty-five years later the Cheysuli were hunted exiles in their own land. All of Homona was raised to fear them, acknowledge the sorcery in their blood, call them *shapechanger, demon.*

This is the story of Alix, the daughter of that ill-fated union between Homanan princess and Cheysuli warrior, and her struggles to comprehend the traditions of an alien race she had been taught to mistrust, to answer the call of magic in her blood, and accept her place in an ancient prophecy she cannot deny.

First of an eight-part dynastic epic of a magical race and the compelling prophecy which ruled them!

0 552 131180

D0854666